The Ballad
of
Frankie Silver

SHARYN McCRUMB

The Ballad of Frankie Silver

For Jeanne—

From a keeper of the legends—

Sharyn McCrumb

May 21, 1999

Dayton

A DUTTON BOOK

DUTTON
Published by the Penguin Group
Penguin Putnam Inc., 375 Hudson Street, New York, New York 10014, U.S.A.
Penguin Books Ltd, 27 Wrights Lane, London W8 5TZ, England
Penguin Books Australia Ltd, Ringwood, Victoria, Australia
Penguin Books Canada Ltd, 10 Alcorn Avenue, Toronto, Ontario, Canada M4V 3B2
Penguin Books (N.Z.) Ltd, 182–190 Wairau Road, Auckland 10, New Zealand

Penguin Books Ltd, Registered Offices:
Harmondsworth, Middlesex, England

First published by Dutton, an imprint of Dutton NAL,
a member of Penguin Putnam Inc.

First Printing, May, 1998
10   9   8   7   6   5   4   3   2   1

Ⓐ REGISTERED TRADEMARK—MARCA REGISTRADA

Library of Congress Cataloging-in-Publication Data

McCrumb, Sharyn
The ballad of Frankie Silver / Sharyn McCrumb.
p.   cm.
ISBN 0-525-93969-5
I. Title.
PS3563.C3527B35   1998
813'. 54—dc21   97-24867
                                                    CIP
Printed in the United States of America
Set in Fairfield Medium
Designed by Julian Hamer

PUBLISHER'S NOTE
This is a work of fiction. Names, characters, places, and incidents
either are the products of the author's imagination or are used fictitiously,
and any resemblance to actual persons, living or dead, events, or
locales is entirely coincidental.

This book is printed on acid-free paper. ♾

The rich never hang;
only the poor and friendless.

   —Perry Smith
    executed in Kansas, 1965,
    for the murder of the
    Clutter family

The Ballad of Frankie Silver

This dreadful, dark and dismal day
Has swept my glories all away;
My sun goes down, my days are past,
And I must leave this world at last.

Oh! Lord, what will become of me?
I am condemned, you all now see;
To heaven or hell my soul must fly,
All in a moment when I die.

Judge Donnell my sentence has passed,
These prison walls I leave at last;
Nothing to cheer my drooping head
Until I'm numbered with the dead.

But Oh! That awful judge I fear,
Shall I that awful sentence hear:
"Depart, ye cursed, down to hell
And forever there to dwell."

I know that frightful ghosts I'll see,
Gnawing their flesh in misery;
And then and there attended be
For murder in the first degree.

Then shall I meet that mournful face,
Whose blood I spilled upon this place;
With flaming eyes to me he'll say,
"Why did you take my life away?"

His feeble hands fell gently down,
His chattering tongue soon lost its sound,
To see his soul and body part
It strikes with terror in my heart.

I took his blooming days away,
Left him no time to God to pray;
And if sins fall upon his head,
Must I not bear them in his stead?

The jealous thought that first gave strife
To make me take my husband's life,
For months and days I spent my time
Thinking how to commit this crime.

And on a dark and doleful night
I put the body out of sight,
With flames I tried to him consume,
But time would not admit it done.

You all see me and on me gaze,
Be careful how you spend your days;
And never commit this awful crime,
But try to serve your God in time.

My mind on solemn subjects rolls,
My little child, God bless its soul;
All you that are of Adam's race,
Let not my faults this child disgrace.

Farewell, good people, you all now see
What my bad conduct's brought on me;
To die of shame and disgrace
Before the world of human race.

Awful indeed to think of death,
In perfect health to lose my breath;
Farewell my friends, I bid adieu,
Vengeance on me you must now pursue.

Great God! How shall I be forgiven?
Not fit for earth, not fit for Heaven;
But little time to pray to God,
For now I try that awful road.

A rumor was prevalent in Burke County that Silver wrote some verses which were tantamount to a confession of her guilt and read them while on the scaffold to the surrounding throng just before she was executed.

The mind of Squire Waits A. Cook, a highly respected justice of the peace in the Enola section, was a veritable storehouse of legends and events of Burke County's earlier days. He told me that the verses Frankie had allegedly written were composed by a Methodist minister whose surname was Stacy.

—Senator Sam J. Ervin, Jr.
Burke County Courthouses and Related Matters

Prologue

I want to show you a grave," the sheriff said.

Three rocks stood alone in the little mountain graveyard: smooth stubs of granite, evenly spaced about four feet apart. The stone pillars were uncarved, weathered from more than a century's exposure to the elements and farthest away from the white steepled church in the clearing at the top of the mountain.

Tennessee deputy sheriff Spencer Arrowood wondered why Nelse Miller had made a detour up a corkscrew mountain road to stop in this country churchyard. He could see nothing out of the ordinary about the old white frame church or the surrounding array of tombstones, ranging from newly carved blocks of shining granite to older markers, tilted askew in the dark earth, scarcely readable anymore. Nearly every burying ground had stones like these.

It was pretty enough up here, Spencer allowed. The view of Celo Mountain across the valley and the blue haze of more distant peaks beyond made a fine sight on a summer morning, but Sheriff Miller wasn't much on admiring scenery no matter how magnificent the vistas before them. He barely glanced at the view. On a hot summer day like this, Nelse was more likely to be in search of a cold drink and a shade tree, and in truth Spencer Arrowood would have preferred such a rest stop to this peculiar excursion to a little mountaintop graveyard. He was twenty-four, and impatience was pretty much a permanent state of mind for him. They could have stopped in the store in Red Hill instead of heading off up Route 80, past Bandana, North Carolina, and up another couple of elliptical miles that spiraled to nowhere. Or they could have headed back across the Tennessee line to Hamelin and got on with the day's work. Spencer was still new enough at the post of deputy sheriff to relish every hour of duty, every moment of patrol in his shiny new '74 Dodge. Much as he respected the old sheriff, he often found himself impatient with Nelse Miller's unhurried serenity. The sheriff, in turn, sometimes seemed to be amused by his eager young deputy, as if he were a new puppy barking at sunbeams.

Spencer looked at his watch. Nearly noon. This old cemetery couldn't have anything to do with business. They were still on the North Carolina side of the mountains, at the Dayton Bend in the Toe River, according to the map. Just over the state line the Toe River would change its name to the Nolichucky and the two sightseers would change into peace officers on duty instead of idlers looking at golden hills on a pleasant summer day.

Their morning's errand had been the delivery of a fugitive to the jail in Bakersville, a little courtesy exchange between peace officers on different sides of the state line. The prisoner hadn't been much in the way of a felon—a car thief, barely old enough to register for the draft. Since he had sobered up after a night in a Tennessee jail cell, the boy had seemed overwhelmed by the consequences of his joy ride. He had wrecked the car in a high-speed chase, and had come out bruised but otherwise uninjured. "God protects fools and drunks," Nelse Miller declared, with some disgust.

The prisoner was handcuffed and shackled in the back of a patrol car, filthy, unshaven, and fighting back tears of panic. The two officers transporting him were not ungentle, but their lack of interest in his predicament was evident.

"What's going to happen to me now?" the young man kept asking.

"You're going to the jail in Bakersville," Nelse Miller had told him. "And after that, we're done with you."

They had delivered the prisoner to the Mitchell County sheriff at ten o'clock, and Sheriff Miller proceeded to spend the next hour drinking coffee and swapping stories with his North Carolina counterpart while Spencer curbed his own thirst and impatience, and smiled at the yarns as if he had not heard them a dozen times before. Finally Sheriff Miller conceded that the prisoner exchange had taken up enough of Tennessee government time. He signaled for Spencer to bring the patrol car around. Nelse Miller seldom did his own driving, a trait that bewildered his young deputy, who thought that driving a cop car was the only childhood dream that had lived up to his expectations.

As Spencer slid behind the wheel of the new Dodge, he felt his impatience slip away. He left the courthouse square of Bakersville, dutifully following Sheriff Miller's directions, taking the twists and turns of North Carolina's back roads, while he wondered just what the old fox was up to this time. He didn't like to ask, though. Nelse Miller had his own way of doing things, and Spencer found that it was usually better to wait him out. Explanations would come at the proper time and place.

Now the deputy stood in the clear mountain sunshine, gazing respectfully at three slabs of quarried stone, as he waited for further enlightenment.

Finally Nelse Miller said: "I come up here when I want to remember why I came into police work. That little piece of trouble we just transported to Bakersville made me feel more like a baby-sitter than a lawman."

Spencer looked around at the peaceful scenery, wondering why Nelse had picked this place for inspiration. He knew the Millers were from this county originally, though. "Family cemetery?" he asked, though he didn't see any headstones marked "Miller."

The sheriff shook his head. "These aren't my people." He pointed to the uncarved markers. "Charlie Silver is buried here. He was a murder victim, a hundred and fifty years back. His wife killed him. Leastways they said she did. You ever hear the story of Frankie Silver?"

"Not in detail," said Spencer. "People mention it every now and then. It's like Tom Dooley, isn't it? More legend than fact. With a tune."

The sheriff smiled. " 'Tom Dooley' is a catchy folk song, I reckon, but the inspiration for it—Tom Dula—was real, all right. They hanged him over in Statesville in May of 1868, and good riddance to him. Everybody has heard about him, but they don't know what pox-ridden trifling pond scum he was. Too bad he survived the war. Tom Dooley's story pales beside that of Frankie Silver. I always thought it strange that not too many people outside these mountains have heard about Frankie Silver, while Tom Dooley is a household word."

"It's the song," said Spencer.

"But Frankie Silver—there's a *story*!" Nelse Miller pointed toward the edge of the churchyard where a thicket of bushes sloped down into a dense forest of beech and oak trees. "Eighteen years old—that's all she was. The Silvers' cabin was back in those woods a couple of hundred yards. That's where it happened. The cabin was burned years ago, and the site is all overgrown now with briers and underbrush, but we could go take a look at it if you want."

"I'm not familiar with the case," said Spencer. "Just heard the name, that's all."

"My people were from up around here, so I cut my teeth on that old story. I think it's the real reason I became a lawman. I remember as a kid hearing my granddaddy tell that tale, and wishing I could have been there to investigate the crime. I always wanted to know *who* and *why*. I still do. I thought I would solve the Silver case when I grew up. Thought if I could just learn enough about criminal investigation, I could figure out the truth."

"Did you?" asked Spencer. "Solve it?"

"Never did. I understand some of what happened and why. But not all of it. Not that last secret that she took to her grave."

"Maybe I'll look into it sometime," said Spencer. "Is there a book about the Silver case?"

"Not that I ever saw. I've fiddled with the notion of writing one myself, except that I'm not much on paperwork. I take a proprietary interest in Frankie Silver, though. It's a hell of a story, Spencer. Starting right here. Starting with old Charlie Silver's grave."

Spencer looked at the three pillars of stone, somber in the mountain sunshine. "Well, which one is Charlie Silver's grave?" he asked.

Nelse Miller smiled. *"All of them."*

Chapter One

SHERIFF SPENCER ARROWOOD had dodged a bullet. At least in the metaphorical sense he had; that is, he did not die. Literally, he had not been lucky enough to dodge. The bullet had hit him solidly in the thorax, and had cost him his spleen, several pints of blood, and a nearly fatal bout of shock before the rescue squad managed to get him out of the hills and into the hospital in Johnson City. He had been enforcing an eviction—unwillingly, and in full sympathy with the displaced residents. The fact that he had been shot by someone he knew and had wanted to help made the attack on him that much more bitter to his family and his fellow officers, but he had not cared much about the irony of it. The injury seemed disassociated somehow from the events of that day, as if he had been drawn into another place and it did not matter much how he got there. He felt no bitterness toward his assailant, only wonder at what had happened to him. Coming so close to death had been a shock to his mind as well as his body, and its effects were so intense that it seemed pointless to consider the cause of the injury; its effect overshadowed all that went before. In the hospital he did not speak of these feelings to anyone, though. They might be mistaken for fear, or for an anxiety that might require the ministering of yet another physician. Spencer kept quiet. He wanted out of there.

That confrontation on a mountain farm had taken place

three weeks earlier, and now, newly released from the Johnson City Medical Center, he was recuperating from his injuries at home.

He was able to get dressed by himself now, and to hobble around the house taking care of his own needs, microwaving what he wanted to eat, walking a bit to keep from getting stiff, and watching movies on cable until he was sick of the flickering screen. Three days earlier he had insisted that his mother go back to her own house and leave him to take care of himself. He understood that she was concerned about him, but her hovering presence had dragged him back into childhood, and he chafed at the old feelings of dependence and helplessness. He had claimed more strength and energy than he had really felt in order to convince her that he was well enough to be left alone. He had walked her to the door, waved a cheerful farewell, and then closed the door and leaned against it for ten minutes until he was strong enough to make it to a chair.

He was better now. His mother still phoned him four times a day to make sure that he was still alive, but he bore that without complaint. He knew how frightened she had been when he was shot, and how many years she had dreaded that moment. He did not begrudge her the reassurance that all was well. In fact he was determined to put an end to his convalescence as soon as he possibly could, to end her worry and his own boredom at his confinement.

He was lying in a lounge chair on his deck looking out at the valley and the mountains beyond, enjoying the spring sunshine and the ribbons of dogwood blooms across the hills, but he was still thinking about death. Physically he was recovering well, but the shock of coming so close to nonexistence had left its mark on him. Although he was past forty, he had never really thought about dying before. As a young man he'd had the youthful illusion of immortality to carry him through the daredevil stunts of adolescence and the rigors of a hitch in the army. When Spencer was eighteen, his brother Cal had been killed in Vietnam, but there had been an unreal quality about that, too: a death that occurred a world away, and a closed-casket funeral in Hamelin. The tiny part of his mind that was only ascendant in the small hours of the morning told him that Cal might not be in that box in Oakdale. To this day he might be roaming the jungles of Southeast Asia, or hanging out in bars in Saigon. Spencer would say that he did not believe any of this, of course, but the tiniest fraction of possibility existed, and he welcomed that doubt because it distanced him from death.

As the years went by, Spencer stayed too busy to think much about philosophical matters. Brooding on death was not a healthy pastime for someone in law enforcement. It was better to take each day as it came without anticipating trouble. Now, though, he found himself with unaccustomed time on his hands, and he was under orders to restrict his physical activity until his body had more fully recovered. He thought too much.

The sound of a car horn in the driveway stirred him from contemplation. He lurched over to the railing of the deck and looked out in time to see a white patrol car coming to a stop in front of the garage doors. Deputy sheriff Martha Ayers got out, and he waved to her, to let her know she should come out to the deck instead of going to the front door.

"Up here, Martha!"

"Figures you wouldn't be in bed!" Martha yelled back, but she sounded cheerfully resigned to his defection from bed rest.

He tottered back to the chaise lounge and lowered himself carefully onto the canvas, allowing himself a wince of pain because Martha wasn't close enough yet to see him grimace. She hurried up the wooden steps to the deck, pausing for a moment as she always did to admire the view. "It sure is peaceful up here."

"I like it," he said.

When he bought the twelve acres of ridge land a couple of years back, he had a local contractor build him a wood frame house, three stories: two bedrooms on the top floor, kitchen and living room on the middle floor, and a den, office, and laundry room on the ground floor, garage attached. Both living room and den had sliding glass doors facing the east, where the slope fell away to reveal a landscape of meadows threaded by a country road, and beyond them the wall of green mountains that marked the beginning of Mitchell County, North Carolina—out of his jurisdiction. He had painted the house barn-red, and he had built the decks himself little by little in his free time. Now they encircled the house on the ground floor and the one above, giving views from every conceivable vantage point. Spencer Arrowood liked to see a long way. The view diminished the problems of a country sheriff, because looking out at the green hills made him feel that it could be any century at all, which made his problems seem too ephemeral to fret about. Just lately, though, that same timeless quality had been showing him just how fleeting and fragmentary his own life was against the backdrop of the eternal mountains. The feeling of insignificance disturbed him. For once he was glad to have company.

Martha Ayers leaned against the back of the other deck chair. "I'm on break," she told him. "Can't stay long, but I thought I'd see if there's anything you needed. Glass of water? Pills?"

He shook his head. "I'm fine."

"I brought you your mail," she said. "But only because you insisted."

"I appreciate it, Martha."

He was still too thin, and his cheekbones were still too prominent, making him look haggard, she thought, but some of the color was coming back to his cheeks. The gray sweatshirt and sweatpants he wore hid the bandages. "Pull up a chair," he said. "You'll excuse me if I don't get up."

Martha snorted. "I'd like to see you try. I'll have your mother over here faster than white on rice. And don't think I didn't see you over there at the railing waving at me when I drove in. I should report you to Miss Jane."

He grimaced. "The training academy didn't do anything for your sweet disposition, did it, Martha? How are things at the office?"

"It's a good thing I came back when I did," said Martha.

She considered the deck chair for a moment, and then sat down in one of the wrought-iron garden chairs. "LeDonne may think he's Superman, but even he can't pull two shifts a day seven days a week. He's nobody's idea of a diplomat, either. But we manage."

"Any arrests?"

"Nothing to speak of." Her tone told him that he wasn't going to get any details from her. "If you had any sense, Spencer, you'd just lie back in that lawn chair and drink your iced tea without giving the department another thought. Lord knows you could use the rest, and I've been telling you so for years now. Trust you to get shot before you'd take my advice."

Sheriff Arrowood smiled. "Well, Martha, all I can say is: I wish I'd got shot at the beach, or maybe in Hawaii, because this business of laying around the house with nothing to do but watch talk shows is about as dull as ditchwater. The view is nice, but it doesn't change enough to keep me occupied. I've taken to spying on the deer in the evenings. I try not to meddle in the department business, but sometimes the boredom is overpowering."

"Sounds like you're feeling better then," said Martha. "This time last week, you weren't nearly this feisty. I guess we'll have to take your car keys soon."

"I'm fine. Cooking my own meals even. You want some lunch? I have a whole freezer full of frozen dinners."

"I can't stay that long," she told him. "This is my lunch break, but I ate an apple on my way up the mountain to check on you."

He smiled as he sifted through the stack of letters— mostly junk mail, brochures for various law enforcement–related products, but among the few first-class envelopes he saw an official-looking one from Nashville with the state seal of Tennessee incorporated in the design of the return address.

"What's this?"

Martha sighed. "I knew I should have left that one on your desk. It looks like the state wants something from us, which means you'll either be filling out more forms in triplicate or else driving all over creation going to committee meetings."

He tore open the letter and began to scan its contents. "I can always plead ill health if they—"

"What is it? What's wrong?"

Spencer's pale face had gone gray, and he was staring at the letter as if he'd forgotten that she was there. Martha clenched her fingers around the iron rim of the garden seat, wondering if she ought to run into the house and phone the rescue squad. The sheriff was supposed to be recovering nicely from the operation that removed a bullet and his injured spleen, but she supposed that even a week later something might go wrong. A blood clot, perhaps? She wondered if her rudimentary knowledge of first aid would be of any use.

"I'm fine, Martha." He didn't look up, and his voice had that perfunctory tone that meant he wasn't listening. He was staring past her, gazing at the white-flowering dogwood tree as if he expected it to walk away.

"Don't give me that," said Martha. "What's in that letter? You looked better right after you'd been shot. Tell me what's wrong."

He handed her the letter. "I've been invited to an execution."

The waiting was the hardest part. Spencer had given his testimony hours earlier, but he was still dressed in his dark suit and starched white shirt, feeling as if he, not the defendant, were on trial.

Closing arguments had ended a little after four, and the jury had filed out to begin their deliberations in the case of the State of Tennessee v. Fate Harkryder. Now there was nothing to do but wait. He sat awkwardly on the bench in the reception room of the sheriff's office, hot and uncomfortable in the unaccustomed business suit. It was just as well that he wasn't set to go out on patrol that night. He was too jumpy to be much good at it.

Spencer had testified in court cases before, of course, but

those trials had been insignificant compared to this one. In previous cases the defendants had faced fines or a few weeks in the county jail at most if his testimony helped to convict them. This time it was a matter of life or death. He felt solemn, weighed down by the fate of the prisoner. He also felt angry at him for committing a vicious and senseless crime and setting this chain of events in motion, soiling so many lives with his recklessness.

"Why don't you go on home?" asked Nelse Miller, sitting down on the bench beside him.

Spencer shrugged. "Can't. The jury might come back early, and then we'd have to take the prisoner back to the courtroom. I figure—what with his family and all—all of us ought to be on hand to escort him over."

"I don't figure the Harkryders to open fire on a crowded courtroom, like folks in that Hillsville shoot-out over in Virginia. No, the Harkryders would prefer to ambush an unarmed man in the dark some night, preferably at odds of four against one. It's their way."

"I'm not worried about them," said Spencer.

"Now, I'm not saying I don't appreciate your offer of an extra guard when we have to walk the prisoner back over to the courtroom, because the Harkryders might be in the same melodramatic mood that seems to have seized you—but that jury isn't coming back tonight."

"You don't think so? The case is open-and-shut. We had enough evidence to convict him twice over."

"Yes, but it's detailed evidence. Complicated for ordinary folks. Blood evidence, and the forensic testimony about the defendant being a secretor. That's a lot for a jury to digest. The jewelry is probably the clincher, but it's circumstantial. Even with an ironclad case, the state wants to make sure it removes any shadow of a doubt, jurors being what they are. It's hard to convince honest average citizens that there are monsters in this world. They look at the defense table and they see a boyish young man in a Sunday suit with a new haircut, and they just have a hard time believing that this soft-spoken lad would have put a knife to the throat of a twenty-one-year-old boy and severed the windpipe and jugular while the victim's girlfriend watched, tied to a tree, crying, screaming for him to stop, and knowing she was next. It just doesn't seem possible."

"I've felt that way myself."

"Give yourself a few years as a peace officer, then. You're young yet. The time will come when you'll count your fingers after shaking hands with the preacher. You'll lose your faith in humanity if you stay in police work long enough. But juries never get seasoned to evil. Every case is tried before a new bunch of innocents, and you have to bury them in evidence to get it through their heads that clean-cut young men can be guilty of the terrible crimes we've charged them with."

"So you think they'll take a long time to deliberate?"

"Did you look at those jurors? Some of them were taking notes like there'd be an exam to follow. They won't want to let that effort go to waste. They're probably retrying the case right now, just to prove to one another that they were paying attention. And reasonable doubt! *Reasonable* doubt, mind you. Some juries would make a cat laugh. Why, they're probably in there looking for loopholes as if this was *Perry Mason* on TV. What if this fellow had a twin nobody knew about who just happened to own a gun exactly like his—all that hogwash not fit for a fairy tale, much less a court of law. Makes them feel important. This is a big event for Wake County, you know. We go years without having anybody tried for murder."

"I could have done without this time," said Spencer.

"It's finished. Your part is, anyhow. You said your piece in court, and the lawyers said theirs, and now the matter rests in the hands of twelve other people. And I know for a fact that the judge has dinner plans. It's over for the night. So go home."

Spencer shook his head. "I wouldn't be able to get my mind off it. Might as well be here."

The old sheriff sighed. "You sure do beat all, boy. Now, if it was me having to testify against that little piece of bull turd,

I'd leave that courtroom with a spring in my step and never give him another second's thought. That boy is trash and trouble, like all his kinfolk up there in the holler, and if he didn't do this crime, he did a lot more we never caught him at, and he deserves what he gets."

"What do you mean *if he didn't do this crime?*" said Spencer.

"Oh, nothing. It's not our job to decide guilt anyhow. That's for judges, lawyers, juries. We just catch the suspects and round up such evidence as we can find. After that, it's their call."

"I know that, but what do you mean *if he didn't do this crime?* Don't you think he's guilty?"

"Well, personally, I don't care," said Nelse Miller. "You could have looked into Fate Harkryder's cradle and told that he was going to end up in prison. If it wasn't one thing, it'd be another. I've known his kin for more than fifty years, and there's not a solid citizen in the bunch. You'd stand a better chance of getting a thoroughbred out of a swaybacked donkey than you would of getting a good man out of the Harkryder bloodline."

Spencer just looked at him, waiting.

Finally Nelse Miller let out a sigh, and looked away. "Oh, hell. I just got a feeling, that's all."

"But the case is ironclad. Blood type. Forensic evidence. The victims' possessions found on him. We have him dead to rights. Everything but a confession."

The sheriff shrugged. "It's not up to me. Or you. We gather the evidence. *They* decide."

"Why didn't you say anything about this feeling of yours before now?"

"Because feelings aren't evidence. They'd have laughed me out of the courtroom. Maybe Elissa Rountree would believe me. Sensible woman. She's the only juror that would have! But nobody cares what your *opinion* is in a murder case. Facts. Evidence. Fingerprints. Then they make up their own minds. We're well out of it."

Spencer nodded. "I think he's guilty," he said. "I was there that night. I'm the one who arrested him. I wouldn't have testified for the prosecution if I thought he wasn't guilty."

"Oh, you'd have testified. You were the law that night, and what you saw and what you did is the state's business. But it helped that you had a moral certainty. Now stop fretting about it."

Spencer wanted to protest that he hadn't been fretting at all about the matter of guilt until the sheriff brought it up, but instead he said, "You've testified in capital cases before. Are you ever unsure of the man's guilt?"

"Well, son, I tell you: I've been lucky that way. The doubts I've had have been in trifling cases, most of them. The punishment was at most a couple of months in jail, and like I said, most of the folks we arrest have that coming to them on general principles. But a capital case? There's only two murder cases in these mountains that I'm not happy with. And I may be wrong on both of them, mind you."

"What two cases?"

"One is the fellow you're about to put on death row. And the other one is Frankie Silver."

"What do you mean, an execution? In Tennessee?" Martha shook her head. "It just doesn't happen."

"It does now." Spencer handed her the letter. "That judge who has been granting automatic stays for all these years finally retired, and now it looks like the state is going back into the capital punishment business."

"After all these years? When was the last time we executed anybody in Tennessee?"

"The early sixties. But we didn't abolish capital punishment. Juries kept handing out death sentences right along. We just haven't carried one out in a very long time. Decades. Apparently, that's going to change in about"—he glanced at the letter—"six weeks."

"Why are they telling you about it?"

"Tradition. The sheriff of the prisoner's home county is usually asked to be one of the official witnesses when the sentence is carried out."

"Can you refuse? Like you said: plead ill health. Or decline the honor—if that's what you'd call it—of being a witness."

He didn't answer for a moment. "I don't think I can do that, Martha."

"Sure you could. Dr. Banner would write a letter to get you out of it. And it wouldn't even be a lie, Spencer. You just had major surgery. Shot in the line of duty. They shouldn't ask you to hand out doughnuts at a choir meet, much less do something as stressful as—as watch a man die."

Spencer didn't answer. He was looking out at the ridge lines, where a bank of dark clouds settled in low on the horizon, adding a new mountain chain at the edge of the mist.

Martha tried again. "How do we do it in Tennessee these days? Lethal injection?"

"No," he said. He watched the cloud lines with even greater attention. "It's still Old Sparky. No options."

"Oh. The electric chair. I see." Martha shuddered. After another stretch of silence she added, "Of course, the victims didn't get any options, either. You've got to remember that."

"I'll try to bear it in mind." Spencer folded the letter and slid it under the rest of the stack of mail.

"You're not against capital punishment, are you? Not after what we see in this job. Not after what happens to children at the hands of some of these people. . . ."

"I can't say I'm against capital punishment, no," said Spencer. "I see the victims, which is a misfortune that most people don't have. It's just this one. Just—this—one."

"Why do you feel like you have to go to this thing, Spencer? You're already upset about it, and it's still six weeks away. If the state of Tennessee insists on having somebody from Wake County present for the occasion, why don't you send LeDonne? It wouldn't bother him to watch an execution. He'd pull the switch himself and never turn a hair."

"I can't."

Martha looked at him. She had known Spencer Arrowood all her life. They had been students together at the local high school. She knew his mother from church. She had been a dispatcher in the sheriff's office, and now she was a newly appointed Wake County deputy, all of which added up to a good number of years of close observation of the man. She decided that his reaction to the summons from the Tennessee Department of Corrections amounted to more than just squeamishness. The sheriff hated cruelty on any level, but he was no coward, and he never shirked an obligation. "You want to tell me what this is about, Spencer?" she said quietly.

"It's been about twenty years ago now. I guess you don't remember."

Martha frowned. "Twenty years ago. I was gone by then. I was off being an army wife in some godforsaken little town close to Fort Bragg, North Carolina. Husband number one."

"I forgot. You wouldn't know about the case then."

"Who is it they're executing?"

"Fate Harkryder. I arrested him. Testified against him. And he got the death penalty. He's been sitting on death row in a Nashville prison ever since. Lord, I haven't thought of him in ages. And now this."

"What did he do?"

"Murder."

He had been planning to leave it at that, but Martha's expression told him that the discussion wouldn't be over until he told her the rest. He sighed. "He killed two hikers from the Appalachian Trail. Boy and girl—college students from the University of North Carolina. He was ROTC; she was a colonel's daughter. Honor students. They were very clean-cut and attractive kids. They were worth ten of him."

In his mind he could hear Nelse Miller's voice. *He might as well have killed Donny and Marie.* The Osmonds. Spencer had nearly forgotten them, too.

"Apparently he ambushed them at their campsite while they were sleeping. He tortured the boy. We . . ." He didn't want to remember about the burn marks. "And he raped the girl before he killed her. Mutilated the body. I think that's what really got him the death penalty. The jury looked at pictures of that smiling girl with the big calf's eyes, and then at

what was left of her in the crime scene photos. . . ." He
shrugged.

He took a deep breath and wished he hadn't started talking about the case, because he had tried hard to forget what
he had seen that day. He didn't want to picture the remnants
of bodies he'd found at that campsite. He hadn't had that
nightmare in a long time. And now he would.

"I don't remember this," said Martha. "What were their
names?"

"Her name was Emily Stanton. I can't remember his."

Martha shook her head. "The name doesn't mean anything to me. I sure do remember the Harkryders, though.
They were memorable, every single one of them. How many
were there? I lost count."

Spencer smiled. "Seemed like dozens, though some of
them were cousins of the other ones. Nobody talked family
with the Harkryders. If you were kin to them, you wouldn't
claim it. Tom was the one in our class, wasn't he? I don't
think he started out with us, though. We caught up with
him."

"Mean as a striped snake. Which doesn't say much to distinguish him from the rest of the litter. Which one was
Fate?"

"Lafayette Harkryder. The youngest. There isn't much to
say about him. He was only seventeen when it happened. I
guess he's been in prison now longer than he was out in the
world. Funny, in my mind, I still see him as a skinny teenage
boy. He must be middle-aged by now, at least in prison years.
You age fast in there. I probably wouldn't know him if I saw
him."

"And you arrested him back then?"

Spencer nodded. "My first murder case. I was a deputy for
Nelse Miller, and the bodies were found late one night on
my watch. . . . Fate Harkryder . . . I'd almost forgotten about
him. I fretted over it enough at the time, though. I guess I
never thought it would come to this."

"Well, I wouldn't worry about it if I were you," said
Martha. "In the first place, I'm sure he has it coming to him,

and in the second place, the way they mollycoddle criminals these days, I doubt very much that he'll keep that date with the executioner. He's probably got a roomful of lawyers writing appeals on everything they can think of. Trust me. An execution hasn't happened in Tennessee in thirty-some years, and it won't happen now."

"Maybe you're right, Martha."

"Of course I am. Now, I have to get back on patrol, so I'm going to leave. You're sure you're all right?"

He nodded. "Just a shock to the system, that's all."

"But I worry about you being stuck up here on this ridge all alone. Thank the Lord it's not winter. Is there anything I can bring you?"

"Yes," said Spencer. "I'd like you to bring me the case file on Fate Harkryder."

Martha sighed. "You're going to wear yourself out worrying about this thing, aren't you?"

"No. I promise I'll go easy. I just want to refresh my memory. And, Martha—one other thing. Have you ever heard of Frankie Silver?"

The old woman stood on the side of the road clutching the letter. She waited there until the pickup truck swirled into dust below the brow of the hill before she took a step toward the small iron gate bordered by tiger lilies. The white frame house at the end of the path sat like a pearl on a seashell, poised as it was on the ridge above the patchwork of fields and river far below. The beauty of the scenery did not gladden her heart, though. She looked warily at the prim little house, knowing that for all the urgency of her visit, she was in no hurry to open that gate.

Nora Bonesteel lived here.

Not that anybody ever said a word against old Miz Bonesteel. She was still a handsome woman, who wore well her seventy years, and she never asked favors of a soul. She stood faithfully in her church pew every week, and she kept to herself, but for doing what had to be done: food taken to the sick, and fine things knitted and sewn for the brides and the babies of the parish, but still . . . Still.

Nobody wanted to have much to do with Nora Bonesteel. She knew things. People said that when you came to tell her the news of a death in the valley, the cake for the family would already be in the oven. The Sight was in the Bonesteel family; her grandmother had been the same. The Bonesteel women never talked about what they knew, never meddled in folks' lives, but all the same, it made people uneasy to be around them, knowing that whatever happened to you, they would have seen it coming.

The old woman looked down at the letter from Nashville. Would she know about that, what with the letter coming from so far away? With a sigh she bent down to open the gate.

When she looked up again, the tall, straight figure of a woman in gray stood on the porch, silently watching her. She clutched the mason jar of peach preserves tighter against her belly. She had brought a gift. She would not be beholden to this strange old woman.

As she neared the porch, she called out, "Afternoon, Miz Bonesteel! I've come to sit a spell."

Nora Bonesteel nodded. "You're Pauline Harkryder."

"I am." She held out the jar of preserves, but the burden of the letter from Nashville was too great for the pretense of a social call. "I've got a letter here," she said. "It's about my nephew Lafayette, down at the state prison in Nashville."

"You'd best come in."

They sat down in Nora Bonesteel's parlor with its big glass window overlooking the river valley and the green hills beyond, but Pauline Harkryder had no time to spare for the glories of a mountain summer. She had seen more than fifty of them, and they had not given her much. Each summer reminded her that the world stayed young, while she wore herself out doing the same old thing year after year, with nothing to show for it. She handed the letter to Nora Bonesteel.

She waited, twisting her hands in her lap, while the old woman read the few typed lines announcing the scheduled execution of Lafayette Harkryder in a few weeks' time.

When Nora Bonesteel had finished reading the letter, she set it down on the table. "You'd better have some tea," she said.

Pauline Harkryder shrugged. It was all one to her. She couldn't remember whether she'd eaten anything today or not. "They say they're going to kill Lafayette," she called out. Nora Bonesteel was in the kitchen now, setting the copper kettle on to boil. It made her easier to talk to, Pauline thought, if you didn't have to look at those blue eyes staring through you.

A few moments passed, and there was no answer from the kitchen. Pauline tried again. "Do you think they will? Kill him, I mean."

Nora Bonesteel appeared in the doorway. "I don't know," she said. "I'll pray about it."

"But—what I came to ask . . . If I could just know for sure . . . Miz Bonesteel—*is he guilty?*"

They stared at each other in silence. At last Nora Bonesteel said, "Do you need me to tell you that?"

Pauline Harkryder covered her mouth with her hand. "I've never said anything," she whispered. "In all these years I never did. Is it too late?"

Nora Bonesteel sighed. "Do you have any kind of proof that would convince a judge?"

"No."

"Then let it be." Behind her the teakettle screeched and rumbled, breaking the silence.

"It's hard to know what's best to do," said Pauline. "He was a sweet young 'un, but he growed up wild, same as the other two. I did what I could for those boys after their mama was gone."

"You can write to him," said Nora Bonesteel. "Ask him what he wants you to do. Aside from that, all you can do is pray and wait, because only one person can save him, and that isn't you."

A plain wooden chair sits on the tiled floor of an otherwise empty room. The chair is dark oak, with wide, flat arms. Its back is a solid plank, except for the three rectangular openings on either side, positioned to accommodate two pairs of blue nylon restraining straps ending in metal seat-belt buckles. Behind the chair a round wall clock familiar to schoolrooms hangs high on the pale cinder-block wall. The chair faces a large glass window covered by blinds, concealing a viewing room with space for perhaps twenty chairs. The only ornament in the observation room is a wall plaque, approximately one foot in diameter: a circle with the words "The Great Seal of the State of Tennessee 1796" encircling a drawing of a plow with "Agriculture" written beneath it, and below that a sailing ship designated "Commerce." The walls to the left and right of the chair are fitted with ordinary doors. One leads to the corridor of holding cells and a kitchen such as one might find adjoining the reception hall of a modern country church. The other door opens into another plain, bright room, containing a small metal cabinet with lights and dials fitted on the gray surface. Beside it a power-supply box containing a transformer converts the standard 220-volt current coming into the room into a charge of 2,640 volts at the proper time. A wall telephone hangs a few feet away.

The chair was made for the state of Tennessee by the firm of Fred A. Leuchter Associates in Boston in 1989, but in style and composition, it looks much older. Parts of it are. The state sent the Leuchter company wood from the first Old Sparky, built in 1916, to be used in the construction of the new one, a ritual that was not without precedent. Some of the wood from the 1916 electric chair had been salvaged from Tennessee's old gallows and used to construct its replacement when hanging went out of fashion. Now its successor contains the wood of both, so that more than a century of tradition has been incorporated into the new device. The new chair cost the state $50,000, and it, too, was called "Old Sparky."

It has never been used.

Once a month, though, it is tested.

Once a month a jar of salt water—a much more accurate

representation of a man than the biblical image of dust—is placed on the flat wooden seat; electrodes are inserted into the water; someone presses a button on the gray machine, and current surges through the water, proving that all is in readiness.

At least that is how the prisoners believe the chair is tested. They recount the story to one another in bull sessions, and engage in private speculations about who among them will be the first to go. Who will christen the new chair with his bodily fluids? But the prisoners also say that there are claw marks in the wide arms of the wooden chair, a chair that was built in 1989 and has never been used.

Even when the power is not turned on, the electric chair generates its own current of legend.

Burgess Gaither

ARREST

I remember the first time I ever heard of Frankie Silver.

Constable Charlie Baker was pounding on the door of the courthouse in snow-caked boots, bawling like a branded calf, "Sheriff! Where's Sheriff Butler? There's been murder done!"

It was January 10, 1832, the Tuesday morning after Twelfth Night. I was shivering in my office, still worn out from Saturday's Old Christmas revels at Belvidere, but determined that a headache and a touch of fever should claim no more of this fine new year, my twenty-fifth year of life and the third year of my profession of law.

I was trying to write legibly in the Burke County record book without removing my gloves. The fire burned bravely in the grate behind me, but it was no match for the wind that knifed through the cracks in the wooden walls, and I could see my breath hanging in the air above the candle flame. This sight inspired in me waves of self-pity as I imagined elegant velvet-curtained offices in the great stone edifices of Raleigh: roaring fires blazing beneath marble mantelpieces and crystal decanters of brandywine on mahogany sideboards. In such palatial quarters, more prosperous young lawyers, those who had read law with statesmen and judges, and who were not eighth sons in genteel but modest families, would practice their calling with an exalted clientele, while I, who had read law with my poor older brother, rest his soul, sat freezing in a frontier courthouse, far from the corridors of power, and likely to remain so.

"Where's Mr. Butler? There's been murder done!"

The shouting roused me from my morning lethargy, and I flung open the door of my office and stalked through the courtroom to see who was disturbing my peace. As I pushed open the outer door, I nearly collided with a hulking figure who seemed composed entirely of snow, fur, and buckskin.

"What's all this noise?" I demanded. In truth, I thought that the man was a drunkard whose Christmas revels had gone on well past New Year's. I grabbed hold of his sodden coat sleeve and he spun around, shaking the muffler from his wind-reddened face. I saw that he was sober enough, but his eyes were wide with alarm. "What is it?" I said.

The man quieted now, content to have someone to hear him out. "I'm a constable, bringing in prisoners," he said. "A man has been murdered, up past Celo Mountain, and we reckon we have the killers." I was too astonished to reply, so he went on. "I brought them with me, but it was a day's ride through deep snow, and I won't put my horse or myself through that journey again yet awhile. I'll be staying the night at the county's expense before I head back up the mountain."

I gave him a patient smile and drew him inside, shutting the door against the wind. "You will get no argument from me about your intention to rest in the tavern before heading home," I told him. "I see the sense in your statement. Nothing could induce me to make such an arduous journey twice without respite."

"And the county will pay for my lodging?"

"I am not the man to rule on these financial matters, or even to accept your prisoners. You want the sheriff, or, failing him, the jailer. I am the clerk of the Superior Court, and you'll have no need of my services until the case comes to trial in the spring term, three months hence."

"No one but you is about," he told me. "A lad on the street said I'd find you here. I brought a man with me. He's watching my prisoners for me now. I thought you might summon someone to take charge of them so that I can go off to a drink and a warm room." He used his teeth to pull the deer-skin gloves from his fingers. "I have the warrant with me," he said, fishing a damp bit of paper out of the cavernous folds of his garments.

I recognized my visitor now. The young man, a constable from the far reaches of the county, was the son of old David Baker, a patriot of the Revolution, one of the prominent landowners to the west. I saw this young constable some-times when court was in session. I scanned the document, an arrest warrant penned by his brother, a justice of the peace in one of those settlements miles from here, past the wall of mountains.

Burke County is more than fifty miles long, and the wild western portion of it lies in steep mountains, with bold rivers too rocky and shallow for riverboat commerce, and an end-less thicket of trees walling out the world beyond. From the Carolina piedmont there are but three portals into that wilderness: the Gillespie Gap, the Buck Creek Gap, and the Winding Stairs; from within it, the Iron Mountain Gap is the way out, leading on into Tennessee. The fortress of hills be-tween the piedmont and the Tennessee settlement was once the hunting ground of the Cherokee and the Shawnee. Now it is the kingdom of the bear and the elk; a land of strange bald mountains, rich forests of oak and chestnut, and, scat-tered here and there across it in makeshift homesteads, the frontiersmen.

A determined man, or a desperate one, could eke out an existence on such inhospitable land, but it would be a lonely life, removed from polite society as I knew it. No gentleman would set his plantation west of Morganton, for here ends the fertile piedmont land of rolling hills and wide flat fields. Some people did live in the western reaches of Burke County, but they kept to themselves. Great tracts of that un-forgiving land had been given as grants to soldiers who fought in the War of 1812, causing scores of land-poor farm-ers to come down from Maryland and Pennsylvania looking to homestead the frontier, far from their prosperous Eastern neighbors who had trammeled the seaboard with their plantations. I supposed that the constable's family was one of these backwoods gentry, but since their holdings were miles west of Morganton, they would not be known to me. Such outsiders as appeared socially at Morganton balls and dinner parties invariably hailed from east of us, for that way lay government, society, and civilization; westward lay only the trackless wilderness, Indian country, and Tennessee.

Murder done, Charlie Baker had said. It hardly surprised me in such a wild place. I scanned the document.

STATE OF NORTH CAROLINA
BURKE COUNTY

This day came Elijah Green before me D. D. Baker an acting justice of the county and made oath in due form of law that Frankey Silver and [something was crossed out here] Barbara Stewart and Blackston Stewart is believed that they did murder Charles Silvers contrary to law and against the sovereign dignity of the State. Sworn to and subscribed by me this 9th day of January 1832.

D. D. Baker   *Elijah Green*

Appended to this document was another few lines from Justice Baker authorizing law officers to take the accused persons into custody and to bring them safely before a justice of the county to answer the charges made against them.

"It all seems in order," I said, handing the paper back to the justice's brother. "And you say you have brought the prisoners? Two men and a woman?"

"Two women, sir," said the constable.

I glanced again at the warrant. "Barbara Stewart and . . . Frankie?"

"Mother and daughter. The daughter, Frankie, is the wife of the deceased. They're all outside with the fellow I brought with me. They haven't given us any trouble on the journey, but all the same I'd better head back directly."

"So you shall," I told him. "Bring your prisoners here into the courthouse, where you may all keep warm, and I will find Mr. Butler for you, or, failing that, Mr. Presnell. And in exchange you must promise to tell me what has happened in those mountains to bring about such a grievous charge."

I was eager to hear more of this news, but in good conscience I could not keep women waiting outdoors on such a bitter day, even if they were wicked murderesses. Barbara Stewart and her two grown offspring. The names meant nothing to me. I pictured a wizened crone and her witless children, caught poisoning some poor traveler, or a pair of madwomen perhaps, driven out of their senses by the cold and isolation of that mountain fortress. I shuddered to think that our fair country could contain such evil. However, news is currency in Morganton, as in any other bustling town, and I wanted to be enriched with the information before the gossips had spread it far and wide. I retrieved my overcoat and accompanied Baker outside. Five snow-dusted horses were tethered to the oak tree near the steps. Constable Baker's companion stood on the courthouse walk, his pistol drawn and aimed at his charges.

Two of the prisoners squatted on the ground beneath the tree, so bundled up in their winter wraps that I could tell little about them except that they seemed indifferent to the gun trained on them, for they did not even glance in our direction.

On one of the horses sat a young girl, so little and pale that at first I took her for a child. She was covered in a hooded woolen cloak, but I could see fair hair at the sides of her face, and her cheeks were rouged with cold. Frankie Silver was small and slight, but she had the wiry body of one who had seen her share of drudgery on a hardscrabble hill farm. She appeared to be about eighteen now, only seven years younger than I, but what a distance there was between us in experience and opportunity! At thirty, when I am still short of my prime, she will be an old woman, if childbirth or sickness does not take her first. Just now, though, she was lovely. Her hair was the color of straw, but her features were even and there was a pleasing aspect to her face, except for its sullen expression. At least she was not weeping, as I feared she would be, but perhaps if you have done what she is accused of, you have no tears within you.

She seemed apprehensive, but from time to time when she would steal a glance at her surroundings, curiosity lit her face, banishing the frown of care. She was fine-featured— not as elegant as my Elizabeth, of course; not a lady; but pretty enough.

She has never been to town before, I thought. There are many such girls in the wildwood, born and bred in log cabins, and strangers to the ways of gentlefolk. What a pity that this poor creature should see the sights on such a sad pretext as this.

"This is your prisoner?" I asked Charlie Baker, still doubting the evidence of my own eyes.

He nodded. "Frankie Silver." He had thanked the man who was minding the horses and the prisoners, and told him to take the mounts to the livery stable. The young fellow holstered his pistol and walked away, somewhat reluctantly, I thought. There was a tale in this strange arrival, and he thought it his due to be in on the telling of it, in return for his services on the trail. He was to be disappointed. Charlie Baker would have the glory all to himself.

"But, Constable, surely this . . . this child cannot be charged with murder."

Charlie Baker turned away, probably to hide a grin at my naïveté. "She's a grown woman, right enough. Married these two years or thereabouts, and left a baby up yonder at the Silvers' place. A fatherless one now." He turned to the shivering young woman and untied the rope that looped under her horse's belly, binding one of her ankles to the other. "Get down off your horse now, Miz Silver. Get up, Miz Stewart. Blackston. We're to wait in the courthouse."

Barbara Stewart and her son trudged toward the courthouse steps without so much as a glance in my direction. The mother leaned against the shoulder of the sturdy youth, whether from weariness or despair I could not tell.

Frankie Silver raised her hands from beneath the folds of her cloak, and for the first time I could see that her wrists were bound with hemp rope. Baker held the horse, and I assisted her in dismounting, for the hands of her brother were tied as well, so that he could not have assisted her. She seemed to add but little to the weight of the cloak itself; indeed, I could have carried her all the way into the courthouse without feeling the strain, but it would not have been seemly, and I did not. I set her properly upon the ground, and then, feeling as if I should pass some pleasantry with this small person who was in such straits, I said, "Well, madam, I hope that a stay in our jail will not be too terrible for you. I could wish you better lodging than this on a cold winter morning. They will not grant you bail, of course, but still, guilty or not, it is a great pity to keep a woman in such a tiny, cold room with no windows and no chair, and hardly room to turn around in."

She looked up at me for a moment, and then she shrugged. "Reckon what do you think I lived in before I came here?"

I had not seen Sheriff Butler that morning, though I thought there was little for him to do on a snowbound Tuesday morning. If he was not at his home, then I thought a tavern the logical place to seek him out. There were several to choose from in Morganton. They offered lodging to those who came to town for the courts, or to travelers heading onward over the mountains; for the rest of us they provided a place to meet and talk and quench our thirst. They also spread the news in a veritable brushfire of words. Tales of this arrest, and of the pretty young Mrs. Silver, would inspire so much talk that it would take a keg of whiskey to quench the dry throats of the newsmongers.

I found Sheriff William Butler in the second tavern I tried. He would leave office in a few months' time, for North Carolina sheriffs are not allowed to serve more than one consecutive term in office. Before the year's end there would be an election to fill the position, although the presidential election was a greater topic of conversation among the townsmen.

This new development would engage the sheriff's attention, I thought, and it might divert the town gossips from the endless discussion of Andrew Jackson and his chances for reelection. Butler was only a few years older than myself, and I knew him socially as well as within our mutual duties to the law, because Will was the younger brother of Mr. John Edward Butler of Locust Grove, a prominent landowner and an active participant in the affairs of Burke County. Both of the Butler brothers were often to be found at the Erwins' social gatherings, and we in turn had broken bread with them at Locust Grove. Will's late wife had been a lifelong friend of my Elizabeth, who still mourned the untimely death of her childhood friend. Such are the bonds of friendship among the men of business in a small town. I wondered what Will would make of this piece of news.

I greeted such folks as I knew in the tavern, and motioned for Sheriff Butler to accompany me outside. "Your duty calls, sir," I said, trying not to make the matter sound important. He knew, though, that something was amiss, for he picked up his hat and coat and followed me to the street without a moment's delay.

"A constable from the west county has brought in three prisoners," I told him, steering him through the frozen carriage ruts toward the courthouse square.

He heard me out in silence while I told of the warrant and the arrival of the constable. "Indeed I know little of what has transpired," I said. "But since the jailer cannot be found at the moment, I have put Mr. Baker and his trio of prisoners in the courthouse to await your pleasure. When we have seen the ladies and the boy safely stowed in your custody, perhaps we can prevail upon the constable to tell us the circumstances that brought her here."

Will Butler permitted himself a smile. My use of the word "us" had not escaped him, but he nodded in agreement to my suggestion. "Yes, we must hear his tale, Burgess."

"He will have to speak with the tongues of angels to persuade me of the daughter's guilt. I cannot speak for the other two, for I barely glimpsed them, but indeed I am convinced that an error has been made in arresting her. Wait until you see her, Butler! She looks scarcely more than a child."

"If the prisoner is, as you say, a pretty young woman, they must be sure enough of her guilt in the west county to bring her in at all. The trial will be in March, though, at the spring term of the court—but if worse comes to worst, the consequences of that trial will not occur until after my time. I don't envy my successor his job."

I took his grisly meaning at once, but I doubted his prediction. "It will not come to that," I told him. "They will not hang a woman."

I left Will Butler to his duty and went back to my office and my record books. I had extracted a promise from him to fetch me when the prisoners had been safely locked away into Gabe Presnell's care. The Morganton jail is but a short walk from the courthouse, a two-story log structure with two rooms on the ground floor for the jailer's lodging, and four rooms upstairs for the incarceration of prisoners. It is hardly a fit place for women to be kept, I thought, but I suppose it is better than the dirt-floored stockade that had served as the jail ten years ago. I had heard my father-in-law, Squire Erwin, speak of it, for he was clerk of Superior Court before me, and for much of his tenure that rude byre was in use as the county's prison. Once he described to me the stench and the straw and the dirt floor.

"Like a stable," I had remarked.

"Not at all," said the squire. "No one would keep good horses in the wet and foul-smelling darkness of that log pen, but Burke County in its wisdom reckoned that such accommodations were good enough for its prisoners. We even locked up debtors in those days, poor wretches. Still, I suppose it was fit enough for most of the villains we got."

The new wooden jailhouse was a far cry better than the old

log pen, and I had made light of its discomforts to the young woman prisoner, but, really, I'd sooner sleep on the court-house lawn than up there in that tiny room, in too close proximity to the stink and the body lice of the other prisoners. Outdoors could be no colder, and at least the air would be clean.

I went back to my ledger, and my breath still clouded the air above my desk. Still, a new year had begun and I had much to be thankful for, most of it due to my late brother, whose untimely death these two years past still grieved me. I had come to Morganton on Alfred's coattails, courted his wife's sister, and won her, though Alfred did not live to see us wed. My bride, Elizabeth, was three years my senior, intelligent, well-spoken, and every inch a lady, for all that she was no great beauty. She was an Erwin, though, and that counted for everything. Erwin was a name to conjure with in Burke County, for the Erwins *were* Morganton. The two Erwin brothers who settled there in the late 1700s were gentlemen planters, and their numerous descendants owned vast expanses of land, commanding positions of respect and authority throughout the community. After more than forty years in residence, the Erwins looked after the people in Burke County with a benignity that was almost feudal. To a newly minted young lawyer, they seemed the epitome of hospitality and noble friendliness, offering lodging to new-comers and hosting dinners and parties at Bellevue and Belvidere for those who came to town for the circuit court in the spring and fall. To a new son-in-law, they were bountiful. They were kindness itself. When Miss Elizabeth Erwin graciously consented to be my wife, I was summoned to the study at Belvidere to face her father, who duly inquired into my prospects. I was obliged to tell him that but for my education, my profession of law, and my family's good name—indeed, I had none.

William Willoughby Erwin was a lawyer himself, and he had been father-in-law to my older brother Alfred, who had married Miss Catherine Erwin in March of 1828, so I felt emboldened to speak frankly to him, since we were brother attorneys, and all but family in kinship. I told him that I had hoped that Alfred and I might have set up a law practice together, but that was not to be, for he died before I had even completed my training for the law, and I was forced to conclude my studies under the tutelage of Judge Caldwell. The Gaithers were educated and wellborn, but we were not well off. My father had died when I was twelve, and Alfred, the eldest child in the family, had taken on the duties of father to the eight younger Gaithers. He had been my guide, my friend, and my companion in the law, and I missed him sorely. With Alfred's passing went my hopes for partnership and prosperity, and I admitted my penury readily enough, as I was sure Squire Erwin knew of it already.

"But," I told him, "I am an honest, God-fearing man, not afraid of hard work, neither accustomed to nor in need of luxury." It was a pretty speech to make, standing on the squire's turkey carpet, surrounded by his library of a thousand leather volumes. I waved my crystal wineglass for emphasis, nearly hitting the cut-glass chandelier that shimmered above me.

William Erwin remained solemn at my declaration, but I fancy that there was a twinkle in his eye. "You'll do," he said. "We'll see what can be done about your prospects, sir."

Perhaps he was thinking of the fact that his daughter Elizabeth had seven sisters, and that eligible young lawyers on the frontier were not so plentiful that one could afford to be too particular about prospective sons-in-law. So Elizabeth and I were married, and within a few months Squire Erwin resigned his post as Burke County's clerk of Superior Court, a position he had held for forty-four years. The job was given to me.

It was a steady income, and a respectable civil position that kept me on good terms with the legal community, and it provided me with a chance to learn more of my craft by observing more seasoned attorneys at work. In a few years' time, my experience and my standing in the community would be such that I could afford to establish a law practice of my own. Until then, I was content to toil as a learned clerk in the halls of justice. I had been clerk of Superior Court for eighteen months, well liked and well content with my profession and my family, for Elizabeth and I had a son, whom we named William, after the old squire. We would name the next one Alfred.

I had been at work for less than an hour when the sheriff and the messenger appeared at the door of my office. "Come with us, Burgess," said Will Butler. "Constable Baker promises us a tale worthy of a tavern, but we had better get the news in private. Come to my house, and warm yourselves by my fire while we learn what this is about."

A short walk took us to Butler's house. He settled us in the parlor, a simple enough room, but as warm and comfortable as a man could wish for. He offered us some corn whiskey that he kept in an earthenware jug—not the crystal decanter of brandy that Raleigh's gentlemen lawyers might have proffered, but it was welcome nonetheless, and it chased away the last of the chill from our bones. Soon enough Constable Baker was sitting by the fire, thawing his muddy boots on the hearthrug and stroking the head of one of Butler's hounds. We waited while the sheriff read the warrant from Justice of the Peace Baker.

After a few moments of silence, Will Butler put aside the documents and looked at his guest. "Now," he said, "tell me what has happened."

Charlie Baker warmed his throat with a swig of whiskey and began: "You know Jacob Silver from the other end of the county—along the Toe River, his land is—"

"I do not know him," I said.

"Has someone killed this Jacob Silver?" asked Butler. He reached for the papers again, but then shook his head, remembering that another name was on the warrant as victim. He settled back in his chair then, seeing that Baker was bound and determined to make a tale of it. We might as well hear him out.

"No, sir. No one killed the old man, though I think the grief of this has dealt a blow to his constitution. Jacob Silver is a well-respected man in the community. He's got a smart bit of land over the mountains from a soldier's grant. He came down from Maryland about twenty years ago, after the English war, him and some of his brothers. With him he brought his boy Charlie, whose mother had died birthing him. Not more than a lap baby, Charlie was then.

"Old Jacob has a passel of children now. He married Nancy Reed over at Double Island, more than seventeen years ago, and they have about eight young 'uns. Charlie, the one that got killed, was that son from Maryland, by Jacob's first wife. He wasn't but nineteen years old. Two years ago he married Frankie—"

"The name is probably Frances," I murmured to Butler, who nodded in agreement.

"That's right," said Baker. "Miss Frances Stewart she was before she married into the Silver clan. The other two prisoners, Barbara Stewart and youngest boy Blackston, live on the other side of the Toe River, about two miles downstream from the Jacob Silver homestead. It's Isaiah Stewart's place. He's from Anson County, and he and his wife Barbara—"

"Tell us about the murder," said Will, losing patience at last. "We can sort out their bloodlines later."

"First sign of trouble was on December 23. That morning Frankie Silver went to her in-laws' cabin, with the baby on her hip, and she told them that Charlie had lit out from home a couple of days back, and he hadn't returned. She was wanting somebody to come feed the cows."

"Why didn't she ask her own kinfolk to do it?"

"The menfolk were gone. At least her father was away from home. She has an older brother, Jackson, who's married to a Howell girl, but he was off with his father. I heard they were on a long hunt over in Kentucky. They weren't back when I left there yesterday. I reckon the younger boy, Blackston, could have helped her. He's about fifteen. But like I said, the Stewarts live two miles from Frankie, and over on the other side of the river, while the Silvers' cabin is just a quarter mile down the hill from Frankie and Charlie's place. The snow was knee-deep and the river was frozen. I reckon she didn't want to chance crossing it, with the baby and all. Anyhow, she showed up at Charlie's parents' house, cool as snowmelt, saying he was gone getting his Christmas liquor. She said he had gone to George Young's house with his jug and his fiddle. Boasted about how she'd been busy since sunup doing her washing and redding the cabin. She didn't seem to mind much that her husband was gone, only she wanted somebody to feed the stock. So the Silvers sent over Alfred, their next oldest boy, to see to the cattle, and Frankie went back home.

"Every day after that, Frankie would stop by, still more peevish than affrighted, saying Charlie wasn't back yet, and the Silvers were growing more anxious by the minute. Charlie was a sunny fellow; always a smile and a song; everybody liked him. Finally Frankie said she didn't care if her no-account husband came back or not, she was going to stay at her mother's house, and she was taking the baby with her.

"By then the Silvers were all-fired worried about Charlie, it being the dead of winter and all. Since Charlie Silver was a great one for drinking and fiddling, they thought it was just possible that he had found a party too good to leave and was holed up drunk somewhere, but it had been more than ten days by then, and it wasn't like him to be gone that long. They sent over to George Young's place, looking to find him, and George said that Charlie had come for that Christmas liquor right enough, and he had got it, but he said that Charlie had come and gone many days ago. The Youngs hadn't seen him since.

"By then the Silvers were hunting the woods for him, and all the trails that led to George's cabin, in case Charlie had fallen or come to harm while he was on his way home from the Youngs' place, and maybe the worse for drink. The Silvers and some of their neighbors and kinfolk even went down to examine the river, but it was frozen solid and covered with unbroken snow. There was no sign that anybody had fallen in. After that, some of the neighbors—my people, Elijah Green, the Youngs, the Howells, the Hutchinses, and

old Jack Collis—kept up the search, and Jacob—he was beside himself by this time—he . . . well, he went over into
Tennessee."

Whatever we had been expecting, it was not this. "Went to
Tennessee?" said Butler. "What did he do that for?"

Baker shrugged. "Advice, I reckon you'd call it. He had
heard tell of a Guinea Negro there, over Jonesborough way,
that people say has the conjure power."

I smiled at this touching bit of superstition, but then I recalled the tragic nature of this tale, and it sobered me at
once. Parents who have lost a child will reach out for whatever comfort they can find. I was interested in this development. Guinea Negroes were said to have occult powers that
they brought with them as a vestige of paganism from their
own lands, but I had seldom heard of anyone asking them
for more than simple fortune-telling: benign promises of a
rosy future. This urgent task of finding a lost youth would
prove a challenge indeed for such a conjure man. "And what
did the African tell Mr. Silver?"

"He asked Silver to draw him a map of the valley where
Charlie went missing, to mark the cabins, the river, the
ridges, the fields—everything. Then that old conjure man
took up a pendant, strung on a leather thong, and he swung
it around in a circle over the map. To hear Jacob Silver tell it,
that ball swung around and around over the map, getting
slower and slower, until it came to a full stop and just hovered there—right over Charlie's own cabin. And the conjure
man, he looked up and said, 'That boy never left his own
house.' "

Butler and I looked at each other. Surely the prisoner was
here on more evidence than a trick of ball and string over a
map? "They searched the cabin then?"

"Already had!" said Charlie Baker, grinning triumphantly.
While Mr. Jacob Silver was gone over the mountain into
Tennessee, and Frankie had quit the place to go home to the
Stewarts, that old bear hunter Jack Collis decided to look a
little closer to home. He never did put much stock in what
Frankie had told him, 'cause he couldn't find no tracks in the

woods, despite the deep snow, and he couldn't think where
Charlie could have got to without leaving some kind of a
trail. While everybody else was out combing the deep woods
and the land over by the Youngs' place, Jack Collis snuck
back to that cabin of Frankie and Charlie's, and he poked
around. There was a goodly pile of ashes in the fireplace, as
if somebody had burned a whole cord of wood without
cleaning out the fireplace, he said. Jack studied about that
for a while, and then he put some of those ashes in clean
water in the kettle over the fire, and what do you think he
found?" Baker beamed at us expectantly.

We waited politely, for it was obvious that he was bursting
to tell us.

"Grease bubbles!"

When my expression did not change, the constable must
have realized that such rustic deductions were wasted upon
gentlemen, for we lacked the requisite frontier skills to recognize the significance of that discovery. After a flash of dis-
appointment, Baker explained. "There shouldn't be any
grease in fireplace ashes. The meat is cooked inside the pot,
don't you see? So when Jack found grease in the grate itself,
he knew that a quantity of—of flesh—had been burned directly in that fire."

This time our expressions were all he could have wished.

"Then Jack Collis took a candle and went to checking that
cabin like a dog on point. He found bits of bone and a shoe
buckle in the fireplace, and blood drops in the cracks of the
puncheon floor. He raised the alarm to the rest of the men,
and we began to direct our search closer in, near the spring,
right there around the cabin."

"Did you find him?" I asked. "Did you find Charlie
Silver?"

Constable Baker swallowed hard. "Most of him."

*They have brought me down from my beautiful mountain in
the white silence of winter, my wrists bound with hemp rope,
my legs tied beneath the pony's belly as if I were a yearling doe*

taken on the long hunt. And perhaps I am, for I am as defense-less as a deer, and as silent. They say that deer, who live out their lives in silence, scream when they are being killed. Well, perhaps I will be permitted that.

The horses are almost swallowed by the snow drifts in the pass. They push forward against the white tide, plunging and pushing with their chests, as if they were fording a swollen spring river in-stead of threading their way down a cold mountain.

No one sings or whistles as we make our way down the trail toward town, and I have only the wind to listen to. Sometimes I think I can hear voices in the torrent, indistinguishable words singing close harmony, and I strain to make out the words, but their sense escapes me. Charlie used to sing when he was coming home from George Young's place, but that was never a pleasant sound for me, though I once thought that he had as fine a voice as ever I'd heard. When we were courting, he used to sing me "Barbary Ellen" and "The False Knight in the Road."

No one sings to me now.

The two lawmen are scared of what I have done, what I might do—a crazy woman, a man-killer. What if I worked free of my ropes, and what if I had a knife hidden beneath my skirts? My brother is sullen as always, and I think my mother is afraid of me, too, but for a different reason. She wishes my fa-ther were not gone from home, for he would be able to tell us what to do now. He always knows what to do, but he was not there to ask. I look at her: her hands are clenched over the sad-dle horn until the knuckles show white, and she takes deep breaths every now and then, as if a scream keeps rising up to the top of her throat and she has to keep swallowing it back. She will not look at me.

I wish my daddy were here. I wish he had not gone to Ken-tucky in search of the elk herds. If he had been home on those days before Christmas, we would not be here now, cloud-breathed and shivering, our horses breasting the snow drifts as we plough our way through the pass, heading for jail in Morganton.

Hemp rope shrinks when it is wet, and its grip numbs my

*wrists even more than the cold already has, but I do not com-
plain, because if I began to speak I might never stop.*

*I see you looking at me, Constable Charlie Baker. I know
you of old. Your daddy fought in the Revolution, and your
brother is the justice of the peace, so you have land and position, but for all that you are a runty fellow with never a smile
for ary soul. Constables get to thinking they are better than
other folks. You used to come to dances at George Young's, but
you never did dance. You came to the cabin raisings in Hollow
Poplar and Grassy Creek, and you'd work as hard as any man
there, but when the toil was over and the eating and the dancing began, you'd hang back, bashful to speak to the girls. You
weren't as handsome as my Charlie, and though I saw you
looking at me a time or two, you never asked me to sit supper
with you. You never asked me to dance. Maybe you figured
you'd never cut out a young buck like Charlie Silver, and
maybe you were right. Now you are wondering what would
have happened if you had. If I had chosen Charlie Baker instead of Charlie Silver? Would you have saved me, or would
you be laying in three graves in a mountain churchyard, wishing you had never seen my face?*

Chapter Two

I GUESS HE'S ALL RIGHT." Martha Ayers was on duty break, eating a quick supper at the diner with Deputy Joe LeDonne, who was scheduled to work until eleven. "He's not as bony-looking as he was, and his color's good. He's going to start raring to come back to work any day now."

"Let him," said LeDonne. "It would probably help him take his mind off himself. Besides, we could use the help."

"His mind isn't on himself, Joe. Spencer is brooding about this upcoming execution. They've asked him to be one of the witnesses—sheriff of the prisoner's home county—and he says he has to go, but you can tell that he's just making himself sick about it." She looked with disfavor at the lump of mashed potatoes and the congealing brown gravy that seeped down toward the green beans and meat loaf. She pushed the plate away with a sigh. *I feel as tired as Joe looks,* she thought.

"Fate Harkryder," LeDonne was saying. "I read about the scheduled execution in the *Chronicle*. Paper said he was local. I didn't realize that Spencer knew him, though. He's been on the row a long time."

"Spencer was Nelse Miller's deputy, remember? He's the one who arrested this guy. I think he had all but forgotten about him—and now this. It couldn't come at a worse time. Spencer's just out of the hospital, trying to recover from a wound that almost killed him, and now the state comes up with this business. He'll worry himself sick over it. You know how he is." She reached for her coffee cup, saw that it was empty, and set it down again. Without a word, LeDonne handed her his. Martha smiled her thanks. "It's just bad luck, is all," she said, sighing. "Out of all the men Tennessee has got on death row, they have to pick this guy to go first."

"It didn't surprise me much that it'd be him, though," said LeDonne.

"Why not? There are about a hundred men on death row. It could have been any of them."

"*Any* of them?" There was no amusement in Joe LeDonne's smile. "Hardly that. This will be Tennessee's first execution in more than thirty years. They're going to choose that first prisoner very carefully—very *politically*. It's not going to be a woman, even if there's one eligible to be executed. *Ladies first* does not apply to the electric chair. It can't be any of the new guys, because the public will say it's unfair to execute one of them ahead of fellows who have been there for decades. And it's not going to be a black man, because the death penalty is a sticky enough issue as it is, without leaving yourself open for a charge of racism. You don't want to enrage any special-interest groups if you can help it. So you check the list of condemned prisoners and you find a poor white mountain boy with no money and no political influence, and there's your pigeon. Nobody's going to kick up a fuss when he's put to death. Nobody cares what happens to poor Southern whites. Nobody gets fired or takes a beating in the press for using words like *redneck* and *hillbilly*. When you think about it, Fate Harkryder was the perfect choice for the electric chair. A nobody without a cause."

"You won't make me feel sorry for him," said Martha. "No matter why they picked him to go first, he killed somebody, and the jury said to execute him. Some people might say that Fate Harkryder got twenty more years of life than he was entitled to."

LeDonne nodded. "You'll get no argument from me. I was just pointing out the logic of it to you."

"All right then." The silence stretched on longer than

Martha could stand it, so she said, "Spencer asked me to bring him some books on Frankie Silver."

"Who?"

Martha shrugged. "It's an old murder case. North Carolina. It must be unsolved. Anyhow, he's looking into it."

"Oh. He must be bored if he's looking for crimes to investigate." He paused for a moment before he said, "Did you tell him about the current investigation?"

"No," said Martha. "He's fine where he is. And I've been keeping the newspaper away from him, too. Let him keep his nose in the history books for at least another week. I don't want him to come back before he's well enough to handle it."

"But the similarities between the two incidents . . ."

Martha shrugged. "Coincidence. Anyhow, he's too ill to concern himself with criminal investigation. We can handle it. I'll get him his books on Frankie Silver. They will keep him busy, and if it keeps his mind off the execution and out of the office, so much the better."

Fate Harkryder. Spencer didn't want to think about him right now. He didn't want to relive those hours at the floodlit campsite, and he didn't want to think about the inevitable conclusion to that chain of events set in motion so long ago.

He stood at the sliding glass doors of his cabin, looking out on the folds of hills stretching away to North Carolina. The sight of the mountains in the morning sunshine always brought to mind the 121st Psalm: *I will lift up mine eyes unto the hills, from whence cometh my help.* Usually he found that gazing out at the mountains soothed him and made the concerns of the day fade away into the haze of geologic time. It was a spiritual experience that he could not explain, except to say that the vista gave him perspective and made his problems seem insignificant when measured against the eternity of the land itself.

He found himself thinking instead about Frankie Silver.

It had been twenty years, but Spencer still remembered standing beside Nelse Miller at the grave in the mountain churchyard on that bright summer day and feeling a chill as the old man talked about the death of Charlie Silver. On the drive back to Hamelin, Nelse had rambled on for nearly an hour about the nineteenth-century murder case and the events that followed, making a tale of it as mountain story-tellers instinctively do. Spencer had forgotten most of the details of the story—the names of the witnesses and the attorneys had passed from his mind almost as soon as Nelse uttered them. He had spoken fluently, from long familiarity with the case, with never a moment's hesitation in his recital. What Spencer chiefly remembered was the passion of the sheriff's interest in that one incident and the power of the spell woven by the tale on the long drive back over the mountain. Nelse Miller seldom talked about his own experiences in law enforcement, and he showed only a perfunctory interest in high-profile crimes reported in the national news. It was only this one obscure, seemingly insignificant case that held him in thrall.

Back then, Spencer Arrowood had thought the story of Frankie Silver was only a captivating folktale, entertaining enough to pass the time on the way home, but nothing that he ever needed to think about again. The story held no lessons about criminal investigation that he could see, since forensic detection was all but nonexistent in those days, and despite Nelse Miller's obsession with the case, he saw no chance of resolving its mysteries after so many years had passed. Spencer had forgotten about Frankie Silver. Sheriff Nelse Miller, by then retired and crippled with arthritis, died in 1984, his book about Frankie Silver unwritten, his questions unanswered.

He could have forgotten all about that little-known murder case if it weren't for one thing that Nelse Miller had said. "There's only two cases of mountain justice that I'm not happy with. One is that fellow you put on death row, and the other is Frankie Silver."

And now she haunted him. It was nothing he wanted to talk about with anybody—except Nelse Miller, who was long dead. He would have understood the fascination of the story.

Three graves in a mountain churchyard.

Spencer wondered if his sudden interest in the case was merely a product of the boredom of an active man forced to sit still for the first time in his adult life, or if it was a displacement of his own anxiety about the approaching death of Fate Harkryder. His great-aunt Til would have said, "You are called to solve the mystery," and he smiled at the memory of an old mountain woman and her simple faith. He would look into the case, he told himself, and of all the whys he had to consider in the matter of Frankie Silver, the one he resolved not to look into was the why of his own interest in her story.

Dr. Alton Banner was checking up on his patient in an after-hours visit to the sheriff's mountain cabin. "I don't generally make house calls these days," he remarked as he examined the stitches on the wound. "It frightens the younger members of my profession. I made an exception in your case, however, because any man who is fool enough to get himself shot for trespassing is probably fool enough to try to drive himself into town for his doctor's appointment."

Spencer did not reply. Useless to argue that in "trespassing" he had been in the line of duty, enforcing a court order, or to protest that he felt well enough to end his convalescence. The old man had his own opinions on everything, and he was unlikely to be deterred by the facts as his patient saw them.

"I don't know why you live up here anyhow," Banner went on, as he continued to poke and prod his patient. "The road up this mountain is a sheet of glass in the wintertime. I wouldn't even try it in a four-wheel drive. It's damned near vertical, that's what it is. You're like all the rest of these mountaineers. Moonstruck over these hills, and willing to sacrifice damn near anything to stay in them. It's incurable, though. Forty years in an east Tennessee medical practice has taught me that right enough. Incurable."

"Well, aside from that, how am I?" asked the sheriff.

Alton Banner peered at Spencer over the top of his glasses. "That depends," he said. "If you were planning to take a couple of weeks off and go to Wrightsville Beach, then I'd say you were making satisfactory progress, considering your age and your indifferent attitude toward your own health, but if you're angling to get back in that patrol car, I would be forced to downgrade your condition to critical. Now, which is it?"

"Neither one at the moment. It's just that they want me in Nashville six weeks from now."

"Six weeks! Well, then. If you continue to progress as you have been, I see no problem with that. You won't be prancing around like Garth Brooks, mind you, but I'd say that if you just want to drive over to the state capital for a meeting with the bureaucrats sometime next month, I could in good conscience allow that."

"I see."

The toneless reply made Banner look up. "What's the matter?" he said, peering at his patient. "Did I give you the wrong answer? If you want to skip a budget hearing, just say the word."

"It's more than that." Spencer handed him the letter from the Department of Corrections.

Alton Banner scanned the letter. "Summoned . . . execution . . . six weeks—my God! Fate Harkryder! Hearing that name is like a goose walking over my grave. I haven't thought about him in years."

The sheriff nodded. "You remember, though, don't you? You were there."

"I was. I never will forget it."

They sat in silence for a few moments, thinking back on a night that they both would have preferred to forget.

"That was the night of Emily Stanton's murder. Gone before I got there, poor thing. You had to break the news to her parents, but I saw them at the trial. I remember her father asking me, *Did she suffer?*—and God help me, I took a deep breath and I lied to that man, because I couldn't stand to utter the truth any more than he could stand to hear it."

Spencer nodded. "They drove over from Wilmington the

next day. So did the Wilson boy's mother, but I can't remember her very well. Just the Stantons."

The flash of headlights on the front window and the crunch of gravel indicated that another visitor had arrived at the sheriff's ridgetop home.

Dr. Banner pushed aside the curtain and peered out. "You've got visitors. Looks like Martha's car," he grunted. "Shall I make myself scarce?"

"No," said Spencer. "She's probably just bringing up some more mail from the office."

"She's got some woman with her," the doctor announced.

"My mother?"

"No. About her age, though." Spencer struggled to his feet, but Alton Banner motioned for him to sit back down. "You're an invalid. You stay put. I'll answer the door. Do-gooders! I reckon it's too late to put the lights out and pretend we're not here."

Spencer laughed. "Who's being a mountaineer now?"

A moment later Alton Banner put on a welcoming smile and flung open the door. Martha Ayers ushered in a timid-looking older woman whose tinted blond hair did nothing to disguise her age.

"I brought you a visitor," said Martha. "This is Mrs. Helen Honeycutt."

Spencer's greeting was almost cordial enough to hide his bewilderment. He had never seen the woman before in his life.

"I could make you some coffee," Dr. Banner said, ushering them to chairs after the introductions had been made. "Since I'm a doctor, though, it is traditional for someone else to go and boil the water."

"None for me, thanks." Martha smiled at the sheriff. "I'm here to report on my assignments."

"Your assignments—?"

Martha smiled and handed him a coffee-stained manila folder. "Here's the case file you asked me about. Took me forever to find it."

Spencer resisted the urge to sit down and open it immediately. He waited for Martha to explain the rest.

"Frankie Silver," she prompted him. "You asked me, remember? The library said that there aren't any books about her. Apparently nobody has ever written one. I've got the Book Place in Johnson City double-checking, and the librarian said she'd see if she could find some articles in local history books, but while we were talking about the case, Mrs. Honeycutt here came up to the desk and said that she'd heard that story as a child from her relatives over in North Carolina."

"I didn't mean to eavesdrop," the older woman assured the sheriff, as if she expected him to scold her for it. "But I heard the name Frankie Silvers, and of course, being from a Mitchell County family, I know all about her, so I thought I'd offer to help."

"That's very kind of you," said Spencer, with the carefully cultivated courtesy of an elected official. He didn't like to deal in hearsay, though. He yearned for a concise listing of facts bound, printed, and documented. *I will go to the library myself*, he thought, but he wasn't well enough to go yet, and he couldn't discourage Martha or hurt this woman's feelings. At least this was a start. Aloud he said, "I'd be grateful for anything you could tell me."

"It's a true story that happened in Mitchell County, North Carolina. At the Dayton Bend in the Toe River is a place called Kona. It wasn't called that when Frankie Silvers lived there in the 1830s, but that's its name now. It wasn't in Mitchell County back then, either. In those days Burke County hadn't been subdivided, and its territory stretched all the way to Tennessee. That's not part of the story, Sheriff. I just know that on my own, from looking up census records. I'm tracing my family back to the American Revolution. The Overmountain Men."

Spencer nodded. "That must take a lot of research," he said politely, and waited. He hoped he wasn't going to hear a discourse on Mrs. Honeycutt's glorious ancestors.

She blushed. "Well, I'll just tell it straight out then," she said. "My grandmother made a tale out of it, and I'll tell it like she did, best I can remember. We're not used to tale-telling any more, what with the TV and all, but I will try."

Dr. Banner sat down on the sofa beside his patient and smiled encouragingly. "I've heard something of this story. I'd like to listen, too, if I may."

Spencer reached for the notepad beside the telephone. "Do you mind if I ask you questions as you go along?"

Mrs. Honeycutt looked startled. "My goodness! You'd better wait 'til I've finished, or I might forget where I was. Being questioned by a sheriff is bound to make me nervous. And when you do ask me questions, I don't know if I'll know the answers, but I'll try to help you as best I can."

Spencer smiled reassuringly at his guest. "Go ahead, then," he said. "I'll keep my mouth shut."

Helen Honeycutt perched nervously on the edge of the sofa, toying with the leather strap of her handbag. "I'm not a storyteller or anything like that," she warned her audience. "I'm just going to say it as I was told it."

"I'd be most grateful if you would," said Spencer. On the lined message pad he wrote: "Frankie Silver, testimony of Helen Honeycutt, resident of Mitchell County." He had already begun a file on the case as if it were one of his current investigations.

"Well, the way I heard it . . . at the Dayton Bend of the Toe River—which in Tennessee we call the Nolichucky— well, you know that. . . . Anyhow, in a little log cabin at Kona in the 1830s, there lived a young couple named Charlie and Frankie Silvers. Now, Charlie was a handsome boy, fond of dancing, and fonder still of the ladies, but he and Frankie had married young, and by now he was nineteen years old, and already they had a little baby, who had just passed her first birthday."

Spencer scribbled notes on his legal pad. All of that information sounded either verifiable or not relevant. Nothing he wanted to quibble about. He nodded for her to continue.

"They say Frankie was a pretty little blonde, but she was the jealous type, and they say that Charlie had a sweetheart.

He didn't care to be stuck at home with a nagging wife and a crying baby. Maybe he was planning to leave them both for good. Anyhow, one winter day, Frankie and Charlie had words about the other woman, and then when they'd wore themselves out with arguing, Charlie lay down on a pallet beside the fire to go to sleep. And he held the little baby Nancy in his arms."

Spencer Arrowood opened his mouth to speak, remembered that he had promised not to interrupt, and closed it again.

"Frankie saw him sleeping there by the fireplace, and she picked up an ax. Some say her daddy was there a-visiting in the cabin with them, and that he told her to do it. He might even have threatened to kill her if she didn't murder Charlie. Family honor, I suppose. Like it says in the song, *He was her man, and he was doing her wrong.*"

With an almost imperceptible shake of his head, the sheriff stopped Alton Banner from interrupting.

"Anyhow, Frankie Silvers snuck up on Charlie, brandishing that ax, but he was holding the baby, and he rolled over and smiled the sweetest smile in his sleep. And she looked down at her handsome young husband, sleeping there so peaceful-like with their little daughter snuggled against him, and she just couldn't do it. She backed away. Three times Frankie crept up close to him, and three times he smiled like an angel and caused her to put down the ax and back away again, but the fourth time, he was sleeping sound, and the baby crawled out of her father's arms, and Frankie brought the ax down—whop!—and she near 'bout cut his head off. Charlie opened his eyes, and he said, 'God bless the child!' And then he was gone."

The first page of Spencer's notepad was full. He flipped to a new page and scribbled on.

Martha Ayers looked at the expression on his face and wished she'd waited for a book.

Helen Honeycutt smiled at the sheriff's diligence, pleased at being given such rapt attention. She picked up the tale again with more enthusiasm in her voice. "So Charlie Silvers was dead, laying there by the fireplace in their little cabin. Then Frankie had to figure out what to do with that body. So she cut him up like a deer, and she put his body into the fire, but she didn't have enough firewood to finish the job, so she took the pieces that were left over and she hid them out in the woods. Her daddy took the ax and threw it in the river on his way home, so they never did find it.

"Well, the next morning Frankie went over to her in-laws' house, and she told them she was worried about Charlie. She said he had gone hunting, and he hadn't come home last night. Every day for three days she went to Charlie's parents' house and said, 'No, he's not back yet.' And his folks were getting frantic with worry, because it was winter and all. They rounded up most of the neighbors and started hunting the woods, looking for tracks or some sign of Charlie. They didn't find him.

"Then one of Charlie's old hunting buddies got suspicious, and he went into the cabin after Frankie left, and he found ax marks on the log walls, and blood all over the floor. Then they started hunting the woods up close around the cabin, and they found Charlie's body parts scattered around, some in tree stumps and over by the creek. So they arrested Frankie and took her on horseback down to the jail in Morganton." She paused for breath, smiling expectantly at her audience.

Spencer reminded himself that he wasn't interrogating a suspect. He managed a polite smile. "Can I ask questions now?"

"Yes, if you'd like."

Spencer glanced down at the scrawled notes. "I appreciate your coming and telling me this story," he said gently. "And I know that folktales are supposed to be heard and not dissected, but this is a true story, which is why I'm interested in it. You see, I have the mind of a policeman, even when I'm not on duty, and so I'm going to ask you some questions about what you told me, just as if I were the investigating officer."

Mrs. Honeycutt looked wary. "Well, I can't promise I'll know the answers, but you can try."

"All right. First of all, where did your grandmother hear this story? Was she kin to any of the principals in the case?"

"Well, everybody's kin to everybody in Mitchell County if you go back far enough, but I don't think we were more than distant cousins by marriage to anybody. I don't know where Nana got the story, though. A lot of people tell it."

Spencer made a note. "Were there any witnesses to the crime?"

"Some say that Frankie's father was there. I told that part, didn't I?"

"Yes, but how do they know?"

Helen Honeycutt looked puzzled. "It's what people say," she told him, as if that settled it.

"Yes, ma'am, but how do we *know* that Frankie Silver's father was present at the time of the murder? You said there were no witnesses. Was he charged as an accessory?"

"No. I believe the mother was, though."

"The *mother* was charged?"

"I think so."

"Not the father?"

"No."

With a weary sigh, Spencer sat back and began scribbling in the margins of his notes. "Why?"

"Why wasn't he charged? I don't know, Sheriff, but it didn't matter anyway. Nobody was tried for the murder except Frankie Silvers herself."

Alton Banner cleared his throat. "About that name, ma'am. I'm acquainted with some of the Silvers from over there in Mitchell. I don't believe they have a final *s* on their name. I believe it's Silver. Singular."

"I always heard it *Silvers*." Mrs. Honeycutt's face had taken on a sullen expression, and no doubt she was regretting her impulse to do good deeds for invalids.

"That can be checked fairly easily," said Spencer, unwilling to quibble about minor points. "Let's go back to the story of the murder itself. Did Frankie Silver leave a written confession?"

"Not that I ever heard of. The books don't mention one."

"I'd be astonished to hear that she could write," muttered Dr. Banner. "Consider the time and place."

Spencer nodded. "I was just wondering how we knew the circumstances of Charlie's death so exactly. Where he was lying when the attack came. How many times she attempted to kill him. Especially his last words. *God bless the child.* It sounds like something out of a play."

Alton Banner chuckled. "*Porgy and Bess,* to be exact."

Mrs. Honeycutt's eyes narrowed. "That's the way I heard the story, Sheriff."

"Speaking of songs, ma'am," the doctor continued. "I noticed you quoted from another one in your recounting of the story. You said, 'He was her man, and he was doing her wrong,' which is from 'Frankie and Johnny.' "

"Oh, yes. That's where that old song came from. It was inspired by this murder case."

Spencer shot a quick glance at Alton Banner. *Later,* his look said. "This is extremely helpful," he said to Mrs. Honeycutt. "Now, tell me, was the murder weapon ever found?"

She thought for a moment. "I don't think so."

"Then how do they know it was thrown in the river?" Spencer consulted his notes. "You said, *maybe the father—* who was not definitely there—*threw it into the river on his way home.* Witnesses?"

"No. It's what people said." She glanced at her watch and then at Martha.

"Okay," said Spencer. "Then she was arrested. . . ."

"I really have to be going," said Mrs. Honeycutt with a plaster smile. "Good luck with your research, Sheriff."

Martha stood up, too, gave him a look, and said, "I'll check on you tomorrow."

Spencer saw the visitors to the door with fulsome thanks and offers of coffee, but his peace overtures were coldly received. When he saw the taillights on Martha's car disappear around the curve of the driveway, he sank back on the couch with a weary sigh.

"I don't blame you," said Alton Banner. "That much pleasant hypocrisy would wear out even a well man."

"No, it was kind of her to come and tell me the story," said Spencer. "I really did appreciate it. She probably told it just the way she heard it. It wasn't her fault that—that—"

"It was piffle."

"I think so. Most of it."

The doctor squinted at him. "What do you want to know about this for, anyhow? Long time ago, not your jurisdiction. You writing a book?"

"No. I'm not planning to. I guess it's just something to keep my mind occupied while I'm home." Spencer tried to make his interest seem desultory. "It's an old story, and I always wondered about it. Heard it from Nelse Miller."

"I hope he had more sense than to tell you that this story inspired the song 'Frankie and Johnny.' "

"He didn't say that. No."

"You don't believe it, either, do you?"

Spencer shook his head. "Stranger things have happened, I guess, but it doesn't seem likely. 'Frankie and Johnny' is an urban song. The woman goes to a bar, finds out that her lover is unfaithful to her, and kills him with a pistol, which she fires through the door of an apartment or a hotel room. Except for the name 'Frankie,' I see no similarities between the two incidents."

"It's like confusing Barbara Bush with Barbara Mandrell," Banner grunted. "A mere coincidence of names. I hear nothing of our mountains in either the tune or the story of 'Frankie and Johnny.' "

"No. I wonder if there is a song about Frankie Silver."

"Bound to be, if anybody remembers it. So, tell me, as a lawman, how do you see the rest of it?" The doctor smiled. "In your professional opinion?"

"I don't have enough information yet. Just offhand, though, I'd say that all that business about her sneaking up on him three times and backing away again is the embellishment of a storyteller."

Alton Banner hummed a snatch of an old tune. *"Three times he kissed her lily-white hands . . . three times he kissed her cheek."*

"Yes, exactly," said Spencer. "It sounds like a ballad-in-the-making. And I don't think her father was there, either."

"Why not?"

The sheriff shrugged. "Just a hunch—and a lot of experience with rural justice. If there was a man around, they sure as hell would have put him on trial for the crime. Charging a little eighteen-year-old girl with an ax murder had to be a last resort for the sheriff of Burke County."

"Well, I'll leave you to it, son," said the old doctor. "I'll check back on you toward the end of the week. See how you and Frankie are getting along."

The sheriff smiled. "You do that. One more thing, though. Can I drive yet?"

"To Nashville in six weeks? You still thinking about that?"

"No. I meant around the county here—soon."

Alton Banner shook his head. "Ask me next time."

In the sheriff's office Jeff McCullough, editor of the county's weekly newspaper, the *Hamelin Record*, sat in the straight chair beside Joe LeDonne's desk, scanning the prepared statement that he had been given.

"So I can use everything in here without compromising the investigation?"

"Of course," said the deputy. "We don't have the forensic evidence back from the lab anyhow. I hope we have an arrest by then."

"You were the investigating officer?"

"I took the call when the bodies were found. Martha came out shortly thereafter to help with the crime scene."

McCullough tilted his glasses to the end of his nose and looked again at the press release. "It's eerie, isn't it?" he said. "I just finished doing a story about Fate Harkryder's upcoming execution, so I had to go back and read the old stories on the Trail Murders. I could just about run them again for this new case with no rewrite."

"There are some similarities," LeDonne conceded.

"Well, we know it isn't Fate Harkryder this time," said McCullough. "Do you have any suspects?"

"Nothing to speak of."

Jeff McCullough smiled. "You wouldn't speak of it, anyhow, would you? But that's okay. I don't want to hinder the investigation. I think my angle for this week is the irony of these murders happening so close to Fate Harkryder's execution date, and bearing such a resemblance to his own crime. What does the sheriff think about it?"

"He's still recovering from his wounds. He's not part of this investigation."

"But I just read those old Harkryder articles. Spencer Arrowood was the arresting officer in that case. What does he think about this one?"

"We haven't told him about this one. He's still weak from surgery, and he's not up to any more strain right now. Martha thinks he's better off not being told."

"So I can't interview him about the new case, and whether he thinks they're related?"

"No. He knows nothing about it. Martha and I will keep you posted on what's happening in this case. And the old one is closed—or it will be in a few weeks, when Fate Harkryder goes to the chair."

Jeff McCullough frowned. "When is the sheriff due back on the job?"

"Couple of weeks. We'll have an arrest by then."

Fate Harkryder was thirty-seven years old and looked fifty. His hair was shot with iron gray. A lifetime of smoking and hard times had etched deep creases between his nose and chin, and had stitched a chain of fine lines around the hollows of his eyes. He had not run to fat, though, as so many of the prisoners did, partly because Harkryder men were built short and wiry, and partly because Fate Harkryder stopped eating when he felt his body thicken. Fat was weakness, and in prison it did not do to give the appearance of weakness. Fate Harkryder liked to be left alone. He was softspoken and courteous to those he encountered, but people who mistook his remoteness for weakness did so only once. He had learned long ago that if you are polite and distant, people will leave you alone. He could fight if he had to, but he avoided it if he could do so without backing down. Shouting and striking people is a form of intimacy, and for that reason alone Fate Harkryder avoided confrontations.

His lawyer had just left. This one was an earnest kid out of Nashville who was working pro bono because he claimed to hate the death penalty. He had offered his services when the state announced its intention of executing Fate Harkryder in six weeks' time. Maybe he was a do-gooder, or maybe he wanted to get his name in the paper by representing an infamous man. It was all the same, though. Fate didn't think there was much the kid could do, but for zero legal fees, he was welcome to try. What the hell.

Fate had lost count of the lawyers he'd gone through in twenty years. Some of them had only been voices on the phone, staying on the case just long enough to find some other sucker to take it off their hands. None of them stayed long. Fate wasn't notorious enough to make a name for an ambitious litigator, and his family was too poor to make it worth anybody's while to defend him. That had been the trouble to begin with. The court-appointed lawyer at his original trial went through the motions of defending him, but his efforts had been all but useless.

He sat on a concrete bench outside Pod Five and looked up at the hill beyond the river. The sun was warm against his skin, and he yawned and stretched, savoring the smell and feel of early summer. If he kept his eyes closed, he could picture the homestead back in east Tennessee. He wondered if it had changed much in the decades that he'd been gone. Probably not. The land had been farmed out two generations before he was born. Who'd want it now? He hadn't even seen any pictures of the home place since he left, and what little news he had from the relatives at home never touched on the farm or the changing seasons, which they all took for granted, while he, deprived of it forever, would have traded them all for a hill and a meadow.

His father's sister was the family correspondent. Her spelling was as haphazard as her narrative skills, but at least she made the effort two or three times a year, which is more than the rest of them did. Scrawled pencil notes on lined paper informed him of the birth of a child to cousins he dimly remembered as infants themselves, or the smudged pages wished him a merry Christmas, with a spidery postscript enumerating the Harkryders' car troubles, job losses, and the illnesses of aging relatives. As if he cared. They were all like characters in a movie he had seen once and only vaguely recalled, without any real certainty about the names or their function in the story. In his memory, time in east Tennessee stood still. Hamelin was a sleepy little seventies community still peopled by folks who were old when he was seventeen and his brothers were still young men in their twenties, with unlined faces and thick dark hair. He knew that they had grown older, as he had in the years since he had seen them. They were as old now as his father had been back then, but somehow his mind would not adjust his memories to accommodate the aging process. He could not picture Tom's cold steel eyes looking out of their daddy's furrowed face, or Ewell with Mama's aging dumpling chins and graying hair. His brothers still grinned out at him from Technicolor daydreams as swaggering youths on the brink of manhood.

Tom and Ewell.

Tom was the oldest, a dark-haired banty rooster with a look of sleepy indifference that masked his intensity. That vacant stare had stood him well in poker games and bar fights. His opponents thought that he would be easy pickings, and by the time they cottoned on to their mistake, it was usually too late.

Ewell . . . Mama's side of the family. Bigger, soft-bodied, with heavy-lidded eyes and fleshy lips, and always that look of *wanting* something. He had looked at girls in church, cars on the highway, and deep-fried drumsticks on other people's plates with that same naked hungry stare.

Tom and Ewell. How long had it been since he'd heard from them? There had been a few letters at first. Just after Fate had been sent away to prison, Ewell sent him a couple of postcards that said things like *Cheer up, kid! The lawyers won't give up. They're bound to get you out.* Eventually. Ewell didn't seem to mind about "eventually," since it was not his life trickling away behind cinder-block walls. Fate wondered, sometimes, who Ewell had turned out to be, but he didn't much care about it one way or the other. Not enough to try to find out. Ewell had drifted away from home, and the family had lost touch with him—not that any particular effort was made by the Harkryders or Ewell to maintain the ties. Maybe he had done well and wanted no reminders of his hillbilly relatives. Maybe he finally had enough money to buy all the things he lusted after in the catalogues and the mall displays. Or maybe he was already dead. It was all the same to Fate. Ewell wasn't real any more.

After the trial Tom did a stint in the army, and ended up with an infantry company in Korea. *I reckon we must be in about the same boat,* Tom had written him. *Both of us government prisoners, only they want me to kill people. It rains here all the time. Rains 'til your feet rot in your socks. You probably eat better than I do.* . . . Fate couldn't remember if he'd bothered to answer.

At first he had thought a lot about his brothers. During the first months of his imprisonment, rage had been his warmth, his comforter, and his friend. He would look at the wall, trying to shut out the ceaseless noise of the cell block, and he would imagine his brothers eating hamburgers at the Dixie Grill, or walking the October woods with rifles in search of deer, or burying their faces in the breasts of sweet-smelling doe-eyed girls. In his imaginings they were always laughing, always free. Fate wanted to destroy them. He would escape from prison, he thought, and he would put a gun barrel into Tom's grinning mouth, and he would make the laughter stop. Or he would recant. Break the silence. Tell what happened that night, but tell it a different way, so that they, not he, would be shut away here until they faded away into nothingness. Except that no one would believe him this time. Nobody cared about the truth any more—if, in fact, they had ever cared at all. The trial was finished, the sentence was passed, and now it was all over but the waiting.

His brothers were beyond his reach now. Gradually he had come to accept that. Eventually the rage flickered out, to be replaced for a while by sweeter memories of home and family. Fate lived for a while on scenes from his boyhood. There hadn't been many happy memories of home, but the few that could be lit with the softer light of reflection he replayed over and over again in his mind until they became a tapestry of warmth and laughter, and the other, darker truths lay discarded and forgotten in the bottom of his mind. He subsisted for months on snapshot recollections: he was six, wobbling down the blacktop on a homemade bike, built by Tom from scraps and scrounged (perhaps stolen) parts. . . . He was eight, in overalls and barefoot on a cold, wet rock, fishing in the creek with Tom and Ewell, the spring woods ablaze with redbud. . . . Ten, chugging his first beer in the cool darkness of the smokehouse, Ewell laughing while he choked and sputtered on the bitterness. Tom stood by with his sleepy-eyed smile, looking as if he were somewhere else.

After a year or so, those memories wore out. They became so tattered with replaying that the magic leeched out of them, and they no longer had the power to take him away from The Walls. Sometimes other, harsher memories crept in to taunt him with glimpses of Tom and Ewell that he would rather not recall. Little by little he let go of the other life, as the voices faded and the faces dimmed.

Only here was real.

He knew every arch of the land and every tree by now. The hill was forested with elms and pine—not the oak, and ash, and hickory trees of home. In the springtime the elm pollen turned the prison into a wheezing nest of watery-eyed allergy sufferers, but Fate didn't mind. He had no adverse reaction to the elms, only a mild resentment that they were not the familiar trees of home. He had been staring at that puny middle Tennessee ridge for years now, ever since he was moved from The Walls to Tennessee's new maximum-security prison, Riverbend. At first he had welcomed the change of scenery, and he had stared at the hill on the curve of the river like a starving man, trying to will the ridge to transform itself into one of the mist-shrouded mountains back home.

Prison is a village, and now it was his hometown. He had lived here for twenty years, and soon now he would die here.

Burgess Gaither

HABEAS CORPUS

Frankie Silver and her mother and brother were under lock and key in the wooden house that served as Morganton's jail, and all the town was talking about the dreadful crimes that had happened in the wild land beyond the mountains. The old folks harked back to the time of the Indian raids forty years ago, and those of a religious turn of mind quoted Scripture verses about demons in mortal form. It would be two months before that fair-haired girl and her kinfolk would answer for the crime, and I wondered where an impartial jury could be found in all of Burke County, and who among my colleagues would be fool enough to defend them. Surely he would never draw up a deed or will for an upstanding client again after linking his name with the infamous one of Frankie Silver. I was well out of it, I thought, for having taken the clerkship instead of establishing a private law practice.

The morning after Constable Charlie Baker brought his prisoners down the mountain to Morganton, he headed home again, back past Celo Mountain and into the valley of the Toe River, named for the legendary Cherokee maiden Estatoe, a star-crossed Juliet of the Indian nation. It was a good day's ride up the Yellow Mountain Road even in high summer. Now, with a foot of snow on the trail, and winds like knife blades whipping through the passes, it was bound to be a bitter journey, but at least the constable could travel faster and easier in his mind without three dangerous prisoners in tow.

Before he left Morganton, though, Charlie Baker must have spent some time in Mr. McEntire's tavern—fortifying himself for the long ride back over the mountains. No doubt an innkeeper's bill for lodging, food, and drink (mostly the latter) would be submitted to the county treasurer with the constable's record of expenses for bringing in the prisoners. Charlie must have told his tale many times before the innkeeper's fire, and I'll wager that he bought very few of his own whiskeys. By the time Baker and his companion had set their horses westward on the Yellow Mountain Road, the town was humming with the news of the gruesome murder in the west county.

With all the conviction of eyewitnesses, the tavern gossips recounted the grim tale of the finding of poor young Charlie Silver: bits of his bones and skin in the fireplace ashes, and sundry limbs and body parts scattered about the woods near the cabin. They never did find all of him. The snow was still deep, and general opinion was that bits of the corpse would continue to turn up well into the April thaw, when the last of the spring snowmelt revealed the most deeply covered pieces.

"They buried what they found," one traveler remarked. "But there'll be more come spring."

"Reckon they'll have to start over," said another.

Even greater than the unseemly interest in the gory details of the tragedy was Morganton's fascination with the widow—and accused slayer—of the murdered man. The jailer's wife had done her share of gossiping as well, letting all and sundry know that a handsome young woman was locked away in the upstairs jail cell. News of Frankie Silver overshadowed talk of the other unfortunates, her kinfolk, for a mature woman and a youth were less interesting subjects for speculation.

Even my Elizabeth pressed me for details about the case, but I was able to tell her only what I had heard from the constable, and even that I softened for the ears of a gentlewoman.

"They say that she cruelly murdered her young husband and chopped his body to bits," said Elizabeth. She had met Constable Presnell's wife Sarah on the street and had stopped to "pass the time of day," the term used by our womenfolk for the giving and receiving of local gossip. "Can this be true, Burgess?"

"That is for a jury to decide," I said, hoping to deflect her attention from the matter. "There are two other souls in custody for the crime."

"But the body was found in pieces?"

"Constable Baker said that it was," I said grudgingly. My efforts to protect my wife from the unpleasantness of this case were proving futile, thanks to the incessant curiosity of the town folk.

Elizabeth leaned forward, her eyes shining, eager for news. "And you have met this creature, Burgess? What was she like?"

"She is small and fair. No more than eighteen years of age. She spoke but little. I saw no hint of madness in her." I shrugged. "She seemed like any backwoods girl."

"So she is not mad." Elizabeth considered this. "That makes the story all the more strange. Whyever can she have done it, then? Or do you think her brother did it to protect her honor?"

"I have heard nothing to implicate the boy," I admitted. "He is but fifteen, I think."

"And the mother?"

"Little has been said about her. It is the young widow Silver who was caught in a lie, saying that her husband was gone from home when in fact he lay in pieces within the cabin."

Elizabeth had obviously heard these details before, for she evinced no dismay upon hearing the particulars from me. "Perhaps her husband was paying court to another woman? That is the only reason I can think of to take an ax to him."

"I shall take your warning to heart, madam," I said, smiling.

"See that you do, Burgess Gaither," said Elizabeth, and she laughed at my expression of mock alarm. But the levity left her almost at once. "It is a terrible crime. Do you know what her motive was?"

"The trial is two months away, Elizabeth," I said. "Let us not convict her or her family just yet. You are a lawyer's daughter. Must I remind you that it is the job of the prosecution—not the town gossips or the clerk of court—to fix upon a motive?"

"I think it must have been jealousy," said my wife, as if I had not spoken. "Men are too cruel. Perhaps he was unfaithful to her. And I have heard that the unfortunate couple has a child. Was anything said about that?"

"The prisoner has a baby girl, according to Constable Baker."

"Poor child! Is it imprisoned with its mother, then? Have you seen it?"

"No. Frankie Silver had no child with her. I suppose it is with its father's family."

"How cruel for both mother and infant!" cried Elizabeth. I knew that she was thinking of our own child William, who was not much older than the Silver baby, and it made me shiver to think that any fellow feeling could exist between my wellborn wife and that ignorant girl in Will Butler's jail. I could not imagine William deprived of his parents and left with a legacy of shame, and I wondered what would become of the child of the murderess.

"Do not forget the fate of the baby's poor young father," I said. "Charlie Silver was nineteen, and his family grieves for him, you may be sure."

"A pretty young woman with a baby daughter," said Elizabeth. "How could she have committed such a crime?"

"They live in a savage wilderness. They are not like the gentlefolk in your society, my dear. How can we hope to understand their ways?"

Two days later I was back in my office, working once more on county legal business. As clerk of court, I had deeds and wills to record, and a thousand points of law to commit to memory, for I was expected to advise the judge and members of counsel in the coming term of the circuit court. My father-in-law had forty-four years in which to make himself an authority on the law and the affairs of the county, while I had only a few months' time to prepare to succeed him in a competent fashion that would reflect well upon his choice of a successor.

Once more my labors were interrupted by more pressing business.

I heard the outer door of the courthouse open and slam shut again, and then the sound of hobnailed boots clattering across the oak floor of the courtroom. I sighed and put down my pen. "Come in!" I called out. My office door was ajar, and presently I saw it pushed open, and a man red-faced in furs and buckskin glared in at me.

"What can I do for you?" I asked politely, ignoring the intruder's belligerent expression.

The scowling man approached my desk. "They've got my family locked up in the jail here, and you can tell me what to do about it."

"Oh," I said, for now I realized who my visitor must be.

This was Frankie Silver's father, returned from his long hunt in Kentucky to find his wife and children imprisoned. I should have considered the shock and anguish of the poor fellow, but in truth my first thought was to wonder uneasily: was he armed, and what did he intend to do about his family's imprisonment?

I looked more closely at the man, and I decided that his anger was born of fear for his family. He was unkempt, as most of the trappers are, with a grizzled beard and hair that had seen neither comb nor soap in a good while, but he was sober, fine-featured, and well-spoken enough. From the look of him I thought that he might have started out life in circumstances more propitious than a log cabin in the wildwood. I felt a sudden pang of sympathy for the poor old fellow. The life of a backcountry farmer and trapper is a harsh one, uncertain at the best of times, and the man before me seemed aged before his time. What a blow—to come back from the cold and pitiless frontier to find that your wife and children are in deepest peril and accused of the worst of crimes. What man wouldn't shout his way into a courthouse on such provocation? He was a stranger here, and he was by no means certain of his welcome.

"I am the clerk of the Burke County Superior Court," I told him, extending my hand with a smile of welcome. "My name is Burgess Gaither, sir. I know who you must be."

He nodded. I could see the weariness etched in the lines on his face. He must have ridden all night to get here. "Isaiah Stewart," he said. "I got back last night. Me and my oldest boy Jackson. We was hunting over to Kentucky way. The Howells told us my family had been taken. Have you seen them?"

"Only for a few moments when they first reached the town," I told him. "They waited here in this courtroom until the jailer could be found. They are all well, though. I would have heard otherwise."

Isaiah Stewart sat down in the cane chair beside my desk. His boots made a puddle on my polished floor, but he was too anxious in his mind to notice such a thing. "What must I do?" he asked me. His look was as guileless as a child's, and again I felt a twinge of pity for this poor bewildered fellow. I had no doubt that Stewart would be fearless against an attacking bear, or in defending his pelts against a band of Shawnee, but here in the county town, with all the intricacies of the law in a maze before him, he was powerless, shackled by his own ignorance and his rusticity.

"You know the circumstances of their arrest?" I asked, hoping dearly that it would not fall to me to break the news to him.

"I heard. Charlie Silver's been kilt."

"The trial will take place in March," I told him gently. "You must secure an attorney to defend your family, for they are charged with the crime."

"March! That's two months away. Do they have to stay in jail 'til then?"

I hesitated. In the wake of such a gruesome murder, no

bail would be granted. I was sure of that, but I hated to give such bleak news to this careworn man.

"I fear for their safety, sir," he said.

I was about to protest that Dr. Tate was an excellent physician who lived in the very shadow of the courthouse. He attended prisoners at the county's expense if needed. Before I could blurt out this information, I suddenly took his meaning. He was concerned not that his family might succumb to disease during their confinement, but that their lives might be threatened by vigilantes in the town. I had heard wild talk in the taverns about doing away with the murdering savages in Butler's jail; perhaps Isaiah Stewart knew of such sentiments from his neighbors up-county, or else he had met with such a harsh welcome upon his arrival in Morganton.

"They are drunken louts who make such threats," I told him. "No one here would harm helpless women and a young boy in custody, no matter what they are thought to have done."

He looked unconvinced by my speech, and indeed I had spoken more out of hope than conviction. "I must look after my family," he said at last.

"Did they tell you what happened to Charlie Silver?"

"I heard from them that found him."

I had the feeling that Isaiah Stewart had more to say on the subject of his son-in-law, but nothing more was forthcoming. He seemed impassive for one whose kinsman had met such a brutal end. "It was a shocking crime," I told him, for I was not sure that a backwoodsman would understand the degree of horror that had been generated here in Morganton by the news of the murder.

He nodded. "It sounds so."

"The poor young man was hacked to pieces, Mr. Stewart! They have not yet recovered all of him for a Christian burial. People are enraged."

"They are quick to judge without knowing the facts of the case," said Stewart.

"The fact of the butchered corpse speaks for itself," I said. "I must tell you that there is very little sympathy for those who have committed this crime. The killing was brutal, and the attempt at concealment was pitiless, some say cowardly."

He winced at that, but he gave me no argument. "Is there not some way to free them?" he asked me.

I considered the matter. "Would it be wise, Mr. Stewart? Think about what you are suggesting, regardless of the guilt or innocence of the prisoners. Feelings are running high concerning this case. Even if you succeeded in securing their release on bail, it is possible that a mob would overtake you as you attempted to leave town, or perhaps those nearer to home—the family of the victim—would seek a private vengeance for their wrongs."

"We can take care of ourselves," said Stewart. "My son Jack is twenty-four, and married to a Howell girl. I reckon the Howells will stand with us."

"You could cause the deaths of the very persons you are attempting to save."

Stewart grew impatient. "My wife and my children have been locked away on the word of the Silvers. I want somebody here—somebody who isn't beholden to the damned Silvers—to see if there's any cause to accuse my family of this crime. I'm not saying it wasn't a terrible thing. I liked young Charlie well enough. But besides the Silvers' say-so, I want to know on what proof the Stewarts stand accused."

Fair enough, I thought. Perhaps the family of the murdered man had fixed upon a handy scapegoat to assuage their grief and to settle old scores in the bargain. From what Constable Baker had told us, I did not think it likely, but Isaiah Stewart was correct: his family was entitled to face their accusers.

"If you are set on securing their release," I told him, "and if you are correct about their being unjustly arrested, there is one possible way to free them. You could seek out the magistrates and request a hearing of habeas corpus."

Isaiah Stewart blinked uncomprehendingly. "Can it be done quickly?" Another anxious thought darkened his face. "Will it cost much?" he asked. "I reckon I can raise some cash, but—"

I shook my head. "You must look ahead to the trial in March, for then you will have greater lawyers' fees to pay, but this hearing is a simple matter before the magistrates. Its purpose is to see if there is enough evidence to charge the prisoners with murder. You must request this hearing, though."

"How can I do that?"

"You must find the magistrates—Mr. Hughes or Mr. Burgner, our justices of the peace—and you must formally request the hearing for a legal reason. I will tell you exactly what you must say. The phrases will be strange to you, but you must get them off by heart. Can you manage that?"

"Yes, sir."

"All right. I could write it down for you. . . ."

"Memory will serve."

"Find Thomas Hughes or John C. Burgner—either will do—and say that you wish to take an oath that the prisoners Barbara Stewart, Blackston Stewart, and Frankie Silver have been *imprisoned without the legal forms of trial and without the parties having it in their power to confront their accusers before any legal tribunal.*"

He made me say it twice more, and then he said, "They'll let my family go, then?"

"No. The magistrates will then order a hearing with witnesses to testify, just like a trial. Then the magistrates will determine if there is enough evidence to keep the accused persons in jail. Or they may release them on bond. Do you understand?"

"Well enough," said Stewart. "Say those legal words again."

I drilled him on the form of the request until I was sure that he had committed the phrases to memory. I then gave him directions to John Burgner's house and wished him well.

Isaiah Stewart thanked me gravely, and before he turned to go, he said, "Are you a lawyer, sir?"

"I am," I said, "but I may not represent you in this matter. As the clerk of Superior Court, my part in the case is already assigned. I will be present at the trial as the record keeper, and to advise the members of counsel on points of law. Take heart, though! There are half a dozen qualified attorneys in this town, with much more trial experience than I have. I am sure you will find a good one to take the case. The habeas corpus matter can be handled by any lawyer worthy of the name."

He nodded. "I'll see about that hearing now."

NORTH CAROLINA—BURKE COUNTY

Whereas Isaiah Stewart hath complained to us, John C. Burgner and Thomas Hughes, two of the Acting Justices of the Peace in and for the county of Burke aforesaid, that Barbara Stuart, Frankey Silver, and Blackstone Stuart have been suspected of having committed a murder on the body of one Charles Silver, and whereas it has been made to appear on oath of the said Isaiah Stuart that the said defendants have been committed to the common Jail of the County without the parties having it in their power of confronting their accusers before any legal tribunal:

These are therefore to command you, the Sheriff of Burke County or any other lawful officer of said county, to arrest the bodies of Barbary Stuart, Frankey Silver, and Blackston Stuart, and them safely keep so that you have them before us at Morgan within the time prescribed by law, then and there to answer the charge and to be further delt with as the law directs. Herein fail not at your peril. Given from under our hands and seal, this 13th day of January, A.D. 1832.

Thomas Hughes, J.P.   *John C. Burgner, J.P.*

I returned the document to Will Butler. "Poor Tom Hughes. His command of the language leaves much to be desired, but he's a good man for all that."

Butler tapped the writ. "I see your hand in this, my learned friend."

"Surely I spell better than that, Will," I said, smiling.

"*Isaiah Stewart doth make oath that his family has been de-*

nied the right to face their accusers! Those are fine ten-shilling words to come out of the mouth of a backwoodsman! Why, you could engrave on the head of a pin all that fellow knows about the law. I'm thinking that someone put him up to it."

"Some good Samaritan, perhaps," I said. "Stewart is within his rights in this. Surely you don't object to a hearing."

I watched my breath make mist in the air between us. Will Butler had waylaid me on the street near the Presbyterian church. I had been admiring a churchyard snow scene of red-berry bushes flanked by snow-laden boughs, and thinking that even the dead had their seasonal finery, when Butler hailed me to discuss his newfound fame as the keeper of the most notorious murderess since the Lady Macbeth.

Will Butler had been considering my question. "Object to a hearing? Not I. Tongues are already wagging about this case. Perhaps a dose of the facts would put the matter to rest. Besides, the magistrates may grant bail to some of the prisoners anyhow. The boy is mighty young. I suppose I wouldn't mind having fewer prisoners to guard until the March term of court."

"Are you worried that someone may try to harm the Stewarts before then? I have heard talk."

"We are vigilant," said Butler.

"I have spoken with one of your charges, but only glimpsed the others. What are the prisoners like?"

"Quite ordinary." Butler shrugged. "Backwoods people, of course. They are not the leering savages that the taverners make them out to be. Mrs. Stewart is a small woman, a faded version of her daughter. The son is a sullen fellow—not an uncommon condition for lads of sixteen, though, and hardly an indication of guilt. They are peaceable enough in their quarters. Young Mrs. Silver weeps now and again, and she often asks about her baby. The others sleep or pray or talk in low voices as the mood takes them. The jailer's wife is quite taken with them, I hear. She will have had worse guests to contend with, I'll warrant."

"Have they said anything about the death of Charlie Silver?"

"Nothing for my ears. Perhaps the hearing will enlighten us. Will you be there, Burgess?"

"In my official capacity, no. But I am as curious as the next man. As a private citizen, nothing could keep me away."

The court system of a frontier town is a wonderful thing. Morganton, on the very fringe of civilization, has little in the way of public entertainment. We have a fair at harvesttime, but indeed the highlight of the year is the annual Fourth of July celebration staged by the Morganton Agricultural Society, with its stirring patriotic speeches, a spirited reading of the Declaration of Independence, and the ragtail parade of surviving veterans of the Revolution through the streets of the town—a smaller procession each year, as time thins their ranks. Among the gentlefolk, there are supper parties and balls, with music and dancing, but week in and week out, there is little but hard work to occupy the mind of the common man.

Court is our theatre.

There may the most humble citizen view the dramas of their neighbors, whether it be the small comedies of a squabble over a stray calf or a fence line, or the life-and-death tragedy that will end at the gallows. And not a penny of admission is charged to view this spectacle; indeed it is our right as citizens to view the judicial process at work. The lawyers are the principal actors, and they are accorded respect and an increase in business in proportion to their degree of showmanship. Since it was January—midway between the harvest festival and the Fourth of July revels, and a time of idleness for farmers—I knew that the little courtroom would be packed to the rafters with spectators. There was scarcely a soul in Morganton who had not heard of the dreadful fate of Charlie Silver, and those who could walk would not miss a single performance of the legal process that brought retribution to his killers. It was reckoned to be a three-act play spread out over the next several months: hearing, trial, and hanging. The audience for each would be prodigious.

This was my one chance to be a spectator in the drama. Henceforth I would be playing a supporting role on stage, prompting the lawyers and keeping track of the progress of the trial. I would be too busy with my duties then to be able to savor the action for its own sake. Only now could I sit among the crowd and observe the faces of the principals in the drama. Only now could I listen to their stories as a mere observer. It was not to be missed.

I arrived early, but already there was a goodly crowd milling around outside. They seemed cheerful enough—not the angry mob that Butler and I had feared only three days before. All I saw in the faces of the men was a happy anticipation of an afternoon's entertainment. Perhaps it was unfeeling of them to think so lightly of an event that could mean life or death for a fellow human being, but the Stewarts were strangers among us. Also, there could be no real grief over the death of Charlie Silver, for he was not known to anyone in the town. Only the circumstances of his death had acquainted us with him, and the only feelings stirred by his passing were a general regret that a young man had died a terrible death, and a wish that justice should be served on the perpetrators of that foul deed. Life was hard enough for everyone. Death was nothing out of the ordinary. Indeed, it was a regular visitor in every family I knew. There was nothing remarkable about a young man cut down in his prime, as the sorrowful passing of my brother Alfred had taught me not two years ago.

I pushed my way into the courtroom with the general rabble from town and contrived to take a place next to my wife's kinsman Colonel James Erwin, a tall and powerful man of fifty-six, renowned for his horsemanship. Colonel Erwin, who was himself the county's clerk of the Court of Pleas and Quarter Sessions, was not a lawyer, but he was the squire of lands totaling twenty thousand acres, stretching all the way from the Catawba River. Like me, he was present at the hearing not in his official capacity, but as a pillar of the community taking an interest in all events that touch the welfare of its citizens. The other thing we had in common was the

way in which we secured our positions in county government: Colonel Erwin's father had been the clerk of Pleas
and Quarter Sessions for more than a decade, and he had resigned to let his son take over the job. There was talk in the
family that the process would be repeated within the next
few years, for just last year Colonel Erwin's son Joseph had
graduated from Washington College in Lexington, Virginia,
and now he was preparing to become a lawyer.

"Good afternoon, Colonel," I muttered as I squeezed in
beside him. "A grim business, this."

"Indeed. All Morganton wants a look at the devils who
would defile a man's body after depriving him of his soul."

The crowd parted a bit to allow the two justices of the
peace to take their places on raised chairs at the front of
the courtroom. I saw that the two gentlemen presiding were
John C. Burgner and Aaron Brittain. Burgner had signed the
warrant for the habeas corpus hearing, but Brittain had
taken the place of Thomas Hughes, the other signing justice
of the peace. The five witnesses were escorted in, and I studied them closely, trying to guess at who they were, for all of
them were strangers to our part of the county. There were
three men, a somber-looking matron, and a wide-eyed young
girl, who looked no more than fifteen. Her hands plucked
continually at the folds of her skirt, betraying her nervous-
ness, and she huddled close to the other woman, evidently a
relative, nodding solemnly at the other's urgent whispers—
exhortations of courage, I thought, for the girl looked as if
she needed encouragement to endure the proceedings. Her
eyes were red and swollen. She stole occasional glances at
the crush of spectators, which seemed to frighten her so
much that I was afraid she would faint before the hearing
could even begin. Another maiden who is unused to town
ways, I thought. This bedlam was indeed an ordeal for a
young girl, especially one who had suffered a shocking bereavement not many days ago.

"That young girl is a sister of the murdered man!" I murmured to Colonel Erwin.

"And the other one—her mother?"

"No. There is little likeness between them. Besides, she has not a sufficient look of grief to be closely involved in the tragedy. She is a neighbor, perhaps, or another kinswoman. We'll know soon enough, for here comes Gabe Presnell with the prisoners."

A sudden hush fell over the spectators, and I turned to view the entrance of the principals in the drama. Our local constable Gabriel Presnell had escorted the prisoners on the short walk from the jail, for they were no longer in Constable Baker's jurisdiction. He herded before him a scrawny, faded woman and a scowling, fair-haired youth shackled together, more for show than security, I thought. They made their way along a path that had opened up on their account, for the crowd shrank back from them, not so much, I thought, from the stink of unwashed confinement, as from the thought of the deed of which they stood accused. The prisoners ignored the silent throng. With their heads high and their backs straight, they made their way to their appointed positions before the judges. There was no hint of madness or craven guilt in their demeanor, and I could tell from the silence that the crowd was puzzled by the forthright look of them. The hostility lessened by degrees.

Another murmur began when Mr. Thomas Wilson strode through the crowd and took his place at the rail beside the prisoners. Wilson is one of the town's most prominent lawyers, although he has been in Morganton just over a year. He is a former state legislator, and another of my kinsmen by marriage, though he came to it late, as befits a prudent man, I suppose. Thomas Wilson is forty, while his wife Catherine is but twenty-two. She is the first cousin of my Elizabeth, for their mothers are sisters, daughters of the late William Sharpe, an Iredell County patriot and statesman who served in the Continental Congress.

Wilson, in his black suit and silk cravat, made an elegant and poignant contrast to the two shabbily dressed prisoners he represented. Here was the majesty of the law reaching out to the lowest and least of its citizens. He took his place beside them, courteously distant, as if to make it clear that

duty alone had placed him in their company. I was glad that
Isaiah Stewart had found such distinguished counsel for his
wife and children, but I did wonder what town sentiments
would be toward the Wilsons at the coming trial, and Wilson's demeanor suggested that he, too, worried about the
unpleasant association. These thoughts reminded me to look
for Isaiah Stewart in the crowd, but I could not spot him in
the crush of more than a hundred avid spectators.

When the assembly began to close ranks behind the principals, I suddenly realized that something was amiss.

"There are only two of them!" I said, rather louder than I
had intended. Fortunately, a rising tide of muttering covered
our conversation. "The victim's widow is not with them," I
told the colonel. "Frankie Silver herself is not present. Can
you see beyond the crowd, sir? Is there another constable
approaching?"

"None that I can see. Perhaps the widow will wait to take
her chances in court."

I thought about it. "That is certainly possible. This is a
hearing to determine if there is enough evidence to keep the
prisoners in jail. From what I have heard from Constable
Baker, there are witnesses aplenty to see that Mrs. Silver will
stay confined until the trial, for she has lied to every one of
them in saying that her husband had not returned home
when—"

"Yes. I have heard the tales," said the colonel hastily. "No
doubt you are right. Why should she demand evidence of her
complicity when half the neighborhood stands ready to condemn her? Her trial is inevitable. What about the others?"

I thought back to Charlie Baker's recital of the facts of the
case. "The others were scarcely mentioned," I told him.
"Perhaps he has left out some details of the events."

John Burgner called the hearing to order, adding an acer-
bic warning to the rabble that he would have order and silence in his court, or else he would empty it. He needn't
have worried. When the witnesses began to testify, those eager to listen would enforce the silence.

The first witness called to the stand was Thomas Howell,

a kinsman by marriage of the oldest Stewart son, Jackson. I wondered if the family tie was close enough to cause difficulty for the young couple. Howell seemed ill at ease on the stand, but he took his oath in a clear voice and began his testimony without flinching. His story echoed the one I had heard from Charlie Baker: Frankie Silver reports that her man has gone missing, followed by days of searching through forest snowdrifts, only to be summoned to the missing man's own cabin by Jack Collis.

At the end of Howell's recital, the defense attorney rose and approached the witness. "Did the Stewarts have anything to say about the disappearance of Charlie Silver?"

"Never saw them," said Howell. "They didn't come help us search, that's certain."

"But they did not lie to anyone about the whereabouts of Charlie Silver?"

"Not that I know of."

"And did you see them near the cabin of Charlie and Frankie Silver?"

Tom Howell answered, "I did not."

William Hutchins, Elendor Silver, and Miss Nancy Wilson said much the same. I missed some of their testimony because it was after Howell's turn on the stand that I noticed a flash of red among the spectators and turned to see a familiar but formidable lady caped in black. She was thrusting her way forward in order to get a better look at the proceedings, and her expression suggested that if matters were not handled properly, the court would hear about it. I nudged Colonel Erwin.

He looked in the direction I indicated, and groaned. "Damn! Cousin Mary is poking about, is she? Never a moment's peace, is there?"

"She does take an interest in civic matters," I said tactfully. I was, after all, a rather new connection to the Erwin clan.

Colonel James Erwin snorted. "Your father-in-law ought to marry her off, Burgess. Preferably to someone heading west."

I permitted myself a discreet smile. "It would serve the Indians right, wouldn't it?"

"Maybe having a house to run would keep Mary's nose out of everyone else's business. She would have made a lawyer for sure, if she hadn't been born female. Be glad you didn't marry that one, Burgess!"

Mary Erwin is an elder sister of my Elizabeth, but I can see little resemblance between them. Where Elizabeth is gentle and reticent, Mary is a strong-minded woman with intellectual pretensions and more opinions than God gave Congress. If she was taking an interest in this cause célèbre, then all her connections in the legal profession would be grilled upon the matter at great length, probably at the next dinner party. Heaven help us all—her list of victims included the colonel, Mr. Wilson, and myself. I wondered what Miss Mary made of this case, and from which quarter she planned to stir up trouble.

The young girl was the last witness to be called. There was a murmur of sympathy from the crowd as the slight, fair-haired girl stood up to take the oath.

Thomas Wilson turned to Magistrates Burgner and Brittain. "I consider Miss Margaret Silver the most important of my witnesses, sirs. I would like her to tell her story in her own words, without being interrupted by questions from me. The witness is understandably nervous to be speaking before such a congregation, and I think she will come through it better if she can lose herself in the telling of her testimony."

The justices of the peace had a brief whispered conference. Then John Burgner said, "We'll allow it. This is merely a hearing, and we may relax the rules a bit, especially to accommodate a young lady in distress."

Mr. Wilson turned to the witness and gave her a reassuring smile. "Now, Miss Silver, just a word or two to begin with, so we'll know where we are. Would you state your age, please?"

"Sixteen."

"And your relation to the deceased?"

"Sister. Well, half. Half sister, that is, but we didn't take any notice of that. We were all just family. Our daddy was a widower when he married my mother, Nancy Reed, that was, in October of 1814, when he first came into the Carolina backcountry to settle. Charlie was two years old. That first wife in Maryland, she had died in 1812, giving birth to Charlie. I was born on December 2, 1815."

Young Margaret seemed to be reciting these facts to herself, for she did not so much as glance at the audience. Wilson must have decided that he had let her ramble enough to put her at ease, for he stopped the flow of family reminiscences. "Now, Miss Margaret, I'd like you to remember the events of just a few short weeks ago, when your big brother Charlie went missing. Can you speak up loud and clear now and tell us exactly what happened?"

The girl took a deep breath and nodded, closing her eyes for a moment to compose herself before relating the difficult tale. Thomas Wilson handed her his linen handkerchief and she wound it around her fingers, tugging and picking at it until I thought it would unravel into threads.

"Tell us about your brother Charlie going missing," Wilson prompted.

"Reckon it was two days before Christmas when Frankie showed up at our log house with the baby on her hip, and Charlie nowhere to be seen."

"The day before Christmas Eve."

"Yes, sir. I wasn't thinking on it being nearly Christmas Eve at the time, mind you. We don't make much of Christmas up home, so there was no decorating or presents, no fancy dinner being prepared. Menfolk mostly use it as an excuse to get liquored up. They shoot their guns in the air to make a joyful noise unto the Lord, I reckon."

There was a ripple of amusement in the audience, but the witness ignored it and plunged ahead into her story. "Us women didn't pay Christmas much mind, unless there was a church service near enough to go to, so it was just an ordinary day in the dead of winter, but real cold. The ground was hard as slate under drifts of snow, and the Toe River that runs brash past our mountain land was so hard froze that a body could walk on water. It was a day to run for shelter, if you had any call to be out in the elements at all, but I watched her coming, and Frankie Silver was walking slowly down the track in the frozen hillside, in no hurry to reach our place. And she may have been shaking, but we would have blamed that on the cold."

Here the witness faltered, as if dreading what was to come.

"Tell us about Frankie Silver," Wilson prompted her. "Your sister-in-law."

"She's just two years older than me, but prettier—I'll give her that. I turned sixteen last month. Not that much was made of that, either, except that my brothers Alfred and Milton teased me about being their old-maid sister, seeing as how my sister-in-law Frankie was already expecting a young 'un by the time she was my age, and I hadn't so much as kissed a man yet. I wasn't studying to be like Miss Frances Stewart, I told them."

Margaret Silver blushed. "The truth is, sometimes I wished I was more like her. She was little and fair, and she worked hard, too. Of course, she had to. Being married to Charlie and all."

Margaret Silver ignored the rumble of laughter from the back of the court, but the noise drew scowls from both magistrates.

"Go on," said Burgner. "And I'll have less noise from the gallery, gentlemen."

"About Frankie. Well, she kept that cabin clean, saw to the baby, tended the cows and the chickens, and did the cooking and the washing and kept the fire going. There are three of us girls to help Mama do what Frankie did all by herself. That set me against marrying up early, too."

The two prisoners sat up straight when they heard these words, and they looked as if they might be about to chime in, but the lawyer silenced them with a shake of his head, and Margaret Silver hurried on.

"Charlie wasn't much to bestir himself around the place, no, but he was dashing. People took to him. He and Frankie made a likely pair. It's no wonder they married so young, and, of course, Charlie always did have an eye for beauty."

"A man of refined tastes," murmured Wilson, and I heard no hint of irony in his voice.

Margaret Silver nodded. "I guess Charlie must have taken after his mother's people. We liked him fine, but we weren't like him. He was handsome, and he could charm squirrels out of a gum tree with that smile of his, and he never said no to a jug or a fiddle tune, but . . ."

The magistrates gave Thomas Wilson a look, and he leaned in close to the witness and said softly, "It's time to tell us what happened to Charlie, Miss Margaret."

She took a deep breath and blinked back tears. "We were working when Frankie showed up. Of course, we always are, with ten folks to be fed at mealtimes, and a fire to be kept going, and young 'uns to be tended—my brother William, the youngest, isn't but two years old.

"It was early morning when Frankie came in. She stood there on the threshold, stomping snow off her shoes and shaking the ice flints out of her hair. She handed me the baby, and began to untie her wraps and rub her hands together to warm them. I took the little Nancy over by the fire, peeling off her blankets and checking her fingers and toes for frostbite. It isn't more than a quarter mile over the hill to their place, but the wind was fierce." Her voice softened as she spoke of the child. I had to lean forward to hear her.

"Charlie's baby is just over a year old."

"And what is the child's name?"

Margaret Silver smiled. "Why, it's Nancy. Maybe Charlie named her after our mother that raised him, or maybe the name came from one of Frankie's people, or maybe they just liked the sound of it. I don't know what Frankie thought about that, but maybe she didn't like her own mother's name—Barbara—or maybe Charlie didn't give her any say in the matter. Charlie would have his own way: if he could charm you into doing his bidding, he would, but if not, he could get ugly about it. It's a pretty name, though . . . Nancy Silver. . . . Folks said that if she got her mother's looks and her father's charm, she'd be a force to be reckoned with a dozen years hence."

Talking about her young niece seemed to comfort the poor girl, but Wilson could not allow her prattle to take up the court's time.

"You are dutiful to tell us so much, Miss Margaret," said Wilson, and this time he was smiling gently. "But we do not require such detail, only the bare bones of the tale. Frankie turned up at your parents' house that morning, then, with the baby, did she not?"

"She did."

"And what did she say?"

"She was bragging. She said she had been working since sunup, chopping wood and scrubbing the cabin floor. . . ." She faltered a moment when the gasps from the spectators nearly drowned her out. Perhaps it was the first time the poor girl had realized the significance of those words.

"What else did she say?"

"She wanted one of the boys to feed the cattle. Said Charlie was gone from home. So we sent Alfred back with her."

"Did she say where Charlie was supposed to have gone?"

"Over to George Young's. Most of the men get their Christmas liquor over at George's place."

"So you had no reason to doubt her story?"

"No. It sounded like Charlie, all right."

Thomas Wilson permitted himself a perfunctory smile. "Tell us what happened then, Miss Margaret."

"Well, Frankie took herself off then, but the next morning she was back, saying Charlie still hadn't turned up. After a couple of days we took to searching the woods, but we never did find no trace of him. Not 'til Mr. Collis went to the cabin, after Frankie went home to her people."

"Did you see the Stewarts at any time during all this?"

Margaret Silver thought about it. "I never did," she finally admitted. "They didn't stop by to sit a spell with us, or to ask after Charlie, not one bit."

"But they said nothing about his disappearance? They were not seen at Charlie and Frankie Silver's cabin?"

"Don't reckon they were."

Beside me Colonel Erwin stirred in his seat. "There it is, Mr. Gaither," he murmured. "Wilson has established that there is not one whit of evidence linking the Stewart woman or her boy to this case. They said nothing and no one saw them. They will have to be let go. Wilson has done his best for that poor family, no doubt, but at what a cost!"

"What do you mean?" I whispered back.

"He has put a rope around the neck of Frankie Silver."

I am alone now, but I do not mind the solitude.

I have lived all my life in one-room cabins, first with Daddy and Mama and my brothers, and then with Charlie and the baby. It seemed strange at first to have so much space on my own, and so much quiet. I had Mama and Blackston to talk to for the first week or so, but they were afraid that someone was listening, and we found that apart from that one big thing, we had not much to say to one another. Fear is like a stone in your mouth. When you have it, you cannot talk of anything else. So we passed the days in near-perfect silence, with dread kicking in our bellies. Then there was the hearing, and Mama and Blackston got bond and were let go. After that it was only me, to sit here and wait 'til spring.

I think I would not mind the prison cell but for the idleness. I don't know what to do with my hands. They move in my lap and will not stay still. I asked the jailer's wife if I could help her do the chores so as to pass the time, but she said I mayn't be let out, and that she could not let me have an iron or a needle, for fear that I would use them for mischief. Her name is Sarah. She has a baby, and I ache to hold it, for it reminds me of my Nancy, but of course she will not bring it near me. I watch her sometimes when she plays with it out in the garden. Its golden curls glint in the sunshine, but if she looks up and sees me watching them, she frowns and takes the baby away. Her man has told her that I am mad, and although she sees that I am as mild as milk and never angry, she is still afraid, and hangs back, well away from the door of my cell, whenever she has cause to speak to me. I am a killer.

"You can have a Bible," she said.

I shook my head and she went away, thinking that this was proof of my wickedness, perhaps even a sign that I am a witch. I did not tell her that I refused the Good Book because I cannot read.

I pass the time at the barred window, looking down on the muddy road that passes through the center of the town. There are more people here than I have ever seen in my life. Some of the women have velvet cloaks and bonnets with white feathers. I wish I could see their shoes. Sometimes the people pause and look up toward my window, and I step back into the shadows because I don't want them looking at me. I wonder where they are going, and what the fine houses look like on the inside, and what fancy goods are to be had over there in the store. I had me a store-bought china bowl up home. Someone gave it to us for a wedding gift—one of Charlie's kinfolks, that was. It didn't get broke, in spite of all that happened there in the cabin. I remember it sitting on the pine table when I went away, down to Mama's, not knowing for sure that I was leaving that place for the last time, but thinking I probably wouldn't want to sleep there ever again. When Daddy got home from Kentucky, I'd make him take me back there to get my things, I thought, but that wasn't to be. I wonder what happened to that bowl. It was white with three marks like blue feathers painted on one side. I would like for the baby to have it when she is grown.

Chapter Three

THE MANILA FOLDER lay on the wrought-iron table, untouched but not unnoticed by the invalid in the lawn chair. While he drank his morning coffee on the deck overlooking the mountains, Spencer Arrowood stared at the thick manila folder that Martha had brought him the night before. He had felt too tired to tackle it on the previous evening, but now his curiosity about it was almost overpowering. He had not touched that file in nearly twenty years. Its contents would be strange to him, even though he had written most of the entries himself—and yet he hadn't. The author of those police reports had been a swaggering young deputy, sure of his place in the world and of his superiority over his prisoners. He was the white knight upholding honor and justice in a tarnished world; they were cartoon bad guys, without excuses or families or feelings. He remembered how that young deputy had looked at life. He saw a world inhabited by only two kinds of people: criminals and cop groupies. He had viewed both types with suspicious condescension. It had taken Spencer a long time to learn how narrow the range of his experience was. Most people's lives never touched the orbit of a police officer: they went through an entire existence as neither victim, nor devotee, nor perpetrator, and so he had never seen these folk.

Spencer could remember thinking like that, but he could no longer summon up the arrogance of youth that made such belief possible. He had perspective now. He had arrested a wife beater and recognized him as the skinny kid from sixth grade who used to show up at school with a black eye and bruises and mumbled excuses about how he got them. He arrested a pretty young cheerleader for drunk driving, only now she wasn't the pretty young cheerleader: she was blowsy and forty-four, and sometime in the intervening years since high school she had turned into her own mother. Although he would seldom admit this, especially to himself, Spencer had felt inside himself the same rages and impulses that got people arrested, and now he thought that most law-abiding citizens were as fortunate as they were virtuous. Any one bit of luck—loving parents, a knack for getting good grades, enough money, a faithful spouse—could derail the kind of tragedy that happened to people less blessed.

He knew that Fate Harkryder had not been an upstanding member of the community, but he had not been lucky, either. Spencer looked again at the manila folder containing the biography of a killer, wondering how it would read to him now that he was no longer the arrogant young deputy who thought that his gold shield made him a knight.

He half remembered typing the final reports, two-fingered, on an IBM electric typewriter that at the time had seemed to be the last word in technological wonders. The machine was probably still down in the basement of the sheriff's office, along with the broken staplers, the rotary-dial telephones, the boxes of old paperwork, and all the other detritus of previous administrations which they had always meant to discard but never quite got around to carting off to the landfill.

The first item in the folder was a yellowed newspaper clipping from the *Hamelin Record* relating to the Harkryder case, with a photograph of the state's key witness, a twenty-four-year-old deputy named Spencer Arrowood. Spencer stared at the picture of himself as an impossibly soft-faced kid. His cheeks were plump, his eyes unlined, and for all the air of menace he had tried to invoke, with his narrowed eyes and his mean-cop scowl, he looked like the rawboned adolescent he was, fresh out of the army but still looking for a fight. His sandy hair had brushed his collar in those days, fashionably long but a continual source of irritation for Nelse Miller, whose childhood impressions of masculinity had fixed on the close-cropped doughboys just back from the lice-ridden trenches of the First World War. Spencer had wasted many coffee breaks arguing the point of fashion and hygiene with the old sheriff, but it had been a waste of breath. A waste on both sides, he thought ruefully, for now he kept his graying hair as short as Nelse Miller could have wished for.

Had he ever been that young?

The thought worried him more than he would ever admit. That arrogant young deputy, the Spencer Arrowood of twenty years ago, had made decisions that would cost a man his life. What if he had been wrong?

He hadn't thought so at the time, but back then he had been so angry, and so eager to see someone punished for what had happened to Emily Stanton, that he never paused to question his conclusions for an instant.

Her face smiled out at him from the faded newsprint. He had never seen her smile. The newspaper photo was a year-book shot from her university. They couldn't have used the crime scene photo in a family newspaper. No one would have wanted to remember her as she was when they found her. This was better. The picture was black and white, but Spencer remembered it in color: long red curls, clear green eyes. He remembered other colors, too, ones he would have liked to forget: streaks of mud across her left cheek, a purple bruise on her forehead, rivulets of blood, and a white splinter of bone poking through skin that should have been pink but wasn't any more.

The caption beneath the picture said: "Army Colonel's Daughter Killed in Hiking Tragedy."

To the right of Emily Stanton's lovely face, the plain features of Mike Wilson looked out at him with the buzz hair-cut and the glazed stare of the student soldier. ROTC—a "Rotsy," as the students in the university's Reserve Officers' Training Corps were called. Mike Wilson was headed for a hitch in the air force after college, but he never made it. He had fought a brief, private battle in a clearing in the Tennessee mountains, and he'd never had a chance. There had been defense wounds all up and down his arms, and nicks on his fingers that showed he'd tried to grab at the knife as it came at him. Those were the least of his injuries, of course, but at least they said something about how he had died. Bravely. Everyone clung to that. "Brave Mike Wilson" the news accounts invariably called him, as if that would make up for the waste of his life. Mike Wilson had died first that night. Quickly. At least, Spencer hoped it was quick.

Mike Wilson and Emily Stanton had met at college, the article said, and they had become good friends—the newspaper of twenty years ago would not have said "lovers," but most of its readers would figure it out for themselves. They had decided to hike the Appalachian Trail together as a chance to get to know each other better, and to see if they could work well as partners. Mike liked the idea of roughing it in the wilderness to toughen himself up for the military. He had not been armed, though. Back in those days no one thought that the Appalachian Trail was a dangerous place. Hikers knew to give snakes a wide berth, and they were assured that black bears were not really a threat to people, as long as you didn't menace them or try to approach the cubs. No one gave much thought to human predators in those innocent days.

She was only nineteen that night. She had been dead for twenty years. Spencer tried to picture Emily Stanton growing old, fading from a radiant beauty into an aging woman. Either way, he reasoned, that pretty young girl would not exist any longer, but at least she would have had a chance to become somebody else. He wondered if she had been robbed of a happy future or spared a more protracted tragedy.

At least he could try not to compound the tragedy by letting an innocent man go to his death. But how could he investigate the case at such a remove? The fading documents in this manila folder were all he had to go on. The physical evidence had long since been destroyed. A few months or years after the trial, the blood samples, the hair and fiber evidence, the clothing exhibits, and all the other mementos of the tragedy would have been incinerated in the interest of space management. After all, a small sheriff's office could not keep everything, just on the off chance that it would someday be needed again. The state had won its conviction. Clear out the detritus of that investigation and move on to the next. Don't look back.

Besides, physical evidence deteriorates. Even if the Wake County Sheriff's Department had managed to keep the samples, the results from a retesting would not be reliable, and surely they would not be accepted as new evidence by the court. There was no DNA testing at the time of the Trail Murders. Perhaps then he would have known for sure; now he must investigate with only uncertainty to guide him— that, and his will not to let any mistakes be made.

Spencer leafed through the rest of the contents of the folder. He had the crime scene photos—that was encouraging, but beyond them, he had only his notes to go on, and a short list of witnesses. He wondered how many of them were still alive, and if their memories of that night had faded with time. He would have to find out.

Spencer took out the photos. Some of them had been taken with the department's Polaroid, a state-of-the-art camera back then, and an excellent device for producing fast shots of the crime scene. Had he known then of their impermanence? He could barely make out the images in the faded prints. Heat and age had long since neutralized the developing chemicals of the instant camera, making the prints as imperfect as memory. The 35-millimeter shots were better preserved, but the exposures were inexact, a testament to the inexperience of the photographer, who had been himself.

He had been called to the crime scene by Willis Blaine, the forest ranger for their district. The sequence of events was all there in the witness statement that he'd typed himself so long ago but now could only dimly recall. Spencer scanned the lines of faded type.

The call came in well past midnight: two hikers found

dead, but not on the Appalachian Trail, which was federal
land. A couple of firemen from Alabama had decided to
spend their two weeks' vacation hiking the North Carolina/east
Tennessee section of the Appalachian Trail. They were nearly
at the end of their journey, and that night they had gone off
the trail to spend Friday night at a beer joint. At 11:20 P.M.
they were making their way back through the fields to their
campsite when they stumbled over something soft and sticky
in a moonlit clearing.

Emily Stanton.

The startled firemen had stopped just long enough to determine that the victim was past any efforts at rescue. That
decision had taken only a few seconds. They checked for
breathing and a pulse, but really they had known it was useless the moment they touched her. "Dead people's skin doesn't
feel like flesh," one of them said at the trial. "It feels like
lunch meat wrapped in plastic." The journalists had omitted
that comment from their stories out of consideration for the
families, and because it served no purpose to make a good
guy sound silly in the newspaper when they already had a
surfeit of villains: the Harkryders.

The two hikers hadn't lingered to investigate further. They
ran down the path in the moonlight, back to the beer joint to
call the forest ranger.

A body? he'd said, a little disbelieving. It wouldn't be the
first time anyone tried to play a telephone prank on a forest
ranger. *Where?*

In the woods at the edge of a field, they told him. Just
down from the Appalachian Trail, across the dirt road from
the white frame church. The snake handlers' church.

Yes, he told them. He knew the place. It wasn't a snake handlers' church, of course, but the trail has its own mythology,
and it wasn't important that he should correct their theology.
He knew the place they meant. Would they wait for him in
the parking lot and lead him to the scene of the accident?
No point in calling it murder, yet. It wasn't his call anyhow.
If the hikers had described the site correctly, that clearing

was a couple of hundred yards west of the Appalachian Trail, not federal land. It was in Wake County.

He got in his truck and drove to the roadhouse. The hikers were easy to spot. They were slender young men in their early twenties, huddled together in a pool of light beneath an electric pole, shivering in flannel shirts, although the night was warm. When he parked in the gravel lot and began to walk toward them, they backed away, darting glances toward the open door of the roadhouse, where jukebox music spilled out into the darkness. At last they noticed his ranger's uniform, and they rushed toward him, both talking at once. *We're not armed,* they told the ranger. *Whoever did that might still be there.* The ranger nodded. He showed them his pistol and told them that there was a shotgun in the truck. They could bring it along if it would make them feel any easier. Then they were willing to lead him to the site. They were trained to handle emergencies, and they were already getting over the shock of their find.

Willis Blaine took his flashlight out of the truck and followed them down the road to the church, and then up the dirt road, past the field, and into the woods.

When he aimed the spotlight at the clearing, his mind registered several things at once. Homicide. Not a fight or a failed robbery, this one. A very sick individual was loose out here. Young adult victims, one female, one male—their clothing indicated that they were probably hikers from the trail, but they were no longer on it.

I have to secure this crime scene, he told the young firemen. They nodded. They knew about crime scenes. *You need to go back to the roadhouse and make another call. Wake County Sheriff's Department. Tell them Willis Blaine sent you. Tell them where I am. Tell them it's murder.*

Spencer remembered the call. He wasn't supposed to be in the office at all, because they were a two-man department in those days, and after eleven, calls were forwarded over to Unicoi County, whose sheriff's department had twenty-four-hour patrols. But Spencer was a hotshot in those days. He would have worked twenty-hour days if Nelse Miller had let him, and that night Nelse Miller wasn't there to send him home. Where had the sheriff gone? On vacation to Wrightsville Beach? To a bureaucrat's meeting in Nashville? To a cousin's wedding in Ohio? Spencer couldn't remember anymore. The whereabouts of the sheriff was not a detail included in the official report on the case, but it was duly noted that the officer in charge of the investigation was Wake County sheriff's deputy Spencer Arrowood.

He had been sitting at the oak desk in the darkened office. Only the paperwork and a white china coffee mug were illuminated by the desk light. He had been up since six, and he was so exhausted that the letters were beginning to wiggle on the page, so that he could no longer make out what he had just written. He might lay his head down on the desktop and catch an hour or two of sleep before finishing the reports. The soothing monotony ended with the ringing of the telephone. A calm steady voice with a Deep South drawl delivered the message with only a tinge of emotion shading the words. The fireman told him where they were and what they had found. Spencer made the caller say it twice so that he could be sure he had heard him right.

Murder on the Appalachian Trail. Well, not on it. Near it. In his jurisdiction. Mr. Blaine, the forest ranger, was there with the bodies, waiting to turn the investigation over to him. Did he know where the clearing was? Spencer shook himself to clear his head and to banish the weariness from his muscles. *Wait by the phone,* he told the hikers. *You can save me time by showing me where to go. And I'll need statements from you.*

He had called Alton Banner and asked him to meet the patrol car at the roadhouse. The caller had assured him that the victims were dead, but Spencer wanted to take every precaution.

He took both cameras, the Polaroid and the 35-millimeter; the notebook; and all the paraphernalia that had to be carried to a crime scene. Spencer knew the drill: he had done it often enough before; he had even been in charge of investigations in the past, but they had been trifling occurrences of no real consequence. Murder itself was uncommon enough in this rural mountain county. A case like this was almost unheard of. You would have to go back decades to find another one. God help him, had he been eager? Had he been excited to have a terrible case dumped in his lap after weeks of routine and paperwork?

He locked the office and headed down the steps toward his patrol car, wondering if in his grogginess, he had forgotten some crucial point of police procedure. *Oh shit,* he thought, as his hand touched the car-door handle. *The TBI.*

He was running now. Unlock the office—his fingers seemed to have grown two sizes in as many minutes as he fumbled with the lock, swallowing the urge to kick in the door. A few more minutes wouldn't matter. The real pros wouldn't be there for another three hours at least, because Knoxville was 120 miles away. The Tennessee Bureau of Investigation. You called them out for any serious crime, because they had all the toys. The TBI had a fully trained death squad of officers who did nothing but crime scenes, and who knew how to check for fingerprints, hair and fiber evidence, bloodstains. They also had the lab to process the evidence, which meant that they would get it all anyway, so he might as well let them collect the samples themselves so that there would be no question about tainted evidence when the case came to court. *When* the case came to court. Spencer wouldn't even consider the possibility of a stalemate.

He checked the county map before he made the call, because he would have to give directions to someone unfamiliar with the county back roads. He couldn't say, "Turn left at the Evanses' place, and go past that field where the white horse is usually grazing." No. He located the church and the roadhouse on the map, noted down the road numbers, approximated the distances from the main road. Then he made the call.

The officer from the TBI would meet him at the crime scene in a couple of hours. Say, 3 A.M. Spencer would secure the area and do the photography and the site mapping while he waited. When the sun came up, they would be better able to determine what they were dealing with. Nobody was getting any sleep that night. That much was a given.

He left the office with the taste of cold coffee still in his mouth. He found an all-night country station on the radio and turned it up as loud as he could stand it, so that the noise would keep him awake. He was hoping for happy songs that would drive away the darkness outside and the darkness to come.

One of the vacationing firemen was waiting for him at the crossroads beside the church. When he recognized the patrol car, he stepped out of the shadows of an oak tree and flagged him down. Spencer parked in the church's gravel lot and followed the young man down the road and through the field toward the dark woods beyond.

The fireman's name was Al Hinshaw, and he said that his buddy Neil was waiting at the site with the ranger. He explained about their hiking vacation, and how they'd stumbled over the bodies on their way back to the shelter. Hell of a way to end your vacation, he'd said, shaking his head. The trail was supposed to be a peaceful place, wasn't it?

"It usually is," said Spencer. Now he saw the glow of a Coleman lantern, and he knew they were within hailing distance of the crime scene. He had met Willis Blaine a couple of times, when their paths had crossed in other investigations, but he couldn't remember anything about the man that would be fodder for small talk during the long wait for the pros from Knoxville. *How's the wife and kids, Willis?* Who knew if he even had any? Spencer wasn't much good at small talk anyway, in those days. The demands of the job seemed to overshadow all the rituals of everyday life for him, leaving him without anything ordinary to say.

Blaine did not seem interested in conversation, either. He stood up and nodded a greeting when Spencer came into the clearing. Spencer shook hands with him and with the other fireman, Neil Echols, and that ended the civilities of the evening. "I didn't touch anything," the ranger told him. "It's not my jurisdiction anyhow. But I'll stay if you want me to."

Spencer nodded. He could tell from Willis Blaine's tone of

voice that he wasn't trying to take over the investigation. He was extending a courtesy to a fellow officer, and Spencer would have accepted the offer, realizing with some surprise that he really didn't want to be all alone in the woods in this terrible place waiting for help to arrive, but Alton Banner had joined them by then, so he would have company. He wasn't afraid; he decided that the proximity of death had made him realize how little time we all had in this world not to be alone. Instead of expressing these sentiments, he said: "You go on home. I'll call you and let you know what we find out."

Then he went to hold the light on the bodies while Alton Banner examined them.

"Well, they're past my help," the old doctor declared after a moment's silence. "You don't need me to tell you that."

"No, sir. But your presence makes it official."

Spencer had written the words "Crime Scene Log" at the top of the first page of the notebook. He would record the names of every person who went in and out of the area, so that if a question arose later about a fingerprint or a bit of fiber evidence, they could check the sample against those who had been present at the scene. He took the names and addresses of the two vacationing firemen and sent them on their way. It was just possible that they had been responsible for this crime, but Willis Blaine hadn't thought so, and neither did Spencer. The two men had seemed genuinely upset by their discovery of the bodies, and they hadn't shown the signs of uneasiness or cockiness he'd have expected from the perpetrators. They acted, as far as he could tell, normal, under circumstances that were far from normal.

"They were killed separately," Alton Banner remarked when the hikers had gone.

Spencer blinked. "What?"

"The bodies. There's a difference in body temperature that suggests one has been dead an hour longer than the other. The male victim went first. He was off in the weeds. The killer probably took him there for—what? Privacy? To get him out of the way without letting the girl know what had happened to him?" The doctor shrugged. "Figuring that out is your job, I guess." He turned the flashlight toward the second body, letting the beam play on the ropes that still bound her wrists. "The girl was tied to the tree at that point."

"Cause of death for the male?"

"Exsanguination, suffocation. His throat is cut." He shined the light on the male victim's head and neck. "Windpipe is severed. Watch how you move the body when the time comes. There isn't much holding the head on."

"And the other one?"

"I'm coming to that. I don't think the first victim, the male, was the primary target. The killer got him out of the way first, but that killing was fairly perfunctory. Bludgeonings. Defense wounds. Then the quick slash that puts an end to it. Like swatting a fly." He pointed to the body of Emily Stanton and sighed wearily. "He took his time with her."

Spencer nodded. He wondered how much of it she had been conscious for. At some point in unbearable pain, he'd heard, the mind simply drifts off to somewhere else. He hoped she went there quick and never came back. The blood looked black in the moonlight. "I think I'll wait for the TBI guy," he told the doctor. "He'll have to take samples."

"That's what I'd do," Banner agreed. "My investigation was perfunctory, but he'll do the evidence collecting. You might as well photograph the scene while you wait. I'll hold the light."

Spencer willed himself not to register what he was seeing as he photographed the area—roll after roll of black-and-white 35-millimeter film, backed up by a dozen Polaroid shots. The recording of a crime scene is a methodical process closely akin to archaeology in the precision of the measurements and the use of grid markings to measure off the area. The body was "twelve o'clock" on the site map. He began photographing the body, shooting clockwise around the scene, taking every angle, every degree of rotation, until he returned again to the starting point. When he had finished photographing the scene, Spencer went back to his notebook and began to sketch the scene—pinpointing the position of the bodies, the objects nearby, and so on. Investigators were taught to be thorough. He wasn't much of an artist, but he was diligent.

It was just past three when the officer from the Tennessee Bureau of Investigation showed up. Spencer knew that he was a veteran investigator not so much by his age as by the way he approached the area. He introduced himself to Spencer and the doctor.

"Guess I'll head on home," said Alton Banner. "Office hours come mighty early. You know where to find me if you need anything. I'll get a report typed up for you in the morning."

Spencer thanked him. When he turned to explain the situation to the TBI man, he found the investigator already bending over the body of the young woman. "Oh my," he said in a calm, conversational tone as he trained the beam of his flashlight across her upper body. "What *have* you got loose in your neck of the woods, Deputy?"

Spencer was startled by the question. Surely a bear couldn't have done this? "We're pretty sure they were killed by a human being, sir," he said.

The investigator laughed. "Oh, it was a person, all right. I might be willing to debate you over how *human* he was, though, considering his handiwork. I hate to claim him as part of our species, but, yeah, he's one of us, all right."

He had brought a thermos of coffee, and he didn't even turn away from the bodies while he poured it out and gulped down his first cupful. Then he set down the coffee and surveyed the scene again. "A hard day's night," he said with a sigh.

He signed in on the site log and glanced at Spencer's sketches of the area. "It'll do," he remarked to no one in particular. Then he stood up and stretched. "Drink your coffee. Take your time. I'll have to collect some samples, and then we'll do the grid work together, okay?"

"Sure. Fine."

"Have you identified the victims yet?"

"No. I was waiting for you."

"Maybe we'll turn up something on the grid work. They're not local, are they? Look like trail bunnies to me."

"Hikers. I think so, too," said Spencer. "I don't think they were killed because of who they were. I mean, not by anyone they knew."

"Oh Lord, no," said the TBI man. "Of course, we're pissing in the wind at this early stage of the investigation, but in my far-from-humble opinion, this wasn't a crime. It was a sport. To whoever did this, I mean."

The crime scene photos were spread across Joe LeDonne's desk, in the spotlight of his reading lamp, but he barely glanced at them. At the moment, a hamburger in greasy waxed paper was occupying the one spot on the wooden surface not covered with photographs.

"I've stared at those pictures until I can see them in my sleep," he said. "If I got any these days, that is."

"I thought we'd have solved it by now," said Martha, setting a cup of cold coffee down untasted. "We've put out the word to the informers and talked to everybody within a mile of that field."

"The lab work will help."

"Only if we have someone's blood type and DNA to compare it to."

"It's a start."

"I was so tempted to tell Spencer about it when I took him the mail today, but he still looks awful. The Harkryder case is really getting to him. I don't think he's sleeping much."

"You took him the mail? What about the newspaper?"

Martha smiled. "I took him the *Knoxville Journal*. I told him I'd forgotten to bring the *Record*, and I'd try to remember it next time. He doesn't need anything else to worry about. Besides, there's nothing he can do about it now. The site investigation is done, the lab work isn't back, and he's in no shape to do the legwork of a criminal investigation."

LeDonne leafed through another folder on his desk: the photocopied files of the Fate Harkryder case. Martha had made a copy before taking the originals to Spencer Arrowood. "I wish we had a murder weapon," he said, for perhaps the tenth time.

"Well, it isn't a twenty-year-old knife," said Martha. "The TBI investigator agrees with Dr. McNeill: the wounds are similar to those in the Trail Murders case, but not identical. He thinks it may be a copycat crime, based on the fact that Fate Harkryder's case is back in the news."

"We have Fate Harkryder's blood type on file somewhere, don't we?"

"I think so."

"When the lab work comes back, let's compare them."

"It isn't him," said Martha. "Riverbend is the best alibi there is."

LeDonne nodded. "Besides, he's too old. We're looking for someone under thirty-five. This kind of violence is a young man's sickness."

"I think I'll drop by the high school tomorrow," said Martha. "See if anybody wants to talk about the murders."

Fate Harkryder was thinking about death.

It seemed strange to know that you were going to die when you felt perfectly sound. When he came to consider the matter, it seemed not so much strange as . . . improbable. Ridiculous to believe that after twenty-odd years of sedentary monotony, the very people who had wished him good morning and to whom he had passed the occasional remark about a basketball game or a change in the weather would come for him, strap him into a plain wooden chair, and kill him.

Strange to think that the ridge he had watched day in and day out for so many years would go on changing from green to gold with the seasons without his presence as the observer. He liked to think that the ridge was there on his account, and he found it hard to believe that his death would go unheeded by his ridge.

Of course, he knew that deep down he didn't believe in

death at all. Not for himself, that is, and certainly not by execution in the state of Tennessee. He was still young and strong. He did push-ups every day for exercise, and despite a twenty-year pack-a-day smoking habit, his lungs and his blood pressure were fine. He trusted his body to keep him around for many more years, and he trusted the Tennessee legal system to spin its wheels for at least that long before they got around to trying to execute him. By then, maybe the voters would abolish the death penalty altogether, and someday, when his crime was so far in the past that nobody cared anymore, he would be granted parole. He intended to be hale and hearty enough to enjoy that freedom when the time came.

Even with lawyers who were mediocre at best, Fate Harkryder had been able to stave off the death penalty for twenty years already. It wasn't difficult. There was always some objection that could be made in the appeal process, and any little quibble could tie the court up for a year or more, so slowly did the mills of justice grind. His lawyers had argued that his original counsel hadn't been any good. That fellow was now quite a prominent attorney in Knoxville, but no one seemed to notice the discrepancy, and Fate figured that it was just one of the moves in the game: a formality. Anyhow, it bought him more time. When that objection played itself out a few years down the line, his legal advisers objected to the expert witnesses who had testified at his trial. They had now spent years nitpicking through a stack of transcripts and documents that would fill a pickup truck, but each legal dispute ate up a few more months: filing time, waiting time, court time, awaiting-the-decision time, appealing the decision, and then back to square one to begin again.

Fate sometimes thought that the delaying tactics would go on even if he dropped dead in his cell, so impersonal and relentless was the process. He was not the quarterback in this legal scrimmage; he was the football. It had been years now since anybody had mentioned the names Mike Wilson or

Emily Stanton to him. The paperwork just rolled on, oblivious to real time and real people. Sometimes it seemed that the judicial process had taken on a life of its own, independent of any actual, long-ago crime.

Burgess Gaither

Choosing Counsel

The snows of January deepened into a bleak February chill, and we town folk gathered at our firesides, passing the time away in desultory conversation. We discussed the presidential election coming in autumn, and what the reelection of Andrew Jackson boded for the Western lands. Since the time of the Revolution, the landholdings of the Cherokee nation had shrunk from many thousands of acres stretching from Alabama to Virginia to the present remnant of their past glory: a few townships in the steep mountains to the southwest of us. Now, even that pittance was begrudged them. Since the recent discovery of gold in those mountains, the United States government had been besieged with demands to move the Indians westward so that better use could be made of their mineral-rich acreage. The Indian Removal Act had passed in 1830, ordering all Indians to be resettled on lands west of the Mississippi, but so far it had not been enforced. People were growing impatient. Andrew Jackson, who rose to fame as an Indian fighter, was said to be sympathetic to the plight of the settlers, and people claimed that he'd see to the eviction of the Cherokee to win the support of the voters on the frontier. Gold fever had swept the mountains.

There was much local speculation about the gold fields, and what effect the discovery might have on our own prosperity. Old John Tate, who is seventy if he's a day, has already taken his family off to the hills of Georgia to seek their fortunes, and other folk talk of joining him. They are waiting to hear if he strikes it rich.

Aside from the economics involved, there is much concern among my colleagues that Andrew Jackson may ruin the country if his presidency continues. Most of the gentlemen of my acquaintance think that Jackson is a lout, an uncouth peasant who would turn the country over to the mob rule of uneducated dirt farmers. He is an Antrim Irishman who prides himself on his common touch.

He is also a lawyer. He read law not far from here—with Spruce MaCay in Salisbury, North Carolina. In 1787, when my father-in-law the squire was a young clerk of court in Morganton, Andrew Jackson was the public prosecutor for the Western District of North Carolina. The older gentlemen remember him as a hard-drinking, quick-tempered scarecrow who would sooner fight than gamble.

People still talk about the incident that occurred when Jackson was practicing law over the mountain in Jonesborough in the months before he moved on to Nashville. He was invited to an elegant ball at the home of one of the county's prominent families. Jackson asked if he might bring a companion, and the request was granted, no doubt in hopes that he might introduce another eligible frontier gentleman to polite society. Instead Andrew Jackson arrived at the home of his host in the company of five bawds, tavern women of easy virtue whom he tried to pass off as "ladies." The shock and outrage of those present meant nothing to Andrew Jackson; it only satisfied him that the gentry had correctly interpreted his message of contempt.

Now gentlemen everywhere talk bitterly of President Jackson's 1829 inaugural party, when a drunken mob of his beloved "common people" were allowed to rampage through the White House, leaving a trail of mud and broken china in their wake. The aristocrats are afraid that if this ruffian is allowed to run the country for another term of office, ruin will follow. There is talk of placing tariffs on imported goods, which worries a good many people. They do not criticize the president so publicly, however, for Jackson was a hero in the war with England twenty years ago, and his ties to western North Carolina are cherished by many. Jackson's popularity with the local farmers and backwoodsmen is as undeniable as it is bewildering. I confess, though, that I sometimes wonder what it would be like to be independent of rich and powerful old men, and to be able to oppose them with impunity. Andrew Jackson is every inch a self-made man, and it heartens me to see that such a feat is possible, although I would wish to have more respect from educated and wellborn gentlemen were I in his place.

Besides these political and economic topics, and the ever-present discussions about the weather, we all spoke endlessly, obsessively, perhaps even morbidly, of Frankie Silver. Her trial was but a month away.

She alone of her family languished in the Burke County jail now. Her mother and brother had been let go after the hearing before the magistrates in January. Mr. Burgner quite rightly set them free, declaring that no one had offered any evidence to show that they had known of or participated in the death of Charlie Silver. They were, however, to be witnesses in the forthcoming trial, and to ensure their appearance in court on the appointed day, he made them post a bond of one hundred pounds to secure their liberty. Isaiah Stewart paid the requested sum, and he lost no time in putting forty miles of mountains between them and the law in Morganton, for he took his wife and son back up the Yellow Mountain Road to their land on the Toe River. Frankie Silver was well and truly alone in her prison cell, for the journey across the mountains was too great for a family visit, especially in winter. She must have missed her baby daughter dreadfully, but we did not speak of that. The ordinary folk of Morganton recounted the crime to one another, thrilling anew to the horror of it with each retelling, while we in the legal profession had a more prosaic matter to contemplate. Which of us would defend this wretched young woman?

We had gathered at a secluded table in McEntire's tavern to discuss this delicate matter. I was there as an impartial participant, for as clerk of Superior Court, I could not have defended her even if I had wanted to. And I most certainly did not want to.

Nobody did.

I looked at the faces of my fellow lawyers gathered round the table. Their expressions ranged from wariness to mulish obstinacy. We were here to decide what must be done about her, and I thought that someone was bound to dislike our solution. For a frontier town, Morganton had a goodly number of lawyers, but not all of them cared to practice their calling in court. The fact that the western circuit court met in Morganton was reason enough to have a fair crop of lawyers about, but that was not the only reason they were plentiful. Wealthy planters sent their sons off to study law because a knowledge of legal matters was considered to be the final polish on the education of a gentleman. A trained legal mind made a man proficient in his business affairs, well able to understand deeds and contracts. Perhaps it was a vestige of the old pioneer spirit that inspired the elderly gentlemen to make lawyers of their sons: in that way, the family's commercial ventures would not be at the mercy of outsiders when it came to interpreting and utilizing the law. The family would not have to take anyone's word for the rightness of a business transaction or the meaning of a statute. If knowledge was power, then legal knowledge meant commercial and fiscal supremacy.

Some of these "gentlemen" lawyers, who practiced law for their own benefit only, did not attend our tavern conference, for the present legal dilemma was no concern of theirs. Others were there perhaps out of curiosity, but it was very much a family discussion. There were but six of us to settle the matter—it would have been seven if my brother Alfred had lived, and how I wished he had been there to offer his counsel. I was the youngest man present by a decade. My colleagues were my father-in-law Squire William Erwin; his eldest son and my brother-in-law Adolphus Erwin; Colonel James Erwin, their cousin; Mr. Isaac T. Avery, a former state legislator, who is married to my wife's sister Harriet; Mr. D. J.

Caldwell; and Mr. Thomas Wilson, who had represented Mrs. Silver's relatives at the habeas corpus hearing with great success. Mr. Wilson's wife Catherine is a niece of the Erwins, as her mother is Mrs. Erwin's sister Ruth.

"You ought to take it on, Cousin James," Adolphus suggested. "You could make a name for yourself with this case."

"Yes, but not a name to be spoken in polite company," growled Colonel Erwin. "The woman is an object of loathing to the entire county. Whoever takes her part in court will be branded with her villainy. The criminal cases are tried but twice a year, gentlemen, and they constitute at best a few weeks of work. What would become of the rest of my practice?"

"He's right," said my father-in-law. "Deeds and wills and civil lawsuits are the bread and butter of every country lawyer. Defend that woman, and no honest citizens will cross the threshold of your office thereafter."

"What about you, Mr. Avery?" asked Adolphus.

The silver-haired gentleman shook his head. "I am the bank president now. I have no wish to dabble in criminal law. Particularly not in this case."

"You ought to defend her, Wilson," said Colonel Erwin. "You represented the family at the habeas corpus hearing. An admirable performance."

"And so I have done my part," Wilson growled. "Let someone else take up the burden. Any of you could afford the loss of income better than I."

Thomas Wilson was the next youngest of the group, and not the least distinguished. He had served a term or two in the North Carolina legislature before he moved west to Morganton to set up his law practice, and as I have noted, he is related to the Erwins by marriage, which is useful. Wilson's older brother Joseph, a prominent circuit court judge in Charlotte, had died within months of my own brother's death, and because of this loss so similar to my own, I had always felt an unspoken bond of sympathy with the man. He had been kind in my bereavement, talking of his own loss and offering wise counsel about what I should do now that I had lost my future as a junior partner in a family law firm. Wilson was a good man, well respected by the community. Still, I had misgivings about him for such a momentous case. Thomas Wilson was a competent enough fellow for ordinary matters, but he always struck me as humorless and unimaginative. In my heart I knew that if I were ever in the dock in fear of my life at the whim of a loutish jury, I would want someone other than Thomas Wilson pleading my case.

"Regardless of one's financial circumstances, it would be a pity to put a lifetime's work on the rocks for the sake of a two-day trial with a foregone conclusion," said Adolphus. "It would be folly."

"Surely this one case could not harm a man's career so grievously," I said. "The public must be made to understand that everyone is entitled to a defense in court. Someone must side with an accused person, whether that defendant is guilty or not. I put it to you that our very legal system is built on that premise."

"You might as well teach catechism to a mule," drawled Adolphus. "The layman has no understanding of such matters, and no patience to have it explained to him. I consider myself lucky if I face a jury that is tolerably sober; I don't ask them to think. The fact is, the townspeople are after that young woman's hide. There's not a doubt in anybody's mind that she's as guilty as Jezebel and twice as wicked. That mob will tar Frankie Silver's lawyer with the same brush that convicts her of cruel murder, and while there will be no trial for her attorney, he will be sentenced to poverty as surely as she is bound to die. Let us be clear on that."

"I wouldn't even let my son Joseph take the case if he finished his study of law and passed the bar today," said Colonel Erwin. "Not for the experience or the fame, or even for triple the fee that anyone is likely to get for defending her. No one who is going to practice law in this town can afford the taint of her society."

"I can say the same for my own son Waightstill," said Avery. "He will finish his studies at the university in a few months' time, and he means to make the law his profession, but I would not wish this case on him for any consideration."

The others nodded in somber agreement, and I could not doubt them. Between them they had a good half century's experience in the practice of law, while I was barely past my first year, and, thanks to my clerkship, I was independent of the whims of clients. "But this is unfair, then!" I protested. "How can we ask any man to risk his livelihood by representing a hated defendant who is by all accounts guilty as charged?"

"You are well out of it, Burgess," said Squire Erwin. "And much as I am tempted by the sheer challenge of the matter, I fear that my age and infirmity prevent me from such exertions, so I, too, must be exempted. Gentlemen, we would all be wise to keep out of this matter, but we cannot. We must make some provision for this poor creature's defense, because that same mob who would shun us for defending the woman would be just as quick to condemn us for negligence if we abandoned her to her fate. We must steer a safe course between these two evils."

"But what is the alternative? No lawyer wants this case."

Colonel James Erwin looked thoughtful. "There may be one that does."

"But *who* is Nicholas Woodfin?" Elizabeth asked me when I returned from the lawyers meeting at McEntire's tavern (but for the presence of Mr. Wilson, I might have termed the gathering a family reunion with perfect truth).

"I have met him but once, I think. He has been a licensed attorney now for precisely one year, but we hear good things of him—at least your cousin James says so."

"Woodfin . . . Woodfin . . ." Elizabeth shut her eyes and wrinkled her forehead. A sign, no doubt, that she was flipping through the pages of that great studbook-cum-social register that all the frontier gentlewomen seem to have indexed in their brains.

"Asheville," I said helpfully.

She opened her eyes wide. "Asheville! So near! And his wife is—?"

"He doesn't have one. He's only twenty-one, and doubtless he has been working too hard in his studies to find time for courtship. But there is someone of your acquaintance who may vouch for him, and you will value his opinion even above mine—Mr. David Lowry Swain."

Elizabeth gave me a look. "I might have guessed that, Burgess. Cousin James would not recommend a young novice for an important case unless there was some sign of distinction about him. For an Asheville attorney, that sign could only be a clerkship with the honorable David Swain, who is surely one of the most promising young men on the frontier—excepting yourself, my dearest."

I smiled at her generosity of spirit, but I did not think I merited the comparison. I am a simple country lawyer, content with my lot in life. Never was I as driven to succeed as the tireless Mr. David Swain of Asheville, whose ambition might pass for ruthlessness in the eyes of more humble folk. In the score of months that I had been an attorney in Burke County, I had heard much about him and his aspirations. Although he was not from a prominent family, he had struggled and sacrificed to attain a good education, after which he worked harder than any three so-called gentlemen to better his lot in life. He was barely thirty, yet already he had served five terms in the North Carolina legislature. His days of toil and poverty were behind him, and I daresay he was now as much a gentleman as anyone in Carolina.

"David Lowry Swain," said Elizabeth thoughtfully. "But he is forever traveling, and he stays for months in Raleigh, does he not? One wonders that he would have had time to mentor a lawyer in Asheville. Is he still the member for Buncombe County in the House?"

"No. He refused a sixth term. He is a circuit court judge now."

Elizabeth sighed. "He married exceedingly well."

"Really? Pretty, is she?"

That look again. Elizabeth takes a dim view of my teasing.

"Eleanor White is the daughter of a North Carolina secretary of state," she said primly. "Her maternal grandfather was Richard Caswell, governor during the Revolution. Thanks to Eleanor, and to his own efforts, of course, David Swain has connections that extend well beyond Asheville. That whole family has prospered in state politics. James Lowry of the State House of Commons is his half brother, you know."

I didn't know. Latin verbs are child's play compared to unraveling the tangled lineages of the North Carolina gentry. "David *Lowry* Swain and James *Lowry* are half brothers? Curious coincidence of names."

"Not a coincidence at all," said Elizabeth. "Don't you know that story? It's common talk in the western legal circle. David Swain's mother was Miss Caroline Lane, who as a young woman was married to a Mr. David Lowry. They lived on a farm in north Georgia, and she bore him a number of children. Sadly for his wife and babes, David Lowry was killed in an Indian raid, and poor Caroline Lowry married again—to a Mr. George Swain, who is a merchant and a physician. They had six or seven children—I forget the exact number—"

"Really? I would have thought you'd have their birthdays down by heart."

She waved away the Swain offspring. "They aren't important, except for the youngest. And his mother named him after her first husband—David Lowry. So he is David Lowry Swain. Isn't that a sweet story, Burgess? Such a tender remembrance. The poor woman never forgot her first love."

"One wonders how Mr. Swain felt about the matter," I muttered. "Though perhaps after six predecessors, the happy couple had run out of names anyhow. They might have called the next one after the cat."

"Names are a serious business in good families, Burgess," said my wife reprovingly. "It tells the world instantly and precisely what your connections are— Oh!"

Her lecture on dynastic nomenclature was cut short by a wail from the nursery. Our own son and heir, young master

William Willoughby Erwin Gaither, was in need of his mother's attention.

A few minutes later Elizabeth returned to pursue the topic of Nicholas Woodfin with renewed interest, but I was unable to satisfy her curiosity regarding the young gentleman's antecedents. I said that Colonel Erwin had vouched for Woodfin as a competent attorney, and we were too preoccupied with legal matters to inquire into his suitability for breeding purposes. Elizabeth murmured that perhaps someone in her family would know who he was, and I did not doubt that for a moment. The Erwins of Belvidere have eight daughters; no gentleman west of Wilmington escapes their scrutiny.

After a few minutes of companionable silence, my wife looked up from her embroidery and said, "Something has just occurred to me, Burgess dear."

"Yes?"

"None of you lawyers wants to defend this poor girl Frankie Silver. Is that correct?"

"It is most fervently the case," I assured her.

"Aha! Then why would Nicholas Woodfin agree to take it?"

"I can give you three reasons. First, he is a very young attorney who needs the trial experience, and perhaps even the celebrity that might be gained from this case. Second, he has another case on the Superior Court docket, so he is coming anyway. Another case will only make his trip more fruitful. Third, Woodfin may be well connected by association with David Swain, but your family assures me that he is by no means rich. The legal fees in the Silver case will not amount to much, but I'm sure they will be welcome to a fledgling attorney."

"Those are good enough reasons, I suppose," said Elizabeth. "But what would cause Mr. Woodfin to accept this case when our Morganton lawyers would not?"

"Precisely that, Elizabeth. Nicholas Woodfin is *not* a Morganton lawyer. A local man would lose the community's goodwill and a substantial portion of his income from deeds and wills by associating himself with the infamy of Frankie

Silver. Nicholas Woodfin will suffer no ill effects. He can take the case, show off his legal skills to his fellow attorneys in circuit court, collect his fee, and then ride away to Asheville, some fifty miles away, where few people will know or care about a Burke County murder case. He will not lose a scrap of business for his effort, and if he does well in court, he may even increase his practice by gaining the goodwill of the legal community."

"It seems very suitable for all concerned," Elizabeth conceded. "But what of that poor young woman? Will she be well represented by such young and inexperienced counsel?"

"Your cousin James assures us that Nicholas Woodfin is an able fellow who plans to specialize in the practice of criminal law. He may well be Mrs. Silver's best hope for a defender. Besides, Thomas Wilson has graciously consented to serve as second counsel, so that Woodfin can have the benefit of his experience."

"For part of the fee, of course," said Elizabeth, smiling.

"Of course."

"But he will not speak for Frankie Silver in court?"

"No, certainly not. That is Woodfin's task. Woodfin is to be seen to act as her attorney."

"So all of our local attorneys—"

"Most of which are in your immediate family," I hastened to remind her.

"Thank you, Burgess. I know that. So the Erwins and Mr. Wilson are relieved of the obligation of taking the case, and therefore they will save their livelihoods. And you tell me that Nicholas Woodfin is a good man. I am glad to hear it. My sister Mary is most concerned about the poor young woman."

"She need not worry on Mrs. Silver's account."

"Mary says that she would like to visit the jail. She wants to hear the facts of the matter from the accused woman's own lips." Elizabeth took a deep breath. "And I would like to go with her!"

"Neither of you will be permitted to do anything of the kind," I said, with ill-concealed irritation. "Thomas Wilson is acting as advisory counsel until the trial. He has cautioned his client with the utmost severity against speaking to anyone about her case. I doubt that Sheriff Butler would permit you or Mary to visit. I urge you not to attempt such a thing."

"My sister Mary is quite determined."

"Your sister Mary always is."

"And you are sure that Mr. Woodfin will be a sympathetic and conscientious defender of poor Mrs. Silver?"

"I am certain that he will be excellent, my dear," I assured my wife. But I was thinking, *He is a good deal more than she deserves, for we believe she is a wicked murderess.* I did not tell Elizabeth that her cousin James's parting remark had been, "Won't we look like fools if the young devil gets her acquitted?" And we all laughed heartily at that.

I miss the flowers. I can hardly bear to look out. The ground is so bare and brown now, and the trees look for all the world as if they were dead. "Don't you worry," Sarah Presnell says to me when she brings me my dinner. "The flowers will be back in late March. Everything comes alive then, same as ever."

I must be the opposite of the flowers, then, for they will reappear the very week that my trial is held. They will be coming alive as I commence to dying. They have got me a lawyer, Mrs. Presnell says, and she seems to set a store by them, always going on about what fine gentlemen they are, and big political men, but I cannot see what use that will be to me. I don't trust strangers, and I've seen the way these town-bred folk look at us mountain people—like we were something they caught in a trapline, and they're afeared of catching something off 'n us. I do not want to tell my secrets to such as them, for they are men, and like as not they own slaves to boot. What would they know about being afraid? They think the law looks after people that needs help. They live in a town with a sheriff within hollering distance, and prying neighbors to see that everybody does what he ought. It's easy to die in the wilderness, and there's nobody around to save you.

I dream about Charlie sometimes. He is standing in a field of buffalo grass, and it is summer. He has been picking wild blackberries for me, because he knows I love them so. He lifts a handful of blackberries to his mouth and he bites into them, and the dark juice runs out of his mouth. But suddenly I see that it is not blackberry juice running down his chin, but blood, and there is a gaping wound at the side of his head, matting his brown hair. His eyes are open and staring, but their sense is shut, and he walks toward me, holding out the basket of blackberries. Before he reaches me, though, the dream changes and I am kneeling beside the little branch that runs back of our cabin. The water is so cold that it numbs my fingers, but I am washing white linen in the branch water, and I cannot stop. Swirls of red slide away down the cloth when I hold it up to look at it, but it is not yet white again. I scour it harder on the cold rocks. Someone is behind me, watching me scrub the bloodstains out of the white linen. Someone is watching. It is not Charlie.

Burgess Gaither

THE GRAND JURY

For one week of every September and March, the session of circuit court transforms Morganton from a sleepy frontier village into a boisterous festival of tavern phillipics on law and politics, dinner parties, and, I am sorry to say, more than a few drunken brawls and fistfights, which simply generate more business for the legal community that created the occasion to begin with. The local hostelries teem with travelers come to town for the court. Some of the newcomers are litigants or relatives of the accused, but many others are merely spectators who have come for the sport of it. They see the week of trials as a bit of drama to spice up a humdrum existence. As I have said, court is our theatre.

My wife's parents, the Erwins of Belvidere, offer their hospitality to the visiting attorneys, hosting a sumptuous dinner and even lodging to those who prefer not to take their chances at a country inn. Perhaps this custom of entertaining the officers of the court arose from my father-in-law's long years as clerk of the Superior Court, but I suspect that the family would have done it anyway. The judge and the attorneys who come to town for the court session bring news of the outside world, and they offer fresh opinions on the political intricacies of government in Raleigh. Their society helps to strengthen the ties between the frontier gentry and their peers in the more settled parts of the state. Their town manners and their news of fashion remind us that even in the back of beyond, we are ladies and gentlemen.

Elizabeth always looked forward to these grand family parties, for she never tired of the social round, nor of hearing news about the births and marriages of her far-flung acquaintances, and as she said more than once, she welcomed the chance to show me off to visiting dignitaries who might prove influential in my career. Elizabeth has higher ambitions for me than I have for myself, I fear. Perhaps Morganton is a sleepy backwater village, and someday I suppose I might tire of it, but for now it contents me and I cannot imagine ever wishing to leave it.

We were dressing for the dinner party. I was resplendent in "Archbold" (Elizabeth's playful name for my good black suit), as befitting the importance of the occasion. It is the suit I wore to our wedding and to the funeral of my poor brother Alfred. She will probably insist upon my wearing it to Superior Court next week as well, and perhaps given the solemnity of that occasion, she will be right. Elizabeth was wearing a black gown of some shiny fabric, and a very fetching carved necklace and earrings of jet, for she is still in mourning for her sister Margaret Caroline, who died last year. Elizabeth's hair has been crimped into the sausage curls of current fashion, but because she has a long neck and splendid shoulders, the style suited her better than it did many of the poor overfed matrons who endeavored to wear it. I believe the dress is the one that Elizabeth made from the pattern book from Charleston, though I am by no means an expert on ladies' finery. I am not much better on the vagaries of society's bloodlines and shibboleths, but in this area at least, Elizabeth has been endeavoring to instruct me.

With a worried frown she straightened my cravat before turning again to inspect her own elegant reflection in the pier mirror. "Now, Burgess, do try to keep it all straight, won't you? The two most important guests tonight are Judge Donnell and Cousin William, and they are both from Charlotte."

"Cousin William . . ."

"Alexander!" She fairly snapped at me. "William Julius Alexander. Do try to take this seriously! There is more to the practice of law than passing your exams and winning your share of cases. William Alexander is my kinsman. He is an Erwin on his mother's side, Sophia being the sister of the colonel, that is, Cousin James."

"I'm not likely to forget him," I assured her. "As to Mr. Alexander, I have met him briefly, I think. He is the attorney for the state in this week's trials."

"Yes, but you mustn't talk about the court docket at dinner. It has always been Father's custom never to discuss cases pending before the court. There are outsiders present, you see, and privileged information must not be divulged in general company."

"Of course I knew that," I said with some asperity. Anyone would think that *she* was the lawyer in the family and not I. I forbore to mention that since I was clerk of the court at the forthcoming proceedings, I had no particular need to charm our visiting legal dignitaries. To such a protest of disinterest my wife would no doubt reply that every social connection will prove useful sooner or later, and that one should never lose an opportunity to impress a person of influence. No doubt she is right. The success of the Erwins, socially and otherwise, brooks no argument.

"Besides," said Elizabeth, "all that sort of legal talk is very boring for the rest of us. But even if we stick to general conversation, there are some things you must keep in mind."

"What, for instance?"

"William Alexander is not only our cousin; he is also the nephew by marriage of Thomas Wilson, so be careful that you don't say anything disparaging of the Wilsons in his presence. Not that you would, of course," she added hastily, seeing the glint of annoyance in my eyes.

"I will disparage no one tonight," I assured Elizabeth. "Morganton, which consists solely of strangers and kinfolk, taught me that lesson a long time ago. Still, it surprises me to find such a tangle of pedigrees in the court. It will be old home week in the courtroom, won't it, my dear? All the attorneys kin to one another in varying degrees. No outsiders except the defendants and perhaps a witness or two."

"That is hardly unusual," she said, unimpressed by my wit. "Good families socialize with one another. It is only natural that they should intermarry."

"And the judge? Have we managed to get him into the family yet?"

"Really, Burgess! You are quite dreadful. And I implore you not to adopt this teasing tone with Mr. Justice Donnell. The poor man is quite recently widowed, and I am sure he has no heart for levity. His late wife was only thirty when she passed away, poor thing. She was the former Margaret Spaight, the governor's daughter."

"Richard Dobbs Spaight," I murmured to show willing. "Anything else?"

"You will notice a Scots brogue in Mr. Donnell's voice, by the way. He is a native of that country, but he has spent most of his life on this side of the ocean. He is a graduate of the University of North Carolina, as is Cousin William. The judge is a quiet man, most serene and serious. An altogether superior person, I feel. His home is in New Bern, so we do what we can to make him feel at home and welcome when he is at this end of the state. He has a son and a daughter—"

I took my wife's arm. "No more, please!" I said, laughing. "My memory has reached its limit. Let this poor Christian go down into the den of social lions before I forget every word you have said to me about their pedigrees."

I think I acquitted myself well at the Erwin dinner party. I was solemn and respectful in the presence of the gravely taciturn Judge Donnell, and I chatted amiably about the weather and horses, and the activities of mutual acquaintances with William Alexander, who was closer to me in age but equally distant in interests and temperament. It was not I who brought up the subject of Frankie Silver.

We did manage to get through most of the meal without a

mention of court business by anyone present, but by the
time the dessert wine was being poured into small crystal
glasses, we had exhausted the exchange of news and gossip
about absent friends, and we had settled the mysteries of
weather, politics, and the fate of President Andrew Jackson
to our mutual satisfaction. In the slight lull that comes with
an overwarm room and a sated appetite, Miss Mary Erwin's
voice rang out from the other end of the long mahogany
table.

"Have you heard about our local cause célèbre, Mr.
Alexander?"

William Alexander withdrew the wineglass from his lips
and set it down with only a suggestion of a sigh. "What
cause célèbre would that be, Cousin Mary?" he inquired
with grave courtesy.

"Why, that there is a woman on trial for her life in Superior Court next week! Surely you have been briefed about
the case?"

Mr. Alexander looked around the table for guidance from
his fellow attorneys—the table was rife with them—but we
were all careful to maintain perfectly neutral expressions.
After an awkward silence during which no one leaped to his
rescue, he said, "Oh, yes. The murderess. I hope you are not
learning the domestic art of wifely behavior from that unfortunate example, Miss Mary."

His quick thinking was rewarded with a brace of chuckles
from the gentlemen present, and a clinking of glasses indicated that the tension had eased, but my spinster sister-in-
law refused to let the matter drop.

"So you have made up your mind that she is guilty, have
you?" she demanded.

"So I must. If she is brought to trial, it is my duty as district solicitor to prosecute her," he replied. "If you are worried about her guilt, you had better speak to those who are
defending her." His gaze sought out his wife's uncle, a few
chairs down the mahogany table.

Thomas Wilson glanced nervously at the judge, who remained impassive, apparently in deep contemplation of his

wineglass; then he met the imperious gaze of Mary Erwin. A classical image from my Latin studies at Hull's School leaped to my mind: Ulysses caught between a deadly pair of monsters, Scylla the rock and Charybdis the whirlpool. Although it seemed particularly apt, I decided against sharing this Homeric inspiration with the rest of the party.

"We shall do our best, Miss Mary. Indeed we shall." Wilson tried to strike a note of geniality but his voice rang hollow. "Still, you must see that the evidence against Mrs. Silver is very strong." He glanced warily at the judge, as if he expected that worthy gentleman to rap upon the table with a carving knife and call him to order.

At that point Squire Erwin came to the aid of his struggling dinner guest. "Mary, my dear, you mustn't badger poor Mr. Wilson about his unfortunate client, particularly when his own involvement in the case is indirect. Mrs. Silver will be defended in court by a splendid young lawyer from Asheville, a Mr. Nicholas Woodfin."

Since Nicholas Woodfin was not present at the dinner party, Squire Erwin had succeeded in rescuing Thomas Wilson without throwing his colleague to the wolves. Before Mary could pursue the matter, another guest changed the subject, and we all fell upon a discussion of some trivial matter with more relief than interest.

As we left the table, though, I heard Colonel James Erwin murmur, "Has anyone warned young Woodfin about our Miss Mary, do you think? She is far more menacing than his rustic client."

"Old home week, indeed!" said my wife Elizabeth.

It was Saturday, March 17, the day after my twenty-fifth birthday. I was preparing to leave for the courthouse, where this morning the grand jury was meeting to decide which of the possible cases should go on to trial when the Superior Court met the following Monday.

"Whatever do you mean, my dear?" I murmured, but my attention was on the mirror.

"The grand jury is meeting today, is it not?" I nodded. "And as clerk of court, you selected the jurors?"

"Well . . ."

"And who did you choose to be foreman of the grand jury?"

I sighed. Sometimes I think people in Morganton know things *before* they happen, so quickly does gossip spread through the community. "Samuel Tate."

Elizabeth smiled. "Oh, Burgess, you are such a humbug! After all that fuss you made before father's dinner party about the court being 'old home week,' as you put it, because of the lawyers' family connections. And then, who do you put in charge of the grand jury? Sam Tate!"

"It is a small town, Elizabeth," I said with as much dignity as I could muster. "Nearly every eligible juror is connected in some way—how *is* Sam connected, by the way?"

"Samuel Tate is married to my cousin Elizabeth, the daughter of Peggy Erwin, that was." (Peggy Erwin Tate is the sister of Colonel James Erwin, in case you are as obsessed with family connections as everyone else in Morganton seems to be.) "But that is hardly the point, Burgess, as you well know."

I did know. Apart from his family connections, Sam Tate is hardly the disinterested village yeoman that people seem to think comprise grand juries. Although he is just past thirty and his primary occupation is farming his landholdings at "Hickory Grove," Sam Tate is a former sheriff of Burke County, and now serves as a justice of the Burke County Court of Pleas and Quarter Sessions.

"I think he is a very fitting choice," I said. "I realize that the notion of a former sheriff acting as jury foreman might strike the casual observer as an odd and even suspicious circumstance, but he will be very useful. He has a working knowledge of law and procedure, and he can direct the other jurors in a sensible fashion."

"He is hardly a disinterested party." Elizabeth's questions were serious enough, but something in her tone made me think she might be laughing at me. "And hardly an angel of mercy, either, I fancy."

I knew what she was referring to. Although the incident had happened before I became the clerk of Superior Court, and thus I did not witness it, I had heard the story told more than once. During Sam Tate's tenure as sheriff, a man had been convicted of a felony that required him to be branded upon the thumb with the letter symbolizing his crime. (*M* for manslaughter, and *T* for thief or any other crime.)

There are many crimes on the law books for which the prescribed penalty is death, but in these enlightened times we choose not to execute everyone who steals or commits some lesser crime, even though the law permits such summary justice. First offenders, especially people who are otherwise upstanding citizens except for this one lapse, are often shown mercy by the court, though when I have witnessed the administering of the alternative and heard the screams, I have often wondered if it is indeed mercy that is meted out.

To distinguish between irredeemable sinners and unfortunate transgressors, therefore, capital crimes are divided into two classes: the unpardonable acts in which the offender was denied benefit of clergy and was executed for his crime, and the other, so-called clergyable offenses, in which the convicted prisoner might plead "benefit of clergy" and thus escape the death penalty by accepting the lesser punishment of being branded on the brawn of the left thumb. The term *clergyable* refers to the origin of the practice. In medieval England, the clergy could claim exemption from the punishments of secular courts. Later this leniency was extended to anyone who could read, permitting the offender to escape the death penalty for the lesser punishment of branding. More recently, "benefit of clergy" was extended to citizens irrespective of their literacy, and more depending upon the nature of the offense. One cannot claim "benefit of clergy" twice, however. The law is not given to the eternal mercy of heaven.

When a court had accepted the prisoner's plea of benefit
of clergy, waiving the execution in favor of the lesser punishment, the sheriff's duty was to hold the red-hot branding
iron to the thumb of the criminal for as long as it took the
man to cry out "God save the State" three times. On this occasion, the unrepentant felon, tied to a post and writhing in
his agony, screamed out "God save the State!" twice, and
then sobbed and gasped, "God damn Sam Tate!"

Sheriff Tate carefully removed the branding iron from the
poor man's thumb and began the procedure all over again,
making sure that the requisite phrase was said correctly
three times, as prescribed by law. No, Sam Tate was not an
angel of mercy, but he was faithful to the letter of the law,
and he knew the North Carolina statutes as well as anyone.

"Well," I said, "whatever Sam Tate's biases are toward the
people of Morganton proper, if indeed he has any, he is sure
to be a stranger to all the principals in the Silver case, because they all hail from the back of beyond. Therefore the
proper objectivity will be preserved. Sam knows the law. I
know of nothing fairer than that."

"I suppose it's a foregone conclusion anyway, isn't it?" she
asked as I turned to leave.

"Pretty nearly," I said. "All her hopes must rest on the trial
itself. Perhaps her lawyer can move the jury with his eloquence. Failing that, she is lost."

The grand jury under Sam Tate's able direction considered the case against Frankie Silver, her mother Barbara
Stewart, and her younger brother Blackston. The facts were
presented, and the witnesses heard. When the grand jury retired to begin its deliberations, they argued about what
should be done.

One of the more prominent jurors, George Corpening,
whose brother David is our state legislator, said: "I say we indict the lot of them! They're all in this together. Anyone can
see that."

Other voices chimed in to agree with Corpening.

They finally stopped chattering and noticed that the grand

jury chairman and former sheriff sat conspicuously silent. After a moment's silence, Rucket Stanley said, "What do you think, Mr. Tate?"

Sam Tate considered the matter. "Well, boys," he said, "it's like this. Trials are tricky things. You can indict ever who you want to, but that doesn't guarantee that you'll get a conviction when the trial is over and done with. I've seen a lot of cases go to court in my time, and I'll tell you what's the truth: indicting all three of these suspects would make me uneasy. Yes, sir, it would."

"Why is that, Sheriff Tate?"

"Because it suggests that we don't know who to blame, and that we're arresting everybody just to make sure we get the guilty party. People don't like that. Jurors are so contrary, they might end up feeling sorry for the Stewarts and letting every one of them go. I say we ought to pick one of them—the most obvious one—and let that person take all the blame."

George Corpening was scowling. "But what about the other two?"

"Do you see any proof that they were involved?" The sheriff's eyes narrowed. "I'm not talking about common sense, George. I'm talking about proof that will stand up in a court of law. All I see in this case is what you call circumstantial evidence. Charlie Silver disappeared, and a week or so later his body parts are found in the fireplace of his own cabin."

"But according to the witnesses, Charlie Silver's widow lied!" Corpening protested. "She said he had gone from home, when all the time bits of him were lying in that fireplace." He broke off with a shudder.

"Exactly right," said Sam Tate, unmoved by the thought of gore. "Mrs. Frances Silver was caught in a great and terrible lie. And that means that she is not an innocent party. But what about the other two, boys? What *evidence* can you give me to tie them to this death?"

"It stands to reason that a young girl like that wouldn't have acted on her own," said David Glass.

"I'm talking about proof," Sam Tate reminded him. "Can anybody show me proof?"

No one spoke.

"All right, then. Here's what I propose that we do, boys: we bring back a true bill on Mrs. Frances Silver, and we no-bill her mother and brother. We know she's in it up to her neck, and I'd rather see her punished for her crime than cast the net too wide and risk losing all three. I say we make it easy on the jury and send them a sure thing. Who's with me?"

Hands went up. They all were.

A few hours after they began their deliberations, the Burke County grand jury returned a true bill only on Mrs. Frances Stewart Silver. She alone would stand trial for murder.

In view of the strong feelings inspired by the Silver case, the court ordered each of the subpoenaed witnesses in the forthcoming trial to post a bond, ranging from twenty-five dollars to one hundred pounds British sterling, in order to ensure their attendance at the proceedings. These were staggering sums to be required of witnesses, but we felt that it was necessary to make the consequences of *not testifying* just as terrible as the consequences of testifying. We all knew that when cases involving backwoods families are tried in court, the matter seldom ends there. The losing family continues its search for justice with violence and acts of reprisal, particularly against unfriendly witnesses, often for years after the original matter was settled by the court. The urge to avoid the matter entirely must have been strong for the people of Frankie Silver's community.

The court set the trial date for Thursday, March 29, and Sheriff William Butler was ordered to summon 150 jurors on the Thursday following to be considered for service in the proceedings. This was a larger number of potential jurors than we usually called, but because of the sensational nature of the case, I thought it prudent to have men in reserve in order to provide the lawyers with a satisfactory selection of men from which to choose. Perhaps the notion of mountain justice would convince many of our own citizens that they wanted no part in the proceedings.

Nicholas Woodfin, the young lawyer who was brought in to represent Mrs. Silver in court, arrived in Morganton a few days beforehand in order to familiarize himself with the case and to interview his client. I do not know where he stayed, perhaps at the estate of his cocounsel Thomas Wilson a few miles outside town, or perhaps he took lodgings at the Buckhorn Tavern. Whatever his residence, I know that he did not lack for dinner invitations. One of Elizabeth's sisters had caught sight of Mr. Woodfin, boots shining, brass gleaming, and clothes brushed free of the dust of travel, riding into town on his strapping bay gelding, and she had stopped in her tracks and stared upward like one who has been given a celestial vision.

"Why, he looks for all the world like a foreign prince!" Miss Erwin exclaimed. This pronouncement of the regal nature of Mr. Woodfin's appearance was quickly communicated to every lady in the county, or so it seemed, and they vied with one another to show him every kindness during his visit. I venture to say that the mothers of unmarried gentlewomen in our county envisioned Mr. Woodfin's role of rescuer of damsels extending well beyond his duty to his client Mrs. Silver.

"And *does* he look like a prince, Burgess?" Elizabeth wanted to know. Tending to our infant son and to her duties at hearth and home had kept her so occupied that she had yet to see the distinguished newcomer. She relied on her sisters to keep her supplied with news.

"He is certainly an imposing figure," I said, trying to temper my annoyance with justice. I do not recall such a fuss being made among the ladies when *I* first arrived in Morganton. "Nicholas Woodfin is a man of medium stature, with dark eyes and features in the Greek mold, I believe you would say. His hair is very dark, though already it is flecked with gray."

"What a pity," said Elizabeth.

"Not at all, my dear. The last thing a young lawyer should wish to look like is—a young lawyer. Age suggests wisdom and experience. His clients find his mature countenance very comforting, I expect."

"And has he seen his most important client yet?"

"Mrs. Silver? Yes, I believe so. He must interview her before the trial begins, of course. It must have been an interesting encounter. I wonder what they made of each other?"

"How so, Burgess?"

I shrugged. "I cannot imagine two people more dissimilar than Nicholas Woodfin and the rawboned backwoods girl whom he must defend. It must have been a memorable meeting for both of them. There he is, smelling of lavender soap and pressed linen, standing over her in his spotless wool suit and polished calf-leather boots, an attorney of law, well educated and mannered, conversant in Latin, and acquainted with the most prominent gentlemen in Carolina . . . and there *she* is—greasy-haired, lice-ridden, and unwashed from her months in a straw-floored cell of our Burke County jail: a scrawny, graceless girl, unable to read or write, and scarcely able to understand what is happening to her, I'll warrant."

"The poor girl must see him as a knight in shining armor," said Elizabeth.

"If she has ever heard of such a thing, yes."

"But, Burgess, I have heard that despite all her deprivations in prison, Mrs. Silver is very pretty, too."

"I doubt if Mr. Woodfin would notice if she were the Queen of Sheba," I replied. "He will have quite enough on his mind with a murder trial to prepare for. It is a great responsibility to have someone's life in your hands. And he is such a young man. I do not envy him one bit!" I said these words with all the more force because they were not true.

There were other less notorious cases to be settled in the first few days of the Superior Court session, although nobody paid them much mind. All talk centered on the final

day's business: the State v. Frances Stewart Silver, scheduled
to be tried on Thursday.

I saw Thomas Wilson in court, of course, for he had other
cases on the docket to attend to, but it was several days before we managed to find a moment for conversation other
than the perfunctory courtesies one utters in passing.

I saw him one morning walking from his office to the
courthouse, and I fell into step beside him. After wishing
him good day, I said: "'I hear talk of nothing but the Silver
case, Mr. Wilson. Someone said that if we could sell tickets
to the trial, we could do away with Burke County's property
taxes for a year."

He permitted himself a trace of a smile. "I fear that such
an avid interest in the case is a misfortune for the accused
woman. Strong interest means strong feelings, and the jury
will feel pressured by that, whether they admit it or not."

"At least you will not have former sheriff Tate to contend
with. Having served on the grand jury, his obligation is discharged. I would not have wanted to try a murder case with
his cold stare trained on me."

He nodded. "Well, I will not be pleading this case before the court. The stares are Mr. Woodfin's concern, but I
do not think he minds. He is a great playgoer, is Mr. Woodfin. He says that a defense attorney is the principal actor in
a tragedy. He even went so far as to say that clergymen
ought to attend the theatre and pay close attention to the
dramatic orations, as it would greatly improve their style of
preaching."

"He seems to have some unorthodox opinions for such a
young man."

"Yes, but I think he is very able. And I'm not sure that I
don't agree with him about the importance of being a dramatic orator. Juries *feel* a great deal more than they *think*, it
often seems."

I protested, "Surely a logical argument, well presented—"

Wilson smiled again. "If you ever stand in the dock, Mr.
Gaither, guilty of the crime of which you are accused, I'll

warrant that you will realize the value of making jurors weep instead of think."

On Thursday morning the trial began. The family of the murdered man would be present in court, no doubt making certain that no Stewart kinfolk slipped into the ranks of the jury. By the same token, Isaiah Stewart and his sons, who waited outside the courthouse with expressionless stares, would see to it that none of the Silver clan sat in judgment of Frankie. Since both families were forty miles from home, I thought they stood a better chance than most of receiving disinterested justice.

The thought of all these grim backwoodsmen from beyond the mountains made me uneasy, for their notions of civilized behavior might differ widely from those of Morganton proper. The moment I reached the courthouse I had a word with Constable John Pearson, warning him to keep an eye on the spectators during the trial, particularly the Stewarts. They might all be armed, and they might attempt violence if the court did not rule in their favor. Taking the law into their own hands is a common enough practice on the frontier, where courts are too far removed to serve the needs of the settlers. Men in the wilderness learned to protect their kinfolk and their possessions without the benefit of the legal system.

Pearson narrowed his eyes at my warning. "You think they'll fight, then?"

"I hope not," I said, "but you must be vigilant. Watch everyone. Even our own local citizens. Regrettably, many of them are much the worse for drink on court days. They might become unruly. Feelings are running high over this case."

"So are wagers," grunted Pearson.

"They are betting on this case? On whether she is guilty?"

"No. Her guilt seems evident—at least no one is wagering otherwise. The bet is on whether Mrs. Silver will be acquitted or sent to prison," said Pearson.

"But surely, if she is convicted—"

He shook his head. "She is a woman. They won't hang her."

The first order of business on the day of a trial is the selection of a jury. Today it would be a particularly onerous task, since more than a hundred men had crowded into the courtroom upon the summons of Sheriff Butler. John Pearson was keeping order and quiet among them as best he could, while I readied the tools of jury selection: a wooden ballot box filled with 150 slips of paper, each bearing the name of a Burke County citizen, painstakingly copied from the tax records by me. Of all these men who had been summoned, we required the services of only twelve. The law states that any man between the ages of twenty-one and sixty who is a resident of the county may serve as a juror, provided that he has in his own name or in trust for him a worth of ten pounds in lands or rents, or if he leases for twenty-one years or longer land worth the sum of twenty pounds or more. It is part of my duties as clerk of Superior Court to compile from county tax records the names of those citizens eligible to serve on juries for the year, and to furnish the sheriff with that list, arranged alphabetically, with the place of abode of each man duly recorded by his name, so that the sheriff may easily locate the fellow to summon him.

To select the jurors for the trial, slips of paper bearing the names of the hundred and fifty men summoned were put in a wooden ballot box, and their names were drawn out one by one at random.

I reached into the box and drew out the first name. "David Hennessee!"

There was a stir among the crowd, and a fair-haired young man of short stature and pleasant features stepped forward. David Hennessee told the court that his date of birth was September 3, 1806, adding that he was the son of Mr. John Hennessee, who had substantial land grants along the Catawba River and elsewhere. Thus satisfied as to age and his material qualifications as a juror, Judge Donnell said, "Have you heard about this case?"

"Some," the young man admitted. "People have been talking about it around town."

"Are you acquainted with any of the principals in the case?"

"You mean do I know these folks, the Silvers, or that other family? No, sir. Nary a one. They're from a long way west of here, sir."

"And since you have heard talk about this case, have you made up your mind whether the defendant is innocent or guilty?"

David Hennessee shook his head. "No, sir. Don't rightly know."

Judge Donnell nodded to the prosecutor. "I am satisfied, Mr. Alexander," he said. "You may ask your own questions now."

William Alexander approached the nervous young man. "I shall be brief," he assured him. "Are you aware that the defendant in the case is a young woman?"

David Hennessee blinked. "I reckon everybody knows that, sir."

A trickle of laughter punctuated his statement.

"Well, would you have any difficulty sitting in judgment of a woman?"

The young man hesitated. "It's got to be done. It's the law."

"So it is," said Mr. Alexander with a faint smile. "And if the evidence presented convinces you of this woman's guilt, could you vote to condemn her? Could you vote guilty— knowing the consequences?"

"You mean, that they'd hang her?" said Hennessee.

"Very likely."

"If I thought she done what they said she done, then . . . yes, sir, I could see my way clear to make her pay for it. With her life. Yes, sir."

William Alexander turned to me. "He will do."

This process was repeated nearly two dozen times, until

satisfactory jurors were settled upon by the court. Judge
Donnell thanked the fourscore freeholders who had answered the summons to jury duty. "You may stay and watch
the proceedings if you wish," he told them. Constable Pearson asked the chosen jurors to remain near the front of the
court. The others filed out to mingle with the waiting crowd,
and we were left with a dozen solemn citizens who knew that
a young woman's life rested in their hands.

The jury selection took a little more than an hour. Afterward we took a short recess to stretch our legs, but we were
all back in place in the courtroom before Pearson let the rabble in. I was at my table in proximity to the judge's bench,
surrounded by the books of North Carolina laws and
statutes, with my late brother's leather-bound copy of *Principles of Criminal Law* at the ready. The state's attorney sat re-
viewing his notes of the case, seemingly oblivious to the
noise of the milling crowd waiting beyond the double oak
doors, but after a courteous nod in his direction, I barely
spared him a glance.

I was watching Frankie Silver.

In my record of the proceedings, I would of course write
the defendant's name as Frances Stewart Silver, but she had
been known as "Frankie" in the mountain community she
came from, and whenever her crime was discussed these
past few months, it was that nickname that had been
bandied about in the streets and taverns of Morganton. By
now I had come to think of her this way.

The name suited her, I thought. It had a suggestion of boy-
ishness about it that went well with her slender frame and the
alert angular face that seemed forever watchful. She seemed
little more than a child sitting in the dock, overshadowed by
the dark elegance of Nicholas Woodfin. She was unfettered,
for the law forbids the use of irons or shackles of any kind on
a prisoner during trial, unless there is evident danger of escape. She was wearing a shabby blue dress that seemed far
too large for her slender frame, and too long at the sleeve
ends to have been her own apparel. Sarah Presnell must

have done what she could to make the girl presentable for trial. Her pale hair was clean and pinned up into a knot at the nape of her neck, and she looked too well scrubbed to have emerged unwashed from ten weeks in a prison cell. I wondered if the ill-fitting dress had been a gesture of charity from some Morganton lady, or if it were her own property, and a testimony to the rigors of her confinement. She was unnaturally pale, and though she stared straight ahead without expression, she twisted her hands in her lap, knotting and unknotting her fingers in a continuous display of anxiety. Surely she knew what people were saying about her, and how little sympathy there was for her in that room.

Nicholas Woodfin, by contrast, seemed serene. It was difficult to believe that the Asheville attorney was only three years older than his client. He was as calm and self-assured as a man twice his age. His notes lay in front of him on the small oak table, but he did not glance at them. Once I saw him lean over to his client and say a few quiet words. Then he smiled reassuringly and leaned back to straighten his silk cravat.

I wonder what she has told him of her situation, I thought. *And can he possibly imagine what her life was like?* And if he cannot, how on earth can he defend her? I abandoned this foolish notion at once, for who, I wondered, could truly understand the harsh frontier life that had been the prisoner's existence and yet himself be an able lawyer capable of defending her in a proper court? For some reason a name leaped unbidden to my mind, to be banished by me as quickly as I thought it: Andrew Jackson.

At that moment Constable Pearson threw open the doors to the court, and a seething crowd pushed past him, elbowing one another for the best positions and making loud and uncouth comments about the proceedings. I saw a grim-faced Isaiah Stewart shepherding his wife and sons to a place on the side of the courtroom, a place where the defendant could see them, although they were not near enough to converse. I saw her cast a stricken look at her mother,

but I could not tell what emotion was conveyed in the returned gaze.

At last Judge Donnell took his place at the bench and
called the court to order.

"Frances Stewart Silver."

The defendant stood up, and I fancied that she swayed for
a moment before steadying herself on the edge of the table.
Nicholas Woodfin placed a gentle hand on her arm and held
her attention with a calm, steady stare, much as one might
use to quiet a frightened mare. She took a deep breath and
nodded slightly, and together they approached the bar.

Judge Donnell consulted the indictment that Mr. Alexander had carefully copied out for him. It was substantially
the same document that the prosecutor had prepared for the
grand jury hearing ten days earlier, but in this version the
names of Barbara and Blackston Stewart were omitted, because the grand jury had not seen fit to bind them over for
trial. Judge Donnell read Mr. Alexander's carefully wrought
document, his lips moving soundlessly through the phrases,
which consisted of but a single tortuous sentence, so long
and intricate as to tax the orative powers of even the ablest
judge. After a few more moments' contemplation, he began
to read the document aloud in a steady drone, marked only
by the ripple of his Scots brogue on a word here and there.

"State of North Carolina. Burke County. Superior Court
of Law. Spring Term 1832. The jurors for the State upon
their oath do present that Frances Stewart of said county,
not having the fear of God before her eyes, but being moved
and seduced by the instigation of the devil, on the twenty-
second day of December in the year of our Lord one thousand eight hundred and thirty-one, with force and arms in
the County of Burke aforesaid, in and upon one Charles Silver in the peace of God and of the State, then and there being feloniously, wilfully, and of malice aforethought did
make an assault; and that the said Frances Silver with a certain axe of the value of six pence, which the said Frances Silver in both hands of her, the said Frances Silver then and
there had and held to, against, and upon the said Charles

Silver, then and there feloniously, wilfully, and of her malice aforethought did cast and throw; and that the said Frances Silver with the axe aforesaid so cast and thrown, as aforesaid, the said Charles Silver in and upon the head of him, the said Charles Silver, then and there feloniously, wilfully, and of her malice aforethought with the axe aforesaid, so as aforesaid by the said Frances Silver cast and thrown, in and upon the head of him, the said Charles Silver one mortal wound of the length of three inches and of the depth of one inch; of which said mortal wound he, the said Charles Silver, then and there instantly died; and so the grand jurors aforesaid, upon their oath aforesaid, do say that the said Frances Silver, him, the said Charles Silver, in manner and form aforesaid feloniously, wilfully, and of her malice aforethought did kill and murder against the peace and dignity of the State."

He paused for a moment while the thunder of his final words echoed in the murmurs of the spectators. What a talent for rigmarole Mr. Alexander has got, I was thinking. The *saids* and *aforesaids* rumbled through the air like drumbeats. The prosecutor's carefully wrought indictment was as majestic in sound and cadence as a mass in Latin, and surely as incomprehensible to the majority of its hearers.

Mrs. Silver stood there looking down at the floor, letting the words wash over her head like a mighty river, and understanding not a syllable of their sense, I am certain, for when Judge Donnell said, "How do you plead?" she merely stared up at him, bewildered.

His Honor spoke louder. "How say you, Frances Silver, are you guilty or not guilty?"

There must have been a nudge or a sign from Nicholas Woodfin indicating that this was her cue (they had rehearsed the process beforehand, surely), for suddenly Mrs. Silver stood up straighter, and in a clear, soft voice she said, "Not guilty."

This response came as no surprise to anyone. Since the penalty for murder is inevitably death, there is nothing to be gained by admitting one's guilt. No doubt Woodfin and Wilson had explained to their client that her only chance to escape the gallows was to fight the accusation in open court.

Not guilty.

Judge Donnell nodded to Woodfin and Alexander, and then he uttered the phrase that would begin the trial: "Then let the jury come."

Why must I say I'm not guilty, I asked them. Why can't I just tell them all how it was right then and there, and then they can decide for themselves what should be done with me. Anybody ought to be able to see how it was—even town folk. The old lawyer, Mr. Wilson—he is black and skinny like a crow— he smiled down his beak at me and said, "Proper procedure must be followed in a court of law." His Adam's apple bobs in his throat when he speaks to me, and I wonder if he is dry-mouthed and has trouble swallowing, on account of being in the presence of a wicked murderess. I keep my eyes downcast, and I speak in a soft voice, though, for I do not want them to think me mad—or, worse yet, an ignorant savage from nowhere, for they would hang me without a second thought if they convicted me of that—of being a nobody.

My father has money and can pay for my defense. He comes from good people down in Anson County, near the town of Charlotte, which is where the enemy lawyer hails from. My grandfather William Stewart was a proper man of business in the county, and once he lawed some fellow in court, just like gentlemen are always doing to settle some dispute.

We settle disputes different up the mountain.

I used to speak more ladylike when I was a young 'un, before we came to this place, but I have got out of the way of it now. There wasn't much call for fine words up the mountain. Hard work is what talks the loudest up there.

The young fellow, though—Mr. Woodfin, his name is—he nodded his head, and said, "I wish you could just tell your tale straight out. It must have been possible to do so in a court of law once upon a time, Frankie, but now we have a great book full of rules concerning the conduct of a trial. It is a game we lawyers play, and you must bear with us."

I like him. He has a well-scrubbed look about him, and calf's eyes, and his clothes are right out of a picture book. He is like the prince in the fairy tale. He looks straight into my eyes and says that he will not stand to see me hanged.

So I am safe.

Chapter Four

SPENCER ARROWOOD had watched hours of television, eaten meals he barely tasted, and slept more than he needed to before Martha reappeared with another handful of mail and a stack of library books. She brushed aside his questions about work at the office, announced that she could get her own cup of coffee, and insisted that he look at what she'd brought.

"Nobody has ever written a book on Frankie Silver that I can find," she told him. "But she has rated quite a few chapters in local histories. I brought you a couple of old books, *Dead and Gone* and *Cabin in the Laurels* for starters. I looked over them last night, by the way. They're pretty interesting."

Spencer smiled. "Thanks, but I haven't been to the bank lately. Do you take checks?"

"Consider it a get-well gift, Spencer, I don't do casseroles. Anyhow, they're both used, so the Book Place let me have them cheap. They even marked the pages for you. How are you feeling?"

Spencer sighed. "I've been better. Thanks for the books."

"I brought you something else that you might want to see." She handed him a copy of the *Johnson City Chronicle* open to the headline PARENTS OF SLAIN GIRL DEMAND DEATH OF KILLER. Colonel Charles Wythe Stanton, older and grayer but still in charge, stared out at him from the page of newsprint. He was wearing a dark suit and tie instead of an army uniform, but his piercing expression had not changed. Spencer skimmed the article, already knowing what it would say.

"Colonel Charles Stanton (U.S. Army-ret.), whose daughter Emily was murdered on the Appalachian Trail in 1977, met today with a Tennessee victims' organization to discuss the scheduled execution of the man who killed his daughter. 'Fate Harkryder should be executed at once,' Colonel Stanton told the group. 'His legal ploys have given him twenty years of life to which he was not entitled. I wish he had shown as much mercy to my daughter. He didn't let her live to be twenty.' Colonel Stanton stressed the victims' families' need for closure, so that they can go on with their lives." The article went on for another half dozen paragraphs, but Spencer had heard it all before, and he didn't dispute any of it. That wasn't what worried him.

"Where's the front page of the paper, Martha?" asked Spencer, noting that the part he was reading was section B.

"LeDonne spilled Pepsi on it this morning," said Martha with a shrug. "It wasn't dry yet."

He heard an odd note in her voice, and filed it away for future consideration.

Martha turned her deck chair to face the view of sunlit mountains and sat down across the table from him. "I don't know how you can bear to go inside," she said. "I'd just stare out at these hills for hours at a time."

He smiled. "It gets cold up here after sunset."

"It's always a different scene, though, isn't it? The mountains change color from one day to the next. I can count six shades of green without even turning my head. So peaceful."

"Most of the time." There was a small photo of Emily Stanton accompanying the newspaper article.

Martha took a sip of coffee. "Have you done any more thinking about Frankie Silver?"

"Off and on," he said, shrugging. "It doesn't fit into my experience anywhere yet. She was an eighteen-year-old girl. By all accounts she was pretty, hardworking, and virtuous. Yet she killed her young husband with an ax. Why would she do that?"

"Maybe she was crazy?"

"She seemed sane enough during the trial, apparently. They convicted her anyhow."

"Cabin fever? It was winter when it happened. I remember Mrs. Honeycutt talking about snow on the ground and the river being frozen. Maybe she just got tired of being shut up in that little one-room cage." Martha shivered. "I know I would."

"Yes," said Spencer, "but you hadn't lived in a place like that all your life. Surely Frankie Silver was used to it."

"I guess you're right," said Martha. "Maybe you'll never understand it. Times were different then. I don't see what you can do with a case that's a hundred and fifty years old, with not even a crime scene left to look at, but if it keeps you off your feet for a while longer, then I'm all for it. Better than thinking about that other case."

"Fate Harkryder."

"There's nothing you can do about that one, either. Are you still thinking about going to the—" She didn't want to say *execution*.

He nodded. "I called and told them I would. If it happens."

"Which it won't," said Martha. She stood up and brushed imaginary dust from her trousers. "Well, I wish I had time to sit up here in this pretty place looking at mountains and playing detective, but I guess I have to go prowl for expired car-inspection stickers."

Spencer smiled. "Prowling for expired county stickers isn't unimportant, Martha. The county needs the revenue. How is Joe doing?"

"Oh, he'll be up one of these days. You know how he is."

"Tell him I'm not sick," said Spencer. LeDonne would rather work twenty-hour days than visit sick people.

When Martha had gone, Spencer turned again to the article in the newspaper. He had not wanted her to see how concerned he was about the case. Martha worried too much.

The photograph seemed to be staring directly at him from

out of the newspaper. Charles Wythe Stanton, still alive, still fighting the enemy. Spencer remembered him well. He had been the one to inform the colonel that his only daughter had been murdered.

On the night of Emily Stanton's murder (and Mike Wilson's as well, but people tended to forget about him), Spencer and the TBI officer spent the rest of that night making a grid of the crime scene, stretching twine from one wooden stake to another so that the entire area was marked off into small squares like a checkerboard. They would search each parcel of the site for cigarette butts, gum wrappers, clothing fibers—anything that might have a bearing on the case.

At last the sky lightened to a pall of gray, and the objects beyond the reach of their flashlights began to become more distinct in the haze. The TBI man glanced at his watch. "We'll check the site again in about twenty minutes," he said. "For now, let's check all the approaches to this clearing to see if the assailant discarded anything."

Spencer glanced at the two bodies, which were becoming clearer with every passing minute, and he thought of a photograph taking form in the developing fluid. "When are we going to move them?" he asked.

"Within the hour. They go to University Hospital in Knoxville for a complete workup. I'll give you that information to pass along to the families." He looked down at the two sprawled bodies in the clearing and sighed. "We'll move them before the flies come out, I promise."

"Good," said Spencer. One side of the girl's face looked as if she were only sleeping, and he didn't want to see her covered in insects.

"When it gets light enough, we'll tilt the bodies, see what's under them. I found a tooth under the victim once. Belonged to the killer."

Spencer nodded. He couldn't think of anything to say. He set off on a path that led back into the forest, training his flashlight on the ground in front of it and letting the light play left and right to illuminate the weeds at the side of the trail. He saw no broken twigs or evidence of a struggle, or even of footprints, and his hunch that the killer had not come this way was confirmed a few moments later by a triumphant cry from the other officer. Spencer had forgotten his name almost the instant he heard it, and he would forever think of the investigator as "the TBI man," the embodiment of a faceless state bureaucracy.

He hurried back to the clearing. The officer had laid out the wallets on the log where Willis Blaine, the ranger, had sat for much of the night. The dark brown leather one was worn and scratched, obviously the property of the man. Beside it lay a small red clutch purse containing a compartment for coins, as well as a notepad and a compartment for paper money. "I found them about twenty yards down the hill," said the TBI man with a satisfied smile. "Killer must have taken the money and thrown down the billfolds as he ran. Who knows? We might even get prints." He pried open the two sections of leather with a gloved finger. "Can you read that? I'm no good at fine print in this light."

It seemed perfectly clear to Spencer, who was still a long way from thirty, from bifocals, from having to read the newspaper at arm's length, as he did these days. "Michael Wilson," he said. "Virginia driver's license. He's twenty-one. There's a student ID in there, too. University of North Carolina."

"Yeah, I figured they were college kids. A lot of these hikers are. So they're not from around here. That figures."

"How so?" asked Spencer.

"Stranger killing. They were ambushed out in public land. This wasn't some guy offing his girlfriend, or a fight between two old enemies. Somebody was hunting, and hunters don't care about the identity of the victim. Who was the girl?"

Spencer fingered the soft leather clutch purse. He imagined it still warm from being tucked away in the hip pocket of the girl's jeans, pressing against her buttocks. "Emily Stanton. Driver's license says Wilmington, North Carolina." A solemn young woman with long auburn hair and dainty small-boned features looked out at him from the license photo. He could see tiny gold hoops in her ears, and a pearl necklace against the dark blue background of her dress. *Sorority type,* he thought. *I wonder what she made of the trail.* He said, "There's also a student ID for UNC."

"Yep. I figured. College sweethearts, taking a little vacation together after classes ended. Rich kids, too. At least, she was."

Spencer glanced at the body. The small figure had been wearing jeans and a plain black sweatshirt. Now they lay crumpled a few feet away from her body. "How can you tell?"

The officer smiled. "It helps to have kids, Deputy. I recognize the brand names on her clothing. That outfit may look like old jeans and sneakers to you, but she paid a couple hundred bucks for them. I probably would have known even without that, but it isn't something I could explain." He shrugged. "Her manicured nails. Her hairstyle. After you observe people for enough years, you just *know*."

"A robbery that got out of hand then?"

"No. There won't be any money in the wallets, but taking the cash was an afterthought."

Spencer poked a finger inside the billfold. Empty. The TBI guy was right. "Not the motive, though?"

"Incidentally, sure. I mean, the cash is just lying there. It's not going to do the victims any good. Why not take it? But that's not the real reason the killer did this. He did this for fun, because he's so mad at something that this is his way of striking back."

Spencer said, *"I am reckless what I do to spite the world."* He shrugged. "I always liked that line."

The older man smiled. *"Macbeth,"* he said. "It's nice to hear Shakespeare every now and then from an officer, instead of Kris Kristofferson, which is what passes for philosophy these days."

"I like him, too," said Spencer. "So you think this guy we're looking for is more than a thief whose robbery got out of hand?"

"He's a killer first and foremost. Have there been any other unsolved murders around here?"

"No."

"Any disappearances? Maybe you just didn't find the bodies."

"No missing persons."

"Maybe he's not from around here then. You'd better hope he doesn't decide to stay a while. This kind of thing is habit-forming. There should be more victims sometime . . . somewhere."

"How do we go about looking for him then?"

"Stranger killers are hard to catch. No pool of suspects. Could have been anybody. You have to hope they do something stupid. But we'll do what we can to help you with the forensic evidence. It will take some time, though."

Spencer nodded. "I understand. We have to have a suspect anyhow, before the forensic evidence will do any good."

The TBI man stood up and stretched, yawning into the gray light. "Morning already. You're going to have a long day ahead of you, Deputy, finding out if anybody saw anything suspicious up here. Oh, and when you notify the families, be sure you get a description of the personal effects the victims had with them. They may turn up somewhere. It could be the best lead you get." He yawned again. "Keep in touch. Let me know if there's anything else we can do to help."

Back at the office, Spencer worked through the rest of the dawn hours, organizing his notes, making calls to locate the victims' families. Now it was seven o'clock. He would have to make the notification calls soon, before the families left for work. He stared at the two telephone numbers, wondering which family to call first. He had never had to notify the family of a murder victim. Nelse Miller always took it upon himself to contact the families, and Spencer devoutly wished that the sheriff were here now to take care of it. The thought of coping with weeping and hysterical strangers made him uneasy, and he wondered what questions they would ask him about the circumstances and the condition of the bodies—and what should he tell them?

The most difficult call would be to the female victim's parents, he thought, because no one ever imagines their little girl in danger. Should he get that call over with, or should he begin with the other one and work up to it? He was so tired.

He dialed the Wilsons' number. The phone rang four times before someone picked it up, and a sleepy voice murmured, "—'Lo?"

Spencer took a deep breath. "Mrs. Wilson?"

"Who is this? What time is it?"

He took a deep breath. You never got used to it. "My name is Spencer Arrowood. I'm with the sheriff's department in Wake County, Tennessee. Is there anyone with you, Mrs. Wilson?"

She made a startled cry and said, "What's happened to Mike?" He heard her say, presumably to her husband, "Lyman, it's about Mike." Spencer waited for a man to come to the phone, but after a moment's silence, Mrs. Wilson came back on the line and told him to go on. He plunged into his account of Mike Wilson's death. He repeated who he was and where the bodies had been taken, telling Mrs. Wilson that someone would have to come to Tennessee to identify the body. Spencer made her write down his telephone number, because he knew she would want it later.

At last she said, "I've been expecting this call for a long time, Officer. Funny, though. I always thought it would come from Vietnam."

"Yes, ma'am," said Spencer. "My brother was killed there."

There wasn't much left to say after that. He told her again how sorry he was, and asked if she was sure she was all right, but she was a soldier's mother and she knew how to be brave. She said she was fine, and she thanked him for his kindness, but he could hear the sobs in her throat.

Spencer waited five minutes after he hung up the phone before he placed the second call. He drank cold coffee without tasting it, and wondered if he'd be able to sleep when his day was finally over.

Colonel Stanton had answered the phone as if he had been up for hours, which perhaps he had. His voice was crisp and alert. He picked up the receiver after one ring and said "Stanton!" as if all the calls he had ever received at home were urgent and official.

Spencer identified himself, as he had to Mrs. Wilson, and then he'd asked, for form's sake, "Do you have a daughter named Emily?"

Spencer heard a sharp intake of breath, and then the same calm voice answered, "I do," and then waited. He didn't say: *What is this all about? Why do you ask? Is she hurt?*—all the things that people usually said when Spencer called to break the news to the loved ones. Colonel Stanton's military training had prepared him to meet disaster with an unflinching stare. He simply waited to hear the worst.

The silence at the other end of the phone stretched on as Spencer explained that Emily Stanton and her companion had been attacked while camping near the Appalachian Trail, and that both the young people were dead. He would need a member of the Stanton family to come to Tennessee to identify and claim the body. At this point the silence had become so protracted that Spencer interrupted himself to ask: "Are you all right, sir?"

Charles Wythe Stanton ignored the question. "Are the killers in custody?"

"No, sir. Not yet." The authority in that voice took Spencer back to his army days in Germany. This stranger on the telephone had just taken command of the investigation.

"Is there anything you need from us, Officer?"

"Yes, sir. A description of any jewelry your daughter may have been wearing."

The list was given in the same crisp tones as before. "Is there anything else?"

"Not at this time, sir." Spencer felt that he was more shaken by the news than this stranger on the telephone. *Perhaps he doesn't believe it yet,* he thought. *He hasn't seen her; I have.*

"I will be driving to Tennessee within the hour," Charles Stanton told him. "I shall expect a full report when I arrive."

"Go to Knoxville first," Spencer told him. "Identify the

body, and talk to the TBI. Stop in Hamelin on your way back, after my investigation is under way."

"Hamelin is a little one-horse town, isn't it?"

"You might say that."

"I hope to God you people are up to this investigation," said Charles Stanton. "Because if you aren't, I will find the killer myself."

He hung up before Spencer could respond. He had no intention of explaining to Colonel Stanton that "you people" was him, working alone, with whatever assistance the Tennessee Bureau of Investigation cared to provide. He took another gulp of cold, bitter coffee. Sleep, he decided, was not an option.

Martha Ayers was tired. Running the sheriff's department short-staffed was a tough job even on the slowest days. Now, with a homicide investigation in full swing, she was subsisting on catnaps and cold burgers. She felt as if she had talked to everybody in the county by now, classroom to classroom, door to door, truck stop to café. Had anybody seen something that would help her? She had to keep moving, keep asking. Because sooner or later Spencer was going to find out that they had a double homicide on their hands, and if the pace of the investigation was killing her, she could imagine what it would do to him in his weakened state. She had known him all her life, and he was too intense for his own good, always had been. This case would pull him off that mountain like a logging chain, and if he wore himself out trying to take charge of the case, there'd be hell to pay for it. He might be sick for months. He might even have to resign.

I don't need him, she told herself. *I'm the most recent graduate of the academy. I know all the latest methods of crime solving, and besides, the TBI is doing most of the work. All Joe and I have to do is present them with a suspect.*

"Miz Ayers? Are you awake? Your coffee's getting cold."

Martha looked up from her contemplation of the countertop. "Thanks, Fred," she said to the old farmer who had sat on the stool beside her. "I guess I'm working too hard."

"I heard about it," he said. "You don't expect a thing like that to happen in the country."

"No."

"Of course, it happened here before, didn't it? Twenty years ago." Fred Dayton stabbed his finger at the coffee cup. "Right near that old church it was. Another couple out in the woods, up to no good, like as not."

"The couple in that case were hikers on the Appalachian Trail," said Martha. "These two were grad students from East Tennessee State, studying rare mountain wildflowers."

Fred raised his eyebrows. "At night?"

"Well, they camped out. They were making a weekend of it."

"I saw the girl's picture in the paper. Pretty little thing. Looked like the other one."

"Uh-huh." The female victim, a native of Cincinnati, had been five foot nine with long black hair and dark eyes. She was pretty enough, but that was all she'd had in common with the tiny, auburn-haired Emily Stanton. She had also been married, but the husband, a fourth-year med student, had a hospital full of witnesses to account for his where-abouts on the night of the killings. They had checked him out six ways from Sunday, but the case wasn't going to be that easy to solve. Her partner was nobody's idea of a wife stealer, either: a balding, chubby botanist whose interest in sex seemed to have been confined to honeybees. The case had sounded sensational at first: young couple killed on the Appalachian Trail. But they weren't a couple; they were two botanists who happened to be of opposite sex, and they weren't attractive enough to hold the public's attention. Per-haps that was why the coverage of the case had been light, almost casual. That, and the lack of an advocate like Charles Stanton to keep the media inflamed, had made the interest in the case little more than perfunctory, except to those who had the responsibility of solving it.

"They weren't from around here," said Fred. He felt enti-tled to talk "shop" with her because he had helped her round up strayed horses on a road once, and since then he had engaged her in occasional conversations at the diner. This time he hoped to pick up some tidbits to enliven his trip to the barbershop. Martha was willing to humor him in the hope that something he said would be of value in the investigation.

"No," she sighed. "They weren't from around here."

But the killer was, she thought.

Burgess Gaither

THE TRIAL

Then let the jury come. . . . The words chilled me, familiar as they were to an officer of the court.

The trial had begun.

I duly recorded in my notes: *Frances Silver pleads not guilty of the felony and murder whereof she stands charged and the following jurors were drawn, sworn, and charged to pass between the prisoner and the state on her life and death, to wit: Henry Pain, David Beedle, Cyrus P. Connelly, William L. Baird, Joseph Tipps, Robert Garrison, Robert McEirath, Oscar Willis, John Hall, Richard Bean, Lafayette Collins, and David Hennessee.*

They were all upstanding men of the community as far as I knew, although I was not well acquainted with any of them. By chance, none of them came from the exalted ranks of the town fathers: indeed, I knew of no connections that any of them had to the Erwins, the McDowells, or any of the other prominent families in Burke County, although no doubt Elizabeth could have found a connection somewhere in the wide-ranging roots of Morganton's family trees. No matter if there were connections, of course; the luck of the draw could have packed the jury with Erwin cousins and former sheriffs, and still the trial would have been perfectly legal, but considering the humble origins of the defendant, the common touch seemed appropriate. Surely these plain-spoken men could understand the humble life of this young woman better than the cosseted scions of planter families ever would.

Constable Pearson threw open the doors to the courtroom, and a horde of raucous, clamoring spectators crowded in on an ill wind of whiskey fumes and tobacco smoke. It was a prodigious turnout, even by the standards of Burke County's ordinary court attendance, which was never sparse. Because it was a brisk and cloudy day in early spring, I did not dread the presence of so many sweaty bodies in the confinement of the courtroom, as I often did during the September term of Superior Court. The heat and the noise would at least be bearable today. I hoped, though, that when the new county courthouse was built next year, the courtroom would be larger than the present one.

I recognized many of the men in the crowd: the blacksmith, the tavern keeper, several local farmers. Shabbily dressed frontiersmen elbowed their way in among the dark-suited gentlemen and the townsmen in shirtsleeves, everyone eager for a look at the frail young defendant.

Suddenly a flash of white at the back of the courtroom caught my attention. Surely it wasn't . . . *it was* . . . a parasol. I groaned inwardly and leaned forward in an attempt to discern the bearer of this feminine object among the throng of men. My eyes could only confirm what I already knew, however, and sure enough, a few moments later the crowd parted as if before the staff of Moses, and Miss Mary Erwin sailed in upon a tide of murmuring.

Of course, it was she. What other woman would dare to invade the male bastion of justice? Apart from the danger of unruly crowds, fistfights, and even more serious displays of violence, there is the carnival atmosphere of trial day, with drunken men cheering the lawyers, farmers spitting tobacco juice upon the floor, and a general laxity of decorum that should make any member of the fair sex shun this building when criminal court is in session. No doubt the fact that Miss Mary's father had been clerk of Superior Court for forty-four years gave her a proprietary interest in the proceedings, and I knew that the friendless young woman on trial had aroused her interest and sympathy.

I glanced at Judge Donnell to see if he would order the bailiff to escort Miss Mary from the premises, but he showed no interest in the matter. Her cousin Colonel James Erwin motioned for her to join him, no doubt concluding that if the lady could not be made to leave, then the next best thing would be for a respectable family member to act as her chaperone. I made a mental note to omit this detail from the account of the day's events that I would give to my wife, but no doubt she would know about her sister's boldness already.

What a striking contrast Miss Mary made to the defendant! Her dress and the Spencer jacket that covered it were of the finest material, her hair was perfectly arranged under a fashionable Charleston bonnet, and although she was no beauty, Miss Mary radiated an air of assurance and good breeding that would mark her as a lady and win her respect and deference in any circumstances in which she might find herself. The defendant was a lovely, fragile creature, with a sweet, childish face under a cloud of fair hair, but if Frances Silver lived for a hundred years, she could not attain the commanding poise and aura of gentility that Miss Mary so effortlessly displayed.

Another thought occurred to me as well. Although Frankie Silver was accused of killing her husband with an ax, surely a brutal crime calling for great audacity, I did not think, were the circumstances reversed, that she could have walked into a courtroom full of men and sat down so confident that her presence would be tolerated. I wondered if Elizabeth knew about her sister's daring venture. I resolved not to mention it at home. No doubt she would learn of it soon enough. With a rustle of her skirts, Miss Mary took her place among the gallery and gazed expectantly at the officers of the court as if we were actors. *Let the games begin,* her expression seemed to say.

William Alexander would present his case first. He rose,

and inclined his head toward Judge Donnell with just the suggestion of a bow. The murmuring swelled and then tapered off at a stern look from the bench. Mr. Alexander waved his fist in the air. "We are here to try a wicked and heartless creature for cruel murder!" he announced.

Full of the righteous brimstone that infuses prosecuting attorneys, William Alexander described the finding of Charlie Silver's sundered body, dwelling on the victim's youth and innocence. He let his voice falter as he described the life cut short, the soul sent unshriven into the hereafter, and the fatherless child left to fend for itself in the world. He ended with a thundering demand for justice. "The very blood of Charles Silver cries out for retribution. Let not his killer go unpunished!"

Nicholas Woodfin sat through this harangue, frowning slightly, as if he wondered what his colleague was talking about, his expression suggesting that Mr. Alexander had been misinformed, and that he welcomed the opportunity to rectify the misunderstanding. *Perhaps we are not so far from actors after all.*

Frankie Silver herself sat motionless, staring at the window beyond the jury box, as if she could not hear the tumult taking place around her. *Perhaps she hears but does not comprehend,* I thought. I wondered if Nicholas Woodfin had explained the trial procedure to her, and if so, had he done it in simple enough terms for an unlettered girl to understand? *Surely there are more people here today than she has ever seen in her life; perhaps she is terrified of the sight of so many unruly strangers.* She looked distressed only once, for the briefest moment, when Nicholas Woodfin left her side so that he might address the court on her behalf.

The prince speaks, I thought sourly, remembering the stir that his appearance had caused among the ladies of the community. He stood tall and straight in his black suit, with his classical features composed into a solemn countenance. I was loath to admit, even to myself, that he did make an impressive figure in our simple country courthouse. I wondered what the jurors would make of him.

"Gentlemen, you sit in judgment of a tragedy," he told the jurors. "A young man in his prime has been cruelly struck down, and we compound the sorrow of the family by accusing his widow of his murder, by hauling her into open court to suffer the gaze of strangers, while we accuse her of the basest of crimes.

"My colleague has told you how Charles Silver was done to death, and that his remains were cut up with a knife, as one might butcher a deer, and that his body was burned in the fireplace as if it were refuse. Is this the crime of a *woman*, gentlemen? Can you see even the most pitiless female savage committing such an outrage upon an enemy? I cannot. Yet Mr. Alexander asks us to believe that this gentle young woman, only eighteen years of age, a frail girl who is the tender mother of a baby, could do this awful deed—not to a stranger, but to a man who is her own husband."

Nicholas Woodfin turned and pointed to the defendant, who sat with perfect composure gravely watching him. "This fair young woman whose fate is in your hands is Frances Stewart Silver. Look at her. She is not mad. She is not a savage. She is an ordinary young woman, against whom no word of censure has ever been uttered in her community. She is not lazy. She is not wanton. She is not a drunkard. She is a simple young wife and mother. They say so, all of them in the place she comes from. Yet Mr. Alexander would have us believe that she had the ferocity to butcher a man—her own husband! Where is the sense in it, gentlemen? Where is the strength that would allow her to do it? And—that which concerns us most of all in a court of law—*where is the proof that she did it?* For I saw none. A man is dead, that much has been shown. But by whose hand he met his untimely death—that has *not* been shown."

It was a stirring speech, I thought, delivered in the ringing tones of an actor or perhaps a camp-meeting preacher. I wondered whether the jury would be swayed by it, or whether the enormity of the crime had moved them past the power of persuasion.

The witnesses were waiting in the hall outside the court-room under the watchful eye of Constable Presnell, who would usher in each one in turn as he was summoned to tes-tify. I glanced at the list of names that I had duly copied from the back of Mr. Alexander's indictment. There were thirteen names on the list, members of the Silver clan, their backcountry neighbors who had made up the search party; the two constables involved in the arrest of the defendant; and our own Dr. Tate to provide the medical evidence con-cerning the cause of death and the nature of the wounds.

In my short tenure as clerk of court, I had become quite a connoisseur of witnesses. I never failed to marvel at a great bull of a man who creeps onto the witness stand and squeaks like a mouse, his eyes bulging with fright to be un-der the scrutiny of so great an audience. Other people give evidence in calm, measured tones as if they were ordering up a new suit, instead of swearing away the life of a fellow citizen. Some witnesses seethe with anger as they recount the misdeeds of the accused, or weep piteously if they are compelled to bear witness against a loved one. I wondered what sort of witnesses today's trial would offer, and I was fairly certain that no tears would be shed, for on that list of names I saw not one that could be counted as a friend of the defendant. I wondered why Mrs. Silver's mother and brother had not been called upon to testify, for when we sent them away in January it was under bond, with the understanding that they would return to give evidence in the trial. Perhaps neither attorney feels that he can trust them, I decided. One lawyer must fear that they would lie, and the other is equally afraid that they might speak the whole truth. The trial would proceed without their testimony.

Jack Collis made a good witness. He was a wiry old man with the keen blue eyes of a woodsman. He looked about sixty, and he had lived on the frontier all his life, farming and tracking animals for fur and food. His authority as a tracker could not be questioned. If his clothing was not all that one could hope for in a formal court of law, at least he was tolerably clean. Although he spoke up in a clear voice that carried well in the courtroom, he kept his answers short and to the point. Not a man for social conversation, I thought.

Yes, he had been in the search party for Charlie Silver. No, he had not seen any evidence of the missing man in the woods or in the iced-over river.

"And what did you do then, sir?"

"I figured on searching the cabin."

"Why?"

"Because he wasn't anywhere else."

"Because there was not a sign of Charles Silver between his folks' place and George Young's, where his wife said he had gone?"

"That's right."

"When did you go to the cabin?"

"Sunday morning. The eighth of January, it was. While we were out searching the woods, I chanced to hear somebody saying that Frankie had gone back to her folks' place over the river. I figured it couldn't do no harm to look around in Charlie's cabin."

"Did you go by yourself?"

"Yes. It wasn't but a long shot. I just thought I'd have a look."

"So you went to the Silver homestead. Could you describe the interior of the cabin for the jury, Mr. Collis?"

The frontiersman blinked. "It's just a cabin."

William Alexander favored him with an encouraging smile. "We'd like to picture the scene as you tell your story, sir. Where the furniture was, and so on."

Jack Collis gave the prosecutor a doubtful look, but after a moment's thought, he obliged. "It's an ordinary cabin. Made of chestnut logs, caulked with lime. Fifty paces long, twenty paces wide. Door in the center, front and back, and one little square window next to the fireplace. Puncheon floors. Bed in the corner between the fireplace and the door. Baby's cradle at the bedside. Table and benches—middle of the room. Oak chest against the back wall."

I tried to picture the little house. Surely in its entirety it could have fit into Squire Erwin's parlor at Belvidere; yet I knew that families with eight or ten children lived in similar dwellings, not only in the mountain wilderness but among the humbler folk in Morganton. I glanced at Mrs. Silver to see what her reaction was to hearing her meager possessions thus outlined before a room full of strangers, but she remained impassive.

"It was clean," said Jack Collis, noticing perhaps the faint distaste in Mr. Alexander's expression.

"So you went into this one-room abode to look around, sir. And what did you find?"

"Well, I couldn't see much to begin with. The fire was out. It was almighty dark in there. And cold. I went over to the fireplace to see about starting a fire, so's I could see better, and when I knelt down it struck me that there was too much ash in the fireplace."

"Could you tell us what you deduced from that?" I suspected that the prosecutor's bewilderment was not entirely feigned. William Alexander had never cleaned out a fireplace in his life.

"Somebody had burned up a lot of wood without cleaning out the fireplace. Seemed like a lot of logs had been burned in a hurry, and I wondered how come, so I commenced to sifting through the ashes."

"What did you find?"

Jack Collis told how he lit a new fire to heat the water in the kettle, and how the grease bubbles told him that flesh had been burned upon the logs, which prompted him to make a more careful search of the cabin.

"Once the room warmed up, the smell told me something was wrong."

"What smell, Mr. Collis?"

"The smell of butchering," Jack Collis said, scowling at the memory. The courtroom shuddered with him.

"What did you do then, sir?"

"I went and found Jacob Hutchins with the search party,

and took him back to the cabin. He helped me take up a plank of the puncheon floor next to the fireplace."

"And what did you find, sir?"

"Blood. A dried-up puddle of blood in the dirt underneath that plank."

William Alexander smiled indulgently. "A rabbit, perhaps, or a deer?"

"You butcher animals outdoors."

Several of the jurors were nodding in agreement. Most of them had hunted in the deep forests of Burke County at some time in their lives, and they knew the truth of Jack Collis's words. William Alexander looked pleased with himself as he nodded to Nicholas Woodfin and returned to his seat. "Your witness."

I was watching the defendant. She sat perfectly still, staring past the jury as if she were so deep in prayer or meditation that the words did not reach her. I fancied, though, that I saw her wince when Jack Collis spoke of butchering.

When Nicholas Woodfin stood up to question the old man, Mrs. Silver's blank stare wavered, and for a moment she regarded her lawyer with shining eyes, but the look was gone in an instant, and she resumed her pose of indifference to the proceedings around her.

I wondered what Mr. Woodfin would make of this witness. The legal strategy would be to discredit Jack Collis, if he could, by questioning the old man's eyesight or establishing Collis's close ties to the Silver family and his animosity toward the young widow. I would have hesitated to take such a course of action, though, for I had seen what a forthright fellow the witness was, and I thought that he had won the respect—and therefore the trust—of that simple jury. They would view with disfavor any attempt by a town lawyer to impugn this man's testimony.

Woodfin must have felt as I did, for after one or two perfunctory questions concerning the circumstantial nature of the grisly discovery, he dismissed the old woodsman with grave courtesy.

I looked about the courtroom for familiar faces. Charlie Silver's family was represented by his uncle Mr. Greenberry Silver, himself a prominent landowner in the western reaches of Burke County. One of the constables had mentioned that Charlie's stepmother had a new baby, born only a few weeks ago, and I surmised that either Jacob Silver had chosen to be with his wife, or else he had not cared to venture down from the hills to hear the particulars of his son's murder detailed before uncaring strangers. Other Silver relatives waited in the hallway for their own turn as witnesses.

I caught sight of Isaiah Stewart midway back in the throng. His face bore that look of composed grief that one often sees at funerals, and I wondered whether he had accepted his daughter's guilt or if he thought that she was doomed despite her innocence. I could not decide which burden would be the more terrible for a father to bear.

At Stewart's side was a husky, sandy-haired fellow who looked like a twenty-five-year-old version of his companion. The younger man's emotions were not so well controlled as those of Isaiah Stewart, for I could see rage in every line of his face. His eyes were narrowed, his jaw set in a clenched scowl, and his body put me in mind of a coiled spring as he leaned forward, straining to catch every word of the testimony. I hoped that he had not managed to smuggle a weapon into the courtroom. This is the elder son, I thought. The one who was away on a long hunt with his father at the time of the murder. What was his name? It was not written in any of the court documents, for he was not involved in the proceedings in any way, but someone had spoken of him. I had it now! Jackson. Jackson Stewart, married to a Howell girl, who was surely some kin to the Thomas Howell on my witness list. Surely that would cause dissension in the ranks of the family. I felt that regardless of the outcome of this case, the ripples of pain and ill will would course through that community for years to come. In one sense, a trial is the end of a crime, but in another way it is only the beginning of a protracted torment more cruel than the hangman's rope. The survivors suffer at leisure.

Mr. Alexander took charge again, asking that Miss Nancy Wilson be brought forth to testify. Gabe Presnell opened one of the great oak doors at the back of the courtroom and ushered in a sharp-faced young woman in black. She moved in no great haste, serenely indifferent to the stares and murmurs that arose as she passed. Her head was held high, her countenance white with anger. I noticed that the jurors sat up straighter when they caught sight of her. This is a personage, I thought. She is no older than the defendant, but this is a lady who knows her own mind, and woe betide the traveling drummers, bears, or Indians who get in her way.

On her way up to testify, the stern young woman passed little Mrs. Silver, and I could feel the enmity crackle between them. They glanced at each other, scorn on both sides, and quickly looked away.

When Nancy Wilson had been duly sworn, William Alexander began his questioning with a reassuring smile. "Now, Miss Wilson, speak up. There is no need to be afraid."

She flashed a look at him that said *fool* louder than I could have shouted it, but she made no audible reply. I glanced at the defendant. She did not direct her gaze toward the witness, but her face no longer bore the vacant stare that she had effected for most of the morning; now, although she would not look, she was listening.

"You are Miss Nancy Wilson of the Toe River section of western Burke County?"

"I am."

"And, for the record, are you any relation of Mr. Thomas Wilson, an attorney in Morganton."

This question caught her off guard, for she had been stoking herself up to talk about the murder. She blinked once or twice while she got her bearings, and then said, "I don't believe so. My brother is named Tom Wilson, but he's no lawyer. We don't know any Wilsons in town."

There was soft laughter around the courtroom at the lady's confusion, and I saw Mr. Wilson the attorney shake his head, smiling.

"Well, now we know where we are," said Mr. Alexander

cheerfully. "Let us proceed. Are you acquainted with the defendant Frances Silver?"

"I am," she said in a low voice. "She was married to a kinsman of mine. My mother is the sister of Charlie's father."

"Did you hear Mrs. Silver speak of the disappearance of her husband?"

"I did." An emphatic nod. "Last December I was visiting at Uncle Jacob's cabin when Frankie came in to say that Charlie had not yet come home."

"Did she say where he had gone?"

"She had already told the family that Charlie was gone the day before. She just came to say he wasn't back yet. A day or so earlier he had gone over to George Young's place. To get his Christmas liquor, according to her. Which was a lie." Her tone spoke volumes about the insolence of one who could foully murder a man and then besmirch his memory with cruel falsehood. I saw the jurors glance at one another, though, and their expressions convinced me that all the men in the courtroom had thought in unison, *Maybe Charlie Silver didn't go to George Young's for liquor this time, but he had been on that errand often enough before.* After all, the family had accepted Frankie's story without question. The neighbors had spent days searching the paths between the Silvers' land and the Youngs' homestead. It rang true. Charlie Silver was by all accounts a handsome, high-spirited young man, and it had been Christmastime, a season especially conducive to the imbibing of spirits. Going off to a local distiller for a jug of whiskey would have been a likely custom for an idle youth, but because Charlie Silver was dead, Nancy Wilson must stand up before God and Burke County and deny the possibility of such a thing. Saints had to be dead, according to the tradition of the ancient Church; now ordinary folk have gone them one better, and deem that all dead people have to be saints. It makes for considerable confusion in the courts of law, trying to sort out all the transgressors when no one will admit to any sinning.

"Did Mrs. Silver seem concerned about her missing husband?"

"I suppose she was. She looked like she had been crying."
Young Miss Wilson tossed her head. "She kept saying that
she wished he'd come back, and then she would cry some
more."

"Did Mrs. Silver suggest that the family begin a search for
her husband?"

Nancy Wilson nodded. "She said she was worried about
him being out in the snowdrifts. She was afraid he'd catch
his death, and said would we please ask the men to go and
look for him."

"Who was present when Mrs. Silver appeared to report
her husband's absence?"

Nancy Wilson ticked them off on her fingers. "Charlie's
stepmother and sisters, his brother Alfred and the rest of the
young 'uns, and me."

This testimony had been covered at the previous hearing
by Miss Margaret Silver, the young sister of the murdered
man. I wondered why she had not been called upon to repeat it at the trial. Mr. Alexander had not excused her in deference to her youth, because her cousin was not much older.
More probably the prosecutor thought that Margaret would
be cowed by the proceedings, and that she would not make a
good witness. She might waver upon cross-examination. I remembered her rambling testimony at the earlier hearing,
and the frightened look on her face as she stared out at the
sea of strangers. Nancy Wilson, the iron maiden who took
her place today, was a stronger witness, so armed with self-
righteous indignation was she that the devil himself could
not have made her falter.

"Did Mrs. Silver ask any of the women to accompany her
back to her own cabin, since she was now alone?"

"Well, she may have asked Margaret and me, but we said
the snow was too deep. We told her to bide a while with us,
but she went on back."

I stole a glance at Nicholas Woodfin, who must have
known as well as I did that this was the chain of words that
would hang his client, unless he could somehow dispel the

power of this testimony. Frankie Silver had lied about her husband's whereabouts, and the testimony of this young woman bore witness to that lie. I barely listened to the rest of the interrogation, so occupied was I in second-guessing Mr. Woodfin's next move. I had not long to wait.

Nicholas Woodfin was courtesy itself to the state's witness, but he stood perhaps a shade farther from her than he had from the old woodsman Jack Collis, and something in his expression conveyed the faintest distaste for the lady before him, as if he found her anger vulgar. "You were related to Charles Silver, I believe you said?"

She nodded.

"And no doubt you were quite attached to your handsome kinsman." Something silky in his tone conjured up images of laughing adolescents chasing each other through blackberry patches and stealing kisses beneath a thicket of laurel. One could almost see young Nancy Wilson's ardor turn to bitterness when Charlie's roving eye fell upon the pale loveliness of little Frances Stewart. But Nicholas Woodfin said none of this in plain words, and what had not been spoken could not be denied.

Nancy Wilson looked away from the lawyer's mask of respectful attention. "He was a good boy," she said. "Too good for *her*. She was nobody."

"And had you ever quarreled with Frankie Silver?"

The witness hesitated. "Not to say *quarreled*," she said at last. "Frankie Stewart thought a deal too much of herself, that's all."

"Was she hardworking?"

"And didn't she let everybody know it, too? As if we'd feel sorry for her."

"Was she a good mother?"

An impatient sigh. "She was tolerable."

"And she was a faithful wife?"

A long pause. "I never heard different."

Unlike Charlie. The unspoken words hung in the air, suggested only by a clever lawyer's knowing smile. Nicholas

Woodfin let the silence echo long enough to get inside every-body's head, and then he dismissed the witness with a casual wave, indicating that he had no more use for her than Char-lie ever did.

Had they been lovers? This dark, proud woman and the handsome, careless Silver boy? Perhaps, perhaps not. We would never know. Mr. Woodfin had no interest in letting us know. It was the seed of doubt he had meant to plant, and he was satisfied that he had done so to his client's advantage. Still, I thought, the fact that Nancy Wilson had a metaphori-cal ax to grind did not mean that Frankie Silver had not used one in a more literal sense.

One of our own Morganton physicians, Dr. William Cald-well Tate, was the last witness before the recess. He is an affable young man, only just graduated from the South Caro-lina Medical College in Charleston, and back in Morganton to practice medicine alongside his older brother, Dr. Samuel Tate, who is not the Sam Tate that had served as foreman of the grand jury last week. The two Sam Tates are first cousins, and to the eternal vexation of future genealogists, no doubt, one Sam has married the sister of the other. (Anyone who can keep Morganton bloodlines straight can do square roots in his head.) Of young Dr. William Tate, suffice it to say: his mother was an Erwin.

In the cheerful, impersonal tone of all his kind (as if *he* did not have a skull, or brains to leak out, or a life that would be all too brief), Tate commented on the injuries as they were reported to him by Constable Baker. The young doctor had been chosen to make that arduous two-day journey over the mountains to examine the corpse because the more es-tablished physicians could not have been spared from the care of their own patients in the vicinity of Morganton. "We cannot neglect the living in order to see to the dead," his brother had once remarked in another court case.

After establishing Dr. William Tate's identity and medical qualifications, Mr. Alexander said, "Constable Baker described the nature of the injuries sustained by the victim, did he not?"

"He did, sir. I was able to examine the remains for myself, and my opinion tallied with that of the constable."

"How were the remains found?"

"Some, of course, were burnt, and of those I was able to examine only fragments, but the others had been buried in the snow or concealed about logs in that frozen wilderness, and those parts were tolerably well preserved. The skin had been blanched and shriveled from the cold, but there was no decay or invasion by insects."

I looked at once at my sister-in-law Miss Mary, hoping to see her swooning in the arms of her cousin, but she was as alert and attentive as if a quadrille were being performed. I put it down to a want of imagination on her part, for I felt that the room had suddenly become unseasonably warm.

The doctor continued, "I have taken the liberty of producing a sketch of the placement of various wounds." He drew a sheet of paper out of his coat pocket and handed it to the attorney, who examined it and passed it on to the judge, to Mr. Woodfin, to the jury, and lastly to myself. Dr. Tate had sketched the head and limbs unconnected to a torso, and he had labeled each part with the size and nature of the wound. Many of his notations read: *Sawing marks, made post-mortem.* It was not those wounds that concerned us.

"Were you able to determine the cause of death, Doctor?"

"Any of a number of strong blows with an ax would have served to dispatch the victim, but the one I judge most likely to have done so was a head wound—a gash of several inches' width along the right side of the skull. That blow would have so incapacitated a man that he would be unable to defend himself."

William Alexander considered the matter. "One quick blow to the head—probably delivered without warning—and poor Charles Silver is helpless before his murderer. Would it require great strength to strike a man thus with an ax?"

"Well, sir, a child could not have done it," said Dr. Tate,

"but nearly any able-bodied adult could have managed it. It would take more force than cracking an egg, but less than chopping kindling."

"Would a woman be able to manage it?"

"Oh, easily, I should think. Especially if she was accustomed to doing farmwork."

The prosecutor smiled. "Thank you, Doctor."

The courtroom was a hive of murmurings for a few moments thereafter, and I distinctly heard one man say, "I knew she done it!" before Judge Donnell scolded them into silence.

Nicholas Woodfin took his time approaching the witness. "Dr. Tate," he said slowly, "I know that you have stated that it is physically possible for a woman to have struck this fatal blow. Let me ask you to consider another aspect of that possibility. Have you ever, in all your training and experience, heard or read of a woman killing someone with an ax?"

The physician seemed to be staring straight at me, but I knew that he was not seeing, merely searching the memory behind his eyes for some tale of a murderess. "Poison is a woman's weapon," he muttered at last.

"Yes. Poison," said Nicholas Woodfin. "The ladies don't like untidiness, do they?"

"Not generally, no. But if you were angry or desperate, and you had the weapon to hand . . ."

"But—let me repeat—you know of no case *ever* in which a woman dispatched anyone with an ax. Is that correct?"

"I can't call one to mind. No."

"Such a thing would be unheard of then, in your experience?"

"Well, Charlotte Corday killed Marat in his bath with a knife. Of course, she was French."

When the laughter subsided, the attorney said, "Mademoiselle Corday was not a young girl of eighteen, either, was she? She was a political fanatic killing a stranger, was she not?"

"I suppose so."

"Hardly a parallel to this case, would you say, sir?"

"Perhaps not."

"Doctor, if someone had come in and told you that a young man's head had been split open with an ax, and his body parts strewn about the yard, would you have told the sheriff to look for a slight young woman of eighteen— *working alone?*" He sounded the last two words louder than the rest, and I heard answering gasps from the spectators.

Mrs. Silver stopped staring at the window and blinked. I saw her slender form stiffen within the shapeless mass of that faded gown. Her blue eyes met mine; I was first to look away.

Dr. Tate cleared his throat. "Well, not to expect a thing isn't to say it can't happen."

Nicholas Woodfin shook his head. "Again, Doctor: *Would you have expected such a thing?*"

The physician glanced at the prosecutor and shrugged before responding to Mr. Woodfin's question. "No," he said at last.

A few moments later Mr. Donnell dismissed the buzzing court for the noon recess. I was generally the last person to leave, for I had to gather up my notes and tidy my desk. Beside, I didn't care to be jostled by the rabble in their haste to reach the taverns. Nicholas Woodfin rose, murmured a few words of encouragement to Mrs. Silver, and then took his leave of her. I hoped that he was spending the noon recess in study and contemplation, because things did not look well for his young client. Then I saw Thomas Wilson lingering in the doorway, obviously waiting for his colleague so that they could confer about the events of the morning.

At last the prisoner stood up, preparing to be led back to her cell by Mr. Presnell, but I could see that she, too, was loath to go. She kept looking back at the departing mob, and once she whispered something to the constable, who looked annoyed but gave a grudging assent.

Finally, two men, moving against the tide of humanity, emerged at the rail within arm's length of Mrs. Silver. They did not reach out to her, though. Her father and brother, for it was they, stood together grim-faced and almost shy before this young girl who had suddenly become a presence. They fingered the brims of their hats and shifted uneasily from one foot to another. The constable took a step back from the family gathering, eyeing them warily, his hand on his weapon. I lingered over my papers, straining to overhear what was said.

"Well, Frankie," said Isaiah Stewart.

"How are they treating you?" her brother Jackson asked.

"I get enough to eat," she said. Her frown was directed at the floor. She had appeared anxious enough to see her family, but now that they had appeared, the meeting seemed to afford her no pleasure. They made no move to embrace the girl or to clasp her hand. The three of them stood in awkward silence until finally Frankie Silver asked, "Did Mama send any word?"

"Only that she is praying that God will spare you," said her father.

The sullen look returned. "I see," she said softly. "She didn't come."

"No. We thought it best." Her father would not meet her eyes as he said this, and I strained to hear her reply, but there was none, until after some more leaden silence, she said, "And my baby?"

"She's over to the Silvers' place," said Jackson. "We ain't seen her, but I reckon she's doing all right. Miz Silver just had a new baby boy herself last month, so likely it's as easy for her to do for two as for one."

Frankie Silver's eyes sought those of her older brother. "When you get home, Jack, I want you to ride over there and see she's taken care of good," she said, and as he replied with a shamefaced nod, another thought struck her. "Where's Blackston?"

"We left him home to look after your mama. It's still cold yet up the mountain, and she wanted him to tend the fire and see to the livestock."

I thought that the Stewarts had been wise to keep the other two suspects well out of Morganton, since tempers are apt to run high on court days, but Frankie Silver's eyes filled with tears. Perhaps she wishes to see her dear mother and brother one last time, I thought.

"Alone, then," she murmured.

"We're right here, Frankie," her father said.

"We'll do what we can." The voice of Jackson Stewart carried more conviction. "We'll do *all* we can."

Brother and sister looked at each other and nodded as though an understanding had passed between them. "I'll say no more then," she said, and she turned to Mr. Presnell. "We can go now, mister."

As the constable led her away, I heard her say, "Can we stand off by ourselves on the lawn for a little bit?"

"It's time to eat, ma'am."

"I want to look at the mountains. Can you see them from here?"

I made my way out into the now deserted hall, intending to fortify myself at one of the taverns if space and congenial company could be found, when a shrill voice halted me in my tracks.

"Mr. Gaither! *Brother!*"

I froze. My wife's sisters generally employed the term "brother" only when prefacing a favor, and since I recognized this sister's voice as that of the redoubtable Miss Mary Erwin, I turned slowly toward her with a smile of greeting and a soul of dread.

"Miss Mary," I said. "How are you enjoying the trial? May I take you home to dinner?"

"The trial is a travesty," she informed me, ignoring my pleasantries. "And I do not see how anyone of good conscience could eat after having witnessed it."

I determined not to take this slur personally, even though it was in a sense my court and my trial. I wonder if she would have said such a thing had her dear father continued in the position of clerk of court. "Are things not proceeding to your liking?" I asked politely.

She did not quite reach my shoulder, but she stood there

glaring at me, with her parasol perched musket-like on her shoulder, looking for all the world like an Amazon maiden. At my question, the warrior's scowl gave way to a look of womanly pity. "Oh, Mr. Gaither," she sighed. "That poor lost girl. I cannot make sense of it at all."

"We think she must have killed her husband because she lied and said that he had not come home, and of course . . . he had."

"Not that!" she said, frowning impatiently. "Of course I have followed the trial procedure. I understand perfectly what the witnesses have sworn to. But what we want here is some plainspeaking."

"How so?" I murmured. I looked about for her cousin James, but he seemed to have made good his escape while she waylaid me.

"The girl is the only living soul who knows what happened in that cabin, Mr. Gaither. Put her up in front of the court and *ask* her."

"That we cannot do, Miss Mary," I said.

"Why not?"

"Because defendants may not testify in felony cases. Surely you know that. It is the law of the land, handed down to us from English common law. A venerable tradition that goes back centuries."

"To the Dark Ages, no doubt, where it belongs," she replied. Her gloved hand touched my arm. "Can you not waive the rule in this case? I feel sure there is something we ought to hear. Let the girl speak."

I smiled gently at the flattery implicit in her request. Could I, as clerk of court, set aside codified trial law and age-old tradition because an Erwin wished it so? I shook my head. "Even if I were to attempt such a thing, Miss Mary, neither Judge Donnell nor the prosecutor would allow it. You might even find that the lady's own attorney would wish to keep her silent for fear that with her testimony she might inadvertently condemn herself. She will not speak."

"Then how can we get at the truth?"

Although I had questioned that very stricture in my

own mind often enough, I found myself defending the no-testimony rule to my sister-in-law. "There are those who say that hearing a felon's sworn statement would not avail the listeners of the truth. Such a custom would merely give the accused an opportunity to perjure himself, and to put his soul in further peril by breaking his oath before God."

"You think she would lie under oath and be damned for it?" said Miss Mary.

"So it is argued."

"Is it better that she should say nothing and be hanged for it?"

I had no reply to this, and Miss Mary did not wait to hear one.

When court resumed that afternoon, the prosecutor called more witnesses from the search party that had scoured the woods for Charlie Silver's remains. No new revelations came to light. The only purpose of the afternoon sessions was to hammer home the two themes of William Alexander's case: that the murder was pitiless and horrible, and that the defendant had repeatedly lied.

At last, as the afternoon light thickened into evening, he announced that he had no further witnesses to call. Mr. Nicholas Woodfin might now present his case.

I had doubted that Woodfin would call any witnesses of his own. What on earth could they say? No one had said anything to the detriment of the character of the defendant. Those who took the stand had all admitted, however grudgingly, that young Mrs. Silver was hardworking, sober, altogether a dutiful wife and mother. There were no past incidents of violence or wanton behavior to explain away.

Was she mad, then? I could not believe that anyone present in that courtroom would think so. Frankie Silver had sat solemn and silent through the day's grim proceedings, her behavior unmarked by fits or laughter, and her person as seemly and fair as a maiden in a church pew. He had nothing to deny then, except the sworn testimony of half the frontier community: Frankie Silver had lied. I saw no way around it unless he put her on the stand, and that he was not permitted to do. A bitter outing for a newly minted lawyer, I thought. God help him.

Nicholas Woodfin took a deep breath as he rose to face the judge. "Your Honor," he said, "the defense rests."

Burgess Gaither

VERDICT

By the time the shadows were lengthening on the lawn outside the courtroom, both attorneys had concluded their closing arguments. I had spent much of the afternoon gazing out
the window at the trees and the clabbered sky above them,
letting the words wash over me, as they would surely drown
Frankie Silver.

Judge Donnell delivered his own ponderous summary of
the evidence and the jurors' obligations, and then he sent the
jury out to deliberate. They would report back promptly the
next morning to deliver their verdict. Court was adjourned
until then. I wondered if His Honor would sleep any better
than the rest of us, awaiting the morning's decision. Mrs.
Silver was led out of the courtroom to return to her cell for a
night of dread that could scarcely be worse than the gallows
itself. I watched her square her thin shoulders as she paced
along in front of her jailer, head high, sparing not a glance
for the crowd, and I resolved to murmur a prayer for her that
night.

The jurors trooped off to be sequestered in the courthouse
jury room, which was little bigger than the wooden table
contained in it. For the duration of their deliberations they
would be "without meat nor drink nor fire," as was the custom from time immemorial. Men who are without food or
drink will be more likely to reach a prompt decision. While
the jury was thus deprived, considering the evidence against

Frankie Silver, the rest of Morganton repaired to the taverns
to retry the case in a dull roar over whiskey and tankards of
ale. This convivial court of tipplers argued and analyzed the
fine points of the trial in preparation for a later recital of the
events before the ladies at dinner that evening.

I found the attorneys at McEntire's, all seated together at
a table in the far corner. They had been accorded this semblance of privacy out of respect for the solemn nature of
their task, and the revelers at the bar had thus far not in-
truded upon the members of the bar.

No doubt a layman would have been surprised to see
these men who had been bitter adversaries two hours hence
conversing over tankards of ale with genial complacency, but
as a fellow attorney, I expected nothing else. The battle was
over now; the matter was in the hands of a jury, and the rival
lawyers would live to fight another day. They left their animosity, as always, within the courthouse walls, for legal ca-
reers are long, and today's opponent might be tomorrow's
colleague, or judge, or influential friend in the legislature.
There is no graver courtesy than the respect born of ambitious self-interest.

Even so, Nicholas Woodfin was poor company that evening. He showed no rancor toward his companions, but he
sat before an untouched glass, and stared at nothing, answering only in monosyllables if one addressed him twice—
loudly.

"I thought you did well," I told him, as I settled into the
empty chair beside him. "You spoke eloquently and with
great conviction. Altogether a moving performance."

"But not enough," Woodfin said, resting his forehead on
the heel of his hand. I saw how tired he looked, and how
careworn. There was a stubble of beard on his normally
clean-shaven chin, and his clothing was more full of sweat
and creases than a fastidious gentleman would permit in ordinary circumstances. No doubt he would change before the
dinner hour, but just now he seemed too cast down to care
about how he looked. Anyone would think that he had been

the one on trial today, rather than merely a learned laborer doing the job for which he was hired.

"Come on, Woodfin, give over, won't you? The lady is in God's hands now," said Mr. Wilson, who was considerably more sedate than his colleague. When this bracing speech brought no response, Wilson remarked to the rest of us, "In legal matters, our young friend has not yet learned to keep his heartstrings as tightly drawn as his purse strings."

William Alexander, whose joviality was tempered only by his courtesy, raised his pewter tankard in a toast. "No, no," he said heartily. "Don't scold my colleague for his sensibility, Uncle Wilson. I like a man who believes in his causes. His loyal heart does him credit. To his health—if not that of his client!"

We all laughed politely at his jest. Even Woodfin managed a wan smile, but I could see that he was still troubled. "She may escape the gallows yet," I told him. "The evidence is purely circumstantial."

"So is the evidence that the sun will rise tomorrow," Mr. Alexander drawled. "But I believe it all the same."

Mr. Wilson laughed at this flippancy, and the two of them bent their heads together to talk of other matters, concerning family, I believe, for they were related by Mr. Alexander's marriage to Wilson's niece.

I turned my attention to the anxious young defense attorney. I thought it would be useless to try to cheer him up with a change of subject, so I resolved to be a sympathetic listener to his woes about the case. Besides, the conversation I'd had with Miss Mary Erwin that afternoon hovered in my thoughts. "Has your client told you anything about the death of her husband?" I asked Woodfin. "People feel that there is a great deal to the story that we do not yet know."

Nicholas Woodfin groaned. "I wish she had told me something. I could have used it in her defense. But Frankie Silver keeps her own counsel. She is a brave little thing. I cannot look at her without thinking of the little Spartan boy with the fox in his tunic, gnawing out his innards. She will keep silent if it kills her. And it will."

"Still, you represented her well. You cast what doubt you could. Do you wish that she could have taken the stand herself?"

Woodfin assumed the blank gaze of one who looks at events unfolding in his mind's eye and sees nothing of the world around him. "I wish she could have testified," he said at last. "I'm very much afraid that she would have chosen silence, but by God I wish I'd had the opportunity to let her speak."

"It is a strange case," I said. "She looks like an angel, but her neighbors tell such tales of the crime and her cold-hearted lies about it that I hardly know what to think."

"It's what the jury thinks that matters, Mr. Gaither. And I'm very much afraid that I know that already."

I slept so fitfully that night that Elizabeth declared that I was taking sick from overwork and the uncertainty of the spring weather. She bundled a woolen scarf around my throat when I went off to court that morning, which kept me warm against the March winds but did nothing for the chill at my backbone that told me death was even nearer than spring. The road was thick with crowds surging toward the courthouse to hear the verdict, but I spoke to no one. I bundled my coat tighter about me and trudged along in silence, wishing that I could spend the day in the cold sunshine instead of in a rank-smelling courtroom.

I took my place at the front of the court with only a few minutes to spare—quite later than my customary time of arrival, for I had lingered over an indifferent breakfast and loitered along the road to work like a wayward schoolboy reluctant to begin the day. The jury looked as if they, too, had passed a turbulent night. They shuffled into the jury box with rumpled clothes and that solemn expression of neutrality that jurors all contrive to maintain, perhaps in defense of their privacy, knowing that a hundred strangers are searching their faces, looking for the verdict.

The attorneys came into court together, solemnly, as if they were deacons in a church processional, and I was pleased that they did not laugh and chat among themselves, as lawyers are sometimes wont to do, distancing themselves from the harsh proceedings. Woodfin and Alexander took their appointed places with somber nods to Mr. Donnell and myself, and we waited for the prisoner to be brought in.

She appeared in the doorway, looking small and lost, and I felt a ridiculous urge to stand up, as one does when the bride enters the sanctuary. She wore the same faded blue dress as before, but now she had an old black shawl draped about her shoulders, for the wind was brisk today. The murmur of voices in the courtroom fell away to silence as she made her way to Mr. Woodfin's side. He bent down and whispered a few words to her—encouragement, perhaps, but I saw no emotion in Mrs. Silver's face. She held her head high and looked toward the front of the courtroom; perhaps she, too, was aware of the stares of the multitude.

"Gentlemen of the jury, may we have your verdict?" Mr. Donnell's dour Scots countenance seemed perfectly in keeping with the tenor of the day, and I fancied that I saw the jury foreman blanch under the old justice's withering stare.

"Ah, well, Your Honor . . ." The small man's eyes darted left and right, seeking either support or a way out, but neither was forthcoming. He cleared his throat and began again. "That is to say . . . we don't have one yet."

Judge Donnell waited in a deafening silence during which nobody breathed.

The hapless juror licked his lips, but he resolved to tough it out. "We cannot agree on the matter. We'd like to question some of the witnesses again, sir."

This statement elicited a burst of noise from the gallery, and an answering clatter from the gavel of John Donnell. "This is most irregular," he told the jurors.

"Yes, sir," said the foreman, but he was more confident now. The judge may be the piper of the court, but the jury calls the tune. "We'd like to hear some of the testimony again, sir."

Mr. Donnell sighed wearily, perhaps at his own folly in having left the marble halls of Raleigh to come out to the uncouth hinterlands, where juries didn't even know how to reach a proper verdict. No doubt the judge had wished to get an early start on his travels east, but it was not to be.

One of the other jurors handed the foreman a piece of paper. "We have a list, sir."

The bailiff conveyed the paper to His Honor, who read it twice over with an expression of increasing annoyance. At last he motioned for William Alexander to come forward and take the list of persons to be reexamined. Judge Donnell looked out toward the gallery. "The witnesses are reminded that they are still sworn. They may now exit the court."

Gabriel Presnell gathered up the little band of folk from the mountain wilderness and marched them out into the hall to await their turn on the witness stand.

Over the hum of murmurs from the gallery I heard the upraised voice of Nicholas Woodfin. *"They have not been sequestered!"* He stood up, waving a hand in protest. "Your Honor, the witnesses were not sequestered last evening."

He was right. In trials, those who will testify in the proceedings are kept separate from their fellow witnesses so that they may not compare their stories, and thus, wittingly or not, influence one another's account of the events in question. On Wednesday night before the trial began, the witnesses were indeed kept apart according to procedure, but last night no one bothered about them. We thought they were finished, that the trial was over. We thought the jury had only to deliberate for the evening and then return in the morning to deliver their verdict. Instead the twelve jurors had come back demanding another round of testimony from the witnesses, except that now this jury would be hearing people who had been at liberty to compare notes, to exchange their impressions of the case—in short, witnesses whose recollections were now tainted by the opinions of their fellows. I wondered what Judge Donnell would do about this breach of custom. Suppose a witness's new and altered version of the circumstances affected the verdict?

We waited in silent consternation while the old judge considered the matter. Nothing about this trial was going to be easy for any of us. An unlikely defendant, an unheard-of crime, an inexperienced attorney, and now obstacles strewn in the path of a swift resolution. Henceforth no doubt the very name of Morganton would cause the judge to shudder. At last, having contemplated all the possible ramifications of the extraordinary request, Mr. Donnell turned to me for the first time during the proceedings. "Clerk of court," he said, nodding for me to come forward, "what say you in this matter?"

I stood up. "Well, sir," I said faintly, "I have not seen it done before, but there is nothing in the law books specifically prohibiting the reexamination of witnesses. They have been sworn."

Mr. Donnell's eyes narrowed. "So they have." He leaned forward, addressing his remarks to the two attorneys. "I will permit this, gentlemen."

Woodfin paled. "But, Your Honor, the witnesses may have conferred—"

"They have been sworn, counselor. They have taken God's oath to tell the truth, and we must assume that they will continue to tell the truth as they see it. As they now recall it." His tone brooked no argument, but even so Mr. Woodfin remained standing for a moment or two longer, wide-eyed and gasping, as if he were casting about for some straw of legal redress. It was one of the very few times during the course of the trial that I saw him look around for his co-counsel Thomas Wilson, but that worthy gentleman offered him no help; he merely shook his head as if to say that the point was lost, and that no good could come of arguing about it.

Judge Donnell turned to the prosecutor. "Mr. Alexander," he said, "you may begin, sir."

He consulted the list and nodded to the bailiff. "The state calls Miss Nancy Wilson to the stand."

In the short interval during which we awaited the arrival of Nancy Wilson, I had time to scan the crowd, and I noticed that Miss Mary Erwin was not present among the spectators. Perhaps she had seen her fill of legal chess games on

the preceding day, or more likely, she had anticipated an un-
favorable verdict, rather than the unexpected continuation
of the trial that took us all by surprise.

Nancy Wilson entered the courtroom for her second turn
on the witness stand looking uneasy. Wearing the same black
dress as yesterday but not the same confident demeanor, she
kept close to the bailiff's side, making her way through the
spectators with a worried frown, as if she were wondering
what the jurors wanted from her now.

When the preliminaries were settled, William Alexander
approached the witness with a perfunctory smile intended to
calm her fears. "The jurors would like to hear your testimony
again, Miss Wilson. Let us begin again. I will ask you questions, and you must answer truthfully to the best of your
knowledge. Do you understand?"

She nodded. "Go on, then."

"State your name, please."

"Nancy Wilson."

"You reside in the Toe River section of western Burke
County?"

"That's right."

"No kin to Attorney Thomas Wilson of Morganton."

"No. Not that I ever heard." She shrugged. "Maybe back
in England five hundred years ago."

William Alexander permitted himself a genuine smile.
"There is no need to deny Mr. Wilson so thoroughly, madam,"
he assured her. "We are merely establishing that you have no
ties to the court that might affect your testimony. That aside,
it is no crime to be related to such a worthy gentleman as my
learned colleague."

"Even if he is a lawyer!" someone called out from the
gallery.

This jest proved too much for Judge Donnell, and his own
smile vanished as he banished the levity from his courtroom
with the oak gavel.

"Miss Wilson, are you acquainted with the defendant
Frances Silver?"

"I know her." An emphatic nod.

"Are you related?"

"Her husband Charlie was my first cousin." Nancy Wilson looked as if she intended to say more, or perhaps she meant to remind the prosecutor that he already knew these things, but something in Mr. Alexander's expression must have counseled patience, for she contented herself with that brief reply, and the questioning continued.

"How did you come to hear about the disappearance of your cousin Charles Silver?"

"Last December I was visiting at my uncle's cabin when Frankie"—she nodded contemptuously toward Mrs. Silver— "*she* came in saying that Charlie was gone."

"Did the defendant know where he was?"

"Frankie had already told the family that Charlie was gone the day before. She just came to say he wasn't back yet from a visit to the neighbors over the ridge. We began to think that Charlie had come to harm on the walk home through the snow. He might have fallen through the ice and drowned in the Toe River."

"Did Mrs. Silver seem concerned about her missing husband?"

"Not her. She was angry, more like." Nancy Wilson tossed her head. "She was put out about Charlie being gone, in case he was having a good time without her. And she was all-fired mad about having to do all the chores herself. She wanted the cows fed, as if a big strong woman like her couldn't do it perfectly well herself. And she kept saying that she was going to run out of firewood, and would one of the boys come over and chop some for her."

"Did they?"

She shook her head. "There wasn't no need. Alfred said he had seen a whole cord of oak and kindling already chopped and stacked, sitting right there by the side of the cabin a day or two back. 'You can't have used it all up yet, Frankie,' he told her. Of course, now we know what happened to that wood." Nancy Wilson looked defiantly around the court-room, as if daring anybody to come up with another explanation for the missing woodpile.

"Did Mrs. Silver suggest that the family begin a search for her husband?"

"She did not," said Nancy Wilson. "She knew it wouldn't be no use. She kept saying that there was a party over to the Youngs', and that Charlie would be along home when the liquor ran out, same as always. It wasn't no use to go after him, she said, because he'd rather lay around with those no-account friends of his than do any work anyhow."

"When Mrs. Silver appeared to report her husband missing, who was present in the Silver cabin?"

Nancy Wilson ticked them off on her fingers. "Besides me, there was Mrs. Nancy Silver, Charlie's stepmother; his sisters Margaret, Rachel, and Lucinda; his brothers Alfred, Milton, and Marvel; and the baby, William."

"When she was ready to leave, did Frankie Silver ask any of you to accompany her back to her own cabin, since she was now alone?"

"She did not. She didn't want anybody going near her place at all. That was plain. Charlie's sister Margaret offered to walk back with Frankie, on account of she had the baby with her, and I said I'd go along to keep Margaret company on the way back, but Frankie said she didn't want any visitors. She said she'd go alone. She had an odd look on her face, too. Like she was a-skeered we'd follow her."

This testimony was completely different from the account Miss Wilson had sworn to on the previous day. I had not made notes of the witnesses' recitals, for it was only my job to see that legal procedure was correctly followed, but I remembered it well enough. Nancy Wilson spoke with conviction in a clear, carrying voice, and her words had impressed themselves upon my memory. Frankie Silver had been weeping, she had said. The young wife had been worried about her missing husband. She had asked Margaret Silver and Nancy Wilson to come back to the cabin with her, but they declined, saying that they did not wish to tramp through the deep snow to her cabin. This was the testimony as I recalled it; surely the jury would remember as well?

I scanned the faces in the jury box, but I saw no expressions of surprise or alarm. One white-haired gentleman with cold eyes and a mean-spirited mouth was nodding with satisfaction, as if this story dovetailed perfectly with—with what? His memory of yesterday's proceedings, or his imaginings of the conduct of a guilty murderess? The other jurors listened to the tale with equal equanimity. Had I misheard? I found myself looking about the courtroom, searching for a countenance that reflected my own bewilderment at this turn of events. Did no one remember?

Miss Wilson's revised version of the events of December 22 recast the defendant as a heartless monster, indifferent to the fate of her husband and transparent in her efforts to escape detection. Gone was yesterday's image of the weeping young girl, worried about her lost Charlie and begging his kinswomen to come home and keep her company while the men searched the woods. With a few words, only half a dozen denials, Nancy Wilson had evoked the image of a cunning and cruel killer, someone who deserved no mercy and no pity, and who would surely receive none from those present in the court. The Frankie Silver that was described today deserved to die.

I had no way of knowing which version of the tale was the true one, though of course I suspected that the first telling was the real remembrance. At least I wanted the jurors to realize that they were hearing a vastly different account from the one that had been previously given and sworn to before God.

Surely someone else in this crowded courtroom remembered the previous testimony. Someone would want to know why the facts had altered so completely from the first testimony. *Someone* . . . I found the astonished face I sought at the defense table: it was that of Nicholas Woodfin. He had gone even paler as Miss Wilson spoke, and I saw his lips twitching as if he could control the sound of his outcry, but not the movement.

For an instant our eyes met, and we read dismay in each other's expression. I looked away first, for I could not bear to

see this courageous and idealistic young man in the very beginning of his profession lose all his faith in the majesty of
the law. Juries do not mete out divine justice, I wanted to tell
him. They are the arbiters that we mortals deserve: imperfect, credulous, and above all fallible. He was seeing the end
of his client's hopes, and he knew it. I wondered if *she* did.

Frankie Silver seemed less wounded by this turn of fate
than did her attorney. Perhaps she did not understand the
calamity that had befallen her; perhaps she simply expected
less of her fellow man, or of this witness in particular. She
huddled in her black shawl and listened with the blank stare
she had effected for much of the trial to block the stares of
the curious onlookers, but once I saw her smile. It was a sad,
terrible smile, and I knew that the memory of it would stay
with me always. Such a look might Mary Queen of Scots
have worn upon hearing the death sentence signed by her
cousin Elizabeth I. It was the brave smile of a gambler who
knows she has lost everything, not through any fault of her
own but through the treachery of her companions. For an
instant I found myself wishing that Miss Mary Erwin had
come back to court today. She would not have borne this in
silence. I did, but I had no choice. I was an officer of the
court. I could not stop it.

It was all over but the waiting. The jury had gone out to
deliberate, and the rest of us awaited their pleasure, milling
about inside the courthouse and out, seeking sunshine despite the chill of lingering winter. It was just past noon, but
no one wanted to abandon the vigil in search of dinner.
Some of us were not hungry.

The morning had been taken up with a parade of witnesses, each of whom had shaded his testimony to reflect
the guilt and malevolence of the defendant. The certainty of
Frankie Silver's conviction for murder seemed to seep into
the minds of those who testified, tainting their recollections
with the memory of strange looks or suspicious behavior
where none had been observed before. The girl was a murderer, they reasoned: surely she must have acted like one.

From one day to the next, a young woman who had spent her life in the company of these people, and married into their family, was transformed into a stock villain of melodrama. No one seemed to find it odd.

Nicholas Woodfin had tried to undo the damage caused by the witnesses' premature condemnation. Again and again he asked, "Did you not tell this story differently before?" And always the answer was: "Upon reflection, I remembered more clearly what took place."

At last the questioning was over, the witnesses were dismissed a final time, and Judge Donnell gave his instructions to the jury before sending them forth to begin their task anew. His summation was stern but fair, although he did not touch upon the matter of the altered testimony. He was careful to explain to the jurors that reasonable doubt did not mean conjuring fanciful solutions to the crime, and that although the defendant was a fair young woman, the law was no respecter of persons.

"There is a blindfold around the eyes of the goddess of justice," he reminded them, "so that she may not see who is rich or poor, young or old, fair or ill-favored, and thus base her judgments upon these superficialities. Gentlemen of the jury, see that you, too, are blind to the temptations of offering mercy where none is warranted."

I was surprised by the anxiousness that I felt in anticipation of their verdict. Usually, cases in Superior Court, even quite serious or tragic ones, leave me unmoved. I have no stake in the verdict; nothing that transpires in the courtroom reflects upon my ability as a lawyer or affects my purse. I am merely an observer, a procedural referee, if you will. Somehow, though, this time I found myself wishing with all my heart that Nicholas Woodfin would carry the day, and that little Mrs. Silver would be set free.

I made a point of seeking out Mr. Woodfin, who was standing by himself on the courthouse lawn, seemingly oblivious to the white flowering trees around him heralding spring. It will be winter for him a good while longer, I thought, watching him. His colleague Thomas Wilson had gone home to dine, and none of the spectators had cared to approach the young attorney. The man who defends a heartless killer is not a popular fellow.

"I feel sure that she cannot have done it," I said to him in a low voice, for I did not wish to be overheard by anyone else.

Nicholas Woodfin smiled at the urgency in my voice. He was tired now, and he wanted nothing more to do with hope. "Have you another theory, Mr. Gaither?"

I shook my head. "None. I dismiss all the theatrics of today—all that wild talk of Mrs. Silver's strange looks and malevolent behavior. That was the embellishment of people wishing to enlarge their roles in the one drama of their lives. It is yesterday's testimony that puzzles me. The witnesses were quite firm on the point of her lying. Frankie Silver said that her husband had not come home, and yet pieces of his body were discovered in the cabin. I cannot explain that fact away."

"No."

"Yet it was a crime involving gore and dismemberment, done in stealth rather than in the heat of passion: this argues madness. But the woman I saw in the courtroom was clearly sane. No one could fault her self-control."

"I wish she had a good deal less of it," said Woodfin. "She is keeping back the truth."

"Surely not," I protested. "Do you know what she is hiding?"

He looked uneasy. "I cannot be sure."

"She must speak out. Her life depends on it."

The young attorney nodded thoughtfully. "I wonder if she knows that," he said. "I have told her so often enough, and Mr. Wilson has impressed it upon her in the sternest manner, but I cannot be sure that she believes us. She is so young and pretty that I am sure she cannot take in the enormity of dying. Perhaps she thinks that because she is a young woman with an innocent child, the court will show her mercy."

"Perhaps they will," I said, but my words rang hollow even to my own ears. We stood there in the pale sunshine

and shivered, Nicholas Woodfin and I, for we knew what was
to come.

This time we had little more than an hour to wait for the
return of the jury. The bailiff summoned us all back to court,
and I found myself searching his face for some sign of the
verdict, as if I were the rawest oaf in a crowd of drunken
spectators. His face betrayed nothing; if in fact he even
knew what the verdict would be, he was careful to give nothing away. In his place I would have done the same. We will
all know soon enough, I thought.

I resumed my seat at the clerk's table and arranged my papers over and over to control my apprehension. Out of the
tail of my eye I saw Mrs. Silver led in to take her place beside Mr. Woodfin. She was pale, and I thought I detected a
tinge of red around her eyelids, but she was as composed as
ever, walking slowly, oblivious to all. As she reached the defense table, and the bailiff let go of her arm, she looked up at
her attorney and smiled, as if to reassure him that all would
be well. As if *he* were the one whose life hung in the balance.
He tried to smile back, then looked quickly away.

He is but twenty-one, I thought, and he has tried fewer
than a dozen cases since he was called to the bar. He will
never again feel such pangs of sympathy for a client. He
will never again allow himself to care. I was sure that if God
were to spare Nicholas Woodfin to practice law for yet another fifty years, he would never speak or write of this incident again.

The jury filed in, properly subdued and solemn, taking
their places without meeting the eyes of anyone present.

"Gentlemen of the jury, have you reached a verdict?" He
said. The words *at last* hung in the air unspoken.

"Reckon we have, sir," said the foreman. A glare from
the judge sent him scrambling to his feet as he answered,
"She done it."

Only the solemnity of the occasion kept Judge Donnell
from uttering a blistering rebuke to this stammering yokel
who was so heedless of court procedure. He continued to

glare at the foreman several seconds during which a shocked silence prevailed in the courtroom. A few heartbeats later the gallery burst into a clamoring babble, with even a few whoops of triumph thrown in by some callous drunkards.

Frankie Silver seemed to sway for an instant, steadied by the arm of Nicholas Woodfin. He looked like a man who has steeled himself for a blow and has finally felt it delivered: it was as bad as expected, but at least it was over. He took a deep breath and murmured something to calm his client.

I looked for the Stewarts among the seething crowd, half fearing violence toward them or from them in reaction to the verdict, but they stood still. Isaiah Stewart had bowed his head, whether in prayer or submission I could not tell. His son Jackson stood with clenched fists, red-faced and breathing hard, as if the fight were just beginning, not ending. Neither of them made any move toward the defendant, and I felt a twinge of sorrow for her. She would be alone regardless, though, I thought. In this terrible moment when she has come face-to-face with her own death, she would be alone even if ten thousand hands were reaching out to comfort her. She did not spare a glance for her father and brother. She was looking up at Nicholas Woodfin with a face so full of trust that it made me ashamed of the powerlessness of all professional men. We doctors and lawyers and preachers and judges act as if we hold the power of life and death over those who pass before us, as if nothing frightens or dismays us, but really we are so many pawns in the game. Too often Death brushes past us to claim his prize without even sparing a glance for those of us who have set ourselves up as humanity's defenders. People trust us so much; yet we can do so little.

"Your Honor, counsel for the defense wishes to move for a rule upon the state for a new trial!" Nicholas Woodfin was shouting to make himself heard above the crowd.

Judge Donnell nodded. He had expected some objection. "On what grounds, Mr. Woodfin?"

"That the witnesses were not sequestered."

"Rule granted." Judge Donnell turned to me, indicating

that I should take down his words. I took up my pen and began to make notes.

William Alexander was on his feet, erupting in protest. "A new trial! Your Honor, we have wasted too much time already on this patently guilty prisoner. The witnesses testified under oath. Twice. There is no need to prolong their inconvenience further so that this woman may be convicted yet again."

"She deserves a fair trial," said Woodfin.

"She had one."

"The testimony changed."

"It was lengthened, but not substantially altered. Frankie Silver lied about her husband's disappearance, and all the witnesses have said so from the very beginning."

"That will do, gentlemen."

"The state objects to the waste of time and public money that would be incurred in a new trial. The evidence for the defendant's guilt is overwhelming. Counsel for the defense is quibbling over details."

"Objection sustained," said Judge Donnell, seeing the inarguable point. "Mr. Woodfin, rule for a new trial is denied."

"Prayer for judgment, Your Honor," said the prosecutor, before his opponent could object further.

"The prisoner will rise."

Nicholas Woodfin helped Mrs. Silver to her feet and kept a protective hand at her elbow as they faced the bench.

The judge intoned the sentence in the sonorous voice of a benediction, with nothing in his tone to suggest any emotion on his part toward the defendant or her fate. "Frances Silver," he said, "you have been found guilty of the crime of murder by a jury of your peers. Sentence of the court is that the prisoner, Frances Silver, be taken back to the prison from whence she came and thereby to remain until the Fayday of the July court next of Burke County, and then to be taken from thence to the place of execution and then and there hung by the neck until she is dead. This sentence to be carried into execution by the sheriff of Burke County."

The pronouncement of death was a familiar formula,

never varied, and my hand flew across the page as I noted it down. When I looked up again, Frankie Silver was being led out of the court by Mr. Presnell, with two other constables flanking him as guards in case of trouble. Her cheeks glistened with tears, but she never made a sound.

Woodfin motioned for the officers to stop. "Your Honor," he said, "the prisoner wishes to appeal the judgment of this court to the Supreme Court of North Carolina."

Judge Donnell frowned, and I fancied I knew the cause of his annoyance. It cost money to make an appeal to a higher court, and the defendant did not impress that worthy jurist as a person of means. "And whom does the prisoner give as security for the bond?" he asked.

I think that Nicholas Woodfin would have paid the costs out of his own pocket, for I saw a glint in his eye that spoke of foolhardiness to come, but before he could encumber himself with that reckless pledge, Isaiah Stewart's voice ran out from behind him.

"I'll stand her bond, Judge. Her brother Jackson and I will answer for it."

"Who are you, sir?"

"I'm her daddy," said the grizzled old hunter, looking at his daughter, not at His Honor. I knew that the words had been directed at her.

"Very well, then," said the judge. "If you will guarantee the bond, the verdict shall be appealed." He turned to me. "Mr. Gaither, you will have the goodness to write a summary of the trial to be sent on to the Supreme Court in Raleigh, and have it ready for my inspection before the departure time of tomorrow's stagecoach."

Traditionally the presiding judge wrote a précis of the trial for the appellate court, but in practice they often delegated this task to underlings—that is, to me. Lowly clerks of Superior Court often found themselves wielding the pen and burning the midnight oil to complete the task of summarizing the case for the appeal. "I will do it gladly, sir," I said with careful politeness, but my heart was heavy as I thought of the evening of drudgery that lay before me, when I had hoped to forget about the cares of my office at one of the Erwins' dinner parties.

I lingered over my papers, for I wanted to make sure that I had all the information that I would need to write the trial summary. A few feet away from my table, Nicholas Woodfin was taking his leave of the condemned prisoner.

"We have appealed the conviction," he told her. "Do you know what that means?"

She shook her head. She looked like a poleaxed calf, I thought, for she stood quite pale and still beside him, staring numbly at the ground as if she could envision it rushing up to meet her dangling feet. I put the thought from my mind. It would not come to pass. Nicholas Woodfin is her champion, and he is not without connections.

"An appeal is a request for a higher court to review the trial procedure." He stopped, trying to find simpler words. "We must get the court in Raleigh to say that they cannot hang you."

She nodded wearily, and I thought that she held out no hope, but that she had no strength left to argue about it. Will Butler told me once that after a trial is over, the prisoner sleeps soundly for the first time in weeks, for even if the worst has befallen him, at least the uncertainty is over. Frankie Silver was finished with us now. She had gone to some other place, where we could not follow.

"I haven't given up on you, Frankie," said Nicholas Woodfin. His voice was tinged with urgency, and I was gratified to know that honor as well as skill had comprised the defense of this poor young woman. "We will get you a new trial, and then we will carry the day!"

She nodded once more, and when the bailiff took hold of her arm to lead her away, she went willingly, and with downcast eyes. She did not look back, though Nicholas Woodfin stood and watched until the oak doors of the courtroom swung shut behind her.

She never saw him again.

Chapter Five

DEPUTY SPENCER ARROWOOD was spending another late night working at his desk when the call came in. The hamburger, seeping grease through its waxed-paper covering and onto the paperwork beneath it, was supposed to be his dinner, but it had long since congealed into a sodden lump, and he could not bring himself to touch it, even to throw it away.

When the phone rang, he was so groggy from lack of sleep that he picked it up to reinstate the silence rather than to talk to anyone.

"Uh—Wake County Sheriff's Department."

"Mr. Miller?"

"No. This is his deputy."

"Oh. Spencer. It's Harmon here, out to the truck stop and all. How you been?"

"Fine, Harmon. What can I do for you?" They had been in high school together, nodding acquaintances now, not much more than that then.

"Well, Spencer, the radio station was talking about those murders out on the trail. Terrible thing. I hated to hear that—a pretty young girl and all. And, you know, they said that you wanted people to report anything suspicious."

"Yes?"

"There's been a kid down here at the truck stop. Probably nothing, but I thought I'd better call you."

"A child? How old?"

"Not a child. A *kid*. Well, seventeen or so. Not somebody you'd sell a beer to without having a mighty long look at his driver's license."

Spencer tried to keep the impatience out of his voice. He didn't have time for liquor-law violations. "So what about him?"

"He's been going around trying to sell jewelry to one or two of the truck drivers in here."

"What kind of jewelry?"

"A gold chain, a woman's watch with a band of gold and silver intertwined, and a ring."

"Wedding ring?"

"Looked like a high school class ring to me. Big silver-colored one with a blue stone, and some carving on the side. I didn't get much of a look at it. He shoved it in his pocket when he saw me coming down to that end of the counter."

It was probably nothing, Spencer thought. At best, it would turn out to be evidence of an unreported burglary. Some vacationing couple would call soon to report their hotel room robbed, or their home burgled. Still, he had to check it out. There weren't any other leads to follow.

"Is he still there?"

"Yeah, he's playing pool with a couple of the truckers. I think he's betting on the game. He's putting up the jewelry, and the truckers are betting cash. You'd better get here before he loses it all, and your evidence rolls out of here six ways from Sunday."

"Keep an eye on him. I'm on my way."

Sometimes you get lucky, Nelse Miller had said. In the small hours of the morning, Nelse had been apt to find philosophy at the bottom of a shot glass, or in the glow of his last cigarette. He maintained that for every case that stays unsolved by chance—no one happened to see anything, no one happened to find the weapon—there is another case that is solved by the same random luck. "This time the coin came up your way," he'd said when he got back to find the suspect already in custody and the evidence tagged for trial.

Now Spencer wondered whose luck it had been—his

windfall or Fate Harkryder's misfortune? He found the kid at the truck stop, still shooting pool with a couple of truckers. Harmon pointed him out. Spencer recognized the scraggly youth with the peach-fuzz mustache as one of the Harkryders, and he'd asked to see the jewelry the kid had been trying to sell. The kid had made a move, as if to put his hand into the pocket of his jacket, but instead he had shoved the player with the cue stick against Spencer Arrowood and made a run for the door. He'd been about three truckers short of a getaway, and instead of making it to his car, he found himself facedown on the sticky floor of the truck stop, while the deputy cuffed his hands behind his back.

"It's your move," Alton Banner told his patient, tapping the chessboard with a black pawn.

Spencer blinked and the carved wooden pieces came back into focus, but he had forgotten now what maneuver he had been setting up. "Did we miss anything?" he asked his opponent.

The old doctor shrugged. "Are you referring to my designs on your king's bishop, or are you over there wool-gathering again?"

"I was thinking about the night of the Trail Murders," said Spencer. "When you and I were at the crime scene. Is there anything we overlooked? Anything you'd do differently now— with more experience, I mean."

"Speak for yourself, boy. I was fifty-one back in those days, and I can't say that experience has improved me much since then. As for technology, maybe there's something we could have gained if we'd had Luminol and DNA testing, and all the rest of the new tools, but there's no use worrying about that now. The evidence has long since degraded. It went into the trash the decade before last. What good will it do to dwell on that now?"

"I want to be sure. I've never had anybody executed before— and it's on my say-so. The evidence was circumstantial."

"Circumstantial. Would you listen to yourself? Most of the people in prison are there on circumstantial evidence, aren't they? Even felons are smart enough not to commit the crime in front of a bunch of eyewitnesses. Excepting John Wilkes Booth, that is."

Spencer smiled. "I know that. And most killers are not inclined to think that confession is good for the soul, either. We had a solid case. He had Emily Stanton's jewelry in his possession and was attempting to sell it, which gave us a motive of robbery. His blood—type A-negative—was found at the crime scene. He had no alibi."

"Are you trying to convince me or yourself? Because if you're saying all this for my benefit, let me say now that I never had one moment's doubt from that day until this that you had the killer. He had A-negative blood, Spencer. That's rare enough so that if you walk into a blood bank and offer to give them some, they start dancing for joy and offering you refills on the orange juice."

"I just wondered if there's anything I've forgotten about that case."

"My memory is long. I can still see those two young people crumpled on the ground in that clearing, looking as if they'd been caught in a threshing machine. No, I never will forget that. So don't ask me to spare too much time helping you agonize over Fate Harkryder's execution, because the night we found the bodies of his victims, I could have shot him myself without a flicker of hesitation. I swear I could've."

Spencer pushed a rook forward. "My summons to the execution said that as sheriff of the prisoner's home county, I could appoint another witness besides myself to attend as well. Would you like to go?"

Alton Banner sighed. "I would not," he said. "I have spent a lifetime trying to keep people from dying, and I have no intention this late in the game of watching it happen on purpose. You go, if you feel it's your duty, but my responsibilities in this case were all discharged twenty years ago. I'm done with it."

The sheriff nodded. "I'll tell them I relinquish my second witness, then. The forest ranger, Willis Blaine, is dead. I asked Martha to check on that a couple of days ago. Aside from him, I can't think of anyone else who ought to be there."

A few moments passed in silence while Spencer stared at the chessboard, but Alton Banner knew that chess wasn't on his mind. "What about your other pet case?" he said loudly, hoping to distract him. "Was the evidence against Frankie Silver circumstantial?"

Spencer had finished reading all the material Martha had brought him about the 1830s murder case. So far he saw no reason to question the decision of his nineteenth-century counterpart. Given the circumstances, he could see no choice but to arrest Frankie Silver for murder. "She lied," he said. "When Charlie Silver disappeared, Frankie went to her in-laws and said that he hadn't come back to the cabin."

"Whereas most of him had . . ." drawled Dr. Banner. "I know the story. Doesn't prove she killed him. Maybe she was covering up for someone."

"Then she's not innocent," said Spencer. "Accessories before the fact get hanged, too. There appears to be no evidence of anyone else involved, though. Frankie Silver was never accused of having a lover. And her father and older brother were on a long hunt in Kentucky when the crime was committed."

"You sure about that?"

"All the storytellers say so, and I tend to believe it, because they were never arrested. If they'd been around, they would have been the constable's first choice for suspects."

"All right, she was guilty. I wonder what bothered Nelse Miller about the case then?"

"The fact that it doesn't ring true," said Spencer. "A little eighteen-year-old girl in a cabin with a year-old baby. A one-room cabin. Charlie Silver's body was cut into little pieces and parts of it were burned in the fireplace. How long would that take, anyway?"

The doctor shrugged. "Depends. What do we have to work with?"

"It's 1831. An ax, maybe. A hunting knife."

"A couple of hours, easily. More if she isn't used to

butchering. If you don't hit between the vertebrae just right, it could take you an hour just to get the head off. It would be messy work. I wonder she had the stomach for it. Him being her husband and all."

"She was afraid of being caught," said Spencer. "Fear can make you do extraordinary things."

"Maybe so. But it's not something you'd expect an eighteen-year-old girl to be capable of. I know of no precedent."

"Frankie Silver was a pioneer. People were tougher in those days." Spencer pushed a pawn toward the center of the board. "Your move."

"Checkmate."

Spencer managed to keep the Harkryder case at bay for two more games of chess, both of which he lost, because his mind kept straying to matters of greater consequence. At last he was alone again, having promised to make an early night of it in deference to his weakened condition. Instead he was sitting in his leather chair with the yellowed manila folder in his lap, sorting through the evidence one more time.

The physical evidence tied Fate Harkryder directly to the scene of the crime—no question about that.

That afternoon at the truck stop, Spencer had arrested Fate Harkryder on suspicion of murder. The jewelry was impounded as evidence of his guilt. The items tallied exactly with the list Spencer had written down during his phone call to Colonel Stanton: the woman's UNC class ring containing the initials *EAS*, the silver and goldtone watch, and a gold chain.

Spencer took the prisoner back to the jail in Hamelin for questioning, and he notified the TBI that he had a suspect in custody. He'd also left word with Nelse Miller, wherever it was he'd gone. An arrest in a major murder investigation: that would bring the old fox home. Spencer was sure of it.

Deputy sheriff Spencer Arrowood read the suspect his rights. "Do you understand?" he said as he put the card away. "You can have a lawyer if you want one."

The sullen young man sat with his feet wrapped around

the legs of the chair, scowling up at the officer questioning him. His long hair was unkempt, and his baggy clothes were several days past needing a wash. Spencer had a good mind to hose him down before he put him in the jail cell.

The prisoner shrugged. "What do I need a lawyer for?"

It wasn't the deputy's job to tell him. He said, "I'm just telling you that if you do want one, you can call him now. And if you can't afford to hire an attorney, we can have one appointed to represent you."

He shrugged. "I don't need no help to say I didn't do it."

"Where did you get the jewelry?"

Another shrug. "Found it."

The interrogation had yielded precious little information after that. Fate Harkryder sat there sullen and silent, refusing all offers of food and soft drinks with a quick shake of his head, as if he were determined to say as little as possible.

At first Spencer tried asking simple questions in a firm but courteous tone. When that got nowhere, he switched to shock tactics, describing the mutilated condition of the bodies and declaring that an unrepentant killer would get no sympathy from judge or jury. "If you want to be as dead as they are, you just keep sitting here saying nothing," he said. "You can't talk your way out of having that jewelry in your possession."

"Doesn't prove nothing."

The jury thought otherwise.

Joe LeDonne hated the telephone. Its shrill peal was mechanical nagging as far as he was concerned, and he never answered it without an inward curse at the interruption. If he had not been in law enforcement, he would not have had one in his house. It was ironic, he thought as he stared at the instrument, an electronic spider on his desk, that so much of police work required proficiency in telephoning.

He and Martha had agreed to give it one more day before they told the sheriff about the homicides. The TBI was conducting its own investigation, but Martha and Joe were going to complete all the scut work of canvasing for witnesses, so that there would be little for Spencer to do by the time he was informed of the case. Joe didn't think there was much chance of keeping him on the mountain once he heard about the new Trail Murders, but he reasoned that the sheriff was bound to find out sooner or later, and the news had better come from them.

So far they had played it by the book, with all the thoroughness they could pack into sixteen-hour days. They had investigated the crime scene, and then gone over the site again when the TBI arrived. The next few days had been spent talking to residents in the vicinity of the site, questioning people at the local bars and cafés, and to suppliers of camping goods and army surplus equipment.

Martha had refused to believe that the two Trail Murders, separated by twenty years, were in any way connected, but she had studied the old case file anyway. Willis Blaine, the forest ranger, was dead, but she had questioned Harmon Ritter, still a fixture out at the truck stop. She had even tracked down the two firemen from Alabama, but they had not been able to tell her anything helpful. She had expected no link between the two cases, and she found none.

LeDonne focused his attention on the individuals most likely to be involved in criminal activity. First he checked the list of parolees in residence in the area, phoning the ones whose crimes had included robbery or violence and checking on their current employment status. He had not ruled out the ex-cons entirely, but he was reasonably certain that they would have to look elsewhere for the killer.

That morning he had called the park service and asked that they fax him a copy of the sign-in sheet from the date of the murders from the two shelters on the Appalachian Trail nearest the crime scene. Maybe one of the hikers saw something. Maybe one of them was the man they were looking for. He had spent several hours in the tedious process of tracking down addresses and phone numbers via the Internet and calling the hikers or, in some cases, E-mailing them. Most of those who were hiking all the way to the end of the Appalachian Trail in Maine could not be reached, but he had been able to reach a fair number of weekend campers, and park visitors who had hiked for only a few days. It was now early evening and LeDonne was still at it, reasoning that the dinner hour was the best time to catch people at home. Beside the list of names, the cup of coffee that was his dinner grew cold.

He had just got through to Jeff Garrison in Maryland. LeDonne explained who he was and what he wanted. Days of practice had honed his explanation to a concise summary in the fewest possible words. When he finished, there was a silence on the other end of the telephone.

"Sir? Are you there?"

"I'm thinking." Late twenties, LeDonne thought, analyzing the voice. Educated. White-collar worker. Maybe a lawyer. Not rattled by the idea of talking to a law officer. He waited.

"I'm trying to sort out the different days of the trip."

"We're right on the North Carolina line," LeDonne told him. "Near Erwin. Unicoi. Do you remember anybody who looked—well, out of place—on the trail?"

"Oh, right. Let me see. . . . There was a guy with hunting dogs. I didn't think he ought to be in a national park."

One of the Jessups, thought LeDonne. "They do that around here sometimes," he said aloud, making a note to find out who had been out with the dogs, and to question them also.

"Other than that, there were just the usual folks doing the trail. It's pretty crowded this time of year, you know. Lot of old dudes—the Woodstock leftovers, you know—out communing with nature, and some really buff women doing the Xena thing. All kinds, really. And guys that were obviously locals. Rednecks."

LeDonne resisted the urge to tell Mr. Garrison how much he disliked talking to bigots. He had to be polite to potential witnesses, and besides, the exercise would be pointless. He was sure that the smug young man would be bewildered to be accused of prejudice. Political correctness did not require tolerance or courtesy toward white Southerners.

"Oh, wait. Speaking of locals. There was one guy out there who looked pretty odd."

"How so?"

"He looked like he ought to be going to computer class instead of out backpacking. Skinny little guy with pens in the pocket, and dress shoes. And a necktie. In the woods."

"Did he have a backpack?"

"Yeah. I think so. A bookbag, really. Not serious camping gear."

"How old would you say this individual was?"

"Late teens. Early twenties. Hard to say."

"Can you give me a description of him? Height? Hair color?"

"Not really. I just looked at him and thought: *Nerd,* and I kept walking."

"Nerd, huh?"

"Yeah. Oh, wait there is one other thing I remember. The guy had an earring. You know that science fiction TV show about the space station?"

"No."

"Well, the people from this one planet always wear this odd kind of double earring. And he had one of those. So I knew he was a space cadet. I wondered what he was doing out hiking, instead of shooting down aliens in the video arcade."

"If I find him, I'll ask him," said LeDonne.

Fate Harkryder was having the dream again. It was dark, and he could not see where he was, but he knew, the way one does in dreams, that he was dead. He could not remember how he came to die, or whether there was any pain involved in the leaving of his life: all he knew was that he was dead and it was very dark. He kept still for a moment, listening for his own heartbeat or the sound of his lungs drawing breath, but there was only stillness and silence. He felt the oppression of a confined space, and he knew that he was in a box deep in the ground, but he was somehow conscious. Perhaps there had been a mistake and he was not dead after all. He had heard tales of men on the gallows who were revived after being cut down from the hanging rope, and of an electrocuted prisoner needing two or three jolts of current to finally stop the heart. Ethel Rosenberg—the convicted spy in that fifties atomic-secrets case—went to the electric chair at Sing Sing. Her husband had died on the first round, but they'd had to electrocute her a second time to make her die. Maybe his execution was over and he had been rendered unconscious, but not killed. He would shout for someone to let him out, but when he tried to open his mouth, he found that it had been sewn shut, and he could not open his eyes, because they, too, were sealed with nylon thread. He tried to lift his arms to pound on the lid of the coffin, but he could make no movement with his dead arms. The screams stayed inside his mind, caught behind sewn-shut lips, echoing in the dark.

He woke up then. The same place in the dream that he always awakened, to the same six-paces-by-nine-paces cell, filled with his books and his calendar pictures of mountains.

"Hey, Milton, you out there?" It was two o'clock in the morning, but nobody sleeps soundly on death row. Fate was shivering, even in the breathless heat of a Nashville summer night. It was not completely dark. It is never completely dark here. He listened for a sound from beyond the wall. "Milton?"

Milton, his neighbor, a skinny young junkie from Memphis, who copped the death sentence in a drug hit, didn't answer. Fate didn't like Milton much—but maybe, he reasoned, that was the point. Nobody that you could like very much ever made it to death row these days, because a jury wouldn't ask for the death penalty if they could find any redeeming qualities in the accused. In the old days, maybe, but not now. Public opinion and liberal lawyers were making it harder and harder to execute prisoners, so it was mainly career criminals and second-time killers who made it into Pod Five now. Fate wondered if a new trial would get him taken off the list, but that didn't seem likely now, as the dream reminded him.

"Milton? You up?"

Milton would stab his grandmother in the back and take bets on which way she'd fall, but at least he was there, and awake, and alive, and if anybody could understand what it feels like to dream you're dead and know that the dream is going to come true real soon, it would be another condemned man on the row. He was better than nothing.

"What's eating you, La-fay-ette?" The singsong drawl flowed out of the shadows; made him wonder if Milton could sing.

"Just wanted some company. Bad dream is all."

Silence, and then a rumbling laugh. "Time is getting short, ain't it? You dream you were in Virginia, La-fay-ette?"

"Dreamed I was dead. Buried alive. Couldn't get out. Couldn't scream for help."

"Yeah, you musta been in Virginia all right, then," said Milton. "They been killing prisoners right and left over there. You dead, you must be in Virginia, 'cause they damned sure ain't killed nobody in Tennessee in thirty-some years. I don't reckon they'll start now with your sorry ass."

"The appeals have all been denied."

"I got money riding on your continued existence, homeboy. Well, cigarettes, anyhow. Two packs of Marlboros says you'll be alive and kicking come New Year's Eve."

Fate took a long breath and waited to see if he felt any better. He didn't. "Milton? I want to be cremated."

"After you gone to the electric chair?"

"It's the dream. I'm in a box and I'm dead but I'm still conscious, and it's dark and I can't get out. My mouth is sewn shut."

Milton was silent for some minutes, and Fate had begun to think that he had drifted off to sleep, but then he laughed and said: "Cremated. Don't you beat all?" He laughed again. "*Cremate your ass.* Man, you know what I heard about Old Sparky? They say that the death squad has to wait half an hour before they even touch the body, it gets so hot. It's cooked from all that juice they run through you. Sometimes the skin catches fire, they say, and the eyeballs fry right on your face. And you think you're gonna stay conscious through that, homeboy? You won't have nothing left to think with by the time they put you in the ground to cool off."

"I want to be cremated. If they're going to burn me, they might as well finish the job."

Burgess Gaither

APPEAL

My carefully written appeal went off to Raleigh on New-land's stagecoach, as did Judge Donnell himself. Both would reach the state capital in three days' time, but I knew that many weeks would pass before I received a reply from the North Carolina Supreme Court regarding the fate of Frankie Silver.

I watched the stagecoach lurch along the pike, churning up black mud in its wake, until at last it disappeared into the pines in the distance. I wondered if Mrs. Silver could see the road from the window of her cell. It is a high, barred window, and perhaps she is too small even to be able to reach it, but at least it will afford her a glimpse of the sky, and I must keep reminding myself that it is more than her poor young husband will ever see again. At least she has another summer yet to live, while the learned jurists in Raleigh deliberate. It should not take them long to consider the matter, for my summary of the trial consisted of a single page, simply stating the facts of the case and the nature of the defense's objection to the verdict. I had not written very many appeals in my brief career as clerk of court, but the judge had read over it carefully, affixed his signature to the document, and informed me gruffly that it would do. I did not care to ask him if he thought that my eloquence would win the prisoner a new trial.

I had not seen Frankie Silver since the close of the trial, but I had heard her weeping.

On Friday, when the business of court had ended for the day with the conviction and sentencing of Frankie Silver, I had occasion to walk outside, for the day was mild and sunny, and I was grateful for the arrival of spring, however tenuous its hold on the weather in late March. The crowds had dispersed now, some to make the long ride home, but far too many others would pack into the taverns, celebrating the triumph of justice, or at least their own good fortune in knowing that it was not they who would be hanged. I could hear the sounds of shouting and raucous laughter far off down the street, and I resolved to go straight home tonight, for I did not want to mingle with the revelers. I thought that the sight of spring's new leaf, almost golden in the sunlight, and deep breaths of brisk mountain air would do me more good than all the ale in McEntire's.

The prisoner had been led away by the jailer, still in that walking stupor she had effected since hearing her death sentence pronounced. Now she was locked away in the upstairs jail cell reserved for female prisoners, where she would spend the remaining weeks of her brief life. I wondered if a clergyman had called upon her, for surely she would be in need of spiritual comfort on this bitter day.

Before I could think better of it, I directed my steps toward the frame house that served as the jail. I knocked on the door—just a tentative tap, for I was already thinking better of my impulse and wishing I had not come, but as I turned to leave, Gabriel Presnell himself opened the door with a thundering scowl that eased when he saw that it was I.

"Evening, Mr. Gaither," he said. I saw that he was holding a pistol at his side, and he lowered it sheepishly as he recognized me. "I thought you might be one of them no-account sightseers wanting a look at the prisoner. Offered me money, one of 'em did." He looked as if he wanted to spit.

Presnell opened the door wide enough to let me in, and as I stepped inside the narrow entryway, I could hear a low-pitched wail from above the stairs.

"I didn't mean to trouble you," I said hastily. "Is Mr. Butler here?"

"No. There didn't look to be trouble after the verdict, so he left the watch to me. He's up home, if you're wanting him."

Suddenly I felt foolish. "I just thought I'd inquire—that is, I wondered whether the parson has been to see her. Mrs. Silver, that is. To say a prayer with her, perhaps. It would be a kindness, wouldn't it?"

Gabe Presnell jerked his head in the direction of the keening noise. "She won't be seeing nobody tonight. She's crouched up there in a ball underneath the window in her cell, bawling like a branded calf."

"Has she said anything?"

"No. Just wailing. My wife is up there trying to calm her down, so's we can all get a bit of rest tonight."

"That's kind of her," I said, backing toward the door. "I'm glad to know that the prisoner isn't left alone right now."

"It's more than she deserves," said Presnell.

"Well, I suppose it is," I said, not wanting to debate the matter on the threshold. "But we are bidden to be merciful, except in that last measure of justice which she must shortly undergo."

"That's as may be," said Presnell, "but charity is hard to come by with all these rowdy sots a-knocking on the door every whipstitch, and that caterwauling from herself up yonder to be borne."

"It will all be over soon enough," I told him.

I rode home in the chill March wind, taking no joy in the signs of spring around me. It had been a long, wearying day, and I found that I could not rejoice in the verdict, whether justice had been done or not. The red-tipped branches of the budding oak trees made me think of fingers dripping blood in the forest, and I shuddered, thinking of Charlie Silver's red hand lying in a clump of snow, clutching at nothing. The trial was not over for me. I had yet to write the appeal. I

dreaded an evening of toil by lamplight, while my wife and
her family enjoyed a pleasant conversation by the fireside.

Five of the Erwin sisters and their young cousin Miss
Eliza Grace McDowell were waiting for me in the great hall
at Belvidere, sipping tea and taking turns pacing with anticipation. One of the younger sisters was making a halfhearted
attempt to piece out a tune upon the rosewood piano. When
I appeared in the doorway, they stopped and stared at me
openmouthed, waiting for a sign.

I shook my head and they shrank back with soft cries of
distress, but while I saw dismay upon some of their faces,
and polite regret on others, I did not detect surprise. We
knew, we all knew, what was coming.

I sank down wearily on the sofa and stretched my hand
out for a cup of tea before I let them prevail upon me to tell
what had happened at the trial.

"Please, Mr. Gaither," said pretty little Eliza McDowell.
"Mr. Woodfin seemed so eloquent and so . . . noble. Could
he not persuade the jury to be merciful?"

"He tried, Miss Eliza, but to no avail," I said, suppressing
another spark of irritation at Woodfin's pervasive charm. The
Erwin ladies grouped around me so that I felt like a honey-
bee smothered in the petals of a dozen silk frocks as I told
my tale. They all looked so concerned, but so puzzled, over
the turn of events we had examined in the courtroom that
day. How could a young woman kill her husband? How
could a poor woman receive second-best justice? They knew
no more of Frankie Silver's frontier existence than hothouse
flowers know of ditch lilies. How could I stem their questions when I had no intention of enlightening them about
the realities of the world past Belvidere?

I looked into the sweet, childish face of Eliza Grace
McDowell, so similar in age and feature to Frankie Silver
herself, and found myself wondering what seeds of murder
might lie in that child's innocent heart. Eliza Grace is the
granddaughter of the two McDowell brothers, one a colonel
and the other a general in the Revolutionary War, and the
old folks tell tales of Miss Eliza's great-grandmother Mar-

garet O'Neil McDowell, who faced down the Tory soldiers as they were sacking her very home. With such ruthlessness in her bloodlines, surely Eliza Grace should be capable of the same ferocity that the jury found in Frankie Silver, and yet I could not imagine this cosseted young woman striking anyone in anger, or summoning up any passion that would unleash a whirlwind of violence. That patriot lady Margaret O'Neil McDowell might have understood the hardship and danger of the frontier, but she had lived generations ago, and since then her descendants had known only wealth and privilege.

Is it their upbringing, and the fine character of the aristocrat, that separates them from the sins of the murderess, I wondered, or is it only a matter of simple good fortune? Is Eliza Grace as capable of violence as any murderess, but innocent only because she has never suffered whatever torments led Frankie Silver to her crime? I put the thought aside. The law is my profession, and it must judge people by what they have done, without concerning itself with whether or not life has treated them fairly, for to do so would be questioning God's will. There are some things we are not given to understand. But I did not pity Frankie Silver any the less for it. She was a fair and tender young creature, and she would have a hard life and an early death, while the fine ladies here before me lived measured, ornamental lives, innocent of drudgery or danger. They were no more beautiful or clever than the defendant, but they were wellborn, and that counted for everything. I could find no justice there. Perhaps there is a different kind of justice in heaven.

"Do tell us what happened, Burgess," said my wife Elizabeth, tapping my arm. "You seem quite dazed, my dearest."

"I am weary," I said. I took a sip of my tea and withdrew from my reverie. "The trial was most unusual. Instead of a quick session convened to hear the verdict and set the sentence, there was more testimony this morning."

"Surely that is most irregular." Miss Mary Erwin was watching me closely, and I hoped she would not ask me what I thought of the day's events.

"Well," I said, "it is unusual." They pressed me for more details, and although I hesitated to discuss such delicate matters with gentlewomen, their demand for the particulars overcame me, and I told them as best I could what had happened today in the courtroom.

"The witnesses changed their stories?" said Miss Mary when I had finished. "But this is monstrous!"

"Surely the testimony was a lie," said Elizabeth. "They cannot hang the poor girl on the basis of false witness, can they?"

"What did Mr. Woodfin say about their treachery?" Eliza McDowell wanted to know.

I shook my head. "The witnesses claimed that they had reconsidered their testimony, and that upon reflection they had remembered the events more clearly. This may, of course, be true."

"So they found her guilty," said Miss Mary Erwin. "I feared that they would. Was judgment passed?"

"Yes. Mr. Donnell pronounced the death sentence. In a case of murder, there is no other remedy. Of course, it may not come to that," I added hastily, seeing their stricken faces. "I am writing the appeal myself, and I shall take care to stress the change of testimony and the unsequestered witnesses."

Elizabeth looked around the room triumphantly. "There!" she said. "I told you it would be all right! Burgess will save her!"

Her sisters, undeluded by wifely affection, looked as doubtful as I felt. Juries' decisions are rarely overturned by the State Supreme Court unless grievous errors have been made in the trial procedure. The Erwin sisters, wives and daughters of attorneys, would know this as well as I when they put sentiment aside, but no one contradicted my loyal wife. We found ourselves talking at cross-purposes in our haste to change the subject.

Miss Mary sat in glowering silence for a good while, and then she said, "We must not forget this poor creature who languishes in the jail. We must visit her."

I had opened my mouth to protest this outrageous suggestion when my sister-in-law added, "Did our Lord not instruct us to visit those in prison as well as those who are sick?"

Mary Erwin can cite Scripture for her purpose.

The summer passed uneventfully in Morganton. We reveled in the hot weather, cast our woolen clothes aside, and savored the June tomatoes, glad to be released from the confinement of winter. Then, just when we had put the bitter cold and snow out of our minds as if December would never come again, the flies, the choking red dust, and the breathless heat drove us back indoors once more to wait for the cooling winds of autumn.

I did not speak much about the Silver case, for in truth there was nothing to do but wait upon the pleasure of the Supreme Court in Raleigh, but my reticence about the case did not banish it from the thoughts of the ladies.

One breathless afternoon as I sat in the library at Belvidere reading over a packet of new books just arrived from England by way of Wilmington, Miss Mary Erwin appeared in the doorway, clad in a white morning dress trimmed with lace, and carrying a cloth-covered basket, but she looked no less formidable for this maidenly affectation. She is a spinster of six and thirty years, ten more than my wife, her sister Elizabeth. Some of the awful seniority of an elder sibling must have transferred itself to Miss Mary's attitude toward me, for I always felt like a sweating, lumbering oaf in her presence, and I'll swear that my tongue grew too big for my mouth at times when I had to speak with her.

I covered my confusion, of course, with bluff heartiness. "Good morning, Miss Mary!" I said gaily. "Are you off on a summer picnic to the wildwood?"

She looked at me as a cat might look at a worm. "No, Mr. Gaither," she said. "I hope I have better things to do than waste my days in idleness." She looked pointedly at the illustrated paper that I was reading, and I fought down the urge to stuff it under my coat. "May I trouble you for a few moments of your time?"

Her tone suggested that since I had nothing better to do than to read frivolous tripe, I might at least make myself useful by doing her bidding. I put the paper aside and rose to my feet with a heavy heart. "I am your servant, of course, Miss Mary."

"Thank you." She drew on her gloves with an air of brisk authority. "Catherine and I wish to go and see the prisoner, and we would like the escort of a gentleman to town, and to wait for us at the jail. You will suit the purpose admirably. You need not accompany us upstairs to the poor creature's cell."

"You wish to see . . . the prisoner? Mrs. Silver?"

"Certainly."

"Then I would consider it a privilege as well as my duty to accompany you," I said, inclining my head to suggest a courteous bow. I had been dreading this gambit for weeks, and now that it had finally come, I felt an odd mixture of apprehension and relief. I wondered what the squire would say about his daughters going to visit a murderess, and whether I should have to shoulder the blame for their excursion. Still, I thought I had better go to keep an eye on them. "Is the *other* Mrs. Gaither not to be of the party?"

I meant my wife, of course. Miss Mary's sister Catherine is also Mrs. Gaither, as she is the widow of my late brother Alfred, and so she is doubly my sister-in-law, but my wife was apparently not included in the outing with her older sisters.

"Elizabeth has a dress fitting," Miss Mary informed me. "She may go at another time. We have promised to report the details of our visit to the rest of the household."

We sent for the open carriage, as the day was fine, and we trotted along the few miles to Morganton with little conversation passing among us. Catherine is a meek and gentle lady, almost midway between the ages of her sisters Mary and Elizabeth, but after a few remarks about the weather and other inconsequential topics, I find myself with nothing to say to her. I am always afraid that some chance remark of mine will remind her of poor Alfred, and I live in fear that I will induce a flood of tears whose tide I will be powerless to stem. I contented myself with smiling at poor colorless Catherine, swathed in her purple dress of late mourning. I hoped that my resemblance to Alfred would not make her weep, but she seemed to bear the sight of me calmly enough.

As we drew closer to town, I felt that it was necessary to issue a few words of instruction to my sisters-in-law about prison visitation. "Mrs. Silver may not wish to see you at all," I cautioned them. "And if she does, the jailer will not want you to stay with her long, or to say anything that may upset her."

"Quite the contrary," Miss Mary called out above the clatter of the wheels. "We will set her mind at rest by telling her that petitions are being drawn up to secure her pardon from the gallows."

"Now, you must not give the prisoner false hope, either," I cautioned her. "It is cruel to make her believe that she will be saved from her punishment."

"I hope I never say anything that I do not believe to be true," she said reprovingly.

I saw that she really believed this, and so I did not smile, but I was thinking that no one could exist for even a day in our carefully polite society by telling the unvarnished truth. I kept silent for the remainder of the ride, which was itself a lie, for she thought that I agreed with her.

The Morganton jail was a two-story white house set in a well-kept lawn only a short distance from the courthouse. It was not the foul pit that one imagines for prisoners in Philadelphia or Boston—or even Raleigh, for that matter, but despite that, I suspected that it would seem terrible enough to my sisters-in-law. I wondered if I should prepare them for the scenes to come, but the set of Miss Mary's jaw persuaded me to keep silent. The more unpleasant the experience, the more satisfaction the ladies would derive from having done their duty.

The carriage stopped in front of the jail, and after I had assisted my companions in dismounting, I went to advise the jailer of his distinguished afternoon visitors. "Miss Mary has brought a basket of food to the prisoner," I told Mr. Presnell. "You may, of course, search the contents, but I assure you that it contains only bread and cheese, and, I believe, a slab of blackberry pie. I smelled it baking this morning at Belvidere."

"Good wages for murder," muttered Presnell, but I knew that he would not voice any complaints to the Erwin sisters, so I thanked him for allowing the visit and went back to fetch my sisters-in-law.

Miss Mary marched into the jail like a wolf on the fold and advanced toward the staircase with a fearless and deliberate tread, but Catherine shrank back at the doorway, and I saw that she had gone pale.

"Don't be afraid," I said, touching her elbow. "Frankie Silver is no older than your nephew Waightstill, and she is neither coarse nor mad. It will be all right. I shall go with you upstairs."

Catherine whispered her thanks. "I thought . . ." she said. She took a deep breath and began again. "I came because I thought it might be a comfort to her to meet another woman who has lost her husband."

I nodded, for I did not trust myself to speak. She is a kind woman, and she deserved more happiness in this life than Providence has seen fit to give her.

I indicated to Catherine that she should follow her elder sister up the narrow stairs, and that I would go last and carry the basket.

Mr. Presnell, who had gone up ahead of us, was waiting at the prisoner's cell. He unlocked the door, which was an ordinary wooden door made of stout oak, with a square of bars set at eye level in the middle of it, so that the prisoner could be observed by the guard. "Don't be long in there," he said softly to me as I went past him. "Lice."

We peered in at the straw-covered interior, which contained only a straw-filled mattress on a camp bed and two oaken buckets: a clean one for water and a foul-smelling one for waste. The prisoner was standing at the barred window looking out at the village, or perhaps at the mountains beyond.

"She stands there hour after hour," Presnell remarked. "Just staring out through the bars."

"So should I if I were forced to stay in this place," said Miss Mary, who had overheard him. "At least the air from the window is fresher than the stench in here, and there is something to occupy the mind in the ever-changing view."

Presnell nodded. "Visitors for you, Mrs. Silver," he said, adding as an aside, "I'll be downstairs when you're ready, Mr. Gaither."

Frankie Silver turned to face us, and I saw that she had been weeping. Her eyes were red and swollen, but she dabbed at her cheek with the back of one hand and stood there submissively, wondering, no doubt, what further tribulations she was to endure.

I smiled, hoping to reassure her of the benign intentions of our visit. "Mrs. Silver, I am Burgess Gaither, the county clerk of Superior Court," I said with careful politeness. "You may recall seeing me at your trial. My visit is not an official one, however. I am here as the escort to my wife's sisters, who have come in Christian charity to visit you. May I present Miss Erwin and Mrs. Alfred Gaither? Ladies, this is Mrs. Charles Silver."

She turned her gaze from me to the two Erwin sisters standing uncertainly in the doorway. Her eyes widened, and she nodded, more to indicate that she understood than to convey a greeting. Miss Mary, as always, took charge. She strode forward and inclined her head, as courteously as she would have greeted a gentlewoman in a church pew.

"Good day, Mrs. Silver. We have come to visit you," she said briskly. "And to satisfy ourselves that you are well treated and in good health."

Frankie Silver nodded shyly. Her hair was lank and hung about her shoulders, for she had no means of binding it up, lest she should use a hairpin to pick the lock. She was not wearing the blue court dress, but a plain brown one that looked ancient and none too clean. She put her hands to her hair, as if to smooth it into a semblance of presentability, and as she edged forward a bit toward her visitors, we heard a clattering sound from the floor.

Miss Mary peered down at the straw. "What was that noise?"

"Chain," said the prisoner softly.

"I beg your pardon?"

Frankie Silver lifted the hem of her skirt a few inches from the straw, revealing thick links of chain. She wriggled one small white foot and the chain rattled.

I intervened with a discreet cough. "Mrs. Silver is in restraints. There is an iron shackle around her ankle, which is chained to a ring in the center of the floor."

Miss Mary rounded on me with a look of outrage suggesting that I was personally responsible for this indignity. I think she was on the verge of banishing me from the room when the prisoner spoke up softly, "It's all right. I'm used to it. You can't go too far in this cell anyhow."

Catherine left my side and went to put her hand on the prisoner's arm. "We are very sorry to see a woman in such straits," she said. "Are you well?"

Frankie Silver shrugged. "Reckon I'll live 'til September," she said. September is the time of the next sitting of Superior Court, at which time the judge will set the date for her hanging. *She is unlettered, but she is not stupid,* I thought. Her answer had a pleasing irony that spoke well of her wits.

"Is there anything we can do for you?"

She hesitated for a moment before she whispered, "Can I see my baby?"

They all turned to look at me, and I was forced to play the villain once again. "That is not within our power," I said as gently as I could. "Your child is back up the mountain with her grandparents."

"Am I ever going to see her again?"

"It is a long journey for a young child," said Catherine gently. "I have a little daughter myself, and I would not care to have her travel so far in the summer heat."

"Let us hope that someday you will go home to her," said Miss Mary.

"She'll forget me."

"Your family will not allow that," I said, although I had no idea if this was true or not. I did not want to torment the wretched woman with false hopes, but neither did I want to add to her misery with agonizing thoughts of home.

We stood there awkwardly, trying to think of something else to say to this poor creature. She could hardly know or care about politics or the fashions of the day, and her concerns for her home and family in the wilderness were equally foreign to ourselves.

At last Miss Mary remembered the basket on my arm. "We have brought you some food," she said, motioning for me to set it down on the straw mattress. "Are you hungry?"

Frankie Silver looked away, and I fancied that her pride was struggling with her hunger. The mountain people are shy about accepting favors from anyone; they do not care to be *beholden*, as they call it. A curious attitude, I have always thought, whereas we gentlefolk of the lowlands take care that everyone in our circle of acquaintances should owe us a debt of gratitude for something, be it a dinner party given for a traveling gentleman, or a political appointment arranged for the son of a prominent neighbor. We take care to see that these loans of influence and hospitality are repaid in kind and issued again to a widening circle of acquaintances, for such is the currency of polite society. Frankie Silver would not understand the mechanics of a system of interlacing benevolences. But she was hungry.

"I'm afraid you will have to eat it now," I told her. "Mr. Presnell will not want us to leave the basket or its contents here when we leave."

"Please don't worry about us," said Catherine. "We have had our dinner."

We stepped away from the camp bed to let her approach it, much as one might leave scraps for a stray dog who was shy of people. Mrs. Silver sat down on the straw mattress and began to look through the contents of the basket.

"Thank you," she said softly, looking away from us. "You're right kind to do this." She balanced a chicken leg between her fingers and began to tear chunks out of its brown flesh. We fidgeted in silence, not wanting to stare but finding little else to do.

"Do they feed you well in here?" asked Miss Mary.

The prisoner gulped down a morsel of chicken before she answered. "Tolerable," she said. "A deal of corn mush, and sometimes a little meat in a stew. Hardly nothing fresh, though." She sighed. "I dream about tomatoes and onions. I used to tend the tomato vines up home, and keep the deer out by pelting rocks at 'em, and pick the bugs off the tomato leaves, and I'd watch the little green bobs get bigger every day, until finally they'd get red and soft and you could eat them. I reckon I could eat a bushel of them now. Eat 'til I foundered and my sides swole up with gas, like an old horse in a corncrib."

My sisters-in-law exchanged glances. This was not the sort of discourse they expected to have with a condemned prisoner, and since they had never been hungry in their lives, I am sure that they could find little to add to the conversation. I had been hungry, though, a few times after my father died, and I remembered well that feeling of emptiness that crowded all other thoughts out of one's head.

"With me it was always the apple harvest," I said, smiling. "Sometimes I couldn't wait for them to get ripe, and I'd eat the green ones and be sick as a pup."

She smiled and nodded, "Apples, too!" She looked like a child when the smile illuminated her features, and I thought for a brief moment that some mistake had been made. Surely this little girl was not the wicked murderess everyone talked about? She found the blackberry pie just then, and took a great bite out of the side of it, spilling purple juice down her chin and onto her breast. She wiped the stain away with the back of her hand and blushed. "I ask your pardon," she said. "But it's been a long time since I had pie."

She ate for a few more moments in silence, and then, the edge taken off her hunger, she began to study her visitors.

She swallowed a mouthful of food and said to Miss Mary, "That is one pretty dress, ma'am. I always wanted me a white dress with lace on't. Reckon I oughtn't to have one now." She nodded toward Catherine, in her widow's weeds. "Ought to wear black like you, ma'am."

Miss Mary and I glanced at each other, neither of us daring to enter into a discussion on the proper mode of etiquette for a widow who has become one by her own hand, so to speak. Catherine said gently, "Did you have a white dress for your wedding?"

The prisoner shook her head. "We got married after harvest, Charlie and me. We waited 'til the circuit rider came to meeting so we could stand up before him and make it all legal. Mama cut up one of her old calico dresses from back in Anson County and made me a new frock for the wedding. And Charlie's sisters Margaret and Rachel helped me weave leaves and daisies into a garland for my hair. It was over so quick, I hardly had time to think on it. They give a picnic supper for us, though, after. Folks brought beans, and yams, corn bread, and the last of the summer tomatoes. Silvers killed one of their cows for a barbecue. They roasted it on a spit over an open fire."

"Who butchered it?" The words rose unbidden to my mind, and I said them before I was even aware of it.

Frankie Silver's wide blue eyes turned on me with a careful stare. "I don't believe I've eat that much before or since," she said.

One blazing July day, when the air shimmered like creek water, distorting the shapes of the trees and hills in the distance, a letter arrived for me from Raleigh. It was addressed to *B. S. Gaither, Clerk of Sup. Court, Burke County, Morganton,* in the spidery copperplate script that is the hallmark of professional scribes and minions of the law. I knew exactly what it was, and I took a deep breath before slitting open the envelope, for it is a solemn thing to hold someone else's life in your hands.

A few lines in black ink, nothing more. I stood there in the red dust of the road, reading those words, for, unseemly as it was, I could not wait to walk back to the courthouse to read the verdict contained in that missive.

It is considered by the Court that the judgment of the Superior Court of Law for the county of Burke be affirmed. And it is ordered that the said Superior Court proceed to judgment and sentence of death against the defendant, Francis Silver. On motion judgment is granted against Jackson Stuart and Isaiah Stuart, sureties to the appeal, for the cost of this court in the suit incurred.

Jno. L. Henderson
Clerk of Supreme Court of North Carolina

I folded the letter and put it back among the other letters that had come for me that day. There's an end to it, I thought, but I could not help feeling saddened at this turn of events.

David Newland, the owner of the stagecoach line, stood nearby, watching me. Since he brings most of the news to Morganton, it is not unnatural that he should take an interest in it. "Bad tidings, Mr. Gaither?" he said, ambling over to join me.

"It is very bad indeed for Mrs. Silver," I said. "Her appeal has been denied."

He frowned. "So Mr. Woodfin was not able to persuade the justices to show her mercy?"

I hesitated, but I could see no way to evade the question, and I told myself that it was no business of mine anyhow. "According to the letter, Mr. Woodfin was not there."

"But who presented her case to the justices, then? Mr. Wilson has not left town these past weeks."

I could not meet his gaze, for I knew that I would see the outrage I myself felt mirrored in his eyes. "No one appeared on her behalf before the Supreme Court. The case was judged only on the merits of the written appeal." A document of some three and a half hundred words, cribbed together by me in weariness and haste on the night following the trial. Her life had depended on this brief and colorless cluster of words, and it had failed her.

David Newland's eyes widened. "She had no lawyer to plead her case in Raleigh? No one?"

I studied the wagon tracks in the red dust at my feet. "It's a long way to Raleigh," I murmured.

"Don't I own the stagecoach, by God? I know how far it is, Mr. Gaither. I know exactly. And if I had been hired by that poor girl's family to see her through her troubles, I would have kept my word, so help me I would, even if Raleigh was halfway to hell and stank of brimstone."

I could think of nothing to say that would not cast aspersions on my fellow attorneys, so I merely patted him on the arm and tried to summon a smile.

"Well, what must be done now?" asked Newland.

"Done?" I stared at him. "There is nothing to be done. The jury ruled, and the State Supreme Court has upheld their decision. It is all over now, except for the sentencing, which will come in the fall term of court, and then the execution that must follow."

"We'll see about that," Newland said.

"I beg your pardon?"

He sighed. "You know, Mr. Gaither, when we had that trial back in March, tempers were high around here, and I don't mind telling you that I was as eager as the rest to see that young woman hanged for her crime, but there has been talk around town lately. People are saying that Charlie Silver didn't amount to much, and maybe he got what was coming to him. They've been mulling this case over, and now I hear folks saying that a decent woman doesn't turn to violence but for one reason: to defend herself, or more likely her child. They had a little baby girl, as I recall."

"A daughter," I murmured. "Just over a year old when the murder took place."

Newland nodded triumphantly. "There you are. That set me to thinking, all right. Why didn't her lawyers admit she killed Charlie Silvers and then explain why?"

I sighed. It is difficult to explain the law to laymen. They seem to think that justice has to do with right and wrong, with absolutes. Perhaps when we stand before our Maker on Judgment Day, His court will be a just one, but those trials held on earth are not about what happened, but about what can be proven to have happened, or what twelve citizens can be persuaded to believe happened. Sometimes I think that the patron saint of lawyers ought to be Pontius Pilate, for surely he said it best: *What is truth?*

David Newland tugged at my sleeve. "You're a lawyer, Mr. Gaither. Why didn't they just tell us what happened instead of stonewalling with a plea of not guilty?"

I sighed. "It would have been a great gamble to have admitted her guilt in open court. There was no proof of self-defense, for there is only Mrs. Silver's word for it, and she was not at liberty to testify. Her attorneys must have felt it was safer to make the state prove her guilt on the circumstantial evidence, rather than admit that she did it, with no means to show provocation."

"Someone should have explained the situation to those judges in Raleigh."

"It wouldn't have mattered. The Supreme Court does not decide guilt or innocence. They rule on procedural matters. They cannot pardon as a governor can."

"A governor?" Newland winced. "I had occasion to meet Mr. Montfort Stokes in Wilkesboro last April. The trial was still fresh in our minds, and when I discussed the matter with him, I was dead set against a pardon. I told him she would deserve what she got, and I said the rest of the county was pretty much to my way of thinking. I believe I misspoke, though, and now I must put things right. The governor can be appealed to, and if Montfort Stokes can be made to see reason, she might yet be saved."

"It is worth a try," I told him.

"Will you write him, then?"

I shook my head. "It would not be seemly for a Superior Court clerk to protest a ruling from his own court." I did not like to think what Squire Erwin would say if I had undertaken such a measure. "I suppose I could sign a petition, though," I said. "As a private citizen. The letter will need to be accompanied by a petition showing wide support for the prisoner within the county."

"Who should write the governor then?"

Not I, I thought. I told him: "There is nothing to prevent an honest citizen from taking up the cause, and since you are the one who broached the matter with the governor, surely you are the person to plead her cause with him now. Could you manage such a letter, Mr. Newland?"

He looked at me shrewdly. "I might. There may be one or two gentlemen who could advise me on how to set forth my argument. And I have business in Raleigh in early September, so I shall take care to see that he gets it."

I smiled. "I'm sure that Governor Stokes's door is always open to the citizens of Burke County."

Several weeks later David Newland again waylaid me as I happened to be waiting for the stage. "I have it done!" he said proudly. "That letter to the governor. I have headed it 'Raleigh,' for I shall deliver it when I get there."

He handed me the letter for inspection.

Raleigh, 6 Sept. 1832

His Exelency

M. Stokes, whom I had the pleasure of seeing in Wilksboro some time in April last.

The circumstances of Mrs. Silvers killing her husband was named and you was told that a petition would be presented to you for her pardon. The petition has come in hand for your consideration. At the time aluded to in Wilksboro you claimed you did not know of there ever having been a female executed in N. Carolina & asked if I had—to which I answered in the negative. You then said you would be delicately situated & asked me my opinion. I answered that if rumor be true I thought her a fit subject for example.

But Sir from various information which I have rec'd since her trial I am induced to believe her gilt has been much exagerated which you will perceive by the opinion some gentlemen of the Bar whom has signed her petition & was present & also disinterested during her trial. Upon the whole I realy think her a fit subject for excitive Clemency.

Yours, sinsearly,

D. Newland

"It's a fine letter, Mr. Newland," I said, for if I helped him with its phrasing or altered his misspellings, I would have had a hand in the document, which I did not feel able to do. "I hope it may achieve its purpose."

He nodded happily. "The petition is done as well. You can see it has a goodly number of names on it. Some lawyers, and four of the jurors. The governor ought to sit up and take note of that." He said no more, but he watched me expectantly.

"I'm sorry, Mr. Newland," I muttered at last. I felt my cheeks redden as I spoke. "I do not feel able to add my name to the list of supporters. I do not know the circumstances of Charles Silver's death, and so I cannot say if his widow should go free or not."

Colonel Newland eyed me sadly. "You are dealing in justice, Mr. Gaither," he said. "I am dealing in mercy. I hope some day—before it is too late—you find that Mrs. Silver is deserving of both."

Burgess Gaither

SENTENCING

On the fourth Monday in September, the Superior Court of Burke County convened to hear the fall docket of cases. One minor matter in terms of the court's time, but uppermost in the mind of Morganton, was the sentencing of the convicted murderess Frankie Silver. Her time was drawing nigh, and already people were talking of the crowds that would flock to town for the execution. No woman had ever been hanged before in Burke County, or indeed anywhere that we had ever heard of, and excitement was running high at the prospect of such a cruel yet extraordinary spectacle. No traveling circus or tent revival meeting could rival the thrill of watching a pretty young woman die at the end of a rope, or so the local pundits said in the tavern. I seemed to be the only one present who had no wish to see such a dreadful event, but I kept my opinions to myself.

This was Will Butler's last Superior Court as sheriff. A county election would be held in November in conjunction with the presidential election and various statewide offices, and since sheriffs are not permitted to serve consecutive terms in North Carolina, Butler was already preparing to leave. He looked every inch a gentleman as he entered the courtroom that brisk autumn morning in a russet-colored waistcoat and shining brown boots, but his expression was that of a worried man, and I wondered what was amiss.

The courtroom was not as packed with spectators as it had

been for the trial of Frankie Silver, for no momentous crimes
were set to be tried and no sensational testimony was in the
offing, but since no court day goes unmarked by the curious
and the scandalmongers, there was no shortage of spectators
for the proceedings.

Gabriel Presnell brought the prisoner in through the great
double doors, and my first thought upon seeing her was that
her borrowed dress fit better now. Her collarbone, sharp as a
split rail, no longer protruded above the bodice of the garment, and she was not swallowed in a shroud of blue fabric
as she had been last spring. The months of incarceration
had left her rested and less gaunt than I had seen her at her
trial. *She eats better in prison than she did at home,* I
thought, and this saddened me.

I reminded myself that this woman had killed her husband
without pity or remorse, and that she had cruelly butchered
his body and left it as carrion for the scavengers of the sky
and forest. It is a crime past human forgiveness; only divine
mercy could pardon such a sin. But how odd that the
wickedness had left no mark upon her person: there was no
hardness in her features, no coldness of eye or scowl of unrepentant scorn. Her skin still held the blush of the summer
sun, and her pale hair was bound up into a knot at the nape
of her neck, framing her face with wings of gold. I remembered John Milton's poem *Paradise Lost,* wherein Satan is
described as the most beautiful of all the angels. Surely this
is Milton's parable made flesh, I thought, but I could not
wring any outrage from my heart, only regret and pity for a
frightened girl who would never see her child again. Nearly a
year had passed since the death of Charlie Silver, a man I
had never even seen. It is easy to forget the victim when he
is a stranger; it is especially easy to forget him when the accused is a forlorn and fragile creature who seems incapable
of evil. Perhaps this is why the law is so inflexible in its stric-
tures on punishment for those convicted of murder. The
blindness of Justice protects us lesser mortals from the
weakness of pity.

The prisoner followed the constable into the courtroom

with the same careful detachment that I had seen before, but when Thomas Wilson rose to greet her, she shrank back and I saw her eyes widen in surprise. An instant later her face was expressionless again, and she nodded to him with grave courtesy, but as the attorney turned to sit down again, I saw her eyes searching the courtroom. I did not think she was seeking the faces of her family.

Nicholas Woodfin is not here, I wanted to tell her. *He lives in Asheville, a long way from here, and he had no paying cases before the court here today. Besides, an attorney is not really needed at a sentencing hearing. There is nothing to be argued now.*

I saw her set her lips in a tight line, and I knew that she would not ask for her erstwhile champion, not even if they put the rope around her neck this very minute, but I wished that someone would explain the circumstances to her.

Thomas Wilson was a local attorney. He had attended this session of Superior Court because he had other clients to represent, but out of courtesy, or perhaps sympathy for this poor lost girl, he came to stand by her side for the formal delivery of the death sentence, so that she might have an arm to lean on if she needed it, or someone to comfort her in her hour of need. I was glad to see Wilson there, an unsmiling scarecrow in a black suit, but I liked him all the better for it. What a cruel thing it would be to stand up all alone among strangers to hear your death sentence passed.

I glanced about the courtroom. Although the hour of nine was already upon us, the judge had not yet appeared, which meant that we all must wait upon his pleasure with but little to do. I left the day's notes and papers at my desk and strolled over to Wilson, extending my hand as if it had been days since I had seen him instead of hours.

"Good morning, sir! I hope you and Mrs. Wilson are keeping well."

"Tolerable," said Wilson. A flicker of bewilderment crossed his face at my sudden effusiveness, but he shook my hand with perfect civility.

I inclined my head in the direction of Mrs. Silver to acknowledge her presence. To do more, I felt, would be unseemly, given the sad purpose for which we were assembled. She stared back at me without interest for a moment, and then she looked away, directing her gaze to the courtroom window, as she had throughout most of the trial.

"What do you hear from Mr. Woodfin these days?" I asked Thomas Wilson. Out of the corner of my eye, I saw her shoulders stiffen, and although she looked away quickly, I knew she was listening now.

"Nicholas Woodfin?" Wilson blinked, wondering no doubt what had possessed me to inquire of him. "Why, I believe that he is well. I have not heard otherwise."

"Nor have I," I said heartily for the prisoner's benefit. "No doubt he is very busy with his legal practice these days, for he is an excellent trial lawyer. I think that we shall not see him today, though. I have the court docket, and I know that none of those who stand trial here today are represented by him." I paused to make sure my words had sunk in. "For those who have already been convicted, no doubt Mr. Woodfin can help them more effectively outside the courtroom, with his letters and his influence."

"No doubt," said Wilson with a trace of asperity. "Good day, then." Thomas Wilson is an able lawyer, but not much given to subtlety, and I am sure he thought my conversation was the babble of an eccentric. His client understood, though, for she gave me the faintest smile, and I took my leave of them.

I resumed my place at the front of the courtroom, and we waited for the circuit judge. That dour Scotsman John R. Donnell, who had presided over the trial of Frankie Silver, had served out his tenure in the Western District, and he had been replaced by a newly designated judge who was no stranger to the far reaches of the piedmont: Mr. David Lowry Swain of Asheville. I had never met him, but I knew him by reputation as an able and ambitious man. In anticipation of his visit to Morganton, I had overheard several persons in town mention the story of his naming that I had heard from Elizabeth: Swain was called David Lowry in memory of his mother's first husband, who had been killed by Indians on the Georgia frontier. I remembered, too, that when David Swain was an up-and-coming young attorney in Asheville, Nicholas Woodfin had read law under him before passing the bar himself.

I wondered what Mr. Swain would make of this fragile young woman who waited to be sentenced to death. Had the judge heard about her case from his former associate Mr. Woodfin? I did not see what difference it could make, though. The jury had spoken, the State Supreme Court had upheld their decision, and the judge—whoever he was— would have no choice but to set the date for the execution.

I looked at my watch. Nearly half past. Where was Mr. David Swain? Had anyone seen him in town? I searched the faces in the courtroom until I found Will Butler at the back, near the oak doors, talking with one of the constables. The look on the sheriff's face told me that he was as mystified as the rest of us. I slipped away from my desk and went to confer with him.

"Is there any news of the judge, Mr. Butler?"

He shook his head. "Yesterday's stage brought me no letters. I am at a loss to know what has become of him. The weather is not to blame."

I glanced at the sun-glazed windows above us. The day was fine, as its predecessors had been for a long stretch of Indian summer. No storms had flung down tree limbs in the path of the Raleigh stagecoach, and no swollen rivers had made the fords impassable. "Perhaps His Honor is ill," I said to Butler.

"*His Honor* is thirty-one years old," said the sheriff. "I doubt if his health prevents his coming. It is more likely to be his ambition that trammels him. Something must be afoot in the state capital." He looked at his pocket watch. "I will give him until the hour, and then we will adjourn for the day on my authority. Does that meet with your approval?"

"We can hardly do otherwise," I said. "If there is no judge to preside, the cases cannot go forward."

The voices rose higher and higher as the hour drew

nearer, and I could hear people wondering aloud over the judge's absence. At last Will Butler's voice crested the roar, and he bellowed out: "I hereby declare this session of the Superior Court adjourned until tomorrow, due to the absence of the judge."

There were a few groans of protest, probably from those who had ridden great distances to attend the session, and who would now have to pay for a night's lodging or sleep rough in order to come to court tomorrow. We waited while the spectators dwindled away, until finally only the sheriff, the prisoner, Thomas Wilson, and I were in the courtroom. In the doorway a constable was waiting for the signal to escort Mrs. Silver back to her cell.

I could see that she was puzzled over this turn of events. She touched the sleeve of Mr. Wilson's black coat. "Why didn't he come?"

The lawyer smiled. "Oh, some trifling delay upon the road, like as not, madam. A lame horse, a broken carriage wheel. It is a long way to Morganton, you know. He will turn up this evening, I do not doubt." He meant to be reassuring to the prisoner; no doubt he had not considered the implications of the judge's arrival.

"What if he don't come?"

Thomas Wilson gave her an oily smile. "But I am sure that he will."

The next day the courtroom was again filled with anxious prisoners and idle spectators awaiting justice at the pleasure of the lowland bureaucracy. This time, when the hour of nine had come and gone, there were murmurings about the courtroom. "I suppose the judge has better things to do than to come to our neck of the woods!" someone called out.

"Probably afraid of the Indians!" someone else called, and the laughter overcame the grumbling, for one might as well be afraid of the Phoenicians in these parts nowadays.

Will Butler paced the floor, taking out his watch and glancing at it so often that I wondered why he bothered to put it away. Inevitably a fistfight broke out in the back of the room: bored farmers with a few drinks in their bellies are not the most patient of men. When the sheriff saw that the fright was in earnest, and that it bid fair to spreading among the rest of the congregation, he rapped on the bench for order and bellowed out, "I declare this court adjourned until the spring term—*dammit*." That last word was uttered under his breath, so that only I overheard him, and I did not have time to discuss his ruling before he plunged into the melee wearing a curious look of satisfaction that made me think that quelling the insurrection would serve as a tonic to his own frayed nerves.

It was Butler's last significant act as sheriff of Burke County, for within weeks John Boone would assume the post of peace officer of the county, a duty for which he now had scant enthusiasm. Will Butler's continuance of the case of Frankie Silver ensured that his successor, not he, would have to hang the prisoner. I think, though, that both of them were playing for time, believing that the petitions and letters to Governor Stokes would surely result in a pardon, so that the dreadful sentence would not have to be carried out by anyone.

The courtroom began to empty.

"What does it mean?" Mrs. Silver sat looking up at her black-clad attorney. Her pale face wore an expression of guarded hope, as if she scarcely dared to believe what she thought must be true.

"You have the gift of six months," Wilson told her gravely. "I pray that you will use it wisely, madam, in prayer and meditation. Court will meet again in March."

"It's over?"

"It is called a continuance, madam." The lawyer's voice bristled with annoyance, no doubt because his time was being wasted to no good end by a young puppy of a judge who cared little for the concerns of the western reaches of North Carolina. David Swain's ambitions lay in Raleigh, and no doubt he had deserted our country courthouse to further his own aims.

"What must I do?"

"You must wait, Mrs. Silver, like the rest of Burke County.

Good day." Thomas Wilson gave her a slight bow and nodded
to the jailer, who had come forward with the shackles to take
the prisoner back to jail.

David Newland appeared, with a smile of triumph. "This
has been the best day's work Will Butler ever did!" he announced. "He has managed to stall the case until spring, and
has thus given the governor time to issue the pardon. I have
no doubt that he will do it."

I motioned for him to keep his voice down, for I saw little
Mrs. Silver walking slowly toward the door and glancing
back at us. I knew she was listening to Colonel Newland's
declaration: she lifted her head and took a deep breath, as if
a weight had been lifted from her back.

Newland, oblivious to my warning signal, prattled on. "Or
perhaps the thanks should go to young Judge Swain for this
extra time in which to prevent this execution," he was saying. "Quite providential of Swain not to turn up for this
court date." The colonel turned to Thomas Wilson. "Is it Mr.
Woodfin's doing, do you think, sir?"

The lawyer's face was white with anger. At last he said, "I
believe the word you used just now was *providential*, Colonel
Newland, and I judge it to be the correct one. I should thank
no one but Almighty God for this respite, if you are inclined
to think it a blessing. My prayers on that subject will be that
the prisoner not have her suffering prolonged by false hopes
and a protracted wait for a death that would be more merciful if it came quickly."

And so she was gone, locked away for another season to
pass the harvest, and then the winter, in that narrow cell,
and I'm afraid I gave little thought to her over the next several weeks, for we are busy enough at harvesttime. I know
that the ladies of Morganton continued to visit her, though,
for I have heard Elizabeth speak of it among her sisters.
They have made quite a pet out of the county's most notorious criminal, and I found myself wondering if the ladies
were basking in the melodrama of the doomed woman, or
whether they envied her the courage and determination she
showed in disposing of an unwanted husband. The men of

the county thought she had perpetrated a great wickedness, but I am not sure that the fair sex shared our thoughts on the matter. Many a man in the tavern was uneasy enough when the talk turned round to Frankie Silver, and those who professed the loudest that she should be hanged without delay were the very men who seemed the least respectful of their own wives. I wondered sometimes if brutish husbands behaved a little better that year because of the terrible example of retribution that Mrs. Silver had set before us.

Several weeks after the dismissal of court, elections were held and John Boone took his place as the newly elected sheriff. I am sure he thought that the case of Frankie Silver would be over and done with before he took office, but it lingered still, harrowing him with the dreadful possibility of an execution in his term. Other prominent citizens of the county were still trying to persuade state officials to listen to reason. True to his word, Thomas Wilson wrote a letter to the governor on behalf of his client.

> Statesville
> 19 November 1832

My dear Sir,

I hope you will pardon my troubling you with these few lines. The importance of the subject which I wish to mention will plead my justification. It is the condition of the unfortunate lady who is now confined in our jail at Morganton: Franky Silvers. She has been induced for some little time to believe a Pardon has been granted by your Excellency. This opinion has got abroad through a misunderstanding of Col. David Newland.

It is not necessary that I should multiply in words or reasons why I think she should win a pardon. Suffice it to say that I have no hesitation in saying that the community expect her Pardon and I believe generally wish it. Mr. Joseph Erwin was present at the trial to whom I refer you. He, I know, at one time thought it a case very doubtful. I saw David Newland at Wilkesboro & read the letter which Hugh M. Stokes wrote on that subject. I fully concur in sentiment with him as to the opinion of the community. There is certainly one, but few more, who think or wish her execution. It is believed by many that her Parents was very instrumental in the perpetration of that horrid deed. If so, shurely it is a powerful reason why the executive clemency should be extended to one of her age and condition.

I know, my dear sir, that you have often been reproached for extending the Ordinary Power vested in the Executive. You have nothing to fear from this approach: humanity is certainly one of the greatest attributes.

I do hope and trust, Sir, that if it is consistent with your duty and feelings toward a miserable wretch that you will grant her a Pardon if not already done, and forward same to me at Morganton. I did request our Sheriff Mr. Boone to speak to you on the subject. I know your engagements and fear that I have already wearied your patience.

Please accept the opinion of my highest esteem and regard for your welfare.

Th. W. Wilson

Montfort Stokes, who was in his final days as North Carolina's head of state, declined to reply.

In due course we found out why Judge Swain had not appeared to convene the fall term of Superior Court, and it proved to no one's surprise that our judgment had been accurate: the gentleman had pressing business in grander places than our country backwater. David Lowry Swain was running for governor.

He had resigned his judgeship in order to spend the autumn months campaigning for the office among his influential friends in Raleigh, while his duties to justice in the mountain counties lay forgotten, overshadowed by his ambition. When the news became known, this turn of events was remarked upon by various community leaders in Morganton, with varying degrees of approval. The most charitable remarks I heard concerning Judge Swain's candidacy were to the effect that perhaps it was a good thing, since Swain was a native of Asheville; perhaps, as a westerner himself, Swain could do some good for the oft-neglected mountain areas of North Carolina. Some said they would vote for him, and others were not so sure. Former sheriff Will Butler said that if Judge Swain's attention to duty as a circuit judge was any indication of his concern for his homeland, we would do better to elect a monkey as governor, for we could do no worse. I saw a great deal of sense in the sheriff's estimation of the situation, but I did not say so, for discretion is a lawyer's greatest virtue, and besides, I thought there was very little chance that a man from our part of the state would win anyhow, since the political power is and always has been concentrated in the eastern part of the state.

David Swain did win, though. He was not chosen in the general election, which was held in November. At that time Andrew Jackson was reelected president, much to the consternation of a number of gentlemen in Burke County, and to Swain himself, who had bitterly opposed Jackson's politics, but our local yeoman farmers were happy enough to hear of Old Hickory's success, for he was a man of the people, and from these parts himself, and a few of them even vowed to make the long ride to Washington to attend the party for his inauguration in January. Then, in December, the politicians in Raleigh appointed David L. Swain to a special one-year term as governor of North Carolina, so in the end no one got to vote for him, but he became governor all the same, and in the main Will Butler was wrong about David Swain's attitude toward the mountain counties. He was to prove a loyal friend to his home region, and he favored the advancement of the railroads into the western territories of the state, which would be a great boon to progress for the region, but he did not right all the wrongs in our portion of the state. Not by any means.

"Mrs. Silver is quite delighted to hear of Governor Swain's election to office," Elizabeth remarked at breakfast one morning early in the new year of 1833. "My sister Mary tells me that she wept for joy when she was told."

I replied that I had not realized that Mrs. Silver took such an interest in politics, particularly since she was not likely to live long enough to enjoy the governor's performance.

Elizabeth raised her eyebrows. "You are quite a bear this

morning, Mr. Gaither," she said. "Did last night's rum punch not agree with you?"

"It is wearing out its welcome," I admitted, "but that does not alter the fact that I am concerned about all the attention you ladies are paying Mrs. Silver. She is quite unused to the society to which you expose her in your visits, and I do not know what she makes of all of you. Still, she should be using this time wisely to prepare her soul for the Hereafter, and I think you ladies are at best a distraction from that purpose."

Elizabeth laughed. "But she is not yet twenty! She has a long time to prepare for eternity."

"She has until March, and perhaps six weeks thereafter, for preparations to be made, and the execution to be carried out. A sentencing hearing is merely a formality, Elizabeth. There will be no new evidence, no jury, no appeal. It is a matter of scheduling, nothing more. Her fate has already been decided."

My wife favored me with a tolerant smile. "Her fate was decided before the new governor was appointed. Now, of course, everything has changed."

"Nothing has changed."

"But of course it has, dearest! David Swain of Asheville is now the governor of North Carolina. In short, he is one of us. And you must not forget that Mrs. Silver's own attorney, Nicholas Woodfin, read law under Mr. Swain. A personal appeal can be made. That's how these things are done."

Elizabeth smiled at me, the gentle, condescending smile of an Erwin with four aces. Her grandfather Sharpe had been a member of the Continental Congress, and she counted generals, legislators, and wealthy planters in her bloodline. Who was I to tell her that she was mistaken? So I merely nodded and let it pass. I was thinking, though, that if Mistress Elizabeth Erwin Gaither took an ax to her husband, she could very well get herself pardoned by her father's good friend the governor, but it was not so with Frankie Silver. All the influential supporters in the world could not make her a woman of substance. And the sheltering wing of the Erwin ladies might not be enough to save her.

Chapter Six

Spencer Arrowood had not been to church in many months, but this Sunday, despite his difficulty in getting around and the doctor's misgivings about his leaving the house so soon, he had come. His family had belonged to the little white frame church for generations, and he felt that any thanks offered up for his continued existence should be said here. As usual, though, he came more with the intention of making additional requests than in thankfulness for mercies already bestowed.

The sight of so many people whom Spencer had known for most of his life was reassuring to him in his new awareness of mortality, as if their concern and good wishes could keep death at bay for a little while longer. He sat in the pew beside his mother, uncomfortably warm in his navy sport coat and tie, still pale and weak from his injuries, but trying to seem as if nothing were amiss. From time to time members of the congregation smiled and waved to him from neighboring pews, and he tried to smile back, but perhaps he had ventured out too soon. He felt light-headed, and impossibly tired from the short walk from the car to the sanctuary. It was as if old age had overtaken him in the course of an hour, but this time, when he was well again, he could go back to youth. He wondered what it would be like when he was old for good, past going back. Perhaps he would not live to find out.

When the service began, the comforting rhythm of the ritual washed over him without his being aware of the sense of the words. He stared up at the stained-glass window of the plump Victorian angel guiding a boy and girl over a bridge. As a child he had loved the radiant image, but its cloying sentimentality could not reach him now. He became distracted by the rhythms of his own body: the thud of heartbeat, the prickles of sweat on his forehead, the clump of bandage just above his waist which itched beneath his starched blue shirt. His body had become a clock ticking off the seconds of his allotted time until he reached the abyss, and the bridge that he would have to cross, angel or not.

He was thinking that in twelve more days Fate Harkryder would go to the electric chair. While the opening hymn was sung, Spencer was standing silent, oblivious to the words, working out the number of hours in twelve days. Another part of his mind was wondering if he ought to try to talk to the condemned man on the eve of the execution. What was there to say, though? Please tell me that you did it, so that I'll feel better? Why should he be allowed to feel better when in 288 hours Fate Harkryder would feel nothing at all.

He felt regret at the thought of a man's life being taken from him, and he forced an image of Emily Stanton's body into his mind to remind him that this man deserved his death, but it did not lessen the uneasiness, and he realized that he was picturing the sullen adolescent that he had sent to prison years ago. Let him see the canting, frightened killer who had grown old and hardened in confinement, and perhaps he would resign himself to letting the man go. He would be able to watch it happen.

Spencer had been sitting there thinking about the Harkryder case for some time, while the voices of the other parishioners faded into a hum at the back of his mind, when he realized that he was no longer in the sanctuary of the white frame church. He was standing in the shadows on a trail in the deep woods, and a small blond girl in a white dress was squatting a few yards away from him in the stony shallows of a mountain stream. The creek, forever shaded by deep woods, would be more melted ice than water, and even in summer it would be so cold that wading more than a few feet along the streambed would make your legs ache and your feet tingle, then go numb.

The pale girl was washing a white cloth in the swift, silver water. Her hair was a faded gold, and she was small-boned, a white shadow in the filtered sunlight of the forest clearing. She was leaning over the stream, submerging the cloth in the bone-chilling water. She seemed not to feel the cold on her fingers. She scrubbed the stained cloth against a flat rock in the streambed, intent upon her work and indifferent to the observer. After a moment she looked up at him, without a smile or a flicker of expression, just a look that said he was there, and he knew that she was Frankie Silver.

He tried to move toward her, but he found that he could not. When he opened his mouth to call out to her, she looked straight at him with narrowed eyes and a cold smile. Then she lifted the white cloth out of the water, and he saw the bloodstains that she had been trying to wash away.

When he came to himself, he was standing with the rest of the congregation, and the last strains of a hymn were dying away into silence. Spencer saw that his hymnbook was open to "Are You Washed in the Blood of the Lamb," and his mother had placed her hand on his arm and was shaking him gently.

"I'm all right," he murmured, rubbing his forehead to banish the last fragments of the dream. "I think I dozed off."

"I told you it was too soon for you to be out!" she hissed back.

"No. I'm all right. I just have too much on my mind, that's all."

People were beginning to file out of the pews now, and he realized that the service was over. It seemed to him that only a few minutes had passed since he'd gone into the church. Several of his mother's friends paused in the aisle to wish him well, and he shook white-gloved hands with a tentative smile. He hoped his mother had not invited company over for Sunday dinner. He was not equal to the small talk of village acquaintances.

"Blessed are the poor in spirit, Sheriff," said a soft voice beside him.

He turned to find that Nora Bonesteel, one of the oldest parishioners, had slipped into the pew behind them. She was tall and straight in her blue church dress with the gray wool shawl draped over her shoulders. Her hair, still more dark than silver, was pulled back in two wings framing her face, and drawn into a knot at the back of her head. She touched his arm and he suddenly felt cold. "The poor in spirit," he murmured, recognizing the Beatitudes. Miss Bonesteel had been his Sunday school teacher more years ago than either of them cared to remember. "For they shall see God."

The old woman smiled and shook her head. "You never could keep those verses straight, could you? It's: *For theirs is the kingdom of heaven.*"

He shrugged. "Well, I guess that's why I didn't see God."

"What did you see?"

People told tales about Nora Bonesteel, though nobody ever said she wasn't a good, righteous woman. She knew things, though. She saw things before they happened, and she had a way of knowing secret things no one would have dreamed of telling her. She didn't exactly meddle in other people's lives, but if you went to her for help, she always knew what it was you'd come about. The old folks claimed that Nora Bonesteel even talked to the dead, but Spencer could not let himself believe that, so he chose never to consider the matter at all. He had known her all his life.

What did you see?

"Frankie Silver." He blurted it out before he thought better of it. Nora Bonesteel had always been able to get the truth out of him, even when he was a sullen teenager who passed the few minutes between Sunday school and church sneaking a cigarette in the back of the churchyard with some of the older boys. Nora Bonesteel had put a stop to that one spring morning without so much as a word passing between them.

Frankie Silver.

Anyone else might have said, "Who?" or, "You must have been dreaming!" Or they might have passed the remark off as a joke, but Nora Bonesteel did none of those things. She considered the matter for a moment and nodded slowly.

"I have heard that she walks," she said. "Though I have never seen her myself. It's not surprising, though, is it?"

"No?" He could not believe that he was having this conversation in broad daylight in the sanctuary of the little white church. The place was nearly empty now. His mother had walked toward the door to speak to some of her friends, so there was no one to overhear them.

"They say that those who die by violence often walk. Hers was a cruel death."

"Do you know what really happened that night?"

Nora Bonesteel shook her head. "It's not for me to say. But if you have seen her, she means to tell you something, Spencer. You'd best find out what it is."

That night Spencer Arrowood sat in a circle of light at his dining room table with case-file papers and books of North Carolina history mingling in a pile in front of him. What was there about the Harkryder case that had reminded Nelse Miller of Frankie Silver? He couldn't see it. He didn't think Nelse had known the connection, either. It was a hunch of some sort that had never clarified itself in the old man's mind. Spencer hadn't taken much stock in such things in those days, but now, twenty years older and wiser, he believed that the intuition of an experienced cop could be counted as probable cause. If you lived long enough, you knew things just from instinct and observation.

By now Spencer had read all the material that the libraries could supply on the Silver case. Some of it was speculative, and most of it was repetitive, but he had read it all, and the connection between the legend and the Harkryder boy still eluded him. When he looked at the Silver case as a lawman would, he could see why Constable Baker had no choice but to arrest Frankie Silver for the crime. The jury had no alternative, either. Since the grand jury had not indicted the Stewarts, they were offered no other suspects on whom to cast the blame. During the trial Frankie Silver had given no explanation for the fact that she had lied about Charlie's whereabouts, or for the fact that his remains had been found in their own cabin. "Not guilty," she said. Take it or leave it. They left it. Had to. He understood all that. But his instinct told him that there was something terribly wrong with the case. Eighteen-year-old girls do not kill without provocation, and they don't cut up bodies.

He wondered what had really happened that night. Any explanation—no matter how lame—might have saved her, but she had sat there stone-faced and silent. *Not guilty.*

Lafayette Harkryder had done the same.

He had been given a court-appointed lawyer, not one as young as Nicholas Woodfin, but not much older, either. Perhaps the attorney had lacked the experience to mount a proper defense to the charges, but since the defendant had no money, he also lacked the resources necessary to generate reasonable doubt in the minds of the jury. No private investigators muddied the waters of evidence with favorable findings; no psychiatrists or forensic experts were employed by the defense to refute the state's witnesses. Fate Harkryder had not even been able to afford a suit jacket and tie to impress the jury with his respectability. He had sat in court in a red plaid flannel shirt and gray work pants, looking all the more barbaric in contrast to the sleek attorneys in their dark suits and crisp, starched shirts.

All that was fine with the sheriff, provided the defendant was guilty. Sometimes the law needed all the help it could get to worm a conviction out of bleeding-heart juries, but he didn't want to think that a man had been convicted of murder simply because he had violated the middle-class dress code. The penalty is greatest for breaking the laws that are unwritten.

Spencer pictured the courtroom. Fate in his worn plaid shirt, and his nervous young attorney, correct but bland, and himself in his brown deputy sheriff's uniform. Colonel Stanton had been almost as conspicuous as the lawyers in Wake County's little courtroom. He had understood the symbols of society's unwritten laws. He sat there day after day, ramrod straight, immaculate in his dress uniform, with every ribbon and medal on prominent display: the picture of solemn grief demanding justice. His wife was beside him most of the time, in a little suit and hat that would not have been out of place at a funeral or a church service. She had seemed a bit embarrassed to be there, blushing when anyone spoke to her and never looking at the defendant or the jury, but Colonel Stanton watched the proceedings with the alert gaze of a director viewing the dress rehearsal of the play. He took in everything, nodding when he agreed, and scowling when he did not. He took care to sit where the jury could not fail to see him, and perhaps because of his impressive looks and his air of command, they did seem to be watching him, testing their own reaction to a witness's testimony by checking Stanton's expression for approval.

What about the other victim's parents, Spencer thought. He tried to picture them in the courtroom, but the image would not be summoned. The Wilsons were elderly. They had come to court at least twice, Spencer knew, because he remembered speaking to them in the hall, but they were simple country people, and they had been overshadowed by the elegant Stantons.

Outside the courtroom, Charles Wythe Stanton had also been in command. He radiated confidence, and dignified outrage over his daughter's death. He was always ready to be photographed for the newspaper or to provide a sound bite for the television newsmen, and he would offer each reporter a poignant snapshot of pretty Emily. "She must not be forgotten," he would say with a moist smile. "This trial is not just about that monster in there. It is about what Emily deserves, too, in exchange for her life."

Spencer admired the man for his poise in the face of the media. He'd had the microphone shoved in his face a few

times during the course of the trial, and he knew that pro-
jecting an image of courageous intelligence was harder than
it looked. The old sheriff, though, wanted nothing to do with
the Stantons. More than once he refused their offers to take
the officers to lunch.

"That man is a creature of vengeance," Nelse Miller remarked to his deputy, after court recessed on the third day.
"Lafayette Harkryder might just as well have killed one of
the Disney Mouseketeers and been done with it, because this
smooth-talking snake-oil man is going to hound him to the
outskirts of hell. If you ever kill anybody, Spencer, make sure
that they don't have a damn bloodhound for a daddy."

"That's how I'd want my kin to act if I had been murdered,"
Spencer replied. "Stanton has a right to demand justice."

"I know he does. I'm just not sure that you can take one
day of a person's life, draw a line, and judge him on it."

"We do it every day," said Spencer. "Yesterday I gave a
speeding ticket to a member of the church choir."

Nelse Miller shook his head. "I'm getting old," he said. "I
keep thinking the world would be a better place if there were
less justice and more charity."

Nelse Miller had fulminated through the entire trial,
prompting Spencer to ask more than once, "Which side are
you on?" One day the old sheriff might be carping about
Colonel Stanton holding court before the media. Another
time he remarked: "Have you ever noticed that you can tell
which side a person is on in this case by the way they're
dressed?"

That was true enough.

The Stantons and their supporters always dressed in what
Nelse Miller called "Episcopal uniforms," while the Harkryders, who had no notion of showing their respect for the
court—or perhaps they were—turned up in clothes that
Spencer wouldn't have worn to a yard sale: old stained work
clothes, T-shirts with rude sayings printed on the front, and
occasionally camouflage hunting outfits. Fate Harkryder's
mother was dead, but various other female relatives turned
up from time to time, usually in bright print slacks and

cheap blouses laden with dime-store beads. The jury wasn't supposed to notice such things, but inevitably they did.

Spencer's clearest memory of the trial was the solemn, chiseled features of Colonel Stanton on one side of the courtroom, and sullen, scraggly Fate Harkryder on the other. Every day his two older brothers sat near the front of the courtroom, almost within touching distance of the defendant. They, too, glowered throughout the proceedings, muttering ominously when they disagreed with the witness testimony. Spencer kept his eye on them throughout the trial, watching for the bulge of a weapon in their clothing, or some sign that they meant to cause trouble.

When the verdict was announced, one of the brothers shouted, "It's a damned lie!"

Spencer and the bailiff hurried to put themselves between the prisoner and his family, anticipating more than a shouting match, but Fate Harkryder had simply looked at his brothers for a long moment and shaken his head.

They subsided once more into smoldering resentment. "We'll fight this, boy," one of them muttered.

"You hang tough," said the other one.

Fate Harkryder nodded.

By the time he was led handcuffed from the courtroom, his brothers were already gone. Spencer wondered if he had ever seen them again. Whatever happened to the Harkryder brothers, anyhow?

Fate Harkryder had twenty years' experience in not letting his feelings show. He sat impassively in the blue padded chair, studying the man in the green necktie who sat across from him. He was a stocky fellow in his early forties, with unruly dark hair and a tendency to perspire. He was smiling uncertainly, and creasing the corners of his paperwork. Fate was trying to decide why the man was nervous. Some people felt uneasy in the company of a convicted murderer, but since this man was a state psychologist who often studied prisoners, his current subject didn't think the anxiety stemmed from that particular source. Race was not a factor, either. Fate decided that the man must be uneasy because he was talking to someone who would be dead in a few days' time. Death is considered bad taste in polite society. People do not care to be reminded of it. Now that Fate had an execution date, even some of the guards had stopped looking directly at him, as if they were embarrassed by the presence of someone so close to the abyss.

The psychologist managed a tentative smile as he pushed his glasses farther back along the bridge of his nose. "Now, Mr. Harkryder," he said, "my name is Dr. Ritter. I don't wish to alarm you in any way. I just wanted to have a talk with you to see if there are any concerns you'd like to voice."

"Concerns?" Fate blinked at him. He had found that playing dumb was an asset in prison life. It gave you more time to evaluate your opponent, and sometimes it caused him to underestimate you, which was even more useful.

"Yes. As you know, your—er—your execution is scheduled for later this month, and barring any unforeseen developments, it will take place at that time. I wondered if you'd like to express your feelings."

"I'm innocent, sir."

The psychologist looked away. "I know nothing whatever about the details of your case, Mr. Harkryder. I find it easier to counsel prisoners if I am not apprised of what they have done. My only concern is your peace of mind at this point in time."

"Well, sir, they're going to kill me. How do you think I feel?"

Ritter was ready for that one. "There are many possibilities, Mr. Harkryder. You might feel relief that your long stay in prison is at an end. You might embrace the opportunity to atone for your misdeeds. You might take solace in religion and look forward to peace and joy beyond this life."

"Or I might think that this life is all there is, and I've been cheated out of it by a state that framed me for a murder I didn't commit."

"I had hoped you might be beyond that," sighed the psychologist. "I realize that death is a very difficult thing to accept. That's why we tend to concentrate on the little rituals that precede it as a way of distracting ourselves from the prospect of the death itself. Would you like to discuss some of those items?"

"Like what?"

"Well, to begin with a trivial one—why don't you tell me what you'd like as a last meal?"

Fate Harkryder shrugged. "I haven't given it much thought," he said. He had, of course. Back in Building Two, discussions of his last meal had been going on for weeks. After a while he began to notice that the suggestions from the other men tended to fit a pattern. They urged him to ask for steak and a milk shake; country-style steak, french fries, and strawberry shortcake with double whipped cream; a large pizza and a banana split. It was all comfort food—the dream menus of teenage boys, or of men whose last memories of happiness stretched that far back in their lives. It was food rich in grease, salt, and sugar, proposed by men who had lived for years on a bland, starchy diet that never quite filled them up.

Other suggestions were a poor man's idea of a high-class meal. The farm boy who had suggested a pound of shrimp, a pound of lobster, and a pound of prime rib had never tasted any of those things. Fate had no better ideas about what he should ask for on the night of his execution, and he was by no means sure that he could swallow a single mouthful of whatever was brought to him, but at least he prided himself on knowing why his comrades suggested the menus they did. After twenty years in confinement, he thought he might be as much of a psychologist as the perspiring man who sat across from him now.

"No thoughts on a last meal," Dr. Ritter was saying. He made a notation on his legal pad. "Let's leave that then, shall we? You have plenty of time to consider that option. Now, is there anyone you would like to see in the coming days? Anyone you would wish us to contact?"

A hooker, he thought. Names of various shapely movie stars ran though Fate Harkryder's mind, but he no longer felt in a playful mood. Besides, he was sure that the fat man had heard such feeble efforts at wit before, and was probably expecting them. He probably had his chuckle and his pat answer ready in his froggy throat. Fate decided that the conversation was beginning to bore him. He shook his head. "No one."

"A relative, perhaps? Is your mother still living?"

"She died when I was eight."

"Your father, then?"

"Lung cancer. Ten years back."

"I see. I believe you have brothers, though. Perhaps you'd like a visit from them?"

Fate Harkryder almost smiled. "Perhaps I would," he said. "Why don't you see if they'd like to come and say good-bye?"

"I can certainly do that," said Ritter smoothly. "Now let's talk about you for a moment. Are you experiencing any symptoms of undue anxiety? Loss of appetite, trouble sleeping?"

"*Undue* anxiety?" The prisoner stared at him. "The state of Tennessee is going to strap me into a chair and shoot electricity through my body until I burn to death from the inside out. Just what anxiety would you call undue?"

"You would do well to remain hopeful. You might possibly get a stay of execution," said the psychologist, ignoring the emotional outburst. "Meanwhile, we would hope that you can stay as calm and upbeat as possible under the circumstances. I can recommend sleeping tablets—in carefully controlled doses, of course—and perhaps some sort of tranquilizer for daytime use, if you feel that would help."

Fate Harkryder shook his head. "Keep the drugs," he said. "If I only have a few more days to spend being alive, I don't want to miss any of it. I intend to go down fighting."

Ritter's frown told him that he had misunderstood.

"Legally, I mean," said Fate. "Appeals. Motions filed in every court we can think of. Messages to the governor."

"I see. Meanwhile, if you'd like, we can discuss the incident that put you here. Would you like to tell me your side of it?"

"I don't believe I would."

The psychologist shrugged. "Some men find it easier to go to their deaths having made their peace with this world. Is there any bit of unfinished business that troubles you?"

"Not anything you can put right," said the condemned man.

Burgess Gaither

THE ESCAPE

They'll not hang a woman, folks kept saying, over and over like rain on a roof. You'll not hang, Frankie. I was a young girl, a proper married woman, the mother of an innocent babe. I was no madwoman crazed for blood, nor no town whore robbing a young blade and adding killing to the slate of her sins. You'll not hang. And I carried myself meek and mild every time the court met, with my hair combed smooth, and my dress as clean and fitten as I could get it. "She's a pretty little thing!" the men would say when I passed by. "She don't look like no Jezebel." And I would keep my head down low and pretend not to hear them, for it was all a game, and if I could not tell the truth flat out to that court full of strangers and be done with it, why then I must play their game and take care to win.

I had done good. The fine town ladies brought me pies and came and sat with me and read out the Bible in my cell, and I was thankful, for they were kind, but the tales I liked best were the fairy stories that my mama used to tell me. There was one about a beautiful princess who was walled up in a tower, and a handsome prince rode up and saved her. When my mama told the story, the princess had long golden hair like mine, and the prince was a dark-haired man with a big house and all the money he needed. I didn't ask for the ladies to tell me stories like that, for it wouldn't have been fitten, but I thought about them all the same, to myself, and to pass the time I pretended that I was the princess in that tower, a-waiting to be saved.

The ladies told me that people were working hard to get me a pardon. They were writing letters to Governor Stokes, begging him for mercy, and there was talk of getting up a letter signed by half the county, asking that my life be spared.

Governor Stokes left office at the new year, and the new governor was a man called David Swain, who came from Buncombe County, not far from here. Then the jailer's wife, Sarah Presnell, who wasn't one for making fine promises, she came to my cell with the news, and she said, "Happen you'll be all right now, Frankie, for the new governor is from these parts, and he'll be made to listen to all the folks who won't stand to see you hang." The other ladies of Morganton came and said the same. They told me that even the jury was sorry they had ordered me hanged, and that some of them had signed their name to the paper asking the governor for mercy. I reckoned it would be all right then, just like Mama said. I sat through the winter thinking about how big my baby Nancy was getting and wondering how many teeth she had, and if she was walking good yet. I reckoned I'd see her in the spring. She'd have to get to know me all over again, but at least we'd be together, when I got shut of this old town.

But then in March a new judge came, and he was old and sour, with a pinch-prune face and eyes like the pebbles in the creek bed, and he looked at me as if I were a shriveled-up old woman, and you could tell that he didn't think me a pretty little thing, but only a wicked murderess to be damned and sent to hell, and he was the one to do it.

He fixed the twenty-eighth of June as my day to die.

I never figured on dying in tomato time. Leaving my baby without a mama or a daddy to look out for her. Going into the cold clay while my teeth are still strong and my hair is yellow as moonlight. It don't seem right.

The ladies tell me that Daddy has been stumping around the county like a bear tied to a stake, trying to get some help for me. He went hat in hand to this colonel and to that gentleman, and they all gave him advice, but sometimes they'd say the opposite of one another. At last I reckon Daddy figured it was up to him to look out for his own. And what could I say when they came for me? I wanted to live. I wanted to feel the grass again on my bare ankles, and drink spring water.

So when they stood there in the night with the key to my cell a-dangling from Jack's hand, I didn't spare a thought for the governor or the fine ladies of Morganton with their pies and their petitions. I put on Jack's old shirt and breeches and blacked my face with coal dust, and I went with them.

The people in that town meant well, most of them, trying to help me with letters and such, but we don't take charity from strangers if we can help it. It's not our way. I'd rather trust a surefooted horse and a steep mountain than all the fine words in the world.

I know that people have said I must have known something about it, but upon my oath I did not. Though I should have guessed, perhaps. I had heard the story often enough, when people spoke of Eliza Grace McDowell. The family is proud of it, and perhaps they should be, but just lately it troubles me all the same.

It was a warm evening, the seventeenth of May, and I was pleased to see a red sunset, a sign that we should have no more of the spring rains that had blighted our days, muddied our roads, and made ponds of our fields for a good many days. I lingered on the courthouse lawn, talking with Sheriff Boone in the glow of the spring twilight. We were merely exchanging pleasantries, as I was leaving to go to Belvidere for dinner. I do not think we spoke of Frankie Silver, for her execution was still some weeks away, and I knew that the sheriff was uneasy in his mind about having to perform the grim task, and he did not care to talk about it. So it was apropos of nothing in particular when Boone said to me, "You know, Mr. Gaither, I have been thinking about John Sevier these past few days."

My mind was on other matters, I suppose. I was thinking of the baby's cough, and of whether my old black coat would see me through another season, and I was wondering whom

I should be put next to at dinner this evening, for I was too tired for sparkling inanities with the ladies or the sober political doomsaying of my elders. "John Sevier," I said, to show that I was listening. I barely glanced at Sheriff Boone, for I was anxious to begin the evening, if only to see it over with. "A hero of the Battle of King's Mountain. Sevier was a fine, bold fellow, and a patriot."

"Perhaps too bold," said the sheriff. "But I believe he was a good man nonetheless."

I nodded. There were those who said that Sevier had been too cruel in his treatment of the Indians, but I hardly thought that John Boone would be concerned about such matters some thirty years after the fact. Then I recalled that Sevier had run off with another man's wife over in Tennessee, and I wondered if the sheriff was hinting at some domestic trouble of his own as yet undreamed of by his neighbors. Surely not! Not wishing to hear treacly confidences from this somber old fellow, I eased the subject along a new path. "John Sevier. Indeed, sir, Old Nolichucky Jack was a credit to this country, whatever his personal faults, but, Sheriff, I believe that if we talk of the region's favorite sons, surely it is your uncle whose fame has spread throughout the world, and whose star will burn the brightest and longest in memory. Rightly so."

John Boone blushed and nodded. The sheriff is the nephew of the great pioneer Daniel Boone, but he himself is a kindhearted and modest man, not much given to boasting about his lineage, and I wondered what had prompted his musings on long-dead heroes. I made one or two other inconsequential remarks praising the pathfinder of Kentucky, to which he made little reply, and then I took my leave of the sheriff. I left him standing in the twilight, and now that I think back on it, the old fellow looked as if he had something more to say to me but didn't quite know how to begin. I left him thus, with his piece unsaid.

I realize now, of course, what had put the thought of John Sevier into his head. It was not Sevier's exploits in the Revolution that John Boone had been thinking of, nor of his elopement with Susannah Tipton, but a later incident, much closer to home. Nearly fifty years ago—before the time of Sheriff Boone and myself, but an incident still talked about—John Sevier and his supporters had wanted the mountain country to rid itself of North Carolina's owner-ship. He had ample justification for this, I am sure, because North Carolina had been willing to cede the western lands to the federal government in payment of its war debt from the Revolution. We are a neglected section of the state even to this day. The State of Franklin was formed from the east-ern counties of what is now Tennessee, and Sevier became its governor. Four years later the bold endeavor to form a new state collapsed in political infighting, and in 1788 the state of North Carolina sent a party of armed men to arrest John Sevier, to be tried on a charge of treason.

He was brought in chains over the mountains to Morganton—a sad plight for one of the great leaders in our war for independence. The sheriff of Burke County at the time, William Morrison, had served with Sevier at King's Mountain, and he was appalled that his old commander should be treated thus by order of the craven politicians in Raleigh. Sheriff Morrison struck off the prisoner's chains, and granted him bail so that he might remain in Morganton, but not under lock and key, awaiting trial. The bond money was put up by the grandfathers of Eliza Grace McDowell. These old soldiers, Charles and Joseph McDowell, were themselves brothers, and also brother officers of John Sevier's, one a colonel and the other a general in the Revolution.

Sevier must have had powerful enemies in North Carolina government, or perhaps the politicians merely wished to make an example of anyone who would question the state's authority. They meant to hang John Sevier, right there in Morganton, but that faithful old soldier-turned-sheriff William Morrison would have none of it. Before the court could be convened, word went out to John Sevier's son that his father was at liberty within the town, but in peril of his life come the trial date. By and by, Sevier's brother and his son John Jr. rode into town with some of his supporters, leading Sevier's favorite saddle horse. Young Sevier found his father in the tavern with his old comrades, the McDowells of Quaker Meadows. "I've come to take my father home, sirs," the young man told his father's companions.

The McDowells wished John Sevier Godspeed, and they watched him ride off with his faithful friends toward the Yellow Mountain Road, which would take them at last into Tennessee and away from the jurisdiction of the state of North Carolina. No posse ever set out to bring them back. Nothing more was ever done by the sheriff of Burke County or by the state of North Carolina to prosecute John Sevier. Indeed, in the autumn of the very next year, Sevier was elected to the North Carolina Senate, and he took his place in that august body and was present when the legislators voted to reinstate his rank of brigadier general. It was as if he had never been a shackled prisoner and the object of North Carolina's vengeance.

Surely that was the incident in John Sevier's life that John Boone had been thinking of—not the war, not the attempt to secede from North Carolina, not the incident with the Tennessee lady, but the escape from the Burke County jail. The successful, unpursued escape from the very jail that Sheriff John Boone was now sworn to guard. Sometimes justice can best be served by avoiding the process of the law.

Frankie Silver escaped from jail that night.

Many stories were put about as to how she was able to flee, and I cannot say with any certainty which story is true. Everyone agreed that intruders had entered the building through a basement window and had unlocked the cell by means of a key. It seemed to have been done in stealth, for there was no battle between guards and rescuers. The most fanciful storytellers claimed that Frankie Silver's brother Jack had made a wax impression of the lock of her cell door, and that he carved a key that would fit that lock, but I have never put much faith in that tale myself. I think—though I should never dream of saying it, much less trying to prove it—that a kind and scrupulous man could not bear the thought of hanging that poor, friendless little girl, and so, taking his text from the example of his predecessor Sheriff William Morrison, this gentleman left his own keys where the friends of the prisoner might get at them and thus spirit her away—perhaps, like John Sevier, to Tennessee, and then onward to the great empty Western lands, where she could disappear forever, beyond the reach of North Carolina's terrible revenge. Or justice. Call it what you will.

The next morning word of Frankie Silver's escape spread around the county as fast as a horse could run. I was sitting peacefully at the breakfast table when a commotion in the hall alerted us to the presence of an urgent visitor, and one of the young constables burst in past the servant to tell me the news. I set down my cup and stared at the fellow. He fairly danced on the handwoven rug in his muddy boots, rifle in hand, and he had not even remembered to take off his hat when the servant let him in the front door. "She's fled in the night, Mr. Gaither!" he said, and his eyes were bright with excitement as if he were announcing a fox-hunting party rather than a grim search for a killer. "Frankie Silver has broke out of jail!"

I stared at him for one stricken moment, thinking a dozen thoughts at once. Finally I managed to say, "Was anyone hurt in the escape?"

He shook his head. "No one knew she was missing until they saw her cell empty this morning. Spirited clean away! Some of us are riding out in hopes of picking up her trail. Will you be going with us?"

I looked across the table at my wife's expression of dismay. She had clapped one hand to her mouth, as if determined to keep from crying out in protest of my going. I had no intention of doing so, however. Surely Elizabeth did not imagine that a respectable country lawyer and clerk of court would abandon his day's business to go haring through the mountain wilderness with a horde of vigilantes? After the spring rains, the roads would be indistinguishable from the creeks. And what would her father the squire say if the fine saddle horse he had given me as a wedding gift came back lame from such a fool's errand?

"I leave the chase in your capable hands, Jack," I told the constable. "As an officer of the court, I should stay in town. There may be warrants to be drawn up, or other legal matters that need tending to."

He saw the sense in this—indeed, he saw more sense in this than there was, for I foresaw no legal business that would require my presence—but the excuse satisfied him, and presently Elizabeth and I were able to return to our breakfast in peace, though neither of us had much appetite for it any more.

"She has escaped from jail!" said my wife in a tone of wonder. "I cannot believe it! How could she manage such a thing?"

"With help, no doubt." It was not my place to speculate on such matters, and I keep my thoughts to myself. Elizabeth has too many sisters to confide in.

"But who could have helped her?"

I smiled, thinking again of John Sevier. "Perhaps it was Eliza Grace McDowell, my dear. Her family seems to make a practice of it."

"Oh, Burgess, do be serious!" I don't know whether Elizabeth took my meaning or not. I did not remind her of the incident. At last she said, "Do you think they will catch her?"

"I hope not," I said, before I thought better of it. I realized that my reluctance to see the prisoner recaptured was the real reason that I had been unwilling to join the searchers—though I am sure that I would have been of little use to the seasoned hunters and woodsmen who were on her trail. I did not want her found. So much simpler to let the prisoner disappear into the wilderness of Tennessee, as John Sevier once did a generation ago. Then John Boone would not have to dread the grim duty of hanging a woman, and we could end all of the clamoring to young Governor Swain, whose concerns lie elsewhere. Besides, if they caught Frankie Silver, I felt sure that it would go hard on her father and brother, who surely took her away—but it might also cause harm to the person who let her go. Such a trial would divide Morganton into hostile opposing camps, and such a rift would profit nothing. So, guilty or innocent, I wished Mrs. Silver Godspeed in her flight across the mountains, and I prayed that I might never see her again.

Her escape was a nine days' wonder in our little country town. People seemed to talk of nothing else, and they never tired of speculating on who might be responsible for the escape. I told no one of my conversation with John Boone, and he rode west with a search party, for it was his sworn duty to bring back an escaped prisoner, whatever his private feelings in the matter may have been.

I wonder if any of those searchers wanted to catch the prisoner because they thought she deserved to die, or if they were simply acting on impulse, like hounds who will chase anything that runs, simply because it runs. It was a game of hide-and-seek, with the trackers pitting their skills against the wiles of the elusive prey. I am sure that there was a great deal of shouting and boasting and drinking done by the posse, and that in the end it all seemed such a great sport to them that they forgot the deadly purpose of their chase.

She was not taken easily. Day after day went by with no word from the searchers, and news of the escape spread far beyond the borders of Burke County. Colonel Newland said that even the Raleigh newspaper carried an article about the missing prisoner, and we knew that other lawmen from the neighboring counties had joined in the search. Still, it had been a good many days since her escape, and it seemed likely that she was gone for good.

"Seven days," Miss Mary announced at dinner one night. "Surely she is out of reach by now. The Tennessee border is four days' ride at most, is it not?"

The squire gave his daughter a reproving glare. Such things are not talked of before white linen and crystal. "Are you referring to the escaped murderess, my dear?"

"Of course she is, Father," said Elizabeth. "We can talk of nothing else! We are quite beside ourselves with worry."

"I don't think you need worry," her father replied. "I do

not believe that Mrs. Silver will break in to Belvidere and take an ax to us in our beds."

The Erwin women all stared at him for a moment's consternation before they burst into laughter. It is the squire's way of joking to pretend to misunderstand his wife and children, and then to allow himself to be instructed in the true significance of their remarks.

"Oh, really, Daddy!" said Delia, who is the baby of the family, nearly twenty, and a great pet of her father. "We do not think Mrs. Silver presents any danger to anyone. We are all *so* in hopes that she will get away!"

"Really?" said the squire in mock amazement. "You wish her to escape justice? Delia, my dear, has anyone informed your Dr. Hardy of your feelings regarding husband killing?"

Delia squealed and blushed prettily at the mention of her most ardent admirer, and the others began to laugh and tease her, and so the subject was forgotten. Later, however, as we were leaving the table, Miss Mary turned to me and murmured, "I hope that Delia will be more fortunate in her choice of a husband than Mrs. Silver was."

"There is no doubt of that," I said. "And as for Mrs. Silver, at least it has ended well. She has made her escape, and we can only hope that she deserved this second chance at life that she has been given. Even now she is probably safe in Tennessee, making plans to go west and picking the wild blackberries she spoke of so fondly."

"I hope that you are right," said Miss Mary. "But I shall continue to pray for her deliverance. Indeed, I will not rest easy about it until the hunt is abandoned and the last of the searchers has come back from the mountains."

"Do you not think that the governor would pardon her if she returns?"

My sister-in-law hesitated. "Very likely he would," she said. "But I think it is best not to put too much faith in men—or governments."

I heard the returning search party before I saw them. I had walked down to Newland's to see if the stagecoach had arrived yet, and just as I was crossing the street to have a word with the colonel himself, a mighty whoop and a couple of piercing yells echoed down the street, accompanied by the drumming of hooves. A frail old man on a nearby porch jumped up and reached for his pistol before he remembered himself. The Indians had been gone for a generation or more. No one any younger than the old man would have even considered the possibility of a raid, for such Indians as there were nowadays lived farther to the west, or miles to the south in the Cherokee towns like Chota. These screaming warriors were savages of a different kind, and an instant after I heard their whooping I knew what it meant: the search party had come back, successful in their quest.

I clambered onto the safety of Newland's porch, in case the revelers decided to take a victory gallop along the main street of Morganton. Colonel Newland was emerging from his office just as I reached my vantage point by his doorway.

"What is all this commotion?" he demanded, peering down the street in the direction of the noisemaking.

"I am afraid it is the posse," I told him.

He glanced at me as if he wanted to dispute my theory, but curiosity got the better of both of us, and we jettisoned the argument in favor of leaning across the railings of the stage-office porch, straining for a glimpse of the returning riders. A moment later the procession came into view. Half a dozen mud-caked riders on sweat-soaked horses rounded the bend in the road. The three leaders were waving their hats and shouting to passersby, glorying in the impromptu parade. Three more solemn horsemen followed a short distance behind, each holding the reins of his own mount, each leading a second horse on a short rope. I did not immediately recognize any of the search-party members, but I knew at once the identity of the three ragged and weary persons tied to the saddles of the horses in tow.

Isaiah Stewart sat slumped forward, as if his weariness had overcome even his sorrow and his anger. His clothing was torn and muddy, and there were flecks of blood in his grizzled beard. He had not been taken easily, I thought. Be-

side him, Jackson Stewart sat up, defiantly glaring at the onlookers as though daring them to jeer at his plight. He is a
great bear of a man, six feet in height and not lacking in
girth, and all the welts and bruises upon him I imagined had
been repaid with interest upon the persons of his captors.
He wore iron shackles about his wrists, and over them a rope
tying him to the saddle. Although Frankie Silver would have
been regarded as the main prisoner, it was this accessory to
her escape that the posse most feared. Mrs. Silver herself
rode with eyes downcast, as oblivious to the stares of the
crowd as she had been at her trial. Her hands were bound
with rope, but her feet dangled at the horse's side, not tied
together beneath the belly of her mount, as were those of
her accomplices. She was wearing men's clothing: buckskin
breeches and a homespun shirt beneath a man's coat, and
her blond hair tumbled out from beneath a wide-brimmed
leather hat, although it must have been bound up when the
searchers came upon them. She was small and sturdy
enough to pass for a young boy. I thought the clothes must
have belonged to Blackston Stewart, and I wondered if he
had been left at home to tend the homestead, or if he had
got away into the forest when the lawmen came.

An old man in the crowd called out: "How did ye take her,
boys?"

One of the rear guard reined in his bay mare, and leaned
back in the saddle with a grin of lazy triumph. *Whatever happened,* I thought, *you had least to do with it.* "Well," he said,
"it weren't an easy hunt. It's perilous country out there, and
you could turn around twice and be lost, but we tracked
them well enough, though the going was slow when they
left the trail and took to the woods. We might not have
caught them at all, but for the high water."

Someone laughed and called out, "Come hell or high water, was it?"

"Some of both, I reckon," said the rider. "We reckoned on
them heading west into Buncombe County and then making
for the Tennessee line, but that is not what they done. They

was in Rutherford County when we caught up to them, trying to ford the river, which was so swollen from the spring
rains that their horses could not manage the crossing."

"Did you shoot it out with them?"

The sad little procession had moved on up the street now,
and the rider looked after them as if he wanted to end the
talk and catch up to the others, but after a moment he per-
ceived that they were only a few yards from the jail, and
there were townsmen aplenty surrounding them now, eager
to have a tiny part in the recapture of a notorious outlaw so
that they, too, might become tellers of tales. I watched the
prisoners being dragged from their horses, and I wondered
where it was they were headed. Rutherford County is due
south of us, and not on the way to Tennessee. Perhaps the
Stewarts originally came from down that way, and they were
taking Frankie back to kinfolk there, or in South Carolina.
Anywhere but here, I thought. For if ever they could have
eluded the searchers and made them turn back with no
more leads to follow, they would have got away. The sheriff
had neither the means nor the heart to prolong the search
for her. Another day would have seen her safe.

Seeing that he was no longer needed among the hunters,
the straggling horseman mopped his brow with a muddy rag
and turned his attention back to the little crowd that hung
on his every word.

"Well, now, I can't say that I heard tell of any shooting,"
he said. "The fugitives were hoping to put so much distance
between themselves and Burke County that they would
never have to see us at all, and, failing that, they were thinking they could outsmart us. Old Frankie was dressed as a
boy, and the other two were trying to get a loaded wagon
over the river. So one of the trackers—a fellow name of
Gouge, I think it was—went up to the wagon and says to the
little lad, 'You're Frankie Silver, ain't you?' She ducks her
head and says, 'No, sir. My name is Tommy.'" The rider
paused and grinned. "That big fellow yonder was a-driving
the wagon, and he heard them talking. 'That's right!' he
hollers out. '*Her* name is Tommy.'"

The listeners roared appreciatively, and several of them echoed, "*Her* name is Tommy," to impress it in their minds before they hurried away to regale their friends with the news.

I wondered if it had happened that way, or if the fellow had used the ride back to Morganton to come up with a rousing tale for the taverns. He would drink his fill tonight on the recital of that one, I thought. There would be revelry tonight in the inns of Morganton, I thought as I turned away. The hanging would take place after all.

Burgess Gaither

CONFESSION

Frankie Silver's eight days of freedom had ended in capture, and the arrest of her father and brother for aiding in her escape. I had thought that such an act of disregard for the laws might turn the community against her once more, but it did not. We are a frontier people, still. Our parents' generation comprised their own army to defend themselves against the attacks of the Indians, and they enforced their own laws within the settlements, so we are not yet complacent about taking orders from a far-off government. People seemed to think Frankie Silver's escape was a sensible reaction to an unjust sentence of death. Perhaps they, too, remembered John Sevier in similar circumstances. If anything, the clamor for the prisoner's release was even more strident, and the list of names upon the circulating petition grew ever longer.

I still had not signed it, however. I told myself that whatever I might think of the case, I did not know the facts concerning Charlie Silver's death. Until I was satisfied on that point, I could not in good conscience ask that his killer be reprieved. I said as much to the sheriff, and to a number of well-meaning people who thrust petitions under my nose.

"She wants to confess."

It was the eleventh of June. Thomas Wilson had found me in McEntire's, sharing a pint with young Dr. Tate, who is a learned and kindred spirit in our little country town. Wilson stood looming over my chair like a black-suited crow, as gawky and unsmiling as ever. It is of little wonder to me that Mr. Wilson's political career was short and unpropitious. I stared up at him, endeavoring to make sense of his blast of words. I said stupidly, "She . . . wants . . ."

"The prisoner. Frankie Silver! The wretched girl has finally got it into her head that the state means to kill her, and she has been weeping for hours on end. The sheriff tells me that she has abandoned herself to despair, but that some of her friends have visited with her in the jail—" He paused here and gave me such a meaningful look that I knew at once who the prisoner's friends were, although Mr. Wilson is too much of a gentleman to say the names of wellborn ladies aloud in a public tavern.

"I see."

"I'm sure you do," he said dryly. "Apparently, these friends have convinced the poor creature that her only hope of survival is to tell the truth about what transpired on the night of Charles Silver's death. Her advisors think that if her story is brought to light, the governor can be persuaded to spare her life."

"Do you think so?"

"It is possible, I suppose." He said this with no apparent conviction. "It is worth trying. I have been summoned to hear Mrs. Silver's narrative, and I want another witness. In this situation there should be two listeners to corroborate the testimony."

"That seems fitting," I said. "Will you ask Sheriff Boone?"

"I think not," said Thomas Wilson, after a moment's hesitation. "He is already suspected of being too lenient toward the prisoner. I think you would be the proper witness. As clerk of court, you are the ranking official in the county, since the circuit judge and the district solicitor are not from Morganton. Besides, I was one of Mrs. Silver's attorneys, but you are a disinterested observer—a most desirable thing in a witness. Will you hear her confession?"

"I will, gladly," I said, getting to my feet. "Shall I come with you now?"

"Now is as good a time as any. Bring writing materials with you. We shall want a record of the prisoner's statement."

I stopped by the courthouse to fetch ink and paper, and we proceeded across the lawn to the wood frame building that served as the county jail. John Boone was expecting us, it seemed, for he met us at the door himself and ushered us up the stairs to the prisoner's cell with very little comment beyond a civil greeting.

She must have heard our footsteps on the stairs, for as we neared the second floor, I heard a clank of chain that indicated the prisoner was stirring in her cell. "Can you unchain her while we talk with her?" I asked the sheriff.

John Boone would not meet my eyes. "No," he said.

I did not protest further, for I knew that the escape had forced him to be vigilant. He let us into the cell and locked it behind us, placing the iron key back on his belt. "Really!" I said to Wilson as the door slammed shut. "The sheriff can hardly think we mean to effect an escape with the prisoner."

"He is taking no chances," said Wilson. "I cannot fault him for that."

I thought with sorrow of the pretty young woman who had prattled on about tomatoes and apples last summer. She was gone. The gaunt and haggard creature who huddled near the window of the cell bore no resemblance to that blue-eyed girl who had held her own against the Erwin sisters many months ago. She did not turn to look at us as we came in. I think she no longer cared for visitors.

Thomas Wilson said, "Good afternoon, madam. We have been summoned to speak with you. I believe you know Mr. Burgess Gaither?"

She nodded, and turned to look at me. "I remember him."

"I was asked to witness your statement," I told her. "Do you want to tell this story in your own words, Mrs. Silver, or would you like us to ask you questions?"

"I'll just tell it straight out, I guess. It's been bottled up inside me so long now, I feel like it's poking out my stomach. Let me tell it."

I sat down on the camp bed, took out my writing materials, and set my quill to paper. "Whenever you are ready," I said, with what I hoped was an encouraging smile.

The tears flowed freely down her pale cheeks. "I killed him," she said.

I drew in my breath. I knew, of course, that she must have done it, and the jury had pronounced her guilty more than a year ago, but there is still a chill that comes when one hears a murderer say quietly, *I killed him.* I waited for her to continue, but she simply sat there looking at us.

"We must know more," said Thomas Wilson.

She nodded, and looked back toward the window and the green mountains in the distance. "Charlie . . . I was sixteen when I married him. He was handsome enough, and I reckon that's why I said yes when he asked me. Folks were always saying what a handsome pair we were. And I was wanting to get away from home anyhow. Seems like all there ever was to do was chores, and I thought, I may as well do the washing and the cooking for my own man in my own house instead of letting Mama boss me every whipstitch doing the selfsame tasks at home. I wish I hadn't of now." She looked at me. "You ain't writing," she said.

"No. I will only set down what pertains to the crime itself," I told her. I could not write as fast as she spoke, and at any rate I thought this preamble would be of little value for our purposes. "You may say whatever you like, though, Mrs. Silver. I will read it back to you when we are done."

She nodded. "Where was I? Oh, Charlie. You'd think with his mama dying a-borning him, that he wouldn't be spoiled by his stepmother, but I reckon he was. Or else he was just naturally trifling. He didn't hardly lift his hand to help with the work. He'd chop wood and feed the cattle, and he called himself hunting when he'd slip off for hours at a time while I tended to everything else."

Thomas Wilson scowled at her. "Madam, did you kill your husband because he was lazy?"

She shook her head. "No, sir. I didn't mind him much

most times, but the thing was, Charlie liked to get drunk, and the liquor turned him mean."

"How so?"

"He'd come home cold-eyed and set in his jaw, looking for things to find fault with. I answered him back a time or two at first, but he'd hit me across the face with the back of his hand and split open my lip. Or he'd black my eye and say I'd earned it. I learned to keep out of his way when he was drinking. There's many a woman does the same, sir."

"He had been drinking on the night in question?"

"The night and most of the day as well. He went over to George Young's to get liquor, and he must have put away a jugful before he ever started home. He came in after dark, toting his pistol and letting the cold wind in the cabin when he pulled the door open, and Baby woke up a-bawling."

I wrote: *The prisoner avers that Charles Silver did come home intoxicated on the night of December 22, 1831.*

"We had words then, sir, for I was fit to be tied that he had been gone so long, leaving me to tend the fire and the cattle. I reckon I hollered at him: *It's about time you got home,* or some such words, and he shoved me away. I fell against the cradle, and the baby yelled even louder. Charlie scrunched up his face like the noise hurt his ears, and I was still talking too loud to make myself heard over the din. He pulled out his pistol then, and said, *I'm sick of both of you, by God I am!* I wouldn't have taken much notice of that, for he was always full of talk, except for the look on his face, which wasn't red like anger, but gray, like somebody who was cold all the way to the bone. He looked down at my baby then, sir, and he says to me, *Frankie, if you don't shut that baby up, I reckon I will.*"

"He pointed a pistol at his own child?" I said. Mr. Wilson gave me a withering stare, and I mumbled an apology for forgetting myself and went back to setting down her testimony.

"Charlie pulled the hammer back, and I knew he meant to do it. He wasn't himself at all. He was mad with drink, and we'd been shut up in that cabin most of the winter on account of the deep snow, with the baby colicky and crying day and night. Charlie likes a good time, sir. He wasn't one to suffer bad times. He would have been sorry afterward, most likely, if he had killed the baby, but it wouldn't have been no use then."

Mr. Wilson said softly, "And what did you do?"

"Well, I didn't have more than a heartbeat to think on it, for he was a-steadying that pistol at the baby's head. Next thing I knew, the ax was in my hands and I was swinging at him with all my might. I had to stop him, you see, any way I could."

Thomas Wilson and I looked at each other. There was sorrow in his face and anger in mine, but we said nothing to the prisoner except a calm "Continue, please."

"I hit him. I reckon I did."

"And then?"

"He went down, and there was blood around the side of his head, and he was twitching. I had me a white kitten once, and while it was playing by the hearth, my daddy's hunting dog snapped at its little throat and shook it while I stood and screamed. When that dog dropped my kitten, it lay there twitching, blood coming out of its mouth, with its eyes like ice, staring without seeing. Took it a long, long minute to die. I cried for three days." She looked up at us, as if she had suddenly remembered we were there. "It was like that with Charlie. It was quick."

We sat there in silence for a moment; both Wilson and I were waiting for her to pick up the threads of the story again, for she was no longer weeping, but the silence continued. At last Thomas Wilson said softly, "And then what, Mrs. Silver?"

She stared up at him. "I killed him," she whispered. "And I told you how. That's all I can say."

"But how did you come to burn his body?"

She shrugged. "Just did."

"Surely you realize that it is the destruction of the body that has caused the greatest outrage concerning your crime?"

She nodded. We waited another long minute in silence, but it was clear that the prisoner would say no more.

Wilson's eyes narrowed. "Very well then, madam," he said. "Let us proceed. Tell us what transpired on the night you escaped."

She took a deep breath. "Will them that helped me get in trouble for it, Mr. Wilson?"

"They deserve to," he replied. "They have set the governor's feelings very much against you, for he thinks now that you are an outlaw. You may save yourself, however, if you will hand over those who effected your escape."

"That wouldn't be right," said Frankie Silver.

"It would save you."

"If I told on them that helped me . . . would they hang?" She was looking not at Mr. Wilson, but at me.

"We cannot say what punishment the jury would fix upon them," he said primly, but my expression must have told her my thoughts: they would hang, as surely as I'm sitting here.

"I can't say," she whispered, huddling back against the wall.

Wilson tried to persuade her to confide in us, but she would say nothing further. At last he fairly shouted at her, "Mrs. Silver, without your testimony these people cannot be convicted!"

At that she smiled and shook her head again. I wondered if she really understood what her refusal would cost her.

We left the cell then, for it was clear that nothing more could be got out of badgering the poor creature. She had made up her mind to keep silent. As we descended the stairs, I murmured to Wilson, "She should not be hanged for this crime, sir! It was self-defense."

"I know it," he said. "I thought it must have been, but as she could not testify in court, we could not present that defense to the jury. It is not the killing of Charlie Silver that will hang her, anyhow."

"No, it isn't. It is the cutting up of the body that has outraged the community, and she will not explain that point away. It was panic, I suppose. She wanted to hide the evidence of her crime, for she does not understand legal shadings like 'self-defense' or 'manslaughter.' Poor ignorant girl! What will you do now?"

Thomas Wilson sighed. "I will write to Governor Swain yet again. I must tell you, though, that he is reluctant to intercede. I received a letter from him only last week, and he shows no inclination to mercy. As for the persons who helped Mrs. Silver escape, the governor wants them hanged as well."

"But she should not have been convicted!"

"She was, though. And the state says that verdicts are to be honored, just or unjust. I have shared the governor's letter with the prisoner's father, Isaiah Stewart. I hope it will serve as a warning to him, lest he should get the whole family hanged instead of only the daughter."

"Poor Mr. Stewart. His daughter is wrongly convicted, and he is powerless to save her. Can you wonder that he is driven to desperate measures?"

"I have no sympathy to spare for the relatives," said Thomas Wilson. "It is their meddling that will get her hanged. They should have trusted in the law the moment that Charlie Silver died, instead of now, when it is all but too late." He shook his head. "Well, I will do what I can. I will advise the governor of Mrs. Silver's confession. I must impress upon him that the act was self-defense. Perhaps he will not hang her when he knows the facts of the case. But the escape—that was ill-judged. She is indeed an unfortunate woman."

"You must save her, Wilson."

"Well, I will try. You would oblige me by making several fair copies of Mrs. Silver's confession. We shall need them to accompany the petitions we must circulate around the county. The governor will want reassurance that he is making a popular decision."

"I will write them out tonight," I said.

"Good. Time is short. I will write to Woodfin in Asheville myself. I think when he hears of this new evidence, he will assist us as well."

Downstairs we said our farewells to Sheriff Boone. "I have witnessed her confession," I told him. "And it is a sad tale indeed. I hope that this document will spare you the terrible duty of hanging her."

"I hope so, too," he said. "With all my heart. Though I reckon it would disappoint half the county to be deprived of the spectacle."

"Not I," I said. "If the dreadful day comes, I hope I am far away from the site of the execution, and I shall wish to hear nothing whatever about it then or later."

As I started to cross the threshold into the open air, John Boone called me back. "Mr. Gaither," he said, "you do realize, don't you, that as clerk of Superior Court you are the highest-ranking officer of the court in the county?"

"I suppose so," I said. "Why do you mention it?"

The old sheriff put his hand on my shoulder. "I wondered if you knew that you are the state's witness to the hanging."

Late that night, after most of the household had gone to bed, I sat before the fire in the great hall at Belvidere, copying out the confession that I had taken down. I heard the rustle of skirts and the soft patter of slippers on the oak floor. I had hoped that it was Elizabeth, come to keep me company after putting young William to bed, but I saw Miss Mary in the doorway, carrying the decanter of brandy.

"I thought you might need fortification, Mr. Gaither," she said. "Shall I pour you a glass?"

"Thank you," I said, without troubling to look up, for I did not wish to lose my place.

She set the glass down beside the candle and poured another for herself, at which point I did look up, but although I raised my eyebrows at this impropriety, I said nothing. "I have come to read the confession," she said, taking the chair next to my writing table.

I sighed. At dinner that night I had spoken of my visit to the jail, but before anyone could press me further about the details of that meeting, I had changed the subject to talk of a visit to Charlotte, and the squire had come to my aid, steering the conversation away from the distressing subject again and again. I knew, though, from seeing Miss Mary's thoughtful stare farther down the table, that despite our best efforts at shielding the ladies, I had merely delayed the discussion.

"The document may distress you," I said.

Miss Mary smiled. "Why, Mr. Gaither," she said, "I knew that she had killed him. I merely wish to know why."

Without another word, I handed over the paper and watched as she read my summary of Mrs. Silver's declaration. Her expression did not change. "I thought it must be something like this," she said at last. "A simple girl like that could hardly have been roused to murder for anything less. It is not murder, though, is it, Mr. Gaither?"

"Mr. Wilson says that it was clearly a case of manslaughter, if not justifiable homicide. The law realizes that people must defend themselves. Or it should."

"Yet she was sentenced to death for it."

"That is so. However, we believe that justice was not served in this case, and we are doing everything in our power to have the judgment set aside."

I could see from Miss Mary's expression that she had no doubt that they would carry the day. The Erwins are people of power and influence. They know how to go about these things. They know all the right people in Raleigh, and elsewhere. I was a new member of the family, and I had not the confidence of my new kinsmen.

"People wonder why I have never married," Miss Mary said, taking another sip of her brandy. "There is too much risk in the venture. A woman is quite at the mercy of a fool or a brute, and one can never know the bargain one has made until it is too late."

"We are not all such bad lots," I protested.

Miss Mary smiled. "Not all snakes are poisonous," she said, "but I leave them all alone just the same." She took another quill from the pewter pot on the writing table. "Have you many more copies to make? I write a fair hand. Let me help you."

We spoke very little after that, but sat side by side until the fire burned low, copying the cold words of Frankie Silver's confession until we knew the phrases by heart.

A few days later, I arrived at Belvidere just before the dinner hour, having escaped the premises for most of the afternoon because an afternoon tea was taking place in the great hall. I had no sooner shaken the dust from my boots than Miss Mary appeared, brisk as ever, and thrust several sheets of paper into my hands. "Just the person I wanted to see," she informed me. "Read this and tell me what you think."

I arranged the sheets of paper in order and began to read.

June 29, 1833

To His Excellency David L. Swain:
    Governor of the State of North Carolina

Your petitioners are fully sensible of the Delicacy of presenting to you this petition. Yet they Justify themselves by claiming as a duty peculiar to the Sex to be allways on the side of Mercy towards their fellow beings and to the female more particularly.

The subject of this petition is an unfortunate creation of our Sex, Mrs. Francis silvers who was Sentenced by our court to be executed on the last Friday in June, but by your goodness respited until the second Friday in July. We do not expect to refer you to any information in this that you are not already familiarly acquainted with, only it be the treatment the unfortunate creature received during the life of her husband.

We do not refer you to this with a cause of Justification but wish to reiterate the various unfortunate events which have taken place in the world in consequence of the woman's abuse, indecorous, and insupportable treatment in which the creature now before your Excellency for God's mercy has, contrary to the law of God & the country, yet so consistent with our nature, been her own avenger.

Hear her own wrongs.

The husband of the unfortunate creature now before you we are informed, Gov., was one of that cast of mankind who are wholly destitute of any of the feelings that is necessary to make

a good husband or parent. The neighborhood people are convinced that his treatment of her was both unbecoming and
cruel verry often and at the time too when female Delicacy
would most forbid it he treated her with personal violence.

He was said by all the neighborhood to have been a man who
never made use of any exertions to support either his wife or
child, which terminated, as is frequently the case, that those
dutys nature ordered and intended the husband to perform are
thrown to her.

His own relations admit of his having been a lazy, lady-
trifling man.

It is admitted by them also that she was an industrious
woman, but for the want of Grace, Religion, and Refinement
she had committed an act that she herself would have given a
world to be able to call back.

We refer you to the child who is an infant and needs the
child's mother. We hope that your Excellency will extend to the
unfortunate female all the help you can, even to a pardon, &
wipe from the character of the female in this community the
Stigma, namely of a woman being hung under the gallows.

Yours sincerely,
Mary E. Erwin

Appended to this carefully wrought document were the
signatures of nearly every gentlewoman in the county. I
traced my finger down the list: the attorneys' families were
well represented. Thomas Wilson's wife, Catherine Caldwell
Wilson, who is the Erwins' niece, and Mr. Wilson's mother,
Eunice Worth Wilson, had signed the petition also. The
name of my own dear wife Elizabeth was there, as was that
of her sisters Delia Erwin and Catherine Gaither, my brother
Alfred's widow. My mother-in-law, Matilda Sharpe Erwin,
and her sister Ceceilia Sharpe Erwin had signed the document. There was Martha McEntire Walton, daughter of the
innkeeper and wife of Thomas Walton, a landowner and former justice of the Court of Pleas and Quarter Sessions. I
saw the name of Jane Tate, a relative of our former sheriff

Will Butler, and Goodwin Bousehell, of the Methodist minister's family. Eliza Grace McDowell, granddaughter of a general and a colonel of the Revolution, had signed the petition, as had her cousins Matilda and Elvira Carson, who are McDowells on their mother's side, like their cousin Annie Maria McKesson, also listed. Catherine Carson, the young bride of our United States congressman Sam Carson, had added her name and influence to the petition. I fancied that I could feel the paper growing warm in my hands, and I wondered if the governor would be similarly affected. It is true that women do not vote or hold elected office, but if the old adage is true, that "the hand that rocks the cradle is the hand that rules the world," then there were enough imperial hands represented here to turn the firmament upside down. The daughters and granddaughters of governors, and generals, and congressmen, and wealthy landowners, and lawyers, and signers of the Constitution were all arrayed in a force that made me think of ancient Britain's Queen Boadicea in her war chariot leading the charge against a Roman legion. The respectful request for a political favor was nothing less than a demand, for all its careful phrasing. I did not envy David Lowry Swain his office or his duties that day, or on any day since.

"Well, what do you think?" Miss Mary asked me, when I had set the document aside.

"I hardly know," I said. "Are there no ordinary women who wish to see the prisoner reprieved? No miller's wife, or tailor's daughter?"

Miss Mary had the grace to blush. "Certainly there are," she replied. "I would hope that every woman in the county and indeed the whole state would wish to see this poor creature saved from an undeserved fate, but time is short, and we had no time to spare for collecting signatures far and wide. Besides, I think these names will carry weight with the governor."

I nodded. "The names will be familiar to him, to say the least. It reads like an index of North Carolina history."

"Mr. Bevins has promised to write a letter accompanying

the petition. You see his wife's name there among the others. Surely this will prove to the governor that all the county desires a pardon for that poor wretched woman."

"Did Mrs. Silver ask you to draft such a letter?"

"No. How could she think of such a thing? She knows nothing whatever about it. In fact, it was Colonel Carson who suggested it."

"What? Old Huntin' John?" The colonel was a prominent landowner, and father to our congressman Sam Carson, and I wondered how he came to be dabbling in a backcountry murder case. "What has he to do with it?"

"Poor Mr. Stewart is beside himself with worry over the fate of his daughter, and he appealed to Colonel Carson for advice in the political aspect of the matter."

I frowned. "I think Mr. Stewart should have considered the political side of the case before he broke his daughter out of jail." I raised a hand, forestalling their protests of his innocence. "And if he did not do it, he certainly condoned it, and he certainly knows who did."

"He is a desperate man, Burgess," said Elizabeth, with a look of genuine, if misspent, concern.

"Her unlawful escape from confinement shows little respect for the law, my dear," I said sternly. "I am sure that the governor will be less inclined to mercy than he would have been if she had not shown her contempt for North Carolina justice."

"Why shouldn't she show contempt for it?" Miss Mary demanded. "She has seen little enough of it. She was condemned at her trial without a chance to tell her side of the story. The State Supreme Court considered the case without having anyone present to speak on her behalf. And now you tell me that Governor Swain will judge her harshly because she refuses to sit obediently in her little cell and wait for them to come and kill her?"

I had no more heart to play devil's advocate with her, for she voiced my own sentiments—if, that is, a clerk of court were permitted to have any.

*   *   *

In the weeks since Frankie Silver's escape and return to jail, Burke County had besieged the governor with letters and petitions asking that the prisoner's life be spared. Colonel Newland continued to press his case, and Mr. Wilson wrote as he had said he would, giving Mr. Swain the details of the prisoner's confession. Life went on as usual in Morganton, with weddings and christenings and even a fancy dress ball at Bellevue, but inevitably the talk returned to the prisoner chained on the second floor of the jail. What could be done to save her?

On the twenty-first of June a letter arrived from Raleigh via the Buncombe Mail, granting the prisoner a two-week stay of execution. The governor said in his order, *It has been represented to me that the prisoner has been deluded by false hopes of pardon. Now therefore know so that, to the end that further space may be allowed her to prepare for the awful change that awaits her, and by virtue of the power vested in me by the Constitution of North Carolina, I do hereby respite said Frances Silvers until the second Friday in July next.*

John Boone showed me the letter, so that as the officer of the court, I might make note of the official change in the schedule.

"Well," I said, "we have two more weeks to circulate more petitions."

Boone nodded. "I wonder if it's a kindness, though, to give the girl hope."

Mr. Bevins wrote his letter accompanying the ladies' petition, and even Nicholas Woodfin had come to Burke County to do what he could. Woodfin took one of my copies of the confession, and he spent many days riding through the outlying districts of the county gathering the names of other citizens upon petitions for clemency. I was gratified that Mrs. Silver's young lawyer should take such trouble on her behalf, long after his duties in the courtroom were done, but I thought his time and influence could have been better spent in other ways.

"Nicholas Woodfin is riding from one homestead to the

next up the mountain getting backcountry farmers to put their X on a petition to save Frankie Silver. I cannot understand it!" I was holding forth to Squire Erwin as we took a Sunday afternoon ride along the John's River bottom land that formed one of the boundaries of Belvidere. The plantation runs to nine hundred acres of cultivated land, dotted with smokehouses, sheds, and slave cabins. Beyond that, several thousand more acres of forest and mountain complete the estate, ensuring that William Willoughby Erwin is truly "lord of all he surveys."

When I said again that I did not understand Woodfin's behavior in the Silver case, the squire reined in his mare to a slower pace and gave me an appraising stare, as though I were a schoolboy parsing Latin. "What would you have him do?"

"Why, he should write to the governor, of course! It seems that everybody in Morganton with the means to a goose quill has dispatched a letter to Raleigh. Why doesn't Nicholas Woodfin do the same? Surely he has the most influence with David Swain. He clerked under him in Asheville not three years ago!"

"And you think that the governor would grant Nick Woodfin a great political favor because the man once clerked under him?" William Willoughby Erwin smiled. "Why should he?"

"Why, because they are associates. Because Woodfin is known to him, and so his word may be given higher value than that of well-meaning strangers not known to the governor."

The old man shrugged. "Politics is a form of commerce, Burgess. Never forget that. I assure you that our young governor does not forget it for one moment. What would it profit David Swain to grant a favor to a young pup of a lawyer from Asheville?"

"Why, it would be an act of kindness, a courtesy such as one gentleman shows to another," I protested.

"Too much charity bankrupts commerce. I think young Woodfin knows that he has no claim upon the governor as far as favors go. He thinks that by getting the names of a few hundred voters upon a piece of paper, he may enable his mentor to see the benefit of reaching a popular decision regarding the Silver case. Grateful voters count for more than happy young lawyers."

"So you think that the petitions will save her?"

"No. She will not be saved." William Willoughby Erwin turned his horse away from the river and set forth on his customary path to the western end of his estate, from which he could see the afternoon sun gilding the western mountains in soft, lambent light. After a few moments' contemplative silence, the squire said, "What do you think of James's new bull? Have you seen him yet?"

I was not to be diverted by this change of topic. The minutiae of farming hold no interest for me. When I build a home of my own, it will be in the town, and the few horses that I'll own for carriage and saddle use will be boarded in the livery stable. *Bull, indeed,* I thought. "So you think all our efforts are in vain? Mrs. Silver will not get her reprieve?"

The squire shrugged. "I wouldn't give her one."

I turned to stare at him. In all the months that had passed since the trial, I thought I had heard everyone I knew expressing outrage about the Silver verdict, and half the county seemed to be going to great lengths to keep the girl from being hanged. I had never suspected my father-in-law's indifference to her fate. I was so startled that I could hardly speak. "But—but—have I not told you of her confession? She killed him in self-defense, and to save their child!"

"So she says now, Burgess. She has had a good many months to learn legal subtleties from the likes of Thomas Wilson and my daughter Mary. The fact remains that this frail and ignorant young woman cut the body of her husband into a score of pieces and hid them away. Add to that the fact that she escaped from jail and managed to elude her captors for eight days, and that she will not say who assisted her in the escape. I see no injured mountain dove in need of the protection of the state, Burgess. I see a cold and resourceful woman, who will make use of whatever comes to hand, be it influential but trusting young ladies or the key to her jail cell." He eyed me thoughtfully. "No doubt Frances Silver is very pretty, but I am past caring about that sort of thing."

"But four members of the original jury signed her petition."

"Eight jurors did not sign," the squire replied. "The governor will go with the majority."

"But think of all the names on the entreaties to Swain! Think of the ladies' petition: your wife, and her mother Mrs. Sharpe, Miss Mary, and Mrs. Sam Carson, and all the other gentlewomen in Morganton."

"Ladies cannot vote. What does it matter what they think?"

"But the governor is acquainted with all of them socially. How can he say no to them without seeming like a brute?"

"That is just what I have been asking myself, Burgess. It is what interests me most about the whole affair. He will have to be very clever about it, to be sure."

"There has never been a woman hanged before in the state of North Carolina," I said.

"I daresay that if she were a slave woman you could save her, by pleading that her death would constitute the loss of valuable property to her owner. Then she might be let off with a good flogging. But Frankie Silver is a white woman of no breeding, wealth, or influence. She is of no use to anybody." The squire turned his back on the mountains and the setting sun. "Time to head for home, I think," he said. "Unless you'd care to have a look at James's bull?"

The letters and petitions were duly sent off to Raleigh, and then all Morganton waited anxiously for the official reply, although very few of us doubted that the governor would grant a request so universally favored among the constituency, particularly since a number of prominent people had championed Mrs. Silver's cause. But the days stretched into weeks, and it came time for preparations to be made for the execution, and still there was no word of reprieve from Raleigh.

"The governor is waiting until the last moment," people said. "He wants to make a dramatic flourish of his benevolence." Then they began to worry that he would misjudge the speed of the stagecoach mail delivery, and that the good news would arrive too late to save the prisoner.

At last, though, on Thursday, the eleventh of July, W. C. Bevins received the long-awaited letter. He brought it to me at the courthouse, where I was going over the material pertaining to the duties of a clerk of court in the event of an execution. I had obtained a copy of the death warrant, and I was trying to determine whether there was any set formula by which I should report to the state government that the sentence had been carried out. *I have the honor to inform you . . .* did not seem quite apt under the circumstances.

Bevins gave me a stiff bow of greeting and set the letter on the table atop my law books without a word.

> Executive Department
> Raleigh 9th July 1833

Dear Sir:

I have received your letter without date but postmarked in the 3rd Ins., together with the accompanying Petition of a number of the most respectable ladies of your Vicinity in behalf of the unfortunate Mrs. Silvers, who before this communication can reach you will in all human probability have passed the boundarys which separate us alike from the reproaches of enemies and the sympathies of friends. All that it is now in my power to do, is to unite in the anxious wish, which doubtless pervades the whole community to which she belongs, that she may find mercy in Heaven, which seemed to be necessarily denied upon earth, a free pardon for all the offenses of her life.

I beg you to spare the fair Petitioners, with the most of whom I have the pleasure of acquaintance, that the kindest motives which influenced their memorial in behalf of the unfortunate convict, are duly appreciated and that no one can participate more deeply than I do in their sympathy for her melancholy fate.

> I am, Sir, very respectfully
> your obt. Servt.
> D. L. Swain

To: W.C. Bevins, Esq.

I set down the letter, hardly trusting myself to speak. "The governor appears to think that Mrs. Silver has already been executed," I said at last.

"So it would seem," said Bevins.

"But how can he think that? David Swain himself ordered that stay of execution not three weeks ago. He himself postponed the date of her death from the twenty-eighth of June until the twelfth of July, acting upon a request from Thomas Wilson. I saw the letter myself. How can he write now and say that the sentence has already been carried out?"

"Perhaps he has other things on his mind," Bevins suggested, but I thought I detected a sneer in his voice.

"Very well, let us apprise him of his mistake," I said. "We will go directly to the stage office and draft a letter that Colonel Newland can—"

My voice faltered, and Bevins nodded, seeing that I had realized my error. "Mr. Gaither, you had forgotten the date."

I stared at him. "It is the eleventh of July," I said. "Certainly it is too late to rely upon the stagecoach to send an answer, but—"

"It is too late altogether," Bevins said quietly. "Mrs. Silver is to be hanged tomorrow. And no power on earth could get a letter from Morganton to Raleigh and back again in less than a day. The governor knew that when he posted his reply."

"Then why equivocate with this pretended misunderstanding of dates? Why did he not simply say, *I refuse to pardon the prisoner.*"

"He has said it, Mr. Gaither. As plainly as any politician ever spoke."

Chapter Seven

THE KNOCK at the door brought the sheriff out of his reverie. Spencer hobbled to the door without bothering to peer out the window to see whose vehicle was in his driveway.

There stood Charles Wythe Stanton, holding a potted plant with a yellow satin bow stuck into the soil among the leaves. Spencer had not seen the man for twenty years, except as a face in a news photo or a fleeting image on a television screen, but he recognized him at once. Colonel Stanton looked much as he had at the time of his daughter's death. A little grayer, perhaps, and leaner, so that the lines on his face were more prominent, but he was still as handsome as a recruiting poster. The sort of person of whom people were wont to ask, "Are you somebody?" on the off chance that he might be Oliver North or Harrison Ford, or some other larger-than-life person that one never expected to meet in the flesh.

Spencer stepped back and motioned for him to come inside.

"Hello, Sheriff," he said, holding out the plant as if it were a peace offering. "I'm glad to see that you're up and about."

Spencer set the arrangement on the nearest flat surface and followed his guest into the living room. Colonel Stanton had walked over to the sliding glass doors at the far end of the room, and he was admiring the view of green mountains reflecting cloud shadows in the sunshine. "It's so peaceful up here," he said. "I wanted to bury Emily in a cemetery near Johnson City, so that she could be encircled by mountains. She loved it up here. Anne wouldn't hear of it, though. She wanted to bring our daughter home. To be near us. Perhaps she was right to do that. I don't know."

Spencer didn't see that it mattered. "How is Mrs. Stanton?" he asked politely.

Stanton turned away from the view and did not look at it again. "We divorced some years back," he said. "Emily was our only child. Losing her was hard on us. I expect there was more to the breakup than that, but it was certainly the precipitating cause. Chalk up another death to Lafayette Harkryder. One marriage."

"I'm sorry to hear that," said Spencer.

The colonel shrugged. "These things happen." He seemed for the first time to notice that his host was still standing. "Please sit down," he said, gesturing toward the sofa. "I know you're an invalid at the moment. I didn't mean to keep you on your feet, Mr. Arrowood."

Spencer began, "How did you know—"

Stanton smiled. "How to find you? Or that you were ill? A helpful young lady in your office answered both of those questions. I told her that we were old friends."

"It's been a long time," said Spencer, making a mental note to give the new dispatcher, Jennaleigh, further instructions regarding the privacy of peace officers. He eased himself down in the overstuffed chair next to the sofa and motioned for the colonel to sit down.

"How are you, Sheriff?"

"On the mend. I'll be back on duty by next week, I think."

"A gunshot wound is a sobering experience, isn't it? I took a hit once overseas, and I'll never forget that feeling of stupefaction, followed by the absolute conviction that I was already dead. You never forget it."

"I don't guess I will." Spencer didn't want to swap war stories.

"I hear, though, that the person who shot you was killed in

the capture." The colonel smiled. "Your deputies are to be commended. They saved the state a lot of time and trouble."

Spencer reminded himself that a man who had lost his only child was hardly the most objective observer of criminal proceedings. Besides, since Stanton knew nothing of the case or its participants, he could not realize how deeply the sheriff regretted the death of that particular fugitive. Spencer decided to let it pass. "What brings you to Tennessee?" he said.

Charles Stanton smiled. "The same unfinished business that brought me the first time we met, Mr. Arrowood. Lafayette Harkryder. I'm driving to Nashville to watch him die."

"You're going to be a witness?"

"Oh, yes. I promised Emily that at her funeral twenty years ago. No matter how long it takes, I told her, I will be there when his time comes, and I will watch him die."

Spencer couldn't think of anything to say. He couldn't dispute the man's right to justice, but his evident satisfaction made the sheriff uneasy.

"You'll be there, too, won't you?"

Spencer nodded. "Sheriff of the home county."

"I thought so. I've been studying execution procedures for the last couple of months. There can be only sixteen witnesses at an execution." He ticked them off on his fingers. "The warden or someone designated to represent him, the surgeon of the penitentiary, the prisoner's attorney, relatives, and any clergyman he wishes to be present. *And six respectable citizens.*"

Spencer nodded. "The sheriff, or his representative and one other witness chosen by him. I knew that. I waived my other choice. And the other four are chosen by other law enforcement agencies, aren't they?"

"Right."

"But you're going to witness the execution?" Spencer didn't think the TBI would have appointed Colonel Stanton as one of their official witnesses. The eagerness in his voice would have put them off.

Stanton smiled. "Media witness. Don't forget our friends

in the press. The state press association, the Associated Press, and the radio and television newspeople get a total of five witnesses, and five alternates, in case one of the others can't make it. I got one of the AP slots, in exchange for a promise to write about it."

Spencer repressed a shudder. "Will you write the article?"

"I will. I'm a man of my word. I said I would watch that man die, and if writing an article is the cost of keeping that promise, then so be it."

"I wish this execution would bring your daughter back, sir," said Spencer, choosing his words carefully. "But since it won't, I can't say that I see much point in it."

Charles Stanton narrowed his eyes. "People ought to pay their debts, Mr. Arrowood. Legally and morally. Debts have to be paid. So even if this execution isn't a deterrent to others, even if this man would never kill again, and, yes, even though it will not bring my daughter back from the grave, at least a debt will be paid, and that's something. I worked long and hard for this day. Maybe it even cost me my marriage. So when Fate Harkryder sits down in that electric chair, it will mean that twenty years of my life have not been wasted."

Spencer nodded. He was thinking that there are many ways to serve a life sentence, and he wondered if Fate Harkryder's death would set Charles Stanton free.

"I came to see if you'd like to ride to Nashville," said Stanton. "I'll be going up a day or so early, to pay my respects to the governor and to thank him for having the courage to let this happen on his watch. When I heard that you were injured, I thought I'd offer to take you with me. An invalid shouldn't make a six-hour trip alone."

"That's very kind of you, Colonel," said Spencer, "but I have some things to take care of here before I can leave. I'll go up the actual day of the execution. If it's still scheduled by then."

Stanton smiled. "I can promise you it will still be scheduled. Three network news shows are interviewing me from Nashville between now and the time Fate Harkryder dies.

They're calling the segments things like 'Justice at Last.' The authorities won't dare call it off. I've seen to that."

Spencer wanted to say, *But what if he isn't guilty?* But he kept silent, because guilt or innocence didn't matter anymore to this man with a handsome face and dead eyes. Charles Stanton had hated Lafayette Harkryder for too long to change his mind now; no evidence would ever convince him that the condemned man was not guilty. Someone was going to die for Emily Stanton's sake, and to that end Charles Stanton was a much more cunning killer than any Harkryder had ever been.

Charles Stanton stood up, smiling. "Well, I mustn't keep you," he said. "I know you're not well, and I have a press conference this afternoon in Johnson City. I plan to use the new Trail Murders to draw attention to our cause. I wish Harkryder's execution had come in time to deter this new killer."

Spencer managed to nod. He was able to stay expressionless only because police work had given him twenty years of practice at concealing his emotions, but he felt his muscles tighten and his stomach churn.

"Are you close to an arrest yet, Sheriff?" asked Stanton, making his way to the door.

"I can't say." *What murders? In my county?*

"Too bad. I've actually heard people saying that the two cases might be related. I want to put a stop to that nonsense right away. I wouldn't want the governor to have any excuse for a stay of execution."

Spencer leaned against the door, taking deep breaths until he heard Stanton's tires crunch the gravel in the driveway. He glanced at the telephone. No. He would go in. Holding his side, as if pressure could block the pain, he limped toward the kitchen counter, where his car keys lay in a bowl with his spare change. Alton Banner had not yet given the sheriff permission to drive, but Spencer told himself that it had been a couple of days since he'd asked, and he was confident that he was no risk to anyone but himself behind the wheel. He would get down the mountain, one way or another. And he wanted some answers.

He backed his car out of the garage, around the gravel circle beneath the oak and hickory trees, and headed up the driveway. He was about six minutes from town, but the road led through field and forest, so that it might have been any century at all, but for the black ribbon of road that separated the meadows. Actually, that wasn't true. Frankie Silver would have been bewildered by the missing chestnut trees, the strange kudzu vines, and other changes in the modern landscape, but Spencer was willing to settle for a lack of billboards and power lines. He tried to calm himself by blurring his thoughts into a distant hum, drowned out by the beauty of the surrounding mountains, and for a few miles he almost succeeded, but the sign marking the town limits of Hamelin brought him back to the business at hand. The sheriff's department was two blocks away.

When he saw Deputy Joe LeDonne's patrol car parked in the driveway, he felt his jaw clench. He had hoped to find Martha, but LeDonne would do. He hobbled out of the car, slamming the door until the window rattled. He managed to walk up the front steps without much hesitation, and by the time he reached the front door, he had filled his lungs with a deep breath to ward off any expressions of pain. He must be careful not to seem ill. He intended to take over the investigation, and he wanted to give his deputies no chance to use his injuries as an excuse to exclude him from the case. If he showed any weakness, LeDonne, with the best of intentions, was likely to summon Martha and then Alton Banner, and the pair of them would insist upon escorting the sheriff back home until he had recovered more completely from his wound. There was no time for that.

"What are you doing out?" Joe LeDonne had never got the hang of social amenities. Picturing the deputy at a press conference or a meeting of the board of supervisors made the sheriff wince even more than the pain in his gut.

"I feel fine," Spencer told him. "Consider me back on

duty. Begin with telling me why the hell I wasn't informed about the homicides."

LeDonne was sitting at his usual desk, with the Pepsi that was probably his dinner sitting to the left of the computer monitor. On the screen was a list of addresses and phone numbers. He was doing phone interviews, tracking witnesses. He didn't look so great either, Spencer thought. Long hours and no days off were beginning to wear him down.

"We're doing all we can," said LeDonne. "The TBI is on it, and we're doing interviews. That's about it."

Spencer nodded. "It was Martha's call, wasn't it? *Don't disturb poor Spencer. He's been sick.*"

The deputy shrugged. "Something like that. She may be right, you know."

They mean well, Spencer told himself, swallowing his rage. "We'll leave that for now," he said. "Tell me about the homicides."

With a sigh of resignation, LeDonne picked up the case file and handed it to the sheriff. "At least sit down," he said. "You look awful."

"I'm fine." He sat down, though. "Tell me what is being done."

Step by step, LeDonne took him through the stages of the investigation, from the call reporting the discovery of the bodies to the several lists of possible witnesses being questioned by telephone or in door-to-door canvasing. Spencer nodded as the case began to take shape.

LeDonne paused for breath. After a moment he said, "Is there anything else you would have done?"

The sheriff shrugged. "I don't know. I'd have to think about it. I wouldn't have ignored the possible link between this crime and the Harkryder case, though."

"We didn't ignore it. We questioned all of those witnesses we could find—Harmon, the two firemen from Alabama, even poor Willis Blaine's widow. We came up empty."

"Don't you see what you've done? A man is set to die this week, and you've failed to follow up on new evidence that might save him."

The deputy was silent for a few moments. Confrontations were all part of a day's work in law enforcement, but LeDonne hated to have to quarrel with his boss, who was also his friend. They had known each other a long time now. LeDonne had spent his teenage years in Vietnam with an infantry line company. For a dozen years after that, he had drifted from one job to another, missing the excitement of combat and never succeeding in outrunning the rest of the memories. This little county on the shoulder of a Tennessee mountain was as close as he ever got to coming home. Spencer was obviously in no shape to handle the present situation. At last he said, "We don't see a connection between the two cases. The TBI doesn't see it, either."

"You haven't ruled it out."

"It's a coincidence, that's all."

"What if it isn't?"

"Let it go, Spencer," said Martha from the doorway. She came in, looking more tired than both of them, and perched on the edge of LeDonne's desk. "I saw your car here," she told the sheriff. "I was afraid you'd find out about this, but I kept hoping we'd solve it first. You're in no shape to handle an investigation, and I knew you'd try, because of this Harkryder connection."

"So there is a connection!"

Martha sighed. "Only in your mind, Spencer. Look, you need to trust us. I just finished the academy course, remember? Things have changed in the twenty years since you arrested Fate Harkryder. Back then the film *The Collector* was a creepy fairy tale; now it's used as a training film, because there's a whole new breed of serial killer out there. We know more about murder now than we used to. And one thing we know is that people don't commit identical murders twenty years apart with nothing in between."

"You're betting a man's life on this," said Spencer.

"We're following a good lead right now, and there's no connection to the Harkryder case. This case isn't your answer, Sheriff," said Martha. She so seldom called him by his title that he looked up in surprise. "Why don't you let me drive you home now?"

"No!" He was too forceful. The urgency that he had taken such trouble to conceal was now apparent, and he realized that his emotions were too close to the surface, a sign of his tenuous health. "I won't get any rest anyhow, if I have to worry about this. I know you've checked over the Harkryder case, but let me double-check. For my own peace of mind. You go home. I'll stay here and pull some records."

"You're in no shape to be working," said Martha.

"I can't help thinking."

"It's that damned execution, isn't it?" said LeDonne.

"Yes."

"Stay home then. The state wants a county witness, tell them I'll go."

"It has to be me. Fate Harkryder is on death row because I put him there—and I may have been wrong."

"I doubt it," said LeDonne, as calmly as if they were talking about a bet on an old baseball game.

"Nelse Miller was never happy about this conviction, but I was so sure of myself back then. It was my first big case, and I thought his doubts about it were just sour grapes because he hadn't been here to solve it."

"So why didn't he prove you wrong?"

Spencer shrugged. "I gathered the evidence, that's all. The district attorney and the jury were the ones who decided Fate Harkryder was guilty. And all the evidence was against him. Blood type, lack of alibi. He even had the dead girl's jewelry on him when he was arrested."

"You've got me convinced," said LeDonne. "That's as good as cases get, except on television."

"I know. But it feels wrong."

The deputy smiled. "Well, that's bound to impress the Supreme Court," he said.

"I know. I need something besides twenty years' experience and a hunch. I thought the Trail Murders had the earmarks of serial killings. And they stopped after I arrested the suspect, right? If I had the right man, the killings shouldn't have stopped. But now we have this case."

"Martha told you. Serial killers don't take twenty-year breaks. More like twenty days. Most of them are under forty anyhow."

"I know. I said it was a feeling. It doesn't make sense yet, and I don't have much to go on. But I want to look at some criminal records." Spencer handed LeDonne a slip of paper from his telephone scratch pad. "Can we contact the TBI and get them to run these names through their computers?"

"Sure," said LeDonne. "What are you looking for?"

"I'll know when I see it. Get me everything they've got."

The deputy handed Spencer the telephone. "You might as well go out to dinner with Martha, then, because this will take a while. I take it you want to check more states than just Tennessee?"

"I want everything."

LeDonne nodded at Martha. "You'll have time for breakfast, too," he said.

The officer-in-charge stacked the cardboard boxes on the bunk in Fate Harkryder's cell. "We might as well get this taken care of now, Lafayette," he said, but his tone was apologetic. "They're moving you out of Two in an hour or so. To the quiet cell. I thought you might like some help."

Fate nodded. "Thanks." He noticed that Berry had said, "We're moving you to the quiet cell," instead of "We're putting you on death watch." A small point, perhaps, since it amounted to the same thing, but Fate's existence had long been built upon small pleasures and petty annoyances in the great nothingness of prison time. Little things mattered. Berry wasn't too bad for a guard. He was just doing his job. Maybe he understood things better than the lawyers did. You didn't have to explain poverty to someone who worked as a prison guard.

Fate looked around, measuring his possessions, the accumulation of his entire adult life. They would fit easily into the four cardboard boxes. Now he must decide what to do with them. He began to take things off the shelf. Four bottles of Prell shampoo, a carton of cigarettes, a stack of unused yellow legal pads. . . . He thought how people on the outside would shake their heads at such a pitiful excuse for wealth. "Give those things to Milton," he said, scooping the cigarettes and toilet articles into the smallest box. "God knows he needs it. Especially the shampoo."

It was a feeble joke, but Berry smiled anyhow.

"What happens now?"

Berry shrugged. "You're going to get some peace and quiet," he said. "But the accommodations are a little sparse."

"Compared to what?"

"The quiet cell has bars, like a jail. It has a bed, a sink, a toilet, and a writing table. That's it. You'll be allowed fifteen minutes a day outside the cell to shower; otherwise, that's where you stay."

"No exercise?"

"Not anymore. You'll have someone to talk to, though. There'll be two guards stationed outside the cell at all times. And you can have visitors."

"Good. I want Milton to come over and play cards with me."

"Sorry. No contact with other inmates. You can see your lawyers, your minister, a counselor, or members of your family. Family can go to the regular visitors' lounge. Noncontact visitation."

"Has anybody asked to see me?"

Berry turned away and began to take the posters and photographs off the wall. "Not that I know of," he said. "Of course, that stuff goes through the front office. They might not have told me yet."

"Sure."

"I hear that a bunch of reporters want to interview you, though. Big shots from national TV, even."

"I'll pass." He set the last of his possessions into a cardboard box. "Okay. That's it. Do we move this to the new cell?"

Berry shook his head. "Most of it, no. You can take a

couple of the legal pads with you," he said. "And a Bible if you've got one."

"What do I do with the rest of this stuff?" Fate pointed to the collection of letters, the documents concerning his case, a couple of books, and the signed photograph from one of the film stars who was sympathetic to his cause.

The guard shrugged. "Give them away, I guess. Your family? Your lawyers, maybe? If it was me, I think I'd give my belongings to someone that would want a keepsake to re-member me by."

Fate nodded. "That makes sense." He began to place the objects into the remaining boxes.

"Well? What shall we do with these things?"

"Throw them away."

Burgess Gaither

EXECUTION

My day had come at last. Of all the days that I have lived on this earth—fewer than seven thousand of them, Miss Mary Erwin says, for I once asked her to do the sum for me—of all those days, there were only three that were altogether mine. I do not count the day that I was born, for that was mainly my mother's time, and anyhow I remember nothing of it, so I cannot say if I was petted and made much of, or not. Perhaps they wished for another boy, and were disappointed when I arrived instead.

The first day that I can count as my very own was the day I married Charlie Silver. I suppose I should say that the day was half his, for Preacher said that being man and wife, we were to share our lives and all our worldly goods, but I don't think Charlie wanted much to do with that day. He blushed and stammered, and tried to pretend he didn't care a bit about all the foolishness of the celebration. A man is always a little shamefaced on his wedding day, like a fox caught in a baited trap, ensnared because his greed overcame his better judgment. The menfolk laughed at Charlie that spring day, and said he was caught for sure now. As the bride, I was praised and fussed over, as if I had won a prize or done something marvelous that no one ever did before, and I could not help feeling pleased and clever that I had managed to turn myself from an ordinary girl into a shining bride. Now I think it is a dirty lie. The man is the one who is winning the game that day, though they always pretend they are not, and the poor girl bride is led into a trap of hard work and harsh words, the ripping of childbirth and the drubbing of her man's fists. It is the end of being young, but no one tells her so. Instead they make over her, and tell her how lucky she is. I wonder do slaves get dressed up in finery on the day they are sold.

The second day that was mine was when my baby Nancy came into the world, though that was one day Charlie claimed for his'n loud enough, as if I had nothing to do with it, laying there blood-soaked and spent on the straw pallet, while he strutted and crowed about how he was a daddy now. The way I saw it, she was five minutes his, and nine months mine, but I kept my peace on that, because in my joy I didn't care at all that day who got the praise and the glad-handing. I had Nancy, and she was beautiful, and she was all mine, for I knew that after Charlie had done boasting about his firstborn, she'd see little enough of him. I wearied of her sometimes after that, when she wouldn't leave off crying, or when she spit up on a dress I had scrubbed clean on a creek rock 'til my fingers bled, but for all the little bit of trouble she ever was, I long to hold her one last time, and I count the day that she came into the world as my greatest gift and glory.

The third of my days is now.

This day, the twelfth of July in the year of our Lord eighteen hundred and thirty-three, is well and truly all mine, and I share it with no one. It is my last. In some ways it will be like my wedding day, for I will wear white and put flowers in my hair. A solemn old man will escort me through the staring strangers, and a preacher will read words out of a book. Sarah Presnell has told me all of this about how it will be. She will not speak about what comes after, and it makes her cry when I press her for more, so I do not ask about it any longer. But I think about it. I wonder which is worse—the death, not knowing what comes after, or the wedding, when you think you know, but you're wrong. Perhaps dying is most like childbirth: a terrible, rivening pain, and then a great joy that makes you forget all that came before.

*　　*　　*

It is Friday, an apt day for a public execution killing the innocent, as Miss Mary has remarked more than once. So far no one has rebuked her for the blasphemy of comparing the death of our Lord to the legally mandated execution of a convicted murderess. I think we are all a bit ashamed about what will take place, for we think that the sentence is unjust, and we know that Miss Mary speaks rashly because she feels powerless to stop it. There will be a good many harsh words said of what we do here before it is over.

I find it ironic that of all the wagonloads of people who have come to town from the outlying areas, from the mountain lands, and from Table Rock and Jonas Ridge to witness the spectacle, who will shove and jostle one another for the best view of the gallows, it is only I—the one person who does not want to watch it happen—whose presence is required to see that the execution takes place. I am the eyes of the state of North Carolina, and I must tell the governor that what he wanted done has been done quickly and soberly, and that the county officials accorded the victim the civility and compassion of a solemn ritual.

There was to be no building of a gallows for the hanging of Frankie Silver. Burke County has no permanent scaffold, for although we must put men to death from time to time, such an event is sufficiently infrequent as to need no lasting reminder. Damon's Hill is the traditional site chosen for executions. Our Golgotha, Miss Mary calls it, blasphemous again. I wonder why executions are carried out in high places—Calvary, Tower Hill in England, Gallows Hill in Salem. . . . Is it some dim memory of the old custom of human sacrifice to the gods, or is it merely the state's wish that government-mandated deaths should be as visible as possible, so that others might see the suffering of the offender and be themselves deterred from committing crimes? Whatever our unconscious motives for the choice, Damon's Hill is the place where people are put to death in Burke County.

The hill is high enough to be seen from miles around, and it lies but a short distance from the jail and courthouse. On its summit is the place of execution: a broad, flat field, large enough to contain the great crowd of gawkers, and the dogs and horses and wagons that they would bring with them on gallows day. The field on Damon's Hill is crowned by a towering oak tree whose girth is so vast that ten men hand in hand could not encircle its trunk. It is beautiful in its spreading limbs and luxuriant foliage. Perhaps the oak was already growing on Damon's Hill when the colonists of Walter Raleigh's expedition first set foot upon North Carolina soil three centuries ago. Trees seem to live forever. By comparison, the nineteen years of Frankie Silver's little life seem no more than a flicker in time. That tree has outlived many a man in its long life span, and it has been the instrument of death for perhaps a score of others. That broad oak is the hanging tree.

It takes little enough to kill a convicted felon. A tree and a rope. John Boone procured the rope many days ago—before he could even bring himself to believe he would use it, I think, but he is a prudent man, and he knows that he must provide for every contingency. He has softened the gallows rope with mutton tallow and made sure that it is free of kinks, which would cause the rope to spin when a weight is attached to it. The thirty feet of hemp rope hangs now from a rafter in the barn behind the county jail. One end is looped tight around the rafter, and the other end is suspending a heavy sack of corn three feet above the barn's dirt floor. Ropes stretch when a heavy weight pulls down on them. If they are not stretched beforehand, this may happen at the time of the execution, and the result is said to be terrible to behold.

"Boone has never hanged a prisoner before," Squire Erwin told me when he returned from town one day in early July. "I had to go in and tell him a thing or two about the procedure, so that things will go smoothly when the time comes. Even when all goes well, a hanging is a brutal scene to watch, Burgess, but when something goes awry, it can be cruel beyond imagining. I was clerk of court for forty-four years, you know, and so I've seen my share of hangings, good and bad."

"I know very little about it," I said, with an inward shudder. Nor did I want to. "I believe I have heard that there is some skill required in gauging the length of the rope and the size of the victim."

William Erwin nodded. "That's it exactly," he said. "The ratio is everything, and God help you if you get it wrong. We had a hanging once where the rope stretched out and the victim's weight was not sufficient to the length of hemp. The poor devil landed on solid ground and had to be hoisted up again, crying piteously, while the onlookers moaned and wept to see his suffering."

"That must not happen this time," I said. "Though, of course, I hope that we may avoid the issue altogether with an eleventh-hour reprieve."

"I had a word with John Boone. I think he knows what must be done if he is called upon to do it. He has no heart for it, poor soul, but he recognizes his duty."

I shuddered again, mindful of my own obligation to be state's witness. "Will it take long?"

The old man sighed. "I'll warrant it will seem so to you, Burgess. It may feel like hours if you fix your eyes upon the condemned and watch the death throes, but you need not put yourself through that. Many a harder man than you has stared at the ground until the struggling ceased."

"But how long?"

"A quarter of an hour, perhaps."

"That much! Oh, surely not, sir! A rope around the neck cuts off the victim's air supply, and no one can live so long without drawing breath."

He sighed. "The rope is an imperfect instrument, son. It prevents most of the air from reaching the lungs—but not all of it. What follows is a sort of respiratory starvation—a slow stifling of the body, which fights for every morsel of air, even though the struggle prolongs the agony. We must hope that unconsciousness follows soon after the drop."

"Does it, then?"

The squire looked away. "Often not."

The ladies of the family were not present, of course, when

we spoke of the process of hanging. Neither of us had any intention of discussing such an inappropriate subject in their presence, though I was certainly pressed for details about the matter by my wife and several of her sisters. The Carolina gentlewoman is not the delicate creature that society would have us believe.

"It is monstrous!" my wife announced to the gaggle of family in the hall one evening. "North Carolina actually means to hang a woman. I cannot believe it!"

Her father has little liking for bold talk from the ladies. "What would you have them do, Elizabeth?" he said harshly. "Should we give her a medal for butchering her husband? The state of Massachusetts once burnt a woman at the stake for murder. Would you prefer that?"

Elizabeth turned horrified eyes upon her father. "Burnt a woman? I do not believe that."

I cleared my throat and said softly, "It was a slave woman, my dear. In colonial times."

"Oh. Well. It is terrible nonetheless," she said, stabbing at her embroidery with the needle until I feared for her fingers beneath the fabric. "And I am sure that hanging is no less cruel."

"It will indeed be terrible to watch," said her sister Catherine.

"We shall not go," said Miss Mary Erwin, before her father could utter the same words.

We all turned to her in speechless wonder. Mary Erwin had been the champion of Mrs. Silver from the beginning. I could not believe that she would willingly abandon her cause at the last, although I was certain that the squire would have forbidden her to go in any case. "We shall not go," she said again, and her voice was calm, but it brooked no argument.

"Why not?" asked Elizabeth.

"Mrs. Silver would not want us to see her die—shamed in front of a jeering crowd. The hanging will be her last violation, and then she will be at peace. We must remember her as she was in life. It is the last gift we can give her."

The ladies all nodded in agreement, and the squire very

wisely refrained from adding that he would not have permitted them to attend anyhow. It seemed that I was the only one of the immediate family who would be present at the death of Frankie Silver.

Miss Mary went back to her sewing. I watched her there, haloed in candlelight, making the tiny even stitches on the wool tapestry cloth, and I wondered what she was thinking behind that calm facade. Without looking up at me, she said, "Mr. Gaither, there is something I'd like you to take to the jail tomorrow."

The governor had fixed the time of the hanging for Friday afternoon the twelfth of July, between the hours of one and four o'clock. I thought the actual time of the execution would be close to four: the late hour would allow the prisoner's family time to make the journey if they wished, and it would enable most of the onlookers to travel to town from the farthest reaches of the county to view the spectacle. I arrived at the jail just before noon, to find the town streets already choked with people and horses, churning up great quantities of red dust in their wake.

A guard with a rifle was posted on the porch of the white frame building, but the fellow knew me by sight, and he nodded a greeting, offering no objection when I went past him. I wanted to make sure that all the preliminaries for the execution had been performed, and that no detail had been overlooked. I suppose I was half hoping that a special messenger had arrived from Raleigh granting an eleventh-hour reprieve. Certainly one had done so in my dreams these past few nights, but when I entered the hallway of the jail, I could see that no hope remained.

John Boone looked as old and sick as I had ever seen him. He cannot have slept these past few days, for his eyes were bleak with weariness and his skin was gray as worm flesh. "Is all in readiness?" I asked him.

He nodded. "The preparations are made. The rope and the wagon stand ready, and all the constables will be present in case anyone tries to interfere with the execution."

"Interfere?" The thought of an attack had not occurred to me until then. "The Stewarts, you mean?"

"Perhaps. She will not say who helped her to escape. Feelings are running high about the execution. We can trust no one."

I saw that he was eyeing the white bundle under my arm, and I hastened to assure him that he had nothing to fear from me. "Miss Mary sent this to the prisoner," I said. "It is only cloth. You will want to open it and examine it carefully, of course, but I think I can vouch for my sister-in-law."

Sheriff Boone did not smile. "I can't have anyone slipping her poison," he grunted, unwrapping the package and fingering its contents. "It seems all right. From Miss Mary Erwin, you say? Will you want to give this to her yourself?"

I nodded. "I think I should. The ladies have asked me to say good-bye to her for them. I won't stay very long, if you'll allow me to go up now and see her."

"All right. I think she's calm enough, though she will not eat. Sarah Presnell has been with her most of the morning, but she left a little while ago. I think she's making a last meal for Mrs. Silver. I reckon she'll be glad of some company, to take her mind off her sorrow. The preacher came, but she wouldn't see him."

"What about her family?"

"Her father and brother are here in town, but I cannot allow them in the jail because of the escape. She has not asked for them."

He clambered up the stairs, pausing for breath at the top step. "I hate to see this happen, Mr. Gaither. She's no older than my children, poor lass."

I patted his arm. "I know. We must try to ease her suffering all we can."

I stood back while John Boone unlocked the door to the prisoner's cell. "Visitor for you, Frankie!" he called out. "I'll be downstairs," he told me, and as he walked past me, I saw his eyes glisten with unshed tears in the dim light.

I clutched the bundle to my chest and stepped inside the little room. "Mrs. Silver? It's Burgess Gaither here."

She was sitting on her camp bed, swollen-eyed from weeping, but calm now. When she saw me, she shrank back against the wall and whispered, "Is it time?"

"No. It is early yet. The sheriff will come for you in a few hours, not I. I only wanted to bring you a gift from the ladies of the Erwin family. They send their regards, and they asked me to tell you that you will be remembered in their prayers."

"They won't be coming to see me, then, sir?"

"They thought it best not to, in case their tears upset you. They are grieving. They sent you this." Again I held out the bundle, and this time she took it, walking the length of her chain and stretching her hands out to me like a toddling child. Her face brightened as she accepted the offering, and I thought what sad creatures we mortals are, to delight in gifts even as we are dying. I watched as she set the package down on the camp bed and carefully untied the twine that bound it. She unfolded the fabric and held it up to look at it in the sunlight from the window of her cell.

"Oh, sir," she whispered, pressing the white linen against her body.

Miss Mary had sent the prisoner the dress of white lace and linen that she had worn last summer when the Erwin sisters first visited the jail. "Take her this," my sister-in-law had said, thrusting the bundle into my hands and turning away with the first tears that I had ever seen upon her face. "It's little enough that we can do for her."

I remembered that little Mrs. Silver had admired the garment, touching it reverently as though it were the robe of a queen instead of the ordinary morning dress of a country gentlewoman. It pained me to think that her only hope of ever wearing such a garment was to come to town under a sentence of death.

"It's a handsome dress," said Mrs. Silver, fingering the delicate cloth. "Better than I ever had. She means me to have it?"

I nodded. Miss Mary had spent the evening sewing hour altering the dress to fit Frankie Silver's tiny frame.

"They visited me, and read me stories to pass the time. I thank them for that."

I nodded. "We all wish we could have done more."

She turned her gaze to the window, and I think she was on the verge of weeping again, but after a moment she said, "I wish they'd tell me a story now. The time is heavy on my hands, and I am afraid."

I wanted nothing more than to flee the narrow cell and take refuge in the July sunshine of the Presnells' garden, but I could not leave that poor lost creature to contemplate her death alone. "Has the preacher been to see you?"

She nodded. "I wouldn't see him. Last time he came, I wanted him to tell me about heaven, but he would not. He kept saying that unless I named all my sins I would burn forever. He asked me who set me free that night. I wouldn't tell him, though. Do you think I will go to hell for that, sir?"

"No. I cannot think so."

She sighed. "I'm weary of praying. Reckon the Lord and I will be talking it over face-to-face soon enough. I asked the preacher to tell me a story once, and he told me about the good thief who was crucified with Jesus but went with him to paradise."

I had promised the ladies that I would do what I could to comfort Mrs. Silver, and there seemed no other way that I could help her. "I'm not much use as a storyteller," I said, "but if it will ease your mind, I will do my best."

I searched my memory for some tale that would distract the poor lost girl from the thought of her death, and perhaps it was her maiden name of Stewart as much as her present circumstances that suggested the only one that came to me "It isn't a happy story," I warned her, "but it is about a queen, and it is true."

She nodded. "Happy stories mostly ain't true." She hugged the dress to her and sat down upon her bed to listen.

"Long ago in Scotland there lived a beautiful young queen whose name was Stuart. . . ."

"Same as mine."

"Yes. She was called Mary, Queen of Scots, and her father

had been the king, but he died and left the throne to her. She was said to be very beautiful, but she had a sad life. She married a handsome young man called Darnley, but he was blown to pieces in an explosion at a place called Kirk o' Field, and afterward people said that Mary had killed him."

"What happened to her? Did they hang her?"

"Well, she was put in prison at first." I paused for a moment to collect my thoughts, and then I told her, as simply as I could, the long tale of the intrigue between Mary, Queen of Scots, and her cousin Elizabeth of England.

Frankie Silver sat listening to me, rubbing the sore on her ankle where the chain had rubbed, but her eyes were wide and she seemed transported by my clumsy attempt at telling the tale of two great queens. Perhaps for a moment or two she even forgot her own unhappy circumstances, but as I neared the end of the story, she was reminded all too clearly.

I came to the account of Queen Elizabeth signing the death warrant of her beautiful cousin, after being convinced that Mary was plotting to seize the throne of England. "And so, because she was charged with committing treason by planning to overthrow the rightful queen of England, she was condemned to die."

Frankie Silver nodded.

"She was to be beheaded." I began to wish that I had not embarked upon this particular tale to divert the prisoner, but as there was no turning back, I thought that perhaps Mary Stuart could inspire her fellow prisoner to courage on the scaffold. "They say that she went to her death very bravely. She spent the night in prayer with her ladies, and in the wee hours before dawn she walked to the block with the courage of a martyr."

"She didn't scream or cry when she saw the knife?"

"The ax. No. It does no good to weep at such a time. It only gladdens your enemies. Mary believed that she would shortly be in heaven."

"Did she wear white?"

I remembered the histories I had read, and I recalled seeing an illustration in a book once that showed the Queen of

Scots going to the block in a wimpled headdress and a deep black dress in the Tudor fashion. "Yes," I said, "I believe she wore white."

She considered this for a few moments. "She died then?"
"Yes."

"Do you think she killed her husband?"

I took a deep breath. "If she did, I'm sure that she was very sorry, and I think she made her peace with God before the end. She died bravely."

"Why wasn't she afraid? I am. I have prayed and prayed, but I'm still afraid. So afraid."

"Three years ago I watched my brother Alfred die," I said. "He was a young man—not as young as you, but still in the bloom of his youth. He sickened, and when the doctor knew that all hope was lost, the family gathered at his bedside. Alfred had been in great pain, I think, from his illness, for he thrashed in his delirium and he soaked the sheets with the sweat of his fever, but in the end . . . in the last moment before his soul took flight, he grew calm and still, and a great peace settled over his face, almost as if someone had shone a light upon him, and he smiled at us—or, rather, beyond us—and then he was gone. I had never seen him happier."

She nodded. "But it will hurt."

"Only for a little while. And then it is finished, and you have come out on the other side. You are free."

She nodded. "I will wear the dress, sir. Tell the ladies that. I will wear white for paradise."

I left her then, and spent the hours of the early afternoon pacing the lawn of the courthouse and then sifting through the papers on my writing table, as if my mind could address any matter other than the execution. I stayed close to the courthouse all afternoon, for I wanted to be easy to find. *Surely the reprieve will come to me,* I thought. *They must be able to locate me when the messenger arrives.* I had read the finality in the governor's message, but the death of that gentle young girl seemed so improbable that I could not help persuading myself that she would be saved.

At last the hands on my pocket watch advanced toward the hour of three, and I knew that it was time for the ceremony to proceed. With great reluctance I picked up the copy of the death warrant from among my papers, for it would have to be read to the prisoner before we escorted her to Damon's Hill.

I returned to the jail to find that a small open cart had been drawn up to the porch, and the guard was now engaged in keeping at bay a great crowd of noisy onlookers, who were cheering and shouting for the hanging to commence. I looked for Isaiah Stewart and his eldest son, but I could not find them in that sea of faces.

When I went inside, I found that Sheriff Boone had already brought the prisoner downstairs to make ready for departure. Frankie Silver stood there, small and silent, surrounded by Burke County deputies. Sarah Presnell hovered nearby, shedding silent tears as she watched the preparations.

Mrs. Silver was wearing the white dress that Miss Mary had sent her, and I was reminded once again of a bride, as I had been months before when the prisoner had entered the courtroom with her head held high and proceeded down the aisle almost in triumph. The only hint of mourning in her present attire was a black satin bonnet tied with ribbons under her chin. It was trimmed with one red rose. I knew that the bonnet would have to be removed when we reached the place of execution, but I saw no harm in letting her wear her finery until then. Mrs. Silver's ankles were still shackled in the great iron chain, but her hands were unbound—another kindness on the part of Sheriff Boone, and one that I approved of, for it would only compound the ordeal for all of us if the poor girl became terrified and screamed all the way to the hanging tree. *Please, God, keep her calm*, I thought.

John Boone noticed me then. "We are nearly ready," he told me.

I withdrew the death warrant from my pocket. "I must read her the sentence," I reminded him.

He nodded impatiently. "Be quick about it then, sir. Let's have it over with, if it has to be done."

I turned to the prisoner. "I am required by law to read to you the judge's order for your execution. Do you understand?"

She nodded. "Go on."

I found that the paper was shaking as I began to read from it, and it was then that I realized I was as unstrung as the rest of them. With many pauses for breath and composure, I managed to make it through the few sentences that ordered the death by hanging of Frances Stewart Silver on Friday, the twelfth day of July, in the year of our Lord eighteen hundred and thirty-three.

When I had finished, I looked at the prisoner, but she gave no sign of having heard me. I thought that to press her further would only increase her suffering, so I took my leave of them and turned to go.

"Mr. Gaither?" Frankie Silver's voice called me back. "Do I look fitten?"

I looked at her, a tiny slip of a girl in a cast-off linen dress and a poke bonnet over her flaxen hair. "You look like a queen," I said.

They took her outside then, and bundled her into the back of the little one-horse cart. The shackles around her ankle caught on the side of the cart, and one of the sheriff's men lifted it and laid it gently in beside her. She moved to cover the leg iron with her skirt as if it had been a delicate undergarment. People crowded around for a close look at the condemned prisoner, and some of them shouted encouragement, but she ignored them. She put her hand to her mouth when the rope was placed beside her, but after a moment's alarm she was calm once more. Just as a constable slapped the reins and the cart began to move, Sarah Presnell hurried down the steps of the jail holding out half a fruit pie on a wooden plate. I could not make out the words she shouted above the roar of the crowd, but I saw that the pie was blackberry, and I remembered that Frankie Silver had spoken of her fondness for it. She leaned out the back of the cart and took the plate, with a little smile of thanks for her last friend.

I went to my tethered horse and prepared to ride ahead and await the procession at Damon's Hill. As I walked away, I saw Frankie Silver biting into the wine-dark pie, while Sarah Presnell stood on the jail porch, her apron to her face, and wept.

I was waiting at the top of Damon's Hill when the sad procession arrived some twenty minutes later. I had thought it best to arrive in advance of the prisoner in case any trouble awaited them at the place of execution. I did not dismount yet, for the saddle would give me a greater vantage point to scan the throng for troublemakers, though I saw none. An even greater crowd awaited the arrival of the prisoner, and the atmosphere in that summer meadow was that of a fair day. Children and dogs ran, laughed, and chased one another in and out among the clumps of spectators, and here and there a few cows grazed, untroubled by the mass of people invading their field. I was sorry to see a good many women in the crowd, but they were a very drab and common sort of female, and I saw no gentlewomen present. Such sights are not fit for the eyes of a lady.

Among the onlookers I saw old men selling meat pies and cups of cider from a stone jug. The term *gala* comes from gallows, and now I saw the truth of that word used to describe festivities. Most of those present did not know the prisoner or the victim, perhaps they did not even know the details of the case, but they were happy to have the monotony of their dreary lives broken by a spectacle, however tragic its outcome.

The summer sun beat down on me, and flies buzzed around the tail of my mare, and I realized that I was thirsty. I dabbed at my forehead with a linen handkerchief and vowed silently that my tongue would blacken and burst before I would take cider from those merry scavengers with their tin cups.

More people streamed into the meadow, and I knew that the sheriff's procession must be near. I saw James Erwin break away from the others and canter toward me across the grass. He guided his great bay horse alongside mine. "At least we've a clear day for it," he said, waving his straw hat at the clustering mayflies. "I thought the heavens themselves would open up for this travesty."

"So they should," I said. "This woman does not deserve to hang."

A great roar went up from the crowd as the wooden cart rolled up the dirt path and lumbered across the field. We moved our mounts closer to the oak tree, ready to offer assistance if any were needed. From the top of Damon's Hill, one can see all of Morganton spread out like a child's toy village, and I turned away from the scene in the meadow to look at the deserted streets below.

James Erwin was watching me. "There will be no rider," he said.

He was right. There was not. The dusty streets were as empty and silent as if it were midnight. My last hope was gone.

The cart was positioned beneath the oak tree now, and a deputy tossed one end of the rope over the thickest limb, a great log of a branch about twelve feet above the ground. It took him two tries to get the rope across it, and he suffered the jeers of the crowd for his clumsiness, though I doubted if those that mocked him could have done it any better.

James Erwin nudged me then, and nodded toward the crowd grouped closest to the cart. Isaiah Stewart and his son Jackson had shoved their way to a position near the prisoner, but a constable had stationed himself beside them, and I saw no sign of weapons. Frankie Silver saw them, but she made no move to embrace her father or brother, and her expression had not softened. She was dry-eyed and so were they.

The sheriff had taken one end of the rope and was making the noose: seven loops and a slipknot at the top of them. The softened rope was still greasy with mutton tallow, and flies kept alighting on the length of it. John Boone swatted them away. Tears streamed down his cheeks, and I think he was struck by the indignity of the poor creature's last minutes on earth. I was glad that someone wept for her.

At last all was in readiness. The people swarmed closer to

the cart for a better look, and the lawmen shooed them away again like mayflies. They will want a piece of the rope for a keepsake.

Gabe Presnell took hold of the horse's halter to steady the cart, for the animal was frightened by the crush of people around it.

A minister who had approached the cart laid his hand upon Mrs. Silver's shoulder and spoke to her in an urgent undertone. I knew that he was beseeching her to confess her sins, so that she might be forgiven and be spared the fires of hell in the Hereafter. She made him no reply, however, and a moment later he began to pray aloud in a sonorous voice. "Have mercy upon me, O God, according to thy loving kindness. . . ."

"The fifty-first Psalm," muttered James Erwin. "The Tyburn Hymn, it's called, because they always said it over the condemned at the scaffold in London."

". . . Deliver me from bloodguiltiness, O God. . . ."

Frankie Silver was pale, and her breath was coming in great gulps, but she seemed unmoved by the oration. She looked at the sky. Perhaps her thoughts were elsewhere, and the intonations of the minister were a fly buzz among the roar of the crowd.

". . . For thou desirest not sacrifice; else would I give it: thou delightest not in burnt offering. The sacrifices of God are a broken spirit: a broken and a contrite heart. . . ."

Someone shouted, "Get on with it!" and others in the crowd took up the chant.

A few moments later the parson stepped away from the prisoner's side, and Sheriff Boone clambered into the cart and motioned for Mrs. Silver to rise. She swayed for an instant as she got to her feet, and one of the deputies took a length of rope and bound her hands to her sides. The sheriff, his furrowed face still streaked with tears, untied the black poke bonnet and removed it from her head. The crowd gasped to see that the prisoner's blond hair had been cropped as short as a boy's. It could not be allowed to entwine in the rope, which might have caused her more pain, but nonetheless it was a final indignity, and I grieved to see her shamed so.

The sheriff slipped the noose over her head and tightened it, placing the knot on the left side of her neck.

"Frances Stewart Silver," he intoned, "it is my duty as sheriff of Burke County, North Carolina, to carry out the sentence handed down by Judge Henry Seawall of the Superior Court, that you be taken to the place of execution, and therein hanged by the neck until you are dead. And—" His voice faltered for a moment. He took a deep breath and managed to say, "And may God have mercy on your soul. Have you any last words?"

She had not been able to speak in court. She had kept her silence for the long months after the trial. Even those few of us who had heard her confession had not heard all of it, for she would not talk about the cutting up of Charlie Silver's body, nor would she speak of her ill-starred escape from the county jail. This was her last chance. Her last chance, too, to make her peace with Almighty God so that she might be received into paradise. Many a highwayman confessed his guilt upon the scaffold for fear of torments in the Hereafter. Surely this poor creature would do no less.

She nodded, and took a step away from John Boone, toward the surging crowd, who suddenly fell silent, for she had begun to speak. "Good people . . . I . . ."

"Die with it in you, Frankie!"

Isaiah Stewart's voice rang out across the meadow. The words were a harsh command, and for a moment they hung there in the air, echoing in that charged silence, and then the roar from the spectators resumed louder than ever.

Frankie Silver hesitated for a moment, and a look passed between her and her father. He stared at her, stern-faced, arms crossed, waiting.

She stepped back and nodded to John Boone that she was ready. He was weeping openly now, but she was calm, and I'd like to think that her thoughts were on the Queen of Scots, whose story I had told her that morning, and how that

Stuart woman had died bravely and with the dignity of a queen.

"The father has silenced her," said James Erwin, after a startled silence. "Where was he when the Silver boy was murdered?"

"Miles away," I replied. "In Kentucky, on a long hunt."

"So he cannot be guilty. *Then what did he not want her to say?*"

I shook my head. Frankie Silver would take her secret to the grave. It was little enough to let her keep.

She stood there trembling in her white linen dress, with her hands roped to her sides. They slipped a white cloth hood over her head, so that the eager spectators could not revel in her death agonies. A man on the ground took hold of the end of the rope which dangled from the low branch, lashing it securely to the trunk of the oak.

"I cannot watch this," said James Erwin.

Before I could reply, he had turned his horse and trotted away. He passed behind the crowd, and by the time he reached the edge of the meadow, the bay was in full gallop, and a moment later he had vanished from sight.

So I was left alone: the state's official witness, there to see that the will of the people of North Carolina was done as the governor wished it done. They stood her up until the rope was taut, and then someone took hold of the horse's bridle and led it away, so that the cart was no longer beneath the prisoner. For a moment her tiny feet had teetered on the edge of the cart, and then they dangled in the air above the grass of Damon's Hill. The crowd gave a great shout when they saw her struggle at the end of the rope, swaying gently amid a circle of mayflies.

And I had to watch.

I am afraid now. I count my breaths, knowing how few are left to me. But deep underneath the pounding terror is a disbelief that I am bound to die. I cannot see the way of leaving this world, and I cannot imagine the next one. If I am to go to hell, then where is Charlie Silver? And if we should meet in paradise, will there be forgiveness between us? On your head be this, Charlie, for you are the one who made all of it happen. I reckon you have paid for it dear enough, though, and if God has pardoned you, then I will.

I wonder if there are mountains in heaven. The preacher talks of the city of God, but even if it is peopled with angels, I don't want to go there. I am done with walls. I shall camp in God's wilderness, where it is always summer. Then I will truly be home.

I hope that when they stand me up high with the rope around my neck, they will let me turn toward the mountains. I would like to see them one last time. My Nancy is up there. It's all right if she forgets me, if she is happy in days to come. Let her be happy.

I cannot think about my Nancy anymore. I mean to die like a soldier.

They meant to be kind this morning. John Boone kissed my forehead and said that he would see me in heaven, and dear Sarah Presnell brought me pie as I was leaving on the cart. "I made the hood that will cover your head," she whispered to me as she placed the pastry in my hand. "I soaked it in lavender water, so that when you can see no more, you will still have the smell of flowers to keep up your courage. Take a deep breath."

Yes, a last deep breath. But at least it will smell of flowers.

The earnest young lawyer also tried to comfort me. He told me tales about a queen whose name was the same as mine, but what do I know of queens and far-off castles? What does that tell me about what it will be like to die here, in a field in Burke County? It is terrible not to know what is coming. The white dress told me. Perhaps Miss Mary meant it as a sign to me, and if so I understood, and then I was no longer afraid. I put on the clean white dress, and at last I knew where I was going.

I remembered what was going to happen.

You dress yourself in a white robe, and you go with your kinfolk to the gathering place on the bank of a river. The preacher comes and stands at your side. He says words over you. . . . I have done this before . . . and a great congregation of people is there to witness the change in you. . . . The minister puts his hand on your head, and he plunges you downward into the river of death, and you float there for what seems like forever with your lungs bursting for a gulp of air. At last it is over, and when you rise up again, you will be glad, and free, and purified. And then you will walk with God.

And then you will walk with God.

At last—at long last—it was over, and they cut her down. Her little head fell forward upon her breast, and they laid her on the ground, while Dr. Tate felt her pulse for signs of life. There were none. We had seen the life go out of her, though it went slowly, and the sight was so harrowing that the great loutish crowd were themselves reduced to tears. I hope they were sorry they had come.

The body of Frankie Silver was given to her father and brother, with the hood still mercifully covering her face with its staring eyes and protruding tongue. Still stone-faced and silent, the Stewarts wrapped the tiny form in a blanket and laid it in the back of their wagon. They were heading back up the mountain, they said, to bury Frankie with her own people on Stewart land. But it is July, and the breathless heat makes the flies relentless. Forty miles up mountain is a long journey with a lifeless body in high summer. I think they must have buried her secretly that night somewhere along the Yellow Mountain Road, and it saddens me to think that she lies alone, so far from her loved ones. But she is at peace now in her fine white dress, and she is well away from Charlie Silver, so perhaps she is glad after all.

That night I went to James Erwin's home and sat in silence by his fireside, drinking his brandy and not setting out for home until I was sure that Belvidere would be in darkness, and all the ladies long asleep.

Burgess Gaither

AFTERWARD

After the death of Frankie Silver, I continued in my position as clerk of Superior Court for four more years, after which I went into private practice. My career had prospered, and I like to think that my ability had as much to do with my success as my family connections. Perhaps I never really felt at home in Morganton society, but I learned well enough how to act the part, and there were times when I went so far as to forget that I was an outsider in the ranks of the aristocracy. My family was as good as any of theirs, but the wealth was lacking. After two generations, the lack of a fortune removes one from polite society, so I took care that I should acquire one, for I had my sons to think of.

I represented Burke County in the State Senate in 1840–41, and at the end of that time President Tyler honored me with the appointment of superintendent of the United States Mint in Charlotte. Two years later, I returned to the State Senate, and this year, 1851, I ran for the United States Congress. I lost, though, to Thomas Clingman, so perhaps I shall return to the state legislature next year, if the good people of Burke see fit to send me back.

Despite the time I have spent at the Mint in Charlotte, and with the legislature in Raleigh, Morganton continues to be my home. A dozen years ago I built a little house on North Anderson Street. It is a one-story Greek Revival–style house, designed by Mr. Marsh of Charlotte, nothing as grand as Belvidere, of course, but it has a fine pedimented entrance porch supported by fluted Doric columns, and it is quite suitable for a town-dwelling attorney of modest means and no pretensions to aristocracy. I shall be happy to spend the rest of my days in that house, when I am no longer called upon to serve the citizenry with duties elsewhere.

Old Squire Erwin died in 1837, two years before his granddaughter Delia was born to Elizabeth and me. So now we have two sons, William and Alfred, to carry on the names of our departed loved ones, and our darling Delia, who is a proper little lady like her mother.

I saw Nicholas Woodfin from time to time after the trial of Frankie Silver, of course, for we were brother attorneys in the same district, and our paths were bound to cross both professionally and socially, for he, too, was a Whig in politics. He had prospered in the years since I first knew him. He is a shirttail relative now, for he married Miss Eliza Grace McDowell of Quaker Meadows, my wife's cousin, and though they make their home in Asheville, we see them from time to time.

Woodfin served in the State Senate the year after I left it, but his true renown was as an eloquent trial attorney. By tacit agreement, we did not speak of his first capital case for many years thereafter. I think he was ashamed of his failure to secure a pardon for his client, and I think he was genuinely grieved and blamed himself for her tragedy. Since then, I have heard many of our fellow attorneys remark on the curious fact that Nicholas Woodfin refused to represent clients who were on trial for their lives. I thought I knew the reason why.

It was nearly twenty years after the case of Frankie Silver that we met again under circumstances that called to mind the events surrounding our first encounter.

In November 1851, William Waightstill Avery, a prominent fellow attorney and my own nephew by marriage, was charged with murder.

Waightstill was a student in college at the time of the trial of Frankie Silver, which made him nine years younger than

I, and I had always considered myself an older relative rather than a comrade. He was the son of my wife's eldest sister Harriet, who had married Isaac Thomas Avery of Swan Ponds. Young Waightstill, who was named after his paternal grandfather, North Carolina's first attorney general, was a clever and hardworking fellow who had graduated as valedictorian of his class at the state university in Chapel Hill. He went on to read law with Judge William Gaston, qualifying to practice in 1839, the year that I was elected to represent Burke County in the North Carolina State Senate. In 1851, at the time of his trial, Waightstill had just completed a second term representing Burke County in the North Carolina House of Commons. He was thirty-five years old.

The tragedy that led to his being charged with murder began eighteen days earlier, when Waightstill Avery was arguing a civil case in the McDowell County Superior Court. He was representing a McDowell County man named Ephraim Greenlee, a former client of attorney Samuel Fleming of Marion. Greenlee was accusing Fleming of fraud in connection with some disputed property, and during the course of arguing the case, Waightstill Avery blamed Sam Fleming for the disappearance of a will that was relevant evidence in the matter. I am not sure whether he was arguing that Fleming was careless, incompetent, or deliberately concealing the pertinent documents for his own gain, but one interpretation is scarcely better than the other when a lawyer's reputation is at stake.

Fleming took exception to this slur on his skills as an attorney, for, of course, he denied any blame in the matter. Fleming was a tall, red-faced fellow with a thatch of auburn curls and a fiery temper to match. He towered over young Waightstill Avery, quivering with indignation and shouting that he'd have satisfaction for this insult to his honor.

Avery took this for the usual legal bravado that one hears bandied about in the law courts, but this time he had misjudged his opponent, with fatal consequences. When court was adjourned, Avery gathered up his papers and left the courthouse, but when he got outside, he saw that Samuel

Fleming was waiting in the street for him, shouting abuse and brandishing a rawhide horsewhip in a threatening manner, while the north wind whipped his cape about him, making him look like an avenging devil. There's those who would say that's exactly what he was. Sam Fleming was not rich in friendships.

Now my nephew Avery was a small man, and he had perhaps the more pride and dignity because of it, but he was by no means a coward, nor was he an undistinguished citizen of the Carolina frontier. He had no reason to fear a fellow attorney, for although I say that he was a citizen of the "Carolina frontier," things had changed a good deal in the two decades since the trial of Frankie Silver. True, there were as yet no railroads in the mountains, but the roads were better now. The population continued to grow, and the cities were no longer rustic hamlets dotted through the endless forest. The Indians had been removed across the Mississippi, the economy was flourishing, and western North Carolina was as pleasant and peaceful a place as one could find upon God's green earth. We were civilized gentlemen serving the law, and brothers all by the mutual respect conferred by our profession.

Samuel Fleming cared nothing for the sanctity of the legal fraternity, nor for the peace of McDowell County. He was after blood.

I was not present when the altercation took place, but I heard many accounts of it afterward, and everyone agreed that Samuel Fleming was abusive and reckless in his manner. When Waightstill Avery tried to edge past his tormentor, knocking him down in the process, the enraged Mr. Fleming flung himself upon the smaller man, pounding him about the head and shoulders with a rock until he was stunned into insensibility. While poor Waightstill sat there in the muddy high street, attempting to get his bearings and regain his footing, Samuel Fleming lit into him with the horsewhip, punctuating each slash with an oath.

In his dazed and weakened condition, poor Avery could not defend himself. Indeed he was so much smaller and less robust than his opponent that it is doubtful whether he could have given a good account of himself even if he had been perfectly fit. He lay there in the mire, hands braced before him to shield his face and neck from the blows, while blood from the welts on his cheek dripped onto his broadcloth coat and spangled the mud beneath him with flecks of red.

I would like to think that someone in that great throng of onlookers went to his aid, while other right-thinking citizens pulled Samuel Fleming away and tried to talk sense into him. I never heard of anyone interfering, though, and I am forced to conclude that a crowd watched this shameful performance, and perhaps even cheered it on, with no thought toward rescuing the unfortunate victim.

At last—no doubt when his stream of invective had given out and his arm was tired—Fleming ceased his attack upon my unfortunate nephew and swaggered off, boasting about the thrashing that he had given to the young turkey cock who would question his competence as a lawyer. Waightstill Avery was helped to a house nearby, where his wounds were seen to, while a servant took a damp rag and tried as best she could to remove the streaks of mud from his coat and breeches. He was not badly hurt, but the shame and injustice of that public whipping festered inside Waightstill Avery worse than gangrene ever cankered an injured limb. In Morganton he made light of the cuts and bruises and kept his own counsel about his feelings toward his assailant, but word of Fleming's continual boasting reached us in Burke County, and all of us knew that the incident was not over.

Two weeks after the confrontation in Marion, Mr. Fleming had yet another occasion to appear in court, but this time he was representing clients before Judge Kemp Battle at the new courthouse in Morganton. I call this building the new courthouse even though it is twenty years old, but I am nearly fifty now, and time does not move as slowly for me as it once did. This present courthouse was under construction at the time that Frankie Silver was in jail awaiting her execution, and I remember feeling glad at the time that after the tragic circumstances of the Silver case, we could put the past behind us and begin again the pursuit of justice in a new building. I have since learned that it is not so easy to wipe the slate clean; there is enough tragedy and iniquity in the world to fill any amount of courthouses and judicial buildings.

I was there when it happened, but I confess that I felt no inkling of the tragedy that was to come.

Sam Fleming approached the table where Waightstill Avery was concentrating on a point of law in the case at hand. I did not think that Waightstill had even seen Fleming coming, so intent was he upon the argument before the judge, but the incident in Marion two weeks earlier still rankled, and he must have thought that Fleming intended to torment him further. When Fleming was an arm's length away, Waightstill raised a pistol and pointed it toward his enemy, and before anyone in the courtroom could cry out or attempt to stop him, he fired the weapon point-blank at Samuel Fleming's heart.

He was dead before anyone of us reached him, and Waightstill made no move to flee the consequences of his action. He stood there calmly, handed the pistol over to the bailiff, and said that his honor was satisfied now, and that he was willing to be tried for his actions, because Sam Fleming needed killing. And when the facts were put forth in the presence of a jury, Waightstill thought that justice would be done. They led him away, and took him to the jail for form's sake, but he was out on bond before nightfall. I joined the family council at Belvidere to plan the strategy of my nephew's defense.

The trial was held in November 1851, only a few weeks after the incident. Waightstill would not have to languish in jail for months awaiting judgment as poor Frankie Silver had done. He was neither poor nor friendless. When the day came for William Waightstill Avery to appear before the court in Morganton to answer for the death of Samuel Fleming, he was represented by four members of counsel, all

gentlemen that he could count as friends, and all distinguished attorneys, if I may say that without boasting, for I
was one of their number.

So was Nicholas Woodfin. I knew him better now than I
did all those years ago, when, as a newly fledged attorney, he
had defended Frankie Silver. Now he was counted one of us,
a kinsman of sorts, for he had been married to Eliza Grace
some dozen years now.

The two other members of counsel were even more prominent men in the state, and perhaps they were chosen for
their eminence more than for their legal skills. Mr. Tod R.
Caldwell and General John Gray Bynum of Rutherfordton
were both lawyers, but both had gained distinction in the political sphere rather than in the courtroom.

Tod Caldwell was an Irishman whose grandfather had
been exiled from the old country in the rebellion of 1798.
His father had been a shopkeeper in Morganton, and young
Tod, who was a year or two younger than my nephew
Waightstill Avery, had clerked in his father's establishment
before his own talent and ambition had led him off to study
at the University of North Carolina. He simultaneously read
law under the tutelage of David Lowry Swain, and became
the first person ever to graduate from the university and receive his license to practice law at one and the same time.
Then he went into law practice in Morganton, entering politics about ten years ago, when the county elected him to
serve in the North Carolina House of Commons with our
other county delegates, Mr. O. J. Neal and William Waightstill Avery. The two young men were friends and adversaries
throughout their lives, for a town like Morganton is hardly
big enough to cage two such lions. I have often thought that
one of them will end up being governor. I had not thought
that the other would end up on the scaffold.

"He is to have four lawyers?" I said to Woodfin when we
all assembled a few days before the trial.

Nicholas Woodfin smiled. "There is no one so cautious—
or so rightfully afraid—as an attorney who must face trial by
jury."

"I suppose it is mainly for show," I said. "To demonstrate to the jury that the most prominent citizens of western North Carolina stand behind Waightstill in his hour of trouble."

"Mostly that," Woodfin agreed. "I believe I am to do most of the speechmaking, since I have the most trial experience."

"You have made quite a name for yourself in the court-room since we first met," I told him. "We are all glad that you are making an exception to your rule about not appear-ing in capital cases."

Woodfin nodded. "Waightstill is family as well as a friend and colleague," he reminded me. "Besides, I do not really consider this a capital case."

"Waightstill shot the fellow in open court. I saw it. It was no duel. I do not think that Fleming even saw the weapon. But, of course, as one of Waightstill's attorneys, I cannot testify."

Nicholas Woodfin smiled. "Nor can Waightstill, since he is the defendant, but from what I hear, there were witnesses aplenty to the horsewhipping incident in Marion. I think we can show a jury that Sam Fleming needed killing."

"But why not challenge the fellow to a duel?" I asked. "Lord knows there is family precedent for that. Waightstill's grandfather and namesake once got into just such a quarrel with a fellow lawyer over in Tennessee. They agreed to a duel, and when the time came for the battle of honor, each man carefully fired a shot over the head of the other. They left the field the best of friends—or so the family says."

Woodfin looked thoughtful. "Who was the other lawyer?"

"Andrew Jackson."

"I thought so." Woodfin smiled. "Well, that was a long time ago, my friend, and there were giants in those days, but here in 1851, we are given the task of defending a man whose opponent was even less of a gentleman than Andrew Jackson. Horsewhipping a colleague in a public street! I ask you!"

"And you think you can get him freed, despite the lapse of two weeks between incident and reprisal? Despite the scores of witnesses?"

"Of course I can," said Woodfin. "No one should hang when his offense has been committed in defense of his person or his honor."

"I wish you could have convinced a jury of that twenty years ago," I said with a sigh. It was an impudent remark to make, I suppose, but I was uneasy with the dismissal of Samuel Fleming's murder as a justifiable execution. Also, the memory of Frankie Silver had lain heavily on my mind these past few days, and my words were out before I could call them back.

Woodfin gave me a blank look. "Twenty years ago?"

"In this very court. You lost that capital case, alas."

"Lord, yes. Little Mrs. Silver," sighed Woodfin. "I have not forgotten her. I wish to this day that I could have saved her. You were at that trial, too, weren't you, Gaither?"

I nodded. "I was clerk of Superior Court in those days."

"And old Tom Wilson was my co-counsel. I always pictured him as an unhappy cross between crow and scarecrow. What has become of him, anyhow? I had thought to have seen him here."

I hesitated. "He no longer lives in Burke County," I said at last. "He has taken his family off to Texas."

"Really? How long ago?"

"Only a few months back."

"Thomas Wilson went to Texas? At his age? What was he, seventy?"

"Only sixty, I think," I said, as if that made it any less extraordinary for an elderly lawyer to strike out for far-off territory.

"But I thought he had been practicing law here in Morganton forever," Woodfin protested.

"Twenty years or so. Yes."

"And surely I'm correct in remembering that his wife had some connection to the Erwins of Belvidere?"

"She is Matilda Erwin's niece." I had avoided looking at Woodfin as I made my replies, and he must have realized that I was less than forthcoming about the matter of Thomas Wilson's sudden departure. He was watching me closely.

"So," he said, "Thomas Wilson has given up a twenty-year law practice, and a good farm near his influential relatives. At his advanced age, he has forsaken the state of Carolina to go and seek his fortune in Texas. Does he think that he will have some political future out there in the new government in Austin, now that the territory has become a state?"

"He has not gone to Austin," I murmured. "Really, I know nothing about it."

Nicholas Woodfin was an excellent lawyer. Certainly he was too skilled at cross-examination to let this remark pass, no matter how casually I endeavored to say it. "The Wilsons have *not* gone to Austin?"

"No."

"Where then?"

"I believe my wife has had a letter from Mrs. Wilson a few weeks back. It seems that the family has settled in a little place called Seguin."

"Where in God's name is that?"

"They say that it is in the vicinity of San Antonio, where the Battle of the Alamo was fought."

"Seguin," Woodfin repeated, searching his mind for a familiar ring to the word. He did not find one. "Is it a spa of some sort? A restorative to health?"

"No. It boasts no mineral springs. It is said to be a dry sort of place."

He pondered this. "Gold mining country?"

"I think not."

"Land grants for gentlemen settlers?"

"Not that I have heard. No."

"Is he practicing law, then?"

"I believe he is. Certainly. I have not heard otherwise." I cast about for some other topic to distract my colleague from his interrogation. Even talk of Avery's plight was beginning to seem preferable to our current discussion.

"I believe it is difficult to practice law in Texas," said Woodfin. "One must not only know United States law, now that the territory is a state. One must also contend with old deeds from French jurisdiction, and also with Mexican law, which is based upon the Spanish system. It must be quite a challenge to an old fellow who has never practiced law outside the boundaries of North Carolina."

I had no answer to this.

Woodfin leaned back to watch me as he prolonged the silence, so that I should have ample time to reflect with him upon the absurdity of my statements. Why indeed should a man of nearly sixty leave his farm and his law practice of twenty years to go to a remote village in Texas, removing his only son from a chance at a university education? If I had been an ordinary citizen upon the witness stand, I would have burst forth with the explanation simply to end the awkwardness of the encounter. But I, too, am an attorney. Perhaps I am not the seasoned trial lawyer that Woodfin is, but I hope I can hold my own in a discourse with my peers.

"Well, Mr. Wilson has gone off to seek a new life," I said as heartily as I could manage.

"There is a saying I've heard in recent years," said Woodfin thoughtfully. "Some men come to a time in their lives when they either go to hell or Texas."

I managed a watery smile. "I'm sure we all wish Mr. Wilson luck in his bold new endeavor."

Nicholas Woodfin nodded thoughtfully, for by now he had realized that as a gentleman I could not disclose Thomas Wilson's reasons for leaving Morganton. "Wish him luck, indeed," Woodfin echoed. "So you should, Mr. Gaither, for he will need all of it, and more, I think."

I cast about for another subject to distract my colleague from further inquiries about the Wilsons. "Do you remember Jackson Stewart, the elder brother of Mrs. Silver?"

"I do," said Woodfin. "He glowered at me from ten feet away throughout the trial. He had been in Kentucky with his father when the murder occurred, had he not? What became of him? Not hanged, too?"

I smiled. "Quite the reverse, I'm happy to say. You recall that there has been a new county that has been carved out of the western portion of Burke. Yancey County, it's called. Jackson Stewart is running for the post of sheriff there."

"I had not thought to hear that."

"They say he stands a good chance of winning, too. He is prominent and well liked in the district. Odd that you should mention hanging, though, Woodfin, for I have heard that the other Stewart brother—the younger one who was arrested with his mother and sister—*was* hanged as a horse thief in Kentucky. It may be idle talk, of course, but one of the Yancey constables swears that the whole Stewart family was cursed."

Woodfin smiled at this superstitious extravagance. "Cursed? How so?"

"They have all died violent deaths, apparently. The father— Isaiah Stewart—was killed while felling a tree. Crushed. And a few years after that, Barbara Stewart, his widow, was out picking blackberries, and a rattlesnake bit her. She died a terrible death, I was told."

"The poisoning of snakebite is slow and painful. I'm not sure that I wouldn't prefer the hangman's rope," said Woodfin. "I suppose folks in the hills think that the hand of Providence has struck down the Stewarts for their part in the killing?"

"I suppose some of them do think that," I said, "but I would not agree with them. Life is hard on the frontier. There are a good many ways to catch your death before you succumb to old age."

"Didn't Mrs. Silver have a child? Has it, too, felt the wrath of divine retribution?"

"I don't believe so. The little girl would be twenty-one or thereabout today, as I recall. I know that she lived to grow up. About four years after her mother's execution, the Stewarts appeared in court here in Morganton, petitioning for the right to custody of the child."

I remembered the sad scene in the courtroom. The little girl was her mother in miniature, with a calico dress and flaxen hair spilling out from beneath a little poke bonnet. Her large, troubled eyes that stared at strangers without fear or favor. She clung to the hand of one of Charlie's sisters, but she sat still and quiet through the little hearing, though I am sure that she understood none of it. Perhaps if she had understood, she would not have listened so calmly to the arguments concerning her fate. The Silver family had raised the child from the time her mother was taken into custody, and it must have been difficult for her to be taken from the only home she knew. I hope that she visited back and forth for the rest of her childhood, for I know that the families lived close to each other.

"Was the petition for custody granted?" asked Woodfin.

"Oh, yes. Upon the usual conditions. The girl had to be taught to read, and upon her eighteenth birthday she was to receive certain material goods, and so on. I had occasion to speak to Jackson Stewart once at a political meeting, and he mentioned that his niece had got married."

"To a brave man, no doubt," said Woodfin with a chuckle. Then he sighed. "That was unworthy of me. No one knows better than I that the child's mother was unjustly hanged. I wish the daughter well."

"We might wish that she has made a better choice of husband than her mother did."

"That, certainly," Woodfin agreed. "You know, though, that case haunts me yet. I cannot help thinking that if Mrs. Silver had known more about her own rights under the law, or if she had been able to read, even, she might have been saved."

"Let it go," I told him. "You did your best at the time."

He smiled. "I atone in little ways. I have paid for the education of needy girls and boys, and a good part of the salaries of the Asheville Female Academy are paid by me. I never want another young woman to die because she was unlearned. I look at my own daughters now, and I think of that poor lost little thing."

I was glad to hear that Woodfin is doing charitable works to soften his regret at his first case lost, but privately I wondered if a fine education ever saved a woman from a brutish husband. There are gentlewomen of my acquaintance whose lot in life is little better than Frankie Silver's, for all their silks and lace.

The trial of William Waightstill Avery took place on a bitter Friday in late autumn, before Judge Kemp Battle in the court in Morganton. He had not languished in jail. He was arraigned on Wednesday, a true bill returned by the grand jury on Thursday, and Friday we went to trial.

Nicholas Woodfin spoke for the defense. He argued first that although eighteen days had passed between the original encounter and the homicide, the outrage committed by Fleming was so gross, and Avery's suffering and humiliation so great, that his passions had not cooled, and therefore his shooting of the victim was no more than manslaughter.

"Well, I will overrule that," Kemp Battle declared, and he gave Woodfin a look that said: *Damn your impudence*. "The jury is directed to consider the offense to be murder, not manslaughter, if the defendant is found to be of sound mind at the time of the incident."

Upon hearing those words, Nick Woodfin changed his tack as smoothly as a Yankee clipper. "But of course Mr. Avery was not of sound mind at the time," he protested. "How could he be? He was injured in body and soul by the cowardly attack on his person by Mr. Fleming in the public street of Marion. He went mad with shame and rage. His very honor was at stake."

There was much more of this in the course of the morning. Mr. Caldwell, Mr. Bynum, and I were all called upon to add our words to that of Woodfin's, and we all stood and said much the same: Waightstill is the kindest of men; surely he was mad with the injustice done to his honor and his person; he is very sorry for it now.

I thought, perhaps, that Judge Battle saw our plausible arguments as whitewash over the stain of our friend's misdeed. He heard us out in grim but red-faced silence. Still, it was not for him to decide the fate of Waightstill Avery. Twelve jurors, all men of Burke County known to Waightstill at least on sight, sat in judgment of the murder case.

Woodfin gestured and shouted, waxing high on the indignity of a public thrashing, and then pitching his voice low and steady as a growl when he spoke of the festering anger that followed, and of the shame Waightstill Avery felt when friends told him that Fleming was boasting of his foul deed. What choice did he have but to cleanse his name in the blood of his tormentor?

It was a stirring speech. The theatre lost a titan when Nick Woodfin chose the law instead of the stage as his profession. I could see the jurors, watching wide-eyed as the performance rose in pitch, and I have no doubt that had he been a Plantagenet, instead of a country lawyer, Woodfin could have got them to invade France with the power of his words. He has gained much in skill and style since the days when I first knew him.

At last he judged that the jurors had heard enough. The prosecution got up again and argued that shooting a man in cold blood in the sanctity of a courtroom, in front of six dozen witnesses, was murder, by God, and what else could you call it? The state's lawyer conceded that Waightstill Avery was rich, and well connected, and that he rejoiced in the eloquence of his friends, who stood here now to defend him, but, be that as it may, Avery had—with the arrogance of the rich—appointed himself judge and executioner upon a fellow attorney. Were the honest citizens of Burke County going to let him get away with it?

The jury retired in the early afternoon to deliberate the matter. I watched the twelve men file out of the courtroom. "I suppose we might wait in the tavern," I remarked hopefully to my fellow attorneys, for I felt much in need of a change of air.

Mr. Bynum smiled. "Why don't we wait half an hour so that Waightstill can join the party?"

"But surely—"

Woodfin nodded in agreement. "Unless I miss my guess, we haven't time to leave the premises. The jury should be back within the hour."

They were back in ten minutes. As the jurors filed in, my

colleagues exchanged satisfied glances, as if the speed of the verdict were a tribute to their skills of oratory, but I was still not convinced that the verdict would be a favorable one, for I had seen the shooting take place myself, and I could not call the killing of an unarmed man "self-defense," regardless of the provocation several weeks earlier.

"Has the jury reached a verdict?" asked Judge Battle, in a tone that suggested surprise at seeing them again so soon.

"We have, Your Honor." The foreman handed a slip of paper to the bailiff, who conveyed it to Battle.

"The prisoner will rise."

Waightstill got to his feet and stood there with great calmness, but I saw that he was gripping the edge of the table with both hands. Even the most confident of men must realize that a jury is a capricious creature. No one knows this better than a lawyer.

Judge Kemp Battle studied the words on the paper for an agonizing minute before he looked up and announced, "The jury finds the defendant not guilty." He paused here, as if he wanted to say more, but instead he shook his head and sighed. "Mr. Avery, you are free to go. The jury is thanked for its time."

The color came back into Waightstill's face, and he released his grip on the table. Tod Caldwell pounded his old adversary on the back, shouting, "We've done it!" as a crowd of well-wishers surrounded the defense table. My own congratulations were left unsaid, and I think the omission went unnoticed by my nephew and his supporters.

I gathered up my notes from the trial and made my way upstream against the crowd of spectators, seeking the open air. The day was bleak and colorless, with a spitting rain and gusts of cold wind coming down off the mountains as if to sweep away every last leaf of autumn in their wake. Despite the chill and the damp, I braved the elements on the side of the courthouse lawn, out of sight of the main entrance, through which the spectators and the celebrants would be leaving. I was thinking of John Boone, dead these fifteen years, and of all the trials that had come and gone since I arrived in Morganton.

Presently I heard footsteps approaching from behind me, and I turned to see Nicholas Woodfin in his great black cape coming toward me. "We have carried the day," he said, smiling.

"Yes," I said.

"We are going to the tavern now, as you suggested, to celebrate the jury's good judgment, and I'll wager that our old friend will spend more there than his defense cost him. Walk with me."

I shook my head. In my present mood, the brown stubble of garden beside the courthouse suited me better than the prospect of revelry in the tavern. "I will join you later," I said.

"You are not pleased? Waightstill has a great political future. And we have saved him."

"So we have," I said. I turned away and left him staring after me. The dead leaves crackled under my feet, and the north wind numbed my face until I felt nothing at all.

So William Waightstill Avery went free. We had saved him—for another dozen years, anyhow—and he used them well. He served two terms in the State Senate, and fathered three more children with his wife Mary Corinna, who was the daughter of a governor. But the Bible says that he who sheddeth blood shall his own blood be shed by others. In Waightstill Avery's case, the volley answering the death of Samuel Fleming was fired in June 1864, at a place called the Winding Stairs, where the mountains rise not twenty miles west of Morganton. There the Confederate North Carolina First Regiment troops were overtaken by Kirk's raiders, Federals from Tennessee, and Waightstill Avery was wounded in the skirmish. He died of those wounds on July 3, 1864, and I hoped I mourned the death of a brave soldier as sincerely as anyone that day in the churchyard of our Presbyterian church.

As I stood there in the dappled sunshine of the old cemetery, paying my last respects, I thought that I stood in an ever diminishing circle of light. My dear Elizabeth had passed away, and last year we laid her sister the lionhearted Miss Mary into the earth at Belvidere. So many brave people had left this world, and I was growing old alone.

As they lowered Waightstill's coffin into the earth, I heard the drone of flies about my head and I could not help thinking about another "brave little soldier" who had died on a July day many years back, and who lay in unconsecrated ground somewhere up the mountain, unmourned and unremembered. I wish I could have taken just one rose from the mound of flowers on William Waightstill Avery's coffin and laid it on the grave of Frankie Silver.

Chapter Eight

I WANT TO SHOW you a grave," said the sheriff.

Three rocks stood alone in the little mountain graveyard: smooth stubs of granite, evenly spaced about four feet apart. The stone pillars were uncarved, weathered from more than a century's exposure to the elements and farthest away from the white steepled church in the clearing at the top of the mountain.

Sheriff Spencer Arrowood and Nora Bonesteel had said very little to each other in their journey across the mountain into Mitchell County, North Carolina. Early that morning Spencer had appeared at the door of the white frame house on the ridge on Ashe Mountain.

"I need to know about Frankie Silver," he told her.

He had a longer drive to make tomorrow, but first he needed to go to Kona. At first light that morning, LeDonne had called him, knowing that he slept no more than they did. "We've made an arrest," the deputy told him. "Guy with an earring. One of the other hikers noticed him. We found the murder weapon in his possession. He's eighteen years old."

So the sheriff was back where he started, with no new evidence, only a feeling that there was something he didn't understand about the Harkryder case. He had asked LeDonne to continue the check on the names he had given him, but Spencer could not sit still and wait any longer. They were almost out of time. He promised himself that instead of sitting by the phone, he would see the place where the Silver murder happened, and if there was anything to be learned from that ancient riddle, he would do his best to find it.

Spencer asked Nora Bonesteel to go with him, and without asking a single question, she went. Later he would remember that when she answered the door, she had on her walking shoes and the little blue-flowered hat she sometimes wore to church. *She knows when you are coming,* people said of Nora Bonesteel, but the sheriff did not believe it. He believed in coincidence.

It's unofficial, he told himself. *The case is a hundred years old. It's not as if I'm using a psychic to consult on a police investigation. This is a private thing.* He was not driving the patrol car. He was still officially out on sick leave, and the pain in his side reminded him from time to time that this should be so.

Spencer escorted the old woman to the passenger seat of his white sedan and waited for her to fasten her seat belt before he took off down the winding Ashe Mountain road and made the right turn that would take them east into North Carolina.

Nora Bonesteel said nothing.

She knew. He wouldn't ask himself how, or whether his belief in that statement constituted faith of any kind, but he had to know about Frankie Silver, and there was no one else he could bring here who would be able to understand.

"I've been studying the case of Frankie Silver," he told her, after many miles of silence. "You probably know the story, but I'd like to tell it if you wouldn't mind listening. It would clear things in my mind."

Nora Bonesteel nodded, and the sheriff began to go over the facts of Charlie Silver's murder—haltingly at first, but then with greater assurance, until at last he forgot she was there, and he was simply thinking aloud to align his thoughts. The Harkryder case hovered in his mind, parallel to the story he was telling, but although it flickered through his consciousness from time to time, he could not yet see the link.

They drove the winding back roads of Mitchell County, North Carolina, past settlements with colorful names like Bandana and Loafers Glory. It was just as Spencer remembered it from two decades earlier, when he had made the journey with Nelse Miller. If progress had come in the intervening years, it was treading lightly.

When they arrived at the white frame church in the community of Kona on state route 80, the air was still and the shadows sharp, promising a day of breathless heat. Spencer parked his car in the gravel driveway of the churchyard. A slender blond man came out of the church building and waved to them. "I'll be right back," said Spencer, as he got out of the car and headed toward the old church.

The blond man was a Mr. Silver, the keeper of the family history. He could have been any age, and he had been born here in the county, but his accent had been worn away like a river rock, softened by years spent in Atlanta, Chicago, Los Angeles. Now he had come home to stay, and to tend the legends. He had a serenity now that one did not often find in the big cities in which he had spent his youth. People— mostly distant relatives, but sometimes scholars and writers—came thousands of miles to ask their questions, to look at the little stones, and to compare the list of names on their genealogy charts with the reams of information in the collection at Kona. They wanted to know who they were, and they seemed to think that Mr. Silver could tell them. Sooner or later most of the visitors got around to asking about Frankie Silver. Mr. Silver knew all the questions, and most of the answers. He was used to it by now.

Spencer told him who they were and what they wanted. Mr. Silver spoke with him for ten minutes, pointing out landmarks and telling Spencer Arrowood what he needed to know. When he had finished, the two men shook hands and Mr. Silver went back across the road to the newer church to tend to the family-history collection housed in its basement. Later they could come over and look at the maps and the photographs, he said. Spencer thanked him again and walked back to the car.

"We're in the right place," he told Nora Bonesteel, as he opened the door and helped her out of the car. She nodded without surprise and followed him through the little mountain graveyard.

Spencer walked over to the three uncarved rocks at the edge of the cemetery. "That's Charlie Silver," he said.

Nora Bonesteel nodded again. "Yes."

"They didn't find him all at once."

The old woman was looking at the sheriff, not at the grave, and she knew that he was troubled by more deaths than this one. "It's over now," she said.

Spencer knelt and ran his hand along the top of the weathered stone. "Charlie Silver. He's been nineteen for a hundred and sixty-five years now. I used to wonder what kind of a man he was. Whether he deserved what he got. Do you know?"

Nora Bonesteel considered the question. "The cutting came after," she said at last. "He went quick. She didn't."

"Yes, but did he deserve to die?"

"I won't say that anyone deserves it. Sometimes it has to be done, that's all."

Spencer thought that over. "Yes. Perhaps it did. Frankie said that what happened in the cabin was self-defense. I guess somebody was meant to die that night. The only choice was who."

"Or how many," said Nora Bonesteel.

Spencer remembered the baby. *What was her name?* Nancy. That was it. Nancy Silver. Named for Charlie's step-mother. At least she had been saved. He wanted to see where it had all happened. "The cabin site is back in the woods a few hundred yards," he said. "We can't get to it very easily from here in the churchyard, though."

Nora Bonesteel pointed to a log cabin at the bottom of a hill on the other side of the paved road. "That was the Silvers' cabin, wasn't it?"

"Charlie's parents, you mean? Yes. Some of the family still live there. You see that brownish cut in the hillside across the road, leading to the cabin? Mr. Silver said that was the path that Frankie took when she went to tell her in-laws that Charlie hadn't come home. It's still there after a hundred and sixty-five years."

Nora Bonesteel did not turn to look at the worn path in the hillside. "It would be," she said.

"I hoped that we could go to the cabin site. Mr. Silver said to walk on past the old church, around the curve in the paved road, and take the first logging road to the right." Spencer looked doubtfully at the old woman. "It's a bit of a hike, though."

"I'm accustomed to walking."

They threaded their way past the modern gravestones of latter-day Silvers and their kinfolk, and walked the few hundred yards along Route 80 to the dirt trail that led off into deep woods. "Mr. Silver said to follow that logging road into the woods about half a mile, but from there the way to the cabin site isn't marked. . . ."

Nora Bonesteel sighed. "I'll know when to leave the road," she told the sheriff.

Spencer looked at the thicket of trees lining the old logging road. The underbrush beneath the beech and oak groves was so thick that the ground was completely hidden. Walking through such a tangle of brush would be slow-going. He thought about Barbara Stewart, who had died from snakebite while she was out berry picking in these woods or near them, and he reminded himself to stay close to Nora Bonesteel, and to watch the ground. He had not brought his weapon along, but he thought that the noise of their walking would keep snakes out of their way.

"Strange to think that there was once a farmstead here," he said. "You wouldn't think this had ever been cleared land. I guess a lot can change in a hundred and sixty years."

"Some things don't."

They walked for another ten minutes or more, with only the sound of their feet against the rocks on the road to break the silence. It was cool under the canopy of leaves, and the air had the moist, loamy smell of a forest after a rainstorm. The dirt was soft from the recent rains, and they had to make their way around puddles, occasionally pausing to scrape the mud from their shoes. At last Nora Bonesteel stopped. She shut her eyes for a moment, took a deep breath, and nodded. "Here," she said to the sheriff, pointing down a small, steep slope.

Spencer could see nothing to distinguish this spot from any other point along the road through the woods. He could see no footpath leading from it, no break in the foliage, no remnants of an abandoned building. It seemed a random choice. "Are you sure?"

"Oh, Lord," the old woman whispered. "Can't you feel it?" She was standing stock-still on the red clay road, staring at the underbrush, one blue-veined fist pressed against her mouth as if she were holding back a cry.

Spencer stopped and listened. He heard the trill of a bird far off in the branches of the distant trees, but otherwise he had no sense of being anywhere except in a moist, cool forest on a summer morning. "Can we get to it?" he asked his companion. "If I help you down, would you be willing to take me there?"

"If you are bound and determined to go," said Nora Bonesteel, sighing. "We've come this far. We might as well see it through."

He eased his way down the embankment of the logging road, a three-foot slope of mud and weeds. Bracing his foot against a bush at the bottom, he reached up and took the old woman by the hand, helping her gently down the muddy bank. "Will you be able to find it in all this underbrush?" he asked her, looking at the unbroken tangle of woods. No remnant of a farmstead remained.

She nodded. "It will be near the creek. I'll know."

He stepped aside to let her pass, and then fell in behind her as she made her way through the woods as if she were following a path. She deviated from a straight line only to make her way around a bush or to skirt a fallen log. Spencer scanned the ground around them for snakes and wondered if they would ever find the site. He could have asked Mr. Silver to come with them, but he hadn't wanted to share the experience with a stranger. Either he would feel foolish embarking on this journey with Nora Bonesteel or else he would learn what he came to find out by a means that would not bear explanation. Either way, he knew that he would never talk about this journey to anyone else.

They were just beyond sight of the road in a clump of beech trees interspersed with tall yellow-flowered weeds when Nora Bonesteel turned to him and put her hand on his arm. "Here," she said.

The canopy of leaves was so thick that it seemed to be twilight where they stood, but Spencer's eyes were accustomed to the dimness now, and he began to pace slowly through the weeds, looking for some sign that Nora Bonesteel was right. He had not ventured more than a few yards away from her when he found the rocks. "It's here!" he called, motioning for her to come.

A wide, flat rock lay half buried in the black earth, nearly covered by the branches of a shrub growing beside it. "This must be the hearthstone," said Spencer, kneeling down to examine it. "There are no logs or traces of wood that I can see. I had heard that the cabin burned."

Nora Bonesteel nodded. "What else could they do?" she said. "The blood had soaked into the logs, into the earth. No one would have lived there."

It was a crime scene, Spencer told himself. In twenty years, he had seen hundreds of them. You approached each crime scene in the same way. Picture the scene on the night the incident occurred, and try to work out what had to have happened. "December 21, 1831," he murmured, thinking aloud. "The snow was knee-deep. The river was frozen. According to Frankie Silver, her husband Charlie had been to George Young's place to get his Christmas liquor. But he came home. Yes. We know he came home."

Spencer paused, expecting Nora Bonesteel to say something, but she did not, so he went back to his musings. "Christmas liquor. . . . Everybody said that Charlie liked a good time. Liked music. Liked to dance. . . . He's only nineteen. He's had quite a lot of George Young's brew before he gets home. Of course he has. He comes home stinking drunk, and Frankie gives him hell about it. He hasn't done his chores, and he's been out partying, leaving her home alone with the baby. They get into a shouting match."

"They were children themselves," murmured Nora.

Spencer barely heard her. He was reenacting the crime now, as he had learned to do over the years in his own cases. "Why doesn't Charlie storm out when the quarrel begins? Because it's a bitter cold winter night. Deep snow. Frozen river. Nowhere to go. They're trapped in that tiny, cold cabin. Two angry, shouting adolescents. Maybe the baby is crying. Maybe she's sick, or colicky, or just plain hungry, and she won't hush up." The dark shape of a cabin had begun to appear in his mind, but he knew he wasn't seeing it in the sense that Nora Bonesteel saw. The old woman had the Sight, but the picture in the sheriff's mind was constructed out of cold reason. Cops did it at every crime scene. Medical examiners did it when faced with the map of injuries on the body of a victim. Cast your mind out into the possibility of what might have happened, and search with your educated instinct until you can determine what must have happened.

He plunged on into the narrative. "They're teenagers. Not much self-control." Trapped. Miserable. *If you don't shut that kid up, I will.* He had seen it before. Often. This might as well have been a run-down trailer in a shabby backcountry park. A drunken good old boy, an angry young wife, a screaming baby. Nowadays they pick up the phone and call 911, and then he or LeDonne or Martha would have to go out and try to talk sense into them. Sometimes, to end the danger, they would have to take the raging husband away in handcuffs in the back of the patrol car. But the night that the Silvers fought it out—December 22, 1831—there was no one to call. No time. No time.

If you don't shut that baby up, I will, Frankie!

"He picks up the gun." Spencer was staring at the ground now, at the forlorn slab of hearthstone lost in a thicket of weeds. "He doesn't mean it, really. He's drunk and cold and the crying has driven him past reason. But he would have killed her. I've seen a dozen Charlie Silvers. A hundred, maybe. He would have cried all the way to town in the patrol car. He would have found God in the jail cell before the trial. But as sure as I'm standing here, he would have killed them both. He has a gun. It's over in a second. You can't take it back."

He paced the black earth between the stone and the beech trees. "So she takes him out. She has to. He has the gun pointed at—her? At the baby? She has a split second to react, and she does. She picks up the first thing to hand, and she takes him out." He looked at Nora Bonesteel, doubtful for the first time. "An ax?"

She nods. "I think it must have been. It's metal and heavy."

"So he goes down, like a poleaxed steer. She gets him just above the ear. That's in the indictment. He's lying there on the floor, not moving. It's quiet all of a sudden. Even the baby has stopped wailing. And Frankie looks down at the body of her husband, and she feels—what?" Spencer looked at Nora Bonesteel, unsure of his ground now that emotions were called into play.

The old woman shook her head. "I'd be guessing," she told him. "I think she would be feeling shock first. And then mortal terror. She has killed a man. But I'm not feeling anything from her in this place. She's not here."

Spencer looked at her, interested, suspending disbelief. He had role-played scores of crime scenes, but he sensed that what Nora Bonesteel was talking about was a different kind of seeing. Every mountain family had someone with the Sight, but if your job is modern law enforcement, you prefer to overlook the old ways. You deal in facts and evidence and cold reason: things that will stand up in court. Still, what could it hurt to ask her about the Silvers—this case had been closed for more than a century. He simply wanted to know. "What do you feel?"

Nora Bonesteel closed her eyes for a moment and nodded, as if confirming an earlier impression. "Sorrow," she said. "Deep, wordless sorrow. Great loss felt but not spoken."

Spencer blinked. Sorrow. Someone grieving? "Not Frankie?"
"No."

"Charlie, then."

"I don't think so." Nora Bonesteel closed her eyes, shutting out the here and now and reaching for that remnant of past emotion. "It feels, but it has no words," she said. "I think it is the child."

Spencer dismissed the thought. "Oh, the baby. Nancy. It can't be her. She lived to grow up."

"Yes, but on that night, little Nancy Silver was a toddling child without any words for what she had seen. That is what has been left here, burned in the air. It doesn't matter what became of her later on. What I'm getting is the emotion she felt on the night her daddy died. A deep, wordless sorrow. The anger from that night is gone. I feel no fear any more. Just that great, heavy sadness."

"The baby saw it happen," murmured Spencer, taking up the thread again. "Of course, she did. She had to. It was a one-room log cabin, and her parents are shouting loud enough to wake her." He nodded to himself, recapturing the feeling of being there. "The baby is watching. Mama and Daddy are arguing, and then suddenly Daddy falls down and he doesn't get up. He's asleep. What happens then? What does Frankie do?"

Nora Bonesteel said softly, "Frankie is only eighteen years old. A likely *little* woman, folks said. Not five feet tall. Not ninety pounds."

"Right." Spencer nodded, picturing the girl in his mind. "She can't handle this alone. She's in over her head. She'll want her daddy."

"Daddy is in Kentucky on a long hunt."

"Her mother, then. Someone who will believe her; someone who will be on her side. She goes home to mother. *I've killed Charlie, but it was an accident, Mama.*" Spencer looked around at the tangle of woods. "The Stewarts lived on the other side of the river. Where is the river?"

"Across the paved road," said Nora Bonesteel. "Did you see the dirt road across from the logging trail? Likely that takes you down to the river. From where we're standing it might be a mile or more."

"The Stewarts lived on the other side of the river. The land on this side belonged to the Silvers. There's no bridge. It's the dead of winter."

"She can walk it. The river is frozen. The snow is knee-deep."

Spencer nodded. He felt cold in the pale sunlight that filtered through the Silvers' woods. "It's night. Bitterly cold and dark. Frankie has to walk through the deep snow and across the frozen river to reach her mother's cabin. It will take her more than an hour, but she has to go. She's terrified. But . . . but . . ."

"She can't take the baby," Nora Bonesteel finished softly.

"No. The night is too cold, and the snow is deep. She must hurry. She can't take the child with her. It would slow her down. So she leaves it in the cabin in the woods. No one will hear it cry while she's gone. The baby is alone and afraid—"

"Because Daddy won't wake up." The old woman shivered. "Even now I can feel that little child's bewilderment and sorrow."

It felt right. Spencer could see things falling into place. It must have happened this way, he thought. Of course Frankie would go for help. She was eighteen years old. *I've killed Charlie, but it was an accident. What must I do?* He began to pace again. "And what does her mother say? She's shocked at first, but she's angry, too, that Charlie would get drunk and try to kill Frankie and the baby. Barbara Stewart doesn't waste any tears over him. If only her husband were home. What a time for him to be gone! But Kentucky is days and days distant. There'll be no help from him. They must see to things themselves."

"If Mr. Stewart had been home, we wouldn't be here now," said Nora Bonesteel.

"Right. We wouldn't be out here because there'd have been no legend of Frankie Silver to draw us in. She'd have got away with it! She would have said that Charlie didn't come home from the Youngs' place, and no trace of him would ever have been found. Her father would have seen to that. A strong adult man—a trapper and a woodsman— would have been able to hoist up Charlie Silver's body like a sack of flour and haul him away. Into the deep woods perhaps. Or he could have broken the frozen ground and buried the body whole. But Isaiah Stewart wasn't there that night. Neither was the oldest son, Jack. All Frankie has to rely on is her mother, and her brother Blackston, who can't be more than thirteen."

"But they have to do something." Nora Bonesteel understood what the sheriff was doing now. She saw that she needed only to nudge his thoughts along and he would reach the conclusion on his own. It was all there. You had only to picture the scene and it all came clear, whether you had the Sight or not.

He nodded. "They have to do something. They don't trust the law, and they don't understand that self-defense isn't considered murder. They think they have to hide the evidence that the death ever took place. Two women and a young boy can't lift the dead body. At least not easily."

Nora Bonesteel said, "The snow is knee-deep and the river is frozen."

"Lord, yes. If they try to take the body out of that cabin, they'll leave tracks through the snow that a blind man could follow. Besides, there's no way to dispose of the body once they get him outside. The river is solid ice. They don't have shovels—a pick, maybe, but it's hard to dig frozen ground with a pick. It would take too long. Even the wild animals and the scavengers can't be counted on to devour the remains in deepest winter. So the Stewarts are limited to what they can do with Charlie's body inside the cabin." Spencer ticked off the impossibilities on his fingers. "Can't drag him away to the woods without leaving tracks. Can't bury him. Can't dump him in the iced-over river. *Burn him!*"

"It was bound to occur to them," said Nora Bonesteel. "They were desperate."

Spencer sighed. "I wonder if they knew how useless it was to try to burn him. Probably not. People think of fire as all-consuming. They wouldn't have known that a body is mostly water."

"They ran out of fuel, I expect," said Nora.

"I think so. Yes. One of the legends is that shortly after Charlie disappeared, Frankie asked her brother-in-law Alfred to chop some wood for her, and Alfred replied that he'd seen a whole cord of firewood stacked by her cabin a day or so earlier. The Stewarts used up that cord of wood trying to burn the body, but they ran out of wood before—"

"Before they ran out of Charlie." Nora Bonesteel permitted herself a grim smile.

"That's why the body was cut up. It wouldn't all fit into the fireplace in one piece." Spencer stepped away from the hearthstone and closed his eyes for a moment. *There.* They cut him up *there. And fed him into the fire piece by piece.* Who did? He turned to his companion. "You know, there has never been a case—not one that I can find—*anywhere*—of a woman younger than thirty, working alone, dismembering a human body post-mortem. Not one case."

"Including this one," said Nora, "don't you reckon?"

"Well, I can't imagine Frankie cutting up her husband's body. She's only eighteen. He's her husband, for God's sake! The baby is there."

"Someone else then?"

"Barbara Stewart!" whispered Spencer. "Frankie's mother!" He tried to picture a tiny, faded blond woman, old at forty, staring down at the lifeless body of the man who had beaten her daughter. "She is without pity. It is the living who matter now. *Go stall the Silvers. Your brother and I will take care of this.* Yes. She must have said that. Frankie couldn't do it. She was nearly in shock, and besides, there was the baby to tend to. The mother and brother know that if they make Frankie cut up that body, she will become hysterical, and then all is lost. So come sunup, they send her to the Silvers' cabin to visit. *Pretend like nothing is wrong,* they tell her. *Say that*

Charlie went over to the Youngs' place and he's not back yet. Give us time to take care of this."

"That poor girl, having to sit there and make small talk with her husband's relatives, knowing what she's left back there in the cabin." Nora Bonesteel sighed. "No wonder they thought she was a monster, later, when they found out. But by now she had her mother and brother mixed up in it, too, so she had no choice. She was fighting for all their lives."

"Barbara cut up that body. She must have butchered deer before. Her husband was a hunter. She had the ax and a hunting knife, at least. She had time, I guess. The search for Charlie went on for nine days."

"Yes, but she had to get it done a lot quicker than that," said Nora. "Someone must have dropped into the cabin before then. They had to figure that somebody would stop by as soon as Frankie went back home from visiting. Maybe nobody did come to see her, but the Stewarts couldn't chance it. They had to be ready for company by the afternoon of the first day. They'd have disposed of the body that first night, best they could, and cleaned the blood off the cabin floor." She shrugged. "Leastways, I would have."

"You're right," said Spencer. "Of course you are. Close family—there were a dozen Silvers, give or take a child—living less than half a mile away. Someone could have walked in on them at any time. Besides, Barbara and Blackston Stewart couldn't risk being gone from their own cabin for too long, either. If they were missed, someone might wonder later what they were up to."

"People did wonder," said Nora Bonesteel. "Didn't you tell me that they were arrested at the same time that Frankie was?"

"Yes, but they were never tried. There was no evidence against them. Frankie saw to that. She never implicated them at all. But the cutting up of the body is what got her hanged. That's what shocked people so. I wonder if she could have saved herself by telling what really happened."

"More likely she'd have got all three of them hanged," said

Nora Bonesteel. "The law was in the hands of the towns-people, you know, but the Stewarts were frontier folk. They must have figured there was no telling what townspeople would do."

"There's still some of that," said Spencer. He stopped and listened. The woods were completely silent. No birds sang. No gnats swarmed above the damp earth. "She was brave, wasn't she?" he said at last. "Frankie never told who cut up the body, and she never said who helped her escape. She died protecting her family."

"It must have been hard to die like that, wondering if the truth might have saved you."

"She tried to speak on the gallows. They asked her if she had any last words, and according to eyewitnesses—there was a lawyer named Burgess Gaither who told the story years later—they asked Frankie Silver if she had any last words, and she stepped forward and started to speak. But her father was in the crowd, and he yelled out: *Die with it in you, Frankie!* And she stepped back, and was hanged without saying a word."

"It wouldn't have saved her then. He knew that."

"That's what her father was saying to her then," said Spencer. He pictured the grizzled old man, surrounded by shouting strangers, staring up at his daughter with the rope around her neck, and he's ashamed that his sorrow is mixed with fear for what she might say. *Die with it in you.* Mr. Stewart was saying: "We can't save you, Frankie. We did all we could. We tried to keep you from getting caught, but the blood would tell. Then we hired you a lawyer and paid for the appeal, but we lost the case. We even broke you out of jail. We can't save you. *Don't take the rest of the family down with you.*"

"Yes."

Die with it in you. Spencer shivered in the pale sunshine. "I have somewhere to go tomorrow," he said softly.

"Yes."

"I have to go to Nashville and watch a man die in the electric chair. I put him there."

The old woman nodded. Her face showed no trace of surprise or alarm. She began to retrace their steps back to the logging trail. It was time to go back.

Spencer followed her back through the tall yellow-flowered weeds. He said, "I think I understand what bothered Nelse Miller about the case now. I know why Frankie Silver has been on my mind."

"Yes."

"Will I be able to save him?"

Nora Bonesteel turned to look at the sheriff. "Knowing is one thing," she said. "Changing is another."

It was nearly three o'clock when Spencer reached the sheriff's office. "We've finished interrogating the suspect," LeDonne told him. "He confessed. I think there's some mental deficiency there, so he'll probably end up in a treatment facility."

"Did you ask him about the Harkryder case?" asked Spencer.

"Yeah. It happened before he was born. He never heard of it. There's a press conference at four. Do you feel up to conducting it?"

Spencer knew that he should. Elected officials have to stay visible to let their constituents know they're on the job. He shook his head. "It was your case," he said. "You and Martha handle it. I just came back to get the information you ran down for me on my case."

LeDonne handed him a folder. "You don't have much time," he said.

"No. But at least I know who to ask."

His old desk felt strange to him now, after weeks away from duty. He saw that the plant in his window looked better, since he had not been around to pour cold coffee into it, and there was a tidiness to his desktop that made him uneasy. He read through the laser-printed sheets in the folder, making notes as he went. It was coming together now. Everything was beginning to make sense, but still he had no proof.

He picked up the phone and dialed a number in Kentucky. He wished he had time to go in person, but there were only hours remaining. "Tom Harkryder, please," he said when the ringing stopped. "Mr. Harkryder, this is Sheriff Arrowood from Wake County, Tennessee. I'd like to talk to you about your brother."

There was an intake of breath at the other end of the phone, and then a sigh. "I can't help you with Ewell," drawled the voice. "Bailing him out is a waste of money. Let him sleep it off."

"I meant your other brother, Tom. Lafayette. Remember him?"

After another pause, Tom Harkryder said, "I can't help him, either."

"I think you could," said the sheriff. "I think you could save his life—if you told what really happened on the mountain that night twenty years back."

"Fate said he was innocent. The damned jury didn't believe him."

"I believe him—now. He's scheduled to die tomorrow night. If you meet me in Nashville, I can get us in to see the governor, and we can stop the execution."

"By telling them what?"

"Tell them who killed Mike and Emily. It's your brother's only chance." The silence dragged on so long that Spencer finally said, "Mr. Harkryder—Tom—are you there?"

The voice whispered, "I don't believe I can help you," and the line went dead.

Chapter Nine

So now he knew.

Spencer Arrowood wondered if Constable Charlie Baker had known the truth back in 1832, and if he had ever been tempted to use that knowledge to save Frankie Silver.

Maybe the constable had known a lost cause when he saw one.

The six-hour drive to Nashville had never seemed longer, but at least the sheriff knew where he was going. Someone from Riverbend had faxed him directions with his final instructions for attending the execution ("no cameras, no recording devices . . ."). The sheriff did not play the radio for fear that every country song would sound like an omen. Instead he tried to concentrate on I-40, rather than on the jangle of possibilities that crowded his mind. He had finally received the information he'd asked LeDonne to find for him, and he had spent much of the previous evening making telephone calls and assembling the paperwork on the case. He was already weak from his injury, and he got little enough rest, but he told himself that he would not have been able to sleep anyhow.

It was 7 A.M. By the time he reached Nashville, Spencer Arrowood would have nine hours to save a life.

From I-40W, he took the Robertson Road exit, turning right onto Briley Parkway, and onto Centennial Boulevard. The exit from Centennial put him in sight of "The Walls,"

Tennessee's Gothic-looking old prison, a nightmare in red brick, which had closed its doors to real prisoners in 1989, when the new penitentiary was completed. Now only movie stars in shapeless prison garb walked its corridors while the cameras rolled. The state rented out the old facility on a regular basis to film producers, so that the old building spent its declining years in a grotesque parody of its former existence. Now people only pretended to die there.

The real maximum-security prison of the state of Tennessee did not look like Hollywood's idea of a penitentiary. The new prison, Riverbend, would never look the part.

Centennial Boulevard led to Cockrill Bend Industrial Road, past the MTRC (Middle Tennessee Reclassification Center), where new prisoners were evaluated and assigned to various state facilities—and finally, on a wide bend in the Cumberland River, for which it was named, lay Riverbend itself. Riverbend Maximum Security Institution might have been a community college or a prosperous modern elementary school except for the high chain-link fences and the loops of razor wire surrounding the inner compound. Once past the repetitive, ironclad security of code words stamped on one's hand and a succession of locked doors at short intervals, the place had a peaceful, rural look about it, as if the menace of the old days had been replaced by a brisk, impersonal efficiency. The one-story brick buildings were connected by concrete pathways set in a green lawn, and the view, glimpsed from between buildings, was of the bend in the river and the high wooded hill on the other side.

Spencer parked in the lot outside the main entrance and sat for a few moments in his car, collecting his thoughts and wishing he'd stopped for coffee somewhere along the way. It was past one o'clock, and he still hadn't eaten anything. He couldn't spare the time, he thought. The execution was scheduled for eleven o'clock that night. He wondered how persuasive he would have to be to get them to let him in early. The badge should do it, though; badges opened a lot of doors.

At the glass-covered reception booth, he had to give his

name and show them the paperwork relating to his being summoned as a witness to the execution, but no one seemed to think it odd that he wanted to meet the warden. He told them that he was unarmed, and they gave him a clip-on red badge and told him to wait. After only a few minutes, he was taken down the left-hand hallway and ushered into the warden's office, past an outer room containing a wall-sized aerial photo of Riverbend and its surroundings.

"I'd like to speak to the prisoner," he said, as soon as the preliminary greetings were out of the way.

The warden raised his eyebrows. "You're one of the witnesses, aren't you, Sheriff?"

Spencer Arrowood nodded. "Wake is Mr. Harkryder's home county. In fact, I was the arresting officer."

"That was a long time ago, wasn't it?"

"Twenty years."

"And you want to see him today?"

The sheriff nodded. "Today." They both knew there wasn't going to be a tomorrow for Fate Harkryder.

In the long silence that followed, Spencer studied the walls of the warden's office. The room might have belonged to a college president or an official in a small-town bank except for the two framed drawings on the wall, childlike renderings of the prison, with little stick-figure guards manning large, carefully drawn weapons from the rooftop. The sketches were signed "James Earl Ray."

"I see. You want to talk to Mr. Harkryder now." The warden was watching him closely, waiting for the explanation to tumble out, but Spencer said nothing. Interrogation was an old game to him, easier than chess.

"Fate Harkryder is going to die tonight, Sheriff," the warden said at last. "And I want him to go peacefully. He's been a good prisoner here. No trouble. Kept to himself. I owe him the courtesy of death with dignity. So if you have some old score to settle . . ."

"No. I'd just like to talk to him."

"Well, it's up to him. It's his last day on earth, and a man ought to have a say in who he sees or doesn't see at a time like this. You arrested him. You've come to watch him die. In his place, I don't believe I'd relish the sight of you, Sheriff. But I'll tell you what: I'll send one of the guards in to ask Mr. Harkryder if he wants to see you or not, and we will both abide by his decision. Agreed?"

Spencer nodded. "Can I send a message with the guard?"

"All right," said the warden. "A verbal one. Make it short. What do you want us to say to Mr. Harkryder?"

"Tell him I've been talking to Frankie Silver."

The forty acres of Riverbend were nestled into the curve of the Cumberland River: fourteen buildings, encircled by a road and surrounded by two twelve-foot fences whose separate electronic systems for detection of movement and vibration secured the area. The fences were separated by a no-man's-land of gravel and razor wire. There were no guard towers at the facility, but a twenty-four-hour mobile unit patrolled the perimeter. Only Building Seven, the administration building, lay outside the fences, but its sally port, the one entrance to the prison itself, was the focus of intense security.

A guard checked Spencer's name badge and stamped his hand with the fluorescent code word of the day. No one was permitted in or out of the prison grounds without the code word on the back of his hand, illuminated by a sensor gun pointed at the spot by yet another guard.

The code words were short. They changed every day. Today's code word was *owl*. Very appropriate, Spencer thought, studying the three glowing letters on his hand. The call of a hoot owl was considered a sign of death by the old timers up home. The hoot owls should be calling tonight. There was death in the air.

A pleasant-looking man, who might have been the vice principal of an elementary school for all his lack of menace, accompanied the sheriff through the metal detector, past the checkpoint, through the two electric gates that opened consecutively, and into the compound.

Fate Harkryder had sent back word that he would see

Sheriff Arrowood of Wake County. Spencer wondered if the name meant anything to him after all these years.

"How many inmates are here?" asked Spencer, who was tired of the silence.

"Six hundred and sixty-eight," his guide answered. "Ninety-nine on death row. There are six units housing prisoners. That small building to your far left as we passed through the gates is the industry building, Two-A. There the inmates who are qualified to work put in their hours at assigned jobs."

"Like what?"

"Printing. Data entry. Decals. If you buy a car in the state of Tennessee, the registration is sent to you by an inmate on death row. To your right is Building Nine: Food Services and Laundry." They had reached the one-story brick building beyond the second electronic gate. "Building Eight," said the guide. "We'll check in again here."

"What is Building Eight?"

"Security, and visitation. It looks like an airport waiting room."

Spencer nodded. "I'll see him in there?"

"No. The execution chambers are just behind the back wall of the visiting room."

Spencer held up his hand to the electronic sensor. *Owl* flashed green in the light, and then vanished. *Owls,* thought Spencer. Once, when he was nine, Spencer and his older brother Cal had talked an old mountain man named Rattler into taking them owling, because they were still too young to hunt. Rattler walked the Arrowood boys across every ridge over the holler, teaching them to look for the sweep of wings above the tall grass in a field and to listen for the sound of the waking owl, ready to track his prey by the slightest rustle, the shade of movement. He taught them how to make owl calls, and they became so good at it that they could not tell if an owl was calling to them out of the forest or one of their own. *Look out,* Rattler had told them. *When the owl calls your name, it means death.*

Later on we became owls, Spencer thought. Cal went to Vietnam and died in a jungle of screeching birds, and Spencer grew up to be a lawman, hunting prey of his own by the slightest sound or by one false move. A lot of people had heard him call their name.

He stared at the tile floor, the institutional cinder-block walls, and at the display case of carved ship models made by inmate craftsmen. "I thought Mr. Harkryder would be on death row."

"He was housed in Unit Two. It's directly behind this building. But in the days before his execution, a prisoner is moved to a holding cell in the back of Building Eight. We've never done an execution before at Riverbend, but the procedures have all been outlined so that we would be ready."

They walked through the door and into the empty visitation hall, past a series of functional sofas and chairs of plastic and steel arranged in conversational groupings so that twenty or thirty sets of visitors could have a few feet of privacy with the inmate they came to see. They stopped at another metal door on the back wall. The guide unlocked it. "There's another way in," he said, "but I thought we'd go this way, since Mr. Harkryder is already in his cell. This is where you'll be tonight."

The witness room. Rows of metal conference-room chairs facing a plate-glass window covered by blinds. Straight in front of them was another door. The pleasant-looking man pushed it open. "You might as well see it now, Sheriff." He stepped over the threshold and stood aside so that Spencer could look into the bright, empty room.

Almost empty.

A plain wooden chair sat in the center of the room.

The guide motioned him to the door on the left wall. "This leads to the hallway," he said. "You know: the last mile. The other way is the control room, where the machinery is located, and there's also a room there for the equipment of the prison telephone system. Would you like to see it?"

The guide had given this tour many times before, and an

execution had never happened yet, so perhaps the air of un-reality about this place still lingered for him. Spencer de-clined the invitation to see the other rooms. There was too little time.

They emerged in a tiled corridor that reminded Spencer of the Sunday school building of a modern church. The open door on the left revealed a small kitchen. You could have had a wedding reception or a Scout meeting in the bright empty room beyond—except for the wooden chair in the center.

A few paces past the kitchen doorway, Spencer saw the only three barred cells in Riverbend. The ordinary prisoners' rooms had blue metal doors that they could lock with their own keys. Building Four, where the troublemakers were kept, had solid cell doors with pie flaps for food to be taken to the prisoner, and bars enclosing the various areas of that building as a security precaution, but no cells like these. These were jail cells, much more familiar to a county sheriff than to a modern prison guard.

Inside the last barred cell, a man in jeans and a blue cot-ton work shirt sat on the metal bunk, writing on a yellow le-gal pad. An armed guard sat on a folding chair in the hall, watching the cell with an air of uneasy boredom.

Spencer stepped up to the bars. "Thank you for seeing me," he said.

Fate Harkryder looked up. His hair was gray now, and there were lines in his face, but his eyes were unchanged. He set aside the legal pad and walked over to the bars.

The guide touched Spencer's arm. "I'll be at the end of the hall," he said. "Don't be long." The guard in the metal fold-ing chair contrived to look as if he were oblivious to the scene in front of him.

"I needed to talk with you," said Spencer.

The prisoner nodded. "Frankie Silver," he said. "I hadn't thought about her in years. My daddy's sister married a man from over in Mitchell County. My Uncle Steve. He used to sing that old song sometimes when he wasn't too drunk to remember the words. *This dreadful, dark and dismal day/Has swept my glories all away. . . .*" Fate Harkryder smiled bitterly. "Sure fits the mood for today, don't it?"

"I think so," said the sheriff.

"And then they can play 'The Green, Green Grass of Home.' That's a real tearjerker."

"I didn't really come here to talk about music."

"Yeah, I know. You came for the show, didn't you? You want to make sure they kill me. You're the one who put me here. You think I don't remember that? A man don't forget much in twenty years if there's nothing to look at but cinder block."

"I came because I finally figured out the Harkryder case," said Spencer. "Thanks to Frankie Silver. For a hundred and sixty-four years, people have been wondering what Frankie's father meant when he stopped her gallows speech by saying: *Die with it in you, Frankie.* When I figured that out, I knew what was bothering me about your situation."

"Am I supposed to care what you think?"

"Well, I think you should get clemency."

Fate Harkryder shrugged. "Sign a petition then. There are dozens of them. The Pope sent a nice letter to the governor on my behalf, and the anti–death penalty people are staging a vigil tonight, I hear. Candles and everything. A couple of movie stars have sent faxes to me pledging their support, only they're not exactly sure what it was I'm supposed to have done. Seems like all of a sudden nobody wants me to die. I wonder if that's because they're all pretty sure it's going to happen."

"It doesn't have to happen," said Spencer. "Not if you tell them what really happened that night on the mountain."

"I thought you knew that, Mr. Arrowood. You seemed mighty sure of yourself at the trial."

"I was sure. But I was a kid then. So were you."

"And now you know different?"

"Now I do."

"So you came charging up here to save my life, did you?"

"I'm willing to try. Tell the truth about the Trail Murders. You can stop this."

Fate Harkryder smiled. "Oh, we're already trying to stop it, Sheriff. That's what lawyers are for. Allan is at the governor's office right now, trying to get in to see him to plead for a stay. I forget the grounds. Doesn't matter. Whatever comes into his head, I guess. And the other one, that would be Justin, I believe—hell, they're both kids—Justin got on a plane this morning and flew to Washington to talk to the Supreme Court. I'm famous, Mr. Arrowood. Everybody has heard of me."

"Right. But nobody has heard of Tom and Ewell, have they?"

Fate Harkryder stared up at him for one frozen moment. Then he shrugged and turned away. "I guess they haven't," he said casually. "The black sheep of the family gets all the attention."

"Not this time. I've been doing some checking. At the time of the Trail Murders, you were a minor. Your brothers were both over eighteen. You had no criminal record. They did. So—what did they tell you when you got arrested for the killings? *Take the rap, Lafayette. You're underage. You'll do a couple of years at the most. Just don't implicate your brothers. You can save us. Just don't ever tell.* Was it something like that?"

Fate Harkryder shrugged. "It's your story, mister."

Spencer nodded. *"Die with it in you, Frankie.* It's the same old story. Mountain families stick together, no matter what. You were willing to die to keep from betraying them."

Fate Harkryder said nothing.

"That's why the blood at the crime scene matched yours. Same family. Nowadays, with DNA, we could have got a closer match, but back then the results were less exact. We were close, but not close enough."

Silence.

"Tom and Ewell did it, but they gave you the jewelry to sell. All the evidence that linked you to the crime scene would also link them. Brothers. Same blood type. All secretors. There are just two things I don't know: Why did your brothers kill those two kids with such violence, and why didn't you ever tell the truth about what happened—especially after you were sentenced to death?"

Fate Harkryder was staring at a blank wall, where a window ought to have been but wasn't. Somewhere beyond the cinder block was the river and an elm-covered hill. The hill would be deep green now, a canopy of trees leading you on from ridge to ridge, as if the green wave of forest would carry you home. He sighed. "Who'd believe me, Sheriff?"

"I would. I ran a records check on your two brothers. I wanted to see what had become of them in the last twenty years."

"We don't keep in touch."

Spencer felt the sweat prickle on his neck. *I'm more nervous than he is*, he thought. *Maybe it's because he's been fighting this for twenty years, and I've just begun.*

He said: "I ran the records check through the TBI. At the time of the Trail Murders, both your brothers had two felony convictions apiece. One for shoplifting, and one for robbing a convenience store."

"Shoplifting?" The prisoner's smile was ironic.

"Petty larceny was a felony in Tennessee at that time. We had another funny little law back then, too. The Career Criminal Act. Remember that? Three felony convictions, and you're ineligible for parole. Forever. The law was repealed a few years later, but at the time of those murders, your brothers knew that if they were convicted of that crime, they would get either the death penalty or life in prison with no hope of release."

Fate Harkryder sighed and looked away. Spencer wondered if he was remembering with regret a long ago conversation with his brothers, or if he was just tired of talking about it. Twenty years of prison coupled with twenty years of legal battles would make a man weary of life.

"It must have seemed like a reasonable request at the time," the sheriff said. "Your brothers can't afford a conviction. You have no criminal record, and you're only seventeen. When you get caught with the jewelry, they tell you to say nothing about what really happened. Take the rap if you have to. You're a kid. It'll only be a few years. You can do it. But to everyone's surprise, you got the death penalty. And then you were stuck, weren't you?"

"I said I wasn't guilty."

"All prisoners say they're not guilty. We caught you with the victim's personal effects. You must have known that if you didn't explain that, you'd be convicted." Spencer found himself thinking of Frankie Silver. *We caught you in a lie. Why didn't you tell us what really happened?* Fate Harkryder didn't tell, for the same reason Frankie Silver had kept silent. *Because we're Celts and mountain people,* he thought. *We don't trust authority figures, and we haven't since the Romans landed in Britain and started calling the shots. We never think the law is going to be on our side, and ninety-nine times out of a hundred, we're right. Who am I to change that today?*

"So you took the blame for your brothers' crime, and you've spent your entire adult life in prison," he said. "What a waste."

"Yeah, well, I was seventeen years old. What the hell did I know?"

"You learned fast, though, didn't you? The first time you got raped in your cell, I bet you were real sorry you had been so noble."

The condemned man shrugged. "You get used to anything. I survived."

"They weren't worth it, you know. Those brothers of yours. I ran a records check on them before I came here. You may not want to know what happened to them, but I did."

"Found out, did you? That must have been a thrill."

"I don't know what I was hoping for: whether I wanted them to turn out to be notorious serial killers or missionaries to China. I guess I wanted them to be entirely better than you are or utterly worse. They were neither, of course. Tom is on parole in Kentucky for kidnapping and armed robbery, which makes me wonder what else he's done that he hasn't been caught at. And Ewell wasn't on the computer, but we found him through Motor Vehicles. Your brother Ewell is a drunk who lives on welfare and odd jobs in Knoxville. I doubt his liver will last much longer."

"Tom and Ewell," said Fate Harkryder thoughtfully. "I haven't really paid them much mind in years. In my head, they're still twenty-something. The letters from home don't mention them."

"Didn't you care what became of them? You gave up your life for them."

"I cared at first, but . . . hell: Prison is another country. It's like my old life was another incarnation—that it was me back in those days, and yet not me, so none of the people and places from before are real somehow. Tom and Ewell are no more real to me now than people I saw in movies when I was a kid. Maybe they're less real. I still see John Wayne every now and then."

"You don't have to keep on lying," said Spencer. "Let's just call a press conference and tell what really happened."

For one moment something flickered in the prisoner's eyes. He took a deep breath. "Have you got any new evidence? DNA?"

"No. All the physical evidence is gone. All we have is crime scene photos and witness interviews, but they haven't changed since the trial."

"And what about Tom and Ewell? Will they back you up?"

Spencer looked away. "No. I called them last night. Ewell swears he's innocent, and Tom hung up on me. You're on your own."

"So it would just be my word and your hunch against a twenty year old murder conviction that has withstood decades of appeals?"

"Yes."

Fate Harkryder shook his head with amused disbelief. "So you call your press conference and announce all this, and then what, Mr. Arrowood? You and me go out for a few beers? It won't work like that. Nobody will pay us any mind. My *death* is news, not my legal arguments. Stanton will shout us down. The journalists will assume it's a stunt of some kind. People will think I'm a coward, and they'll sure as hell wonder what *your* problem is." The spark in his eyes was gone. He looked away again, barely interested in the conversation anymore, barely listening.

"But you have to try," said the sheriff. "You can't let yourself be executed for a crime just to protect your brothers."

"It isn't about them anymore. Don't you see that? It doesn't matter why I came here, or whether I deserved it. Twenty years are gone. Who I was is gone. All that's left is a tired old man who doesn't want to be in here another day."

"But we could get you a good lawyer and ask for a pardon."

"I wouldn't get one. I'm a poor, dumb hillbilly, Sheriff. Why should anybody bother to keep me alive? They'd just change the sentence to life and let me stay in here and rot. I had the jewelry on me, remember? I'm not just an innocent bystander. Charles Stanton is never going to let anyone forget that."

"At least you wouldn't die."

"You don't get it, do you? I've been dead for twenty years. I just want to get out of here and be done with it. Tonight."

"In a pine box?"

"Whatever."

"Well, if you won't try, at least I can. I don't want you on my conscience. I have seven hours. I can go and see the governor—"

Fate Harkryder shook his head. "I want it to be over, Sheriff. It's too late. I'm tired of this life. Just let it happen, will you? Consider this a dying man's last wish. *Just let it happen.*"

"But—"

Fate Harkryder tapped on the bars. "Visitor's leaving!" He called out to the guard. In a loud, cheerful voice meant to be overheard, he said, "Thanks for coming by, Sheriff. Wish me luck tonight, okay?"

Spencer Arrowood turned to go.

"Mr. Arrowood! There is something you can do for me." Fate Harkryder flashed his mocking smile, but his eyes shone. "I got nobody else to ask. But it's my last wish, and I hope you'll oblige me."

"What is it?"

"When it's over, I want you to take me home."

Chapter Ten

SPENCER ARROWOOD left the prison a little after three in the afternoon. He had talked to the warden about the final arrangements in case a stay of execution did not come through. There was paperwork to sign, but it didn't take long. Now he had six hours to kill—an idle afternoon for him, but for Fate Harkryder all the time in the world. He could still contact the newspaper or a local television station to reveal his theory about the murders, but he knew that he would accomplish nothing with such theatrics except to brand himself as a crackpot who balked at seeing a man executed. If he made any allegations about the Trail Murders, Charles Stanton would be asked to comment on them, of course, and Spencer had no doubt that the colonel would shred him with a few regretful, carefully chosen words. Stanton would not be cheated out of his long-awaited execution.

He could hear the colonel's snide voice now. *A few days ago, the sheriff was willing to believe that a recent homicide was committed by this mysterious killer. Now he wants to free a legally convicted man on the basis of this mythical evidence. I have every concern for the sheriff, who is a man injured in the line of duty, but I think the people of Wake County should ask themselves if he is still fit for the duties of his office.*

No, he couldn't fight Stanton, the master of the press conference. If Fate Harkryder had wanted him to oppose the execution, he would have tried, but he couldn't fight both sides at once.

Spencer knew that he could expect no corroboration from the prisoner himself. Fate Harkryder had made it clear that he would say nothing on his own behalf, and he was right: a statement from a convicted killer would make no difference to the authorities. Even if the death penalty were set aside, Harkryder would not go free. He might not be a murderer, but he was not blameless. At best, he was an accessory after the fact, and Stanton would see to it that he never left River-bend. If bringing the real killers to justice would have won him his freedom, he might have done it, but it wouldn't—so, what was the point?

When Spencer reached the prison parking lot, television mobile units were already setting up their equipment in preparation for their coverage of the execution. The governor's speech was probably already written, with neatly laser-printed copies in distribution to all the media people. Spencer could feel the tension in the prison, and the controlled excitement among the scrambling technicians in the parking lot. *It's going to happen,* he thought. *It has been gathering momentum for a long time, and nothing can stop it now. Not even the truth. The truth will be what they broadcast from this parking lot, not what happened on the mountain twenty years ago.*

Knowing is one thing; changing is another. Nora Bonesteel was right about that.

He drove out of Cockrill Bend, right on Centennial, right on Briley Parkway, over I-40, and along White Bridge Road. He slowed down at Nashville Tech, thinking for one confused moment that he had reached another prison, but then he realized that it was a college. The prisons were all in his mind.

He saw a billboard for Opryland. Emblazoned across a picture of the amusement park's roller coaster were the words RIDE THE HANGMAN! Spencer looked away. The hangman. Death had even staked out the billboards.

Spencer had intended to drive around Nashville for a

while, but the humid, stale air of the flatlands oppressed him, and when he saw the entrance to the Lion's Head Mall on White Bridge Road, he turned in to the parking lot, finding a parking space near the theater. The movies were as good a place as any to kill the rest of the day. There was nothing he wanted to see, but at least the building was airconditioned, and no one would expect him to make conversation. In the cool darkness of the theater, the sheriff stared up at the screen, registering color and noises, but afterward he could not say what film it was that he had seen. A comedy of some sort, he thought, or an action-adventure movie aimed at teenage boys. The screen could not compete with his own thoughts. He kept running the possibilities through his mind as if they were alternate moves in a chess game. *If I did this, then the governor would say that. . . .* He could devise no scenario that would give him so much as a stalemate. Every hypothesis ended with the death of Fate Harkryder. Spencer began to wonder why he cared so much, in defiance even of the condemned man's own intentions. Was it the condemned man who concerned him, or was he indulging his own desire to be blameless?

He remembered what Nelse Miller had told him long ago. *You could have looked into Fate Harkryder's cradle and told that he was going to end up in prison. If it wasn't one thing, it'd be another.*

He sat through that movie and two others before it was time to return to the prison. By then the sun had set, but it was still July in middle Tennessee, a breathless, shimmering heat unlike the cool evenings on the mountain up home. As he turned onto Cockrill Bend, he could see the lights of the prison, augmented now by the blaze of the broadcasters' lights in the parking lot. As Spencer got out of the car, he took the visitor's pass out of his pocket, but he didn't put it on. He didn't want the reporters to know who he was. A gaggle of protesters with picket signs and candles stood in the far corner of the parking lot, but they did not call out to him as he made his way toward the building. One of the reporters had approached them with a cameraman trailing after him, and their attention was focused on their few minutes of fame. At one of the mobile television units, Charles Wythe Stanton stood in a spotlight, speaking into the interviewer's microphone. "This is not about revenge," he was saying. "It's about closure. The final chapter of the Trail Murders takes place tonight. My thoughts are with my daughter."

It was a few minutes past ten o'clock. The execution was scheduled for 11 P.M., more to discourage demonstrators than to afford the prisoner every possible minute of his last day on earth. In the administration building, Spencer went through the same check-in procedure as before, and when the word *owl* was illuminated in his hand, he was ushered through the sally port in the wake of the others attending the execution.

The witnesses walked through the empty visitors' hall, to the door against the back wall. They were silent and walked alone, except for two young men, who seemed to know each other, and who spoke together in a low undertone. Spencer realized that they must be reporters sent to cover the execution. Colonel Stanton, fresh from his interview, was the last to enter. He had come alone.

No pleasantries were exchanged by the witnesses. They stood uneasily, like strangers in an elevator, unwilling to acknowledge one another's presence. After a few moments' hesitation, they took their seats in the metal chairs facing the plate-glass window, on which the blinds were now shut.

A uniformed guard came in behind them and stood near the door, obviously positioned to make a speech. "Good evening, gentlemen," he said. "We are scheduled to begin in approximately fifteen minutes, so let me just go over a few things with you. First of all, I'd like to repeat: no cameras, no recording devices. Any questions?"

There were none. The witnesses stared at the guard uneasily, but their eyes kept straying to the closed blinds that covered the plate-glass window.

"Electrocution is the only form of execution used in the state of Tennessee. This chair has never been used in an execution, but it has been thoroughly tested. You should know what will take place when the time comes. In an electrocution, the prisoner is given an initial shock of two thousand volts, reduced seconds later to about six hundred volts, and keeping the current steady at that rate for fifty-seven seconds. The process is repeated a second time, followed by a third and final charge of two thousand volts, and then the current is shut off. The doctor will check for vital signs, and if he finds that life is extinguished, the body will be left in place for thirty minutes, checked again, and then transferred to a gurney to be wheeled out of the building for the subsequent autopsy and burial. Or disposal of remains, I should say. I believe Mr. Harkryder has requested cremation."

"Where is Harkryder?" someone asked.

"The prisoner has not yet left the quiet cell," the guard replied. As if anticipating their thoughts, he added, "However, his head has been shaved earlier this evening, and he has had his last meal."

One of the reporters called out, "What was his last meal?"

The guard consulted his notes. "Two cheeseburgers, a milk shake, and a slice of blackberry pie."

"Did he eat it?"

"I believe so."

Charles Stanton narrowed his eyes. "My daughter had her last meal twenty years and ten months ago. Let's get on with it."

The guard looked startled at this outburst. It was his first execution, of course, and he had been unprepared for emotional reactions from the witnesses. He decided to ignore the comment. He cleared his throat and resumed his speech. "About ten minutes from now, the 'tie-down team'—a group of officers in helmets and black body armor—will enter Mr. Harkryder's cell. They will manacle his legs, cuff his wrists in front of his body, and attach a belly chain to the handcuff links. At that time, the prisoner will be marched the forty paces or so from the quiet cell to the room beyond that wall, where he will be seated in the electric chair. At that time I will open the blinds on the observation window. Are you with me so far? If anyone wants out, now is the time to leave."

No one stirred. The two young men in dress shirts and running shoes were making notes on pads of lined paper.

Spencer was sitting on the left aisle of the second row, with a good view of the door that led to the hallway where the quiet cell was located. He wondered if the area was soundproof. He could hear no murmur of voices, no sounds of doors closing or footsteps. If there had been screams, would he have been able to hear them?

He looked at his watch. Two minutes had passed since the last time he checked it. He looked around at the other witnesses, wondering if any of them would be unable to handle the strain of watching a man die in the electric chair. Would the doctor standing by attend to fainting witnesses, as well as checking to see that the condemned man was dead?

Spencer could feel his heart beating, and his breath was coming in gulps. He wondered if he had overtired himself too soon after surgery, or whether he was feeling the anxiety that Sheriff John Boone had felt when the time came to hang Frankie Silver. He thought that Boone's anguish must have been worse: in 1833 the Burke County sheriff had been executing a nineteen-year-old girl whom he knew to be innocent of first-degree murder. In those days, innocent people could and did go to the gallows, but nowadays, only the most heinous of crimes is punished by the death penalty: rarely a first offender or a single-victim killer, rarely an upstanding citizen driven beyond emotional endurance. With few exceptions, today's death row is the pit of the sadist and the psychopath, the paid assassin, and the refuse of the drug world. No innocent young girl defending her child would ever reach death row today. It was harder to feel charitable toward these men than to feel sorrow for the plight of Frankie Silver. Their appeals for mercy were not the shining arguments of innocence but the specious claims of technicalities, loopholes, and political maneuvers. He could wish mercy for some of them, but he could not pity them, even as he grieved for a girl who died a century before he was born. She was not one of them.

Spencer heard the two reporters in the front row whispering to each other. "This is way cheaper, man," one of them was saying. "North Carolina claims that it costs $346.51 to kill a prisoner by lethal injection. But the chair uses only thirty-two cents' worth of electricity."

"It's more painful, though," the other reporter said.

"Nah. Two thousand volts. You're unconscious in two seconds. You never know what hits you."

"You sure about that?"

"Guess we'll find out tonight. See if he yells or anything."

It seemed to Spencer a long time before the hall door opened. Fate Harkryder, hunched over his chains, shuffled into the room, surrounded by guards in black padded armor. A man with a Bible trailed the procession, reading aloud in a steady monotone. No one paid him any mind.

The condemned man wore carpet slippers covering his bare feet. The legs of his trousers were slit to the knee, and he had a close-cropped buzz cut that in any other setting would have made one think of boot camp. He was pale, with beads of sweat on his forehead, and his eyes kept darting around the room, looking for a familiar face, or perhaps a way out.

With practiced ease, the tie-down team backed the prisoner into the wooden chair and fastened the airplane seat belt straps to his wrists, legs, and chest.

"That was fast!" muttered the reporter in the front row. "Wonder who they practiced on."

"Do they still call the chair Old Sparky?" his companion whispered back.

Spencer looked at his watch. Less than two minutes had elapsed since Fate Harkryder had entered the death chamber. They had made him wait twenty years on death row, but at least the end, when it finally came, would be mercifully quick.

The warden, who had been standing beside the right-hand doorway, approached the chair and said a few words to the condemned man. The witnesses could not hear what was said, but they could see Fate Harkryder's face, and he appeared to make no reply. He was staring at the glass window in front of him, squinting a little, as if he were trying to make out individual faces. The guard dimmed the lights in the witness room.

As the warden turned to walk away, a member of the tie-down team placed a dark leather cap on the prisoner's head. The top of the cap contained the metal fitting to which the wire would be attached. The current would enter the body through the headpiece. It was fitted with a snap-on flap that covered the top half of the prisoner's face. Now he was merely a human figure, pinioned in a wooden chair.

As the warden took up his old position beside the control-room doorway, the peal of a telephone broke the silence. One of the reporters yelped and grabbed the arm of his companion. Charles Stanton held up a photograph of Emily. Spencer gripped the sides of his chair. He was holding his breath.

A voice from the other room said clearly, "No. This is the death house." Then silence.

"Wrong number," another witness muttered, with a giggle that was somewhere between embarrassment and terror.

The execution itself began without Spencer's at first being aware of it. He knew that the room lights would not dim, as they did in old black-and-white gangster movies, but he had expected a loud buzzing noise, or some other indication that high voltage had been turned on. He let his eyes stray for a moment to the stricken face of the chaplain, and then a gasp from behind him made him look again at the man in the chair. Fate Harkryder had stiffened, and he appeared to be straining against the straps, or perhaps the force of the current had thrown him forward against them. For about a minute, although it seemed much longer, the current surged through the prisoner's body, keeping him rigid against the restraints, and then the body slumped back.

No one moved.

Fate snuggled against his brother Ewell in the darkness, shivering in the crisp July night, watching the sky and breathing grass scent. He was four years old—maybe five—not the youngest child in the field, but surely the only one out alone with his older brothers instead of cradled on a blanket between doting parents. It was late. Daddy usually chased them off to bed before now, so they had learned to slope off before he started his serious drinking, knowing that as long as the boys were out of sight, the old man did not care whether they were in bed or not. It was better not to be home before the rage took him. They had scars to remind them to find somewhere else to be.

Fate couldn't remember Mama being around; maybe she had already started running around by that time. She died when he was eight, but as far as Fate was concerned, she'd been gone much longer than that.

Tom gave him brown sugar on bread for breakfast, and Ewell made him trucks out of scrap wood and bottle caps. And they took him with them, like a cute but useless puppy, wherever they went. His brothers grew up loving to roam the night, as free as the raccoons and the possums, and often as destructive. Later, in adolescence, they would take to Daddy's ways— drinking themselves into that state just before insensibility, when they became strangers even to themselves. He would come to dread going with them. Afterward, they never remembered the things they had done. He never forgot.

Not tonight, though.

Tonight Tom and Ewell had brought little Fate down the mountain, to the Wake County High School football field, where no one noticed them among the laughing crowd in the dark. They had bought him a package of cheese crackers and a grape Nehi with money swiped from the old man's coin jar, and they'd helped themselves to his stash of beer for the road. It was a night of celebration.

Fate willed himself to be still, but inside he was squirming with impatience to see the wonders his brothers had promised. He held his breath, thinking that surely the magic could not happen unless you kept very still for it and wished 'til your teeth hurt. "Is it time?" he whispered to Tom. He saw a bright flashing speck among the stars far up overhead. "Is that it?"

Tom laughed, and ruffled his hair with an ungentle shove. "Naw," he sneered. "You'll know."

"But what will it—"

A roar. A thunderclap.

Suddenly the sky exploded into a burst of red streaks and white stars, like a fiery dandelion blown apart by the night wind, and for that instant the field was as bright as day. He was so startled that he jerked away from Ewell and struggled to his feet, but then he heard his brothers laugh, and a strong arm pulled him down again to the grass, and he snuggled against the warmth of Ewell's musky sweatshirt, and watched the stars wink out and the red streaks fade to black.

An instant later the second charge began.

Spencer looked away. He saw that the warden's gaze was fixed on the clock high on the cinder-block wall at the back of the room. He was watching the second hand with the careful attention of a man who does not want to see what else is happening around him. Spencer heard one of the witnesses groan, but he did not turn around to look at the man. He knew that it was not Charles Stanton. He had just begun to reflect on the unreality of the scene before him, so familiar from films that it seemed to be merely a staged illusion, but before he could reflect further on the meaning of his own detachment, the people in the death chamber began to move around again, and he realized that it was over.

The people in the observation room stood up, avoiding one another's eyes.

The doctor examined the body and nodded to the guards that it was indeed all over. There had been a wisp of smoke where the leather helmet met flesh, but no flames about the face mask, no smell of burning flesh that he could detect, no malfunction of the equipment. Tennessee's first execution in three decades had gone off without a hitch, Spencer thought. Unless you count the fact that the prisoner was innocent.

"Gentlemen, you may leave whenever you're ready." The guard was opening the rear door of the observation room, allowing the witnesses to pass through the visitors' lounge, and then back through the sally port to the administration building. To freedom. They filed out as silently as they had come, still careful not to make eye contact with one another. Even the two young reporters were silent. Spencer was walking directly behind Colonel Stanton, who was still clutching the picture of his daughter, but he could think of nothing to say to the man except, "Was it worth it?" There could be no answer, and he left the question unsaid.

The other witnesses filed out of the building and into the parking lot full of lights and cameras. Spencer was told to wait.

After a few minutes, an assistant warden came out and shook his hand. "I'm glad it's over," he said.

"Yes."

"You've agreed to take Mr. Harkryder's remains back to the mountains?"

Spencer nodded. "He asked me to. He said he didn't have anybody else."

The assistant warden looked away. "The family was contacted. They expressed a desire not to be involved." He sighed. "A sad life, Mr. Arrowood. A waste." After a moment of silence, he went on, "The body has been taken for autopsy now. A strange formality, I always thought." He shrugged.

Spencer did not reply.

"Anyhow, then we have arranged for the crematorium to receive the body and to process it at once. If you could come back here tomorrow morning . . . Around ten?"

The sheriff looked uneasy. "Are you sure I should do this? Maybe his family—"

The assistant warden shook his head.

"Or one of his lawyers—"

"Well, we asked them. They hadn't been on the case very long, you know. One of them is stuck in Washington, and the other has to be in court tomorrow. They said as long as it isn't out of your way . . ."

Spencer nodded. "Tomorrow. Ten o'clock."

*   *   *

He went out into the starless dark of a city night, walking past the waiting reporters without sparing them a glance, and sat for long minutes in the parking lot, his head resting on the steering wheel. It was midnight. He had made reservations at a Nashville motel, so that he could rest before he began the long drive back to east Tennessee, but now he wished that he did not have to spend another hour in the breathless heat of a Nashville summer. If he drove all night, he could be back in the mountains by sunrise. But he had promised to come back tomorrow, and so he would. He would take Fate Harkryder home. He could have wished for other company on his long drive back to the mountains.

The summer haze lay across the distant mountains like a pall of white smoke, but the nearer hills were tangled skeins of green—the oaks and maples holding their own. The locust trees had already given way to the rusty brown of autumn, the first tinge of death on the wind. Soon the nights would turn cold, and summer would be gone.

In crisp October on this hill, facing eastward, Spencer could see Celo Mountain and beneath it the ridges and valleys of North Carolina. But not today. The humid summer air shrouded the distant peaks now, so that turning toward them was more of an act of faith than a fulfillment of a vision.

Through a glass darkly . . .

He wondered if he ought to say words before he began the task.

The pain in his gut reminded him that he ought not to be climbing hills yet, and he shouldn't have come alone, but he wanted to be released from his promise, so that it would not loom over him in the idleness of his convalescence. He looked down at the small wooden box, not as heavy as it ought to have been to contain the mortal remains of a man, but Fate Harkryder had burned twice, he thought, once alive to satisfy the law, and once by the fires of an impersonal crematorium. The little that was left inspired in him neither anger nor pity, only a vague regret that a life had been spent to so little purpose, and that no one had cared to mourn his passing. Spencer wondered if anything besides duty would take people to his own graveside one day. He put the thought out of his mind.

He would do what had been asked of him, no more. No hymn, no prayer, not even a word of valediction for the dead. He hoped, though, that this would be an ending, that all of the victims of that long-ago night of violence—Charles Stanton, Mike and Emily, and Fate Harkryder himself—could rest in peace. It was not justice, perhaps not even mercy, but at least it was over.

He set the box on the ground and opened it. Then he carried it gently to the side of the hill and emptied its contents into the wind.

AUTHOR'S NOTE

The story of Frankie Silver is true, and the account of it given in this novel is as accurate as I was able to make it at a remove of 164 years from the events themselves. Burgess Gaither, the young clerk of court, and all the other persons mentioned in the narrative were real people. Their actual names are used, and the circumstances of their lives and kinships are faithfully recorded.

My research on Frankie Silver really began when I was a child. In 1790 my ancestors settled what is now Mitchell County, home of the Silvers and the Stewarts. My great-great-grandmother's first cousin Sarah Honeycutt married Swinfield Howell, who was the brother-in-law of Jackson Stewart, the older brother of Frankie Silver. I say that Frankie and I are "connected"; to call us related would be overdoing it.

I became interested in the case as a topic for a novel in 1992, when I went to Mitchell County to research *She Walks These Hills*. Jack Pyle and Taylor Reese, two fellow writers who live near Bakersville, took me all over the county. We went up to Kona and saw Charlie Silver's three graves, and I photographed it. I referred to the case of Frankie Silver in that novel (on page 438 of the paperback edition [Dutton, 1995] of *She Walks These Hills*, Nora Bonesteel says to Jeremy, "The next time you come down the trail, you want to go to Kona . . ."). This reference to Kona in *She*

Walks These Hills was understood by a number of North Carolina readers who were familiar with the story. Carolyn Sakowski, president of Blair Press and a native of Morganton, wrote to me quoting the line about Kona. "So you're going to do Frankie, are you?" she said. I owe a great debt of thanks to Carolyn, who was enormously helpful in the research into the case. She accompanied me to Morganton, and we visited the hill where the hanging took place; we interviewed a descendant of Sheriff Boone, who hanged Frankie; and we found the grave of Frankie Silver near the site of the old Buckhorn Tavern (long gone). I am deeply grateful to attorney Robert Byrd of Morganton for making his files on the case available to me, and for all his insight into the Morganton side of the story.

I have made several visits to Mitchell County, talking to Wayne Silver, who is the Silver family curator, visiting the cabin site, and discussing the case at the Silver family reunion and with various acquaintances/cousins in the area. My cousin Professor Lloyd Bailey of Duke University has been arguing back and forth with me about the legal aspects of the case in letters for years. (We each remain unconverted by the other's logic.)

My research into the documents of the case led me to old census records, microfilm copies of old newspapers, collections of the private papers of North Carolina statesmen, and written accounts of the case by people like Manly Wade Wellman, Muriel Early Sheppard, and Perry Deane Young. Mr. Young did much of the research into the documents in the case, and he sent me a copy of his recent efforts to secure a posthumous pardon for Frankie Silver. Filmmaker Tom Davenport and Professor Daniel Patterson of the University of North Carolina recently completed a documentary on the legend of Frankie Silver, and they very kindly sent me a copy.

Dean Williams, the Appalachian Studies Collection librarian at Appalachian State University in Boone, was very generous with his time, and most helpful in locating census records and biographical information about the lawyers and governors concerned in the case. Rob Neufeld, of the Pack Library in Asheville, was my source for much of the information on Nicholas Woodfin. Tonia Moxley, of Virginia Tech's University Library (Newman), borrowed microfilm and documents from the North Carolina State Archives in Raleigh, from the University of Alabama law library, and from repositories of documents in half a dozen other states. Dr. Frank Steely, a law professor at Northern Kentucky University, diligently searched Kentucky's Supreme Court records in an attempt to verify the hanging of Blackston Stewart. We were unable to document his hanging, but given the incomplete nature of nineteenth-century Kentucky court records, we are not prepared to say that the story is false. The search goes on.

To understand the intricacies of 1830s North Carolina law (based on English common law), I consulted many lawyers, all of whom were extraordinarily patient and helpful in trying to make sense of a system of law no longer used in this country. Jay Brandon, a fellow author and a former district attorney of San Antonio, considered the case as if he were prosecuting it, and walked me through everything from grand jury selection to the appeals process. He even accompanied me to Seguin, Texas, where we consulted tax rolls, census records, and old newspapers, trying to figure out why Thomas Wilson would have given up a twenty-year law practice to relocate to a small town a thousand miles from home. (We concluded that whyever Wilson did it, the result was a disaster for him.)

Robert F. Johnson, district attorney of Burlington, North Carolina, enabled me to see the 1832 Morganton attorneys in the Silver case as real people, working together behind the scenes to solve a public relations dilemma without damage to their own reputations. Mr. Johnson solved to my satisfaction a key question among scholars in the Frankie Silver case: Who represented her at the trial? Senator Sam Ervin of Morganton, whose father was a friend of Burgess Gaither's, said that Nicholas Woodfin defended Frankie Silver, but in letters to the governor asking for clemency, Thomas Wilson clearly states, "I defended Frankie Silver." The record of the trial does not name her attorney. Rob Johnson's explanation, based on current North Carolina law in capital cases, is the one I have used in the novel.

British barrister Sarah Cockburn (a.k.a. author Sarah Caudwell), Virginia attorney H. Gregory Campbell, and James G. McAdams III of the U.S. attorney general's office, all considered various aspects of the legal side of the case, and I thank them for all their help.

Becky Councill of Boone lives in a log cabin that dates from the same era as Frankie's cabin, and it was built only ten miles away from Kona. She allowed me in to photograph it, turn off the electricity, pace the floor, peer up into her fireplace. This was most helpful in allowing me to visualize the crime scene. I learned that even on the brightest day, the interior of a log cabin is extremely dark: bloodstains would be difficult to spot.

For various psychological insights into the case, I am indebted to Charlotte Ross, Sergeant J. A. Niehaus, Laura Wilson Ford, and Becky Huddleston for hearing me out and sharing their wisdom with me; and to Appalachian scholar Loyal Jones for providing me with a copy of the Bascom Lamar Lunsford recording of "The Ballad of Frankie Silver."

The modern component of this novel centered on Riverbend, the maximum-security prison in Nashville. I am grateful to my fellow author Steve Womack for arranging a tour of the prison, and for going with me. Warden Ricky J. Bell, Assistant Warden Thomas A. Joplin, and Bill Smith, who escorted us on our tour of Riverbend, were all generous with their time and information. William Groseclose, who is an inmate on death row in Riverbend, helped me with the characterization of Fate Harkryder, and very graciously provided me with information about prison routine and other details concerning Riverbend and its surroundings. Tennessee attorney Michael McMahan was my guide to modern Tennessee law concerning the court system and the death penalty, and he provided me with excellent material pertaining to Tennessee law. Author David Hunter, a former Knox County deputy sheriff, advised me on police procedure, patiently listening and offering suggestions through many months of planning as I worked my way through the case of Fate Harkryder.

When I began researching the life and death of Frankie Silver, I thought I was looking into a fascinating riddle concerning a long-ago murder on the frontier, a tragic incident but only a minor curiosity in North Carolina's pioneer history. As I delved deeper into the story, I began to think that the case was really about poor people as defendants and rich people as officers of the court, about Celt versus English values in developing America, about mountain people versus the "flatlanders" in any culture. This is why I was careful to include all of the names in the Morganton story—to show the ties of blood and common interest that bound all the town folk and the plantation gentry—a world in which Frankie and her frontier community had no connections at all. I concluded that Frankie Silver had much to tell us about equal justice under the law, and that not much has changed since she went to her death on a bright July afternoon 164 years ago.

BIBLIOGRAPHY

I have several hundred pages of source material on the case, on the individuals involved, and on nineteenth-century law. Below is a list of the more useful volumes, and some more accessible to the reader.

Abbott, Geoffrey. *Lords of the Scaffold: A History of Execution.* London: Headline, 1992.

Avery, Clifton K. *Official Court Record of the Trial, Conviction and Execution of Francis Silvers, First Woman Hanged in North Carolina.* Booklet reprinted from articles appearing in the Morganton *News Herald,* 1944.

Cotton, J. Randall, Suzanne Pickens Wylie, and Millie M. Barbee. *Historic Burke: An Architectural Sites Inventory of Burke County.* Morganton, N.C.: Historic Burke Foundation, 1987.

Dictionary of North Carolina Biography.

Drimmer Frederick. *Until You Are Dead: The Book of Executions in America.* New York: Pinnacle, 1992.

Ervin, Senator Sam J., Jr. *Burke County Courthouses and Related Matters.* Morganton, N.C.: Historic Burke Foundation, 1985.

The Heritage of Burke County. Edited by H. Russell Triebert, Jean Conyers Ervin, and Marjorie Miller Triebert. Morganton, N.C.: Burke County Historical Society, 1981.

Holland, Eliza Woodfin. "A Grand-Daughter's Tribute to Her Grandfather." Article published in the *Asheville Citizen*, May 3, 1921.

Sakowski, Carolyn. "The Life and Death of Frankie Silver." Article, privately printed, May 1973.

Sheppard, Muriel Early. *Cabins in the Laurel*. Chapel Hill, N.C.: University of North Carolina Press, 1935.

Silver, Wayne. *Frankie's Song: A Collection from the Kona Baptist Church Library*. Privately printed, n.d.

Stockton, Dennis. "Diary of a Death Row Inmate." Series of articles published in the *Roanoke Times & World News*, July 26–September 28, 1995.

Toe River Valley Heritage. Edited by Lloyd Richard Bailey, Sr. Marceline, Mo.: Walsworth Publishing, 1994.

Wellman, Manly Wade. *Dead and Gone*. Chapel Hill, N.C.: University of North Carolina Press, 1955.

• A NOTE ON THE TYPE •

The typeface used in this book is a version of Fairfield, designed in 1937–40 by artist Rudolph Ruzicka (1883–1978), on a commission from Linotype. The assignment was the occasion for a well-known essay in the form of a letter from W. A. Dwiggins to Ruzicka, in response to the latter's request for advice. Dwiggins, who had recently designed Electra and Caledonia, relates that he would start by making very large scale drawings (10 and 64 times the size you are reading) and having test cuttings made, which were used to print on a variety of papers. "By looking at all these for two or three days I get an idea of how to go forward—or, if the result is a dud, how to start over again." At this stage he often took *parts* of letters that satisfied him and made cardboard cutouts, which he would then use to assemble other letters. This "template" method anticipated one that many contemporary computer type designers use.